Lula Mae

Bianca Cuie

Lula Mae

This book is dedicated to my grandmother,
Lula Mae Harrison.

Acknowledgments

I take this opportunity to express my deepest gratitude to the people who have been instrumental in the successful completion of *Lula Mae.*

I would first like to give honor and thanks to the Creator for giving me the strength, patience, and resiliency in completing this book.

I wish to express my sincere gratitude to my mother, Gloria Cuie. These measly words will never be able express the amount of gratitude I have for you, but I will try. You were the first person who believed in me as a writer. Throughout this process, you have been with me every step of the way, from start to finish, and beyond. Your insightful critiques, numerous edits, and continuous encouragement is what kept me working. I do not think I would have completed this book without you! I love you more than you will ever know and I humbly thank you.

To my brother, John Cuie. Thank you for your analytical critiques and summarization. It is a good feeling to know that, wherever I am in this world, I have a brother who loves me and will be there for me no matter what. I humbly thank you.

Thank you to my sister, Sabrina Cuie. Your critiques were very insightful. And to my niece, Jalyn Cuie. You left auntie alone when need be and brought me snacks while I worked. It always put a smile on my face when I think about how helpful you were to me. I humbly thank you both.

Thanks to my father for your encouraging words. Thank you Aunt Jackie Cuie and Uncle Leroy Frank for offering support without me having to ask. It brings joy to my heart to know that I have family who cared enough to support me the way you both have done. I humbly thank you.

Thank you Bishop James Harrison for providing me with pictures. We asked for them, and without any question, you sent them in a timely fashion. I humbly thank you.

I take immense pleasure in thanking my ancestors who are gone, but never forgotten. Learning about my family's history helped me to learn more about myself. Without you, there is no me. I humbly thank you.

Lastly, I would like to take the opportunity to thank you, the reader. Thank you for taking the time out of your day to read my book. Enjoy!

Introduction

Lula Mae Harrison-Frank, a southern belle, born and raised in Eunice, Louisiana, walked to her grandmother's house with a blue dress on flowing in the summer breeze. A beautiful young woman with tight pin curls coiled neatly around her head, popped her Doublemint gum with a simultaneous sense of peace and excitement.

Lula noticed not much had changed as she walked along. Gone for many years and still the same wooden houses, dirt roads, unbearable heat, merciless mosquitoes, and familiar faces on porches looked as if Lula had never left. Nonetheless, Lula strolled unfazed by it all. Her main concern was to see her grandmother whom she'd been apart from for far too long.

Prepared to put her grandmother's guilt to rest, Lula was ready to make amends. All was already forgiven in Lula's heart. She wanted her grandmother to live the rest of her days in peace.

Ready to ignite the power of forgiveness, Lula traveled proudly to her grandmother's house to reveal the concealed...

Lula Mae

Chapter 1

In 1944, a small Creole community, newly incorporated forty-five years earlier, had mud-lined dirt roads on Beulah Street in Eunice, Louisiana. Dirt roads were newly paved with small clamshells, adding a pungent fishy odor to the air. The scorching hot, muggy sun spared no one. Humidity thick enough to cut with a knife. Crawfish swam in the deep ditches alongside the roads with a foot of soil bank surrounding it, running past each house. Barefoot children played in those ditches, catching crawfish to bring home to their mothers in hopes of getting a delicious Creole dish cooked for dinner. The one-story houses were built above ground on cement stumps to prevent flooding during the rainy season and stop snakes from entering homes. A rumor amongst town folk was, if one dug too deep, they'd hit water due to Eunice being a part of Louisiana that was below sea level.

The people of Eunice knew each other by name, treating each other as if they were all kinfolks; passing one by without acknowledgement was an intolerable act. Despite the relentless heat and humidity, children played and adults sat on their porches fanning the heat off their bodies, sipping on water or lemonade, sharing the current gossip amongst themselves as if their bodies were immune to high humid temperatures.

The town's people moved slower on this hot Saturday afternoon. Only worries were what to wear for church on Sunday, and for the party goers, the Zydeco Juke Joint that Saturday night. No mention was made about the laborious work, strenuous chores, mile long walks, or schooling in the upcoming week. Evading the monotony of their weeks kept cheerful moods afloat, and mention of Sunday dinner set off a chitchat frenzy.

A wooden whitewashed house, uniformed with the other houses on Beulah Street, sat modestly in the middle of the block. The dirt-filled yard with patches of grass created a divergence with the freshly painted white porch. Four homemade clay vases full of purple and pink Geraniums were spaced against the wall of the porch, in between three wooden chairs. Spider plants hung on both sides of the porch, clinging on rusty nails, growing wildly outside of their pots. The purple, pink, and green colors from the potted flowers and plants against the white porch formed a pleasant aesthetic from the road.

The backyard of the house had an outhouse on the side, as did all the houses, and a huge fig tree full of dark purple figs ready for picking.

Inside the house was a small kitchen with Oakwood floors, a few lower cabinets with linoleum countertops, a sink between the cabinets with a window above it, and an old pantry sat near the kitchen entrance, parallel to the sink. Next to the pantry was a small round table in the corner, stationed there as a second food prepping base. In the window above the sink, a fallen piece of spider plant grew in a canning jar full of water, its roots circling around searching for space.

In the kitchen, Big Ma prepared homemade sweet dough with her granddaughter, Lula Mae, as they did every Saturday despite the heat.

"Oh yeah, dis here gonna make some good sweet dough fo' teacakes, huh, Lula Mae," Big Ma said, mashing the dough in the bowl. She tore a small piece of dough off popping it in Lula's mouth. "Nah, you tell me, what it need?"

Lula closed her eyes, mashing the dough against the roof of her mouth, dissecting every ingredient. "Mo' sugar!" Lula shouted.

Sitting on the counter, six year-old Lula looked like a life-size baby doll, dangling her barefoot feet against the cabinet in her yellow summer dress. Her sugar brown skin glistened from the heat and her hair was combed into neat pigtails with yellow ribbons tied at the ends matching her dress. Her innocent eyes waited for Big Ma's approval as she flashed her small white teeth with two missing at the bottom, hoping her answer was correct. Big Ma tasted the dough and nodded in agreement, giving Lula the approval she wanted. Big Ma smiled proudly at her precocious granddaughter, taking notice to Lula's innate talents.

Before she could talk, Lula was in the kitchen helping along with her older sister, Lillie Mae, who was also a great cook in the making—aside from disappearing from the kitchen in the mist of the heat wave. Their ability to cook was evident. Inevitably, being a pint-size apprentice under the "Greatest Cook" crown bearer in Eunice, Lula was headed in Big Ma's footsteps, along with her sisters.

Big Ma said, "Okay nah go get it out the pantry. I'm gonna start flourin' dis here table."

Lula hopped off the kitchen counter landing on both feet and ran over to the pantry. She grabbed the sugar at arm's length, sat it on the table, and then pulled a chair over to the pantry, climbed on top and began reaching high on her tippy toes. Big Ma saw Lula and hurried to grab her before she fell. "Lula Mae, what yah doin' child? You can hurt yah self," Big Ma said, putting Lula down on the floor. Lula pointed at the top of the pantry. Big Ma lifted Lula up close to the pantry's higher shelves, allowing her to grab whatever she was reaching for, and then put her down. Big Ma bellowed over in laughter, hitting her knee when she saw what Lula had in her hand.

"My baby, why didn't yah say somethin'," Big Ma said, taking the spice from her. "Dis here is called 'nutmeg' and yes, that dough sho' need mo' of it too! Good job, Sha."

Big Ma laughed, lifting Lula back on the counter top and handed the nutmeg and sugar to Lula, allowing her to pour however much she thought the dough needed. After mixing, Big Ma tore a couple pieces of dough off for her and Lula to taste. Both nodded in agreement, the sweet dough tasted perfect.

Cooking and baking with Big Ma was heaven on earth to Lula. She followed Big Ma's every move, observing the ingredients used, and mimicking Big Ma's style of cooking.

Big Ma was an elderly woman who moved lightening fast in the kitchen, yet light as feather on her feet. Keeping up with Big Ma's fast pace was a workout for Lula. Nevertheless, throughout the heat and quick pace, Lula was already becoming accustomed to cooking under any condition.

The "Greatest Cook" in Eunice title didn't come easy for Big Ma. She started young, around Lula's age, and practically lived in the kitchen mastering every dish, adding her own unique flavor, setting herself apart from how everyone else made their food, and using fresh fruits and vegetables from her garden was a must. Heat was never a distraction. She wasn't going to allow lousy heat to deter her from preparing the freshest, tastiest, most talked about meals in Eunice.

Big Ma got her name due to her size. She stood 5'8" with broad shoulders and a thick frame. She was a modest beauty, wearing no make-up since it was against her religion, and she dressed only in long button down dresses or skirts well below the knee. She had soul seeking eyes while age had no effect on her face; only faint lines on her caramel colored forehead revealed the struggles of her life. She had been working hard since childhood, helping her overworked parents raise ten younger siblings.

Nothing changed once Big Ma started a family of her own. She stayed in the church praising God every chance she got, and was no stranger to hard work. She woke up before the break of dawn gardening, cleaning, cooking, washing, and sewing, then went to work a ten hour shift as a maid for a well-to-do Caucasian family to repeat the same task in their homes until she retired due to heart problems. Jack-of-all-trades, master of all, Big Ma had the tenacity and wherewithal to multitask her work, singing and humming every step of the way. When Big Ma returned home from work, she cooked dinner for her family, cleaned, and then attended night service to commune with her God, merely stopping to fix the gray curls in her hair before walking to the sanctified church.

An evangelist missionary for the Church of God and Christ, Big Ma took her title seriously, willing to speak the word of God to fellow church members, friends, and family as a saved Christian woman.

Big Ma's refuge, besides church, was in her garden. It was her way to commune with Jesus and silently pray while working. Carrots, corn, mustard greens, okra, tomatoes, watermelon, sweet potatoes, onions, garlic, parsley, and snap beans grew in rich dark soil. In addition to Big Ma's garden, there were apple, walnut, peach, pecan, and fig trees growing in the back of her and other neighbor's houses which they all shared; yet, Big Ma made the most use of them. The fruits and nuts couldn't ripen fast enough for Big Ma, and after the growing season, she canned the remaining harvest for fruit preserves during the winter months.

Big Ma's garden was like having her own personal paradise. The foliage sprouting in her backyard was the most recognized amongst the small community for having the best yield. Finding the time during night and day, Big Ma never missed a day gardening. In return, the garden provided the tranquility Big Ma needed as a thanks for her efforts. After Big Ma rolled the dough flat on the flour covered table, she began using a thin edge cup to shape out perfect circles while Lula pulled out the cutlets and neatly placed them to the side. Lula mimicked Big Ma's humming, unsure of the song, but still following every tone.

Leroy entered the kitchen, tickled at the sight of his daughter and mother together in his house. In a white chef's jacket and dark slacks, Leroy leaned against the wall crossing his arms enjoying the scene. Lula did a double-take over her shoulder, surprised to see her father against the wall smiling at her. She immediately jumped off the chair and ran with her hands up leaping into Leroy's embrace nearly choking him. He kissed her cheek and said, "What yah been up to, Sha?"

Lula got down from his arms and ran over to the table picking up a cut of sweet dough. "We makin' teacakes, daddy," she said, holding the cutlet up.

"Where've you been?" Big Ma said without lifting her head. Lula put the teacake back down and continued pulling the sweet dough cutlets out, placing them aside.

"Ma'am?"

"Yah heard me."

Leroy hesitated. "One of the cooks called out, so I had to do a double shift."

"Pierre's close at midnight and open back up at six. Where were yah between those graveyard hours?"

"I miss the bus to Eunice, so I slept at the restaurant."

"What yah mean yah missed yah bus? Pierre always gives you a ride!"

"He's out sick."

"Oh please, Leroy, I knew Pierre fo' thirty years and if that man had two broke arms and legs, he'll still be at that restaurant. Try again!" Big Ma said, balling the rest of the dough to roll out again.

Leroy said, "I'm serious, mama, he's been out sick."

Big Ma stopped rolling. She placed one hand on her hip looking over at Leroy. "Well! I guess I betta pay him a visit then since he's so sick. Bring him a pot of vegetable soup," she said, twisting her mouth to the side waiting for Leroy's response. Lula yanked at Big Ma's hand for her to continue rolling the sweet dough.

Leroy exhaled, leaning back against the wall, scratching the top of his head and said in a low tone, "No need fo' that."

"Why not?" She smirked. "Please stop, child," Big Ma said, releasing her hand from Lula's tugs.

Big Ma waited. Leroy scratched at the top of his head. Lula pulled the rolling pin from Big Ma's hand and started rolling the dough herself.

"Ain't nothin', mama. Just had a few things to do after work."

Big Ma grunted at Leroy's answer and turned back around. "I got my own house to tend to yah kno'," she said, resuming to cutting out the sweet dough at a faster, heavier pace. Lula moved faster trying to keep up.

Big Ma continued, "It is somethin' when yah got three chillun and a sick wife here at home. I got my own home to take care of and I've been neglecting my husband and my garden for two days b'cause of your 'things to do'. Nah, I refuse to believe my son is out there sinnin'," she said, stopping everything at once to face Leroy.

Chills ran down Leroy's spine as Big Ma glared at him, making him feel like a young boy again. It was the same stare Big Ma used to give Leroy and his siblings before they had to get a switch off the tree.

Leroy's eyes settled on the floor. "No, ma'am."

Big Ma continued prepping her teacakes in silence. She was getting too old to exert extra energy cross examining her adult son. Leaving the subject alone, Big Ma knew if Leroy was being deceitful, the goose would soon peck him and the Lord would soon expose his actions. She decided to pray an extra long prayer for Leroy at church service that night.

"Where's Mary Lee and Lillie Mae?" Leroy asked, changing the subject.

"Mary Lee nappin'. Lillie Mae out back."

Leroy swallowed at her curt, monotone answer. "How's Beatrice?"

"Go see fo' yah self."

Leroy put his hands in his pocket, hanging his head. Falling out of good grace with the woman he revered most was a tough blow. It was evident that Big Ma's fondness was turning tenuous toward him. She'd placed Leroy on a high pedestal ever since he was an infant. Among all of her children, Leroy received preferential treatment, compelling him to maintain rank by his achievements. Always an impressive, well-accomplished child, Leroy craved the attention, the accolades and high praises from Big Ma, adversely causing Leroy unwarranted beatings from his jealous father, Doc Harrison. Doc singled Leroy out as a troublemaker, always accusing Leroy of misbehaving and beating him as a result. In her own way, Big Ma tried to make up for Doc's mistreatment towards Leroy by praising him every chance she got, unknowingly, adding fuel to the fire.

When Leroy matured into a handsome man, women added to the adulation. His tall muscular frame, brown skin, straight white teeth, square jaws, and deep set eyes made women weak in the knees at the sight of him. Leroy seldom raised a finger to do anything since eager women took turns providing his every need in hopes of a ring in exchange. Big Ma herself was flattered to have a son that women flocked to and was approving of Leroy being the ladies man in Eunice, making it a challenge for Leroy to eat a piece of humble pie.

In the kitchen, Leroy kissed Lula's forehead and hugged Big Ma from behind kissing her cheek. "I really appreciate yah being here in my absence, mama," he said in her ear. Big Ma ignored him, muttering something about Jesus as she released herself from Leroy's embrace and placed the first patch of teacakes in the oven. Leroy stepped away and retreated from the kitchen, feeling himself slowly being nudged off Big Ma's pedestal.

Leroy entered the bedroom he shared with his wife, Beatrice Harrison, and sat beside her on the bed, moving a piece of hair away from her eye. Mary Lee, their youngest daughter, was asleep on the other side of the bed.

Tempted to kiss Beatrice awake, Leroy faltered, rubbing his hands together, wondering if she was going to ask about his whereabouts, too. If Big Ma didn't buy his story, neither would Beatrice.

Their bedroom was small and neat. Beatrice was a meticulous woman. Everything had its place and there was no room for dirt. The bedroom had a dust-free dresser drawer, streak-free mirror, bed with fresh sheets, and a spotless floor with a little hint of lemon and pine in the air enhancing the cleanliness of the room. The double sized bed had a navy blue flower printed bedspread with white sheets and a wooden headboard that Leroy carved by hand. Silver plated prayer hands hung above their bed on a silver nail. Sitting across from the bed was a dresser drawer, three on each side, and in the middle of the floor laid an area rug matching the bedspread. Leroy and Beatrice's wedding picture was on the dresser in a wooden frame surrounded by smaller pictures of their three daughters. Vaseline, shoe polish, and toiletry items were on the other side of the dresser in size order next to the fresh picked flowers in a vase.

Leroy scratched at the top of his head, turning to find Beatrice's sleepy eyes blinking open to the silhouette of her husband in the dim light.

He leaned in closer to Beatrice. "How yah feelin, Bea?"

"I had better days. Big Ma gave me BC's a few hours ago so my head's feeling a little better now," Beatrice said. She looked down at Mary scrunched up beside her and chuckled, "Oh Lord, when did this child get in the bed with me?"

Leroy clapped his hand. "Com'on nah, get up, Mary Lee. Go outside and tell Lillie Mae to come on in."

Mary woke up rubbing her eyes. She looked over at her mother, concerned.

"I'm okay, my baby, you can go," Beatrice smiled. Mary got up sluggishly walking towards the door.

Leroy said, "Um, 'cuse me, little one, and how are you?"

"Hi daddy," Mary said, running over to him, hugging and kissing his cheek.

"That's betta," Leroy said. "Nah scat." Mary left out the bedroom closing the door behind her.

Beatrice squinted in pain after hearing the door shut. She grabbed hold to her forehead. "Leroy, what's happening to me. This headache, it just won't go away!"

"Just relax, baby. I'll go get yah some mo' BC's."

Leroy's knees cracked getting up from the bed. He went into the kitchen where Lillie, Mary, and Lula were enjoying their first batch of hot teacakes while Big Ma did the dishes. Lillie ran up and hugged Leroy.

He said, "And where've you been young lady?"

"I was outside in the tree tryin' to pick figs. Me and Lula Mae wanna make pies."

"You out there in dis here heat, Sha?"

"Yes, sir."

Big Ma said, "Oh no, y'all not makin' nothin' without me or yah mama in the kitchen with yah."

Lillie said, "No, ma'am. We gonna wait 'til mama feel betta."

"Somethin' startin' to smell good in here. What's dis cookin'?" Leroy said, removing the lid off the pot, "Aww thanks, mama. I was gonna go out to the coop and get a chicken fo' dinner."

Leroy breathed in the simmering beans in the pot, already tasting the flavor on his tongue.

"The teacakes done, daddy. Taste one," Lula said, holding one up to him.

Leroy took a bite, closing his eyes and rubbing his stomach. "Mmm, hmm, wow, dis here is delicious. Thank you, Sha."

"Yah welcome, daddy," Lula said, swaying side-to-side bashfully with her index finger in her mouth.

Big Ma disregarded Leroy's exaggerated zeal. The mood wasn't any lighter between the two. He got the BC's out the pantry and a glass of water, ready to make another exit out the hot kitchen.

"Leroy," Big Ma called, "I have to hurry, I gotta make my way to church fo' our prayer meeting t'night. I'm tryin' to get everythin' cleaned b'fore I go. Make sho' yah feed yah chillun and yah wife. Think yah can stay home long enough to do that?"

"Com'on, mama, please stop. Give me a break," Leroy said, making sure enough space was between them out of habit of Big Ma's quick back hand after talking back when Leroy was younger. The look Big Ma gave was enough warning for him to keep quiet.

Big Ma rushed wiping the counters and then started sweeping the floor. Leroy kissed Big Ma on the cheek.

"That's enough teacakes b'fore supper. I told y'all only eat one nah," Big Ma said. Lula, Mary, and Lille dropped their teacakes fast, wiping their mouths and brushing off their clothes. Big Ma opened the oven checking on the next batch. Leroy grabbed the BC's and water and left out of the kitchen, upset at Big Ma's dismissal of him.

Returning back to the bedroom, Leroy disguised his distress with a smile. "Here yah go, baby, I brought the whole box fo' yah."

Beatrice took the glass of water and inspected it for bugs, particles, or whatever else that could've fallen in the cup on his trip to the bedroom. She poured the BC's in her mouth and ferociously drank the water until she noticed bugs crawling from the glass onto her arms and face. She threw the glass against the wall, screaming and flicking the bugs off her.

Leroy jumped back. "What's wrong, Bea!"

"Why'd you put that in my glass?"

"Put what in yah glass?"

"There's bugs in there," Beatrice cried out searching her gown for bugs.

"No it ain't."

Big Ma and the girls ran to the bedroom door. Big Ma quickly put her hand out to stop them from running in the room when she saw the broken glass on the floor. "Go back to the kitchen!"

Mary and Lula clung onto Lillie running back.

Big Ma said, "Lord Jesus, not again!"

Leroy asked, "What yah mean 'not again'?"

"She's been doin' dis all day. I thought she'd sleep it off. I'll get the broom, Lord have mercy!"

"No, mama, go back in the kitchen with the girls. I'll deal with dis here."

Big Ma looked worried at Beatrice, who was smacking at herself. Taking a deep breath, Big Ma threw her hands up heading back to the kitchen, ready more than ever to go to church to pray.

Leroy stepped over the glass to get near Beatrice. She flinched when he reached his hand out. He reached out slower, and Beatrice finally stopped flinching, sighing in relief when the bugs were gone.

"What's wrong with me?" Beatrice asked as Leroy looked at her trying to figure out the question for himself.

After seven years of marriage, the same intense love Leroy had felt for Beatrice when they were teenagers still existed. Leroy's heart pounded for the tall, beautiful, new girl in the church. He was mesmerized by the sway of her hips, her sensual stride, and the allure of her features as she walked with her head held high and shoulders back exuding confidence. Even the Pastor, Henry Evans, skipped over words in his sermon when Beatrice walked up to the front and took a seat in front of Leroy, whose hands turned clammy as she sat down. His knees bounced uncontrollably and beads of sweat formed on his forehead. The smell of her sweet perfume didn't help; Leroy had to loosen his collar for air. This was an unusual state for the ladies' man. Whatever it was, Leroy wanted more of it from then on into eternity. The Pastor, church folks, and the church itself disappeared. The only thing Leroy saw was the young lady wearing a soft pink dress clinging to her thin, yet shapely frame. The white pearls around her neck and wrist, and the beaded barrette holding in her jet black curls made her appear sophisticated and full of elegance. Leroy didn't notice when the congregation rose with hymn books in their hands ready to sing. He remained seated, getting a good view of the beautiful woman from behind. Hearing the young lady's voice sing made Leroy freeze. Big Ma tapped Leroy on the shoulder, shaking him out of his trance. He stood up trying to clap and sing the words to the song he easily sang every Sunday, except this time, the words weren't registering in his brain as he clapped offbeat. Big Ma chuckled continuing on with the song. Leroy gave up. This was more than what he could withstand. He stepped over his siblings, out into the aisle and left out the church. Big Ma let her son go and get much needed fresh air.

Outside the church, Leroy pulled at his drenched wet dress shirt examining the perspiration. He took off his dress shirt, leaving his t-shirt on, and put his hands in his pocket walking home smiling at the clearer blue sky, the greener grass, colorful birds, and everything else he never took notice of before.

Leroy physically and mentally prepared himself for the following Sunday. He was the first person in church dressed in his best suit, shoes, and way too much cologne. He held flowers and a box of chocolates, telling everyone they were for "someone special". By the time church service ended, Leroy sat in the pew holding the box of chocolates and flowers until the last person had left. The mystery woman never showed.

Months passed and each Sunday, Leroy dressed to impress with a different gift in hand, only to leave dejected because of the lady's absence. Taking matters into his own hands, he decided it was time to actively find his lady love. Begrudgingly, Leroy befriended the town gossips whom he normally evaded, spending time with them, listening to their conversations on a whole lot of nothing. Most of them were women—with one effeminate man—that were more than happy to be in Leroy's presence and were candid about information they heard about people in Eunice, giving Leroy a chance to ease in indirect questions about the beautiful woman whom he now could identify as, Beatrice Redeaux. Leroy collected a few facts on Beatrice: she was born in Happy Hill, Louisiana, completed High School at the top of her class, excellent in English, always corrected people's grammar, and got paid for tutoring other students. In another conversation with his "friends", Leroy found out Beatrice moved to Texas in pursuit of becoming a teacher and planned to obtain her college degree. They also informed him that her father, a Creole man named Oscar Redeaux, nicknamed Papa Top, lived in Happy Hill and took kindly to goal-oriented young men. Case closed. Leroy left the town gossips to what they do best and didn't bother with them again, except for a quick greet in passing.

Leroy's brothers, friends, and cousins laughed at him when he spoke about Beatrice, telling Leroy that he didn't stand a chance getting a woman with those credentials. Their doubt fueled Leroy's desire for Beatrice. Nothing was more challenging than an untouchable, classy woman.

Papa Top had an unexpected visit from the young man who called himself, Leroy, asking Papa Top for a job in his repair shop without pay. Papa Top was leery, but agreed, needing an extra hand with the work load. Even though Leroy wasn't the best handy man, and broke things more than he fixed them, Papa Top admired Leroy's effort. For weeks, Leroy worked hard in the hot sun carrying fixed or broken items to and from people's homes, only to come back and have Papa Top give him a mop and broom to clean the floors. Leroy worked from sun-up-to-sun-down. He scrubbed, cleaned, organized, and rearranged Papa Top's entire store by the time Papa Top invited Leroy for dinner with Beatrice when she returned back to town on Sunday, giving Leroy a slap on the back and a wink. Leroy had to laugh at himself for being foolish enough to think he could get one over on a father. Papa Top laughed telling Leroy, he too was a young man once.

That following Saturday night, Leroy rehearsed his lines in the mirror for hours, toning down his southern accent and hitting his head when he said something too stupid. This was a pivotal moment in his life. His one chance to make Beatrice his before she left for Texas for good.

Sunday came and Leroy arrived in church feeling confident, posed, and looking sharp as a tack. The women smiled, waved, and greeted him, trying to catch Leroy's attention, and Leroy cordially greeted them back, but kept a look out for his lady love. Sitting in the back pew for a full view of the church, Leroy saw Beatrice walk through the double doors of the church, and he tensed up when she sat in front of him. He coughed out the tightness from the pit of his stomach, tapping his foot, trying to remain cool.

Beatrice paid no attention to Leroy's coughs, loud singing, hard clapping, and constant clearing of his throat. She grew irritated by the minute at the obnoxious man sitting behind her. Leroy retreated outside to take a break from his silly antics and to get some air. He waited until church was over, and then stood with his brothers and cousins making small talk to stall for time. Beatrice came out hugging her bible, talked to a few church members, and then began walking away from the church where Leroy and his people stood. Leroy blatantly blocked Beatrice's path and stood there speechless. Beatrice looked him up and down, then shoved Leroy out of her way and kept walking, only to stop, turn around, and look Leroy dead in his eye. Leroy swallowed hard, fixing his tie, elated when their eyes met for the first time. Before Leroy could speak, Beatrice flipped him off, rolling her eyes at the audacity of his rudeness, and then continued walking. Leroy's cousins and brothers laughed hysterically at Leroy since they had never seen a woman react to him in such a way. But, in that moment, with the guys pointing and laughing at him, Leroy knew Beatrice Redeaux was going to be his wife. He smirked to himself. Little did they know, he had a supper date with Miss Beatrice Redeaux and her father that evening.

The rest of that day, Leroy couldn't get her chocolate skin, long jet black hair, high cheekbones, and seductive eyes off his mind. That good looking, proper etiquette speaking woman would look perfect on his arm. Leroy sat waiting, watching the clock, angry at it for not moving faster. No other woman lit that fire Leroy so desperately desired and he wanted to capture that feeling for the remainder of his life.

The time neared and Leroy left out the house with flowers, not telling Big Ma, Doc, or his siblings where he was going. When Leroy got to Papa Top's door, he didn't realize he was an hour early. Papa Top came to the door and looked through the screen at Leroy standing there. He chuckled, and then disappeared back in the house as Leroy waited, scratching the top of his head. Beatrice came to the front door and stood behind the screen, shocked to see the man her father invited to dinner was the rude man from the church. Leroy stood there opening his mouth to speak what he had rehearsed, except nothing came out. All Leroy could do was open the screen door, take her hand, and kiss the back of it while staring at Beatrice, baring his truth through his eyes.

Beatrice felt a light flutter in her stomach. She blushed and warmly said, "We're having okra and sausage stew," and grabbed hold of Leroy's hand, inviting him into the house. She remained in Eunice ever since that memorable day and wedded Leroy a year later.

Now, back in the bedroom, it took Leroy a while to calm Beatrice down and convince her that there were no bugs in the bed. He got Beatrice to eat a little beans and rice, and she finally laid down to rest.

Night time came quick. Big Ma was long gone, but had made plans to return in the morning. Leroy fed and put Lula, Mary, and Lillie to bed, then changed out of his work uniform and spent the remainder of the evening hovering over Beatrice while she slept. He spent less time with Beatrice ever since she fell ill, so Leroy took advantage of the quiet moment watching his sleeping beauty and reflecting on how happy his life had been ever since Beatrice said, "I do". Leroy raised a brow, noticing Beatrice's hair was still neat. *Through all that pain, she still fixing her hair,* Leroy chuckled to himself.

In a split second, his face went blank. Eyes widened.

A strange sensation came over him.

Leroy hopped up, kissed Beatrice on the forehead and headed towards the bedroom door. Before he exited, Beatrice woke up. "Leroy, where are you going?"

Leroy thought fast, "Down to the rib shack."

"At this hour?"

"They're open pretty late and I gotta taste fo' boudin."

"Why didn't you come home last night from work?"

Leroy cringed, dreading the question he thought he had evaded. "I had to work a double shift, so I missed the last bus to Eunice and I couldn't get a ride from Pierre, he's out sick, so I slept at the restaurant fo' the night."

She said in a mellow tone, "Are you sure about that?" She began squinting again from her headache.

Leroy walked back over to Beatrice and sat next to her, kissing her forehead. "I'm sho', Bea." He looked down at the ground scratching the top of his head.

Beatrice adjusted her pillow, trying to find a cooler spot to lay on for relief, and asked, "Why can't you look me in the eye?"

No response.

"Stop scratching your head like that. You're going to flake up your scalp," she said, grabbing Leroy's arm to stop. "Leroy, I'm no fool. I know good and well Pierre never call out sick. That man keeps an eye on his restaurant like a hawk. You just don't like being around me while I'm like this, do you?"

"No, I missed my bus."

"I'm going to take your word for it. You never gave me a reason to doubt you before. But, if God is my witness, if I catch you lying, I'm gonna ..." Beatrice motioned Leroy to come closer. She pulled his collar even closer and whispered, "I'm going to rip your head off and shove it up your ass!" She released her grip, sweetly smiling at him, blowing a kiss. Leroy sat motionless. His eyes were wide as saucers staring at her. Beatrice closed her eyes and went back to sleep. Leroy rubbed the top of his head, trying not to scratch, and hurried out the room. Before he closed the front door, Leroy smiled to himself, feeling the warmth build up inside. *That's my baby,* he thought.

Beatrice's sassy tongue always entertained Leroy, making his life more exciting. She was honest about her feelings and never bit her tongue when angry, which seldom happened because she and Leroy got along well. Her fun, vivacious attitude kept things interesting in their relationship because she was so unpredictable. Male family members disapproved of Leroy's lenient behavior with Beatrice, especially Doc, who detested it the most and was disgusted at the sight of Leroy. The men often coached Leroy on a woman's place in a marriage and how Beatrice not only crossed the line, she did a tap dance on his manhood.

Leroy ignored them. He knew they judged the situation without a clue about what went on behind closed doors. Beatrice's motto was: "Indeed, he is a man, but he isn't made of stone." Nobody witnessed, or just failed to regard, the compassion and endless love Beatrice showered on Leroy. She allowed him to be the man of the house and added her opinions when looking out for Leroy's best interest. Leroy's ambitious mentality strengthened because he knew he had a loving wife at home supporting him in life. He tried to defend the slander of Beatrice's character from the men, explaining her sensibility and how he chose to listen to his wife's advice, it was never forced. Nonetheless, Leroy's argument fell on deaf ears. Despite Leroy's efforts to discount their opinions, the constant scolding eventually started to affect him. He couldn't bring himself to take Doc's suggestion to physically harm Beatrice to maintain rank in their marriage since, as a child, Leroy saw Doc take the same disciplinary action with Big Ma. Leroy opted to be a better man than his father by solving problems with Beatrice without getting physical. However, feeling like he still had to defend his manhood, Leroy had to find a way to prove the men and Doc wrong, and that Beatrice didn't control him.

Leroy stepped outside and closed the front door to the house, still amused by Beatrice's abrasive words. He locked the door and put the key in his pocket, whistling and jiggling the change in his pocket, contemplating his next move. Leroy rubbed the top of his head trying not to scratch. Thinking about Beatrice, Leroy felt shamefaced for what he'd been doing and what he was about to do.

Having second thoughts, Leroy took the key back out his pocket and tried unlocking the door, but had trouble opening it. "Damn latch, gotta get dis fixed," he said. Lifting his hand for a second attempt to open the door with his key, Leroy paused, hearing Doc's unsavory words about Beatrice, and then a strange sensation came over him again. Leroy smacked a mosquito on his arm, plucked it off, and rubbed at the lump forming. He adjusted his collar, put his hands in his pocket, and marched down the porch stairs into the night.

***

The sun spared no mercy during the summer months in Eunice, Louisiana. The town folk's immunity to heat struggled to keep a comfort level in this heat wave. They travelled at slower paces during the day and gave thanks to the twilight breeze at dusk. As vile as the humidity and the sun were, that was the least of their worries. Mosquitoes preyed upon them like minuscule vampires, biting those who weren't privileged to have screened porches to shield them from these nuisances, causing the victims of bites to resort to lemon juice, calamine lotion, or baking soda mixtures for relief.

Lula, Lillie, and Mary longed for the August heat wave to end, even though they reaped the benefit of having fewer chores. Big Ma, on the other hand, was able to withstand the heat, carrying on with the chores and cooking while Beatrice was sick and Leroy absent. Big Ma spent the night with Beatrice and the girls, praying on her knees every night, waiting for Jesus to take care of the matter, believing her God wouldn't fail her.

The third night into Big Ma's stay, she entered the girl's bedroom in middle of the night while they were asleep. In a pink robe she had borrowed from Beatrice, and a white scarf wrapped around paper bag rollers in her hair, Big Ma lightly shook Lula up whispering, "Lula Mae?"

"Ma'am," Lula sleepily muttered.

"I need yah help."

Lula leaped out of bed hearing those words. Big Ma tucked the sheet around Lillie and Mary, and left the room in a hurry with Lula trailing behind, moving stealthily to minimize the squeaks on the old wooden floor.

They entered Leroy and Beatrice's bedroom. Lula noticed Beatrice was sleeping alone again. In her tiny undershirt and underwear standing barefoot, Lula tugged on Big Ma's robe. "Where's daddy?"

"At work, Sha."

Lula sighed in relief.

"Yah mama had a little accident, so I need yah help. When I lift her to the side, pull the sheet from under her," Big Ma said, lifting Beatrice to the side. Lula yanked the sheet, flabbergasted at how soaked it was. Big Ma laid Beatrice back down and pulled the rest of the sheet off the bed from the other side, then balled them, throwing them in the corner. She left out the room, leaving Lula biting at her lip standing over Beatrice sleeping, wondering what was wrong.

Wetting the bed was unlike Beatrice. She was overly hygienic and would never lie in her own urine.

"Mama?" Lula said, softly tapping Beatrice on the shoulder. Beatrice didn't budge. Lula nudged Beatrice's arm.

Still no response.

Lula began shaking Beatrice forcefully, calling out for her mother, terrified. Big Ma came rushing back in the room with a pail of warm water, a rag, and a towel over her shoulder.

"Shush child," she said, "yah wanna wake the neighbors?"

"She dead!"

"No she's not, my baby. She just in a deep sleep. You can go back to bed nah. Thank you, baby."

Lula backed away, stopping at the door to watch Big Ma move Beatrice to the other side of the bed and take her gown off to wash her. Lula went back over to help Big Ma get Beatrice's gown over her head. Big Ma didn't object. Lifting Beatrice on her side, Big Ma motioned her head for Lula to grab the towel hanging on her shoulder. Lula slid it off, shook it out, and ran over to the other side, laying the towel down on the wet spot.

Beatrice moaned when she felt the warm rag rubbing across her forehead. Lula perked up moving closer to Beatrice. "Mama?"

Beatrice opened her eyes while Big Ma continued to wash down her body.

"Hi," Beatrice said, running the tips of her fingers softly down the side of Lula's face. "Such a pretty little girl."

"How yah feelin', Sha?" Big Ma said, washing down Beatrice's legs.

"Cold!"

"Yah gonna be warm in a minute, Sha. Just gotta finish washin' yah down."

"Why are you washing me?"

"Yah had an accident."

"Really?"

Lula knelt down and took hold of Beatrice's hand.

Beatrice smiled asking, "Whose child is this?"

Big Ma and Lula paused. Beatrice looked back and forth at them, waiting for an answer. Lula stood up on her feet still holding Beatrice's hand.

"Yah serious, Bea?" Big Ma asked with the rag in her hand dripping water.

"Why you keep calling me Beatrice?"

Everyone was quiet looking at each other, asking the same question with their expressions. Killing the docile moment, Big Ma dropped the cloth in the pail and took Lula by the hand. "Com'on nah, time fo' yah to go back to bed. I'll be in there in a bit to tuck you in." She escorted Lula to the door.

"But, Big Ma!"

"Go, Lula Mae!" Big Ma released Lula's hand out of the room and shut the door. Lula ran through the dark to her room, tripping over a chair on her way there. Hopping on one leg into the bed next to her sisters, Lula rubbed her sore toe before tossing and turning the rest of the night.

***

The next morning, Big Ma sent the girls out to get ice from the store. Lillie walked between Lula and Mary, holding their hands. They walked barefoot, wearing different colored dresses that Big Ma made for them—most of the town's people travelled barefoot, only wearing shoes when required.

Mary wore yellow, Lula had on blue, and Lillie wore green, all with matching ribbons in their hair. Following their religious dress code that pants were inappropriate for females, the girls wore mainly dresses or skirts below the knee which was the proper attire for God fearing Christian girls. Big Ma and Leroy had many debates about religious dress codes since Beatrice and Leroy didn't mind their daughters wearing pants, shorts, or overalls, as long as they were clean. Their argument was, "They're children, let them be." They came to agreement with Big Ma that the girls could wear overalls when they came home from school. But as Big Ma's stay became more frequent due to Leroy's absence and Beatrice's illness, the girls had to abide by her rules meaning dresses only.

On the way to the store, Mary picked up every rock she saw, throwing it into the road while walking. Being the youngest at four years-old, Mary followed Lillie and Lula everywhere, playing and getting into everything, or bringing home things she found on the road, whether it was a unique looking rock or a funny shaped stick. Lula and Lillie always took the fall for the outside objects under the bed, not wanting to see their little sister get in trouble.

Lillie, on the other hand, was prim and proper like Beatrice, always fixing her clothes, stopping to knock off dirt while playing outside. At seven years-old, Lillie was the oldest and responsible for looking after Lula and Mary, taking on the parental role when no adults were present. When Beatrice and Leroy were gone to work, Lillie would pick figs for Lula and Mary, giving them the ripest figs to eat while she settled for the unripe sour figs. Lillie made sure Mary and Lula had the best, even if it meant her walking away with less or nothing at all. Her chocolate skin and wisdom-filled eyes made it look as if she'd lived many lifetimes. The quietest of the sisters, Lillie was an observer who learned a lot about people watching them in action. She spoke mostly to Beatrice and Lula, but when people did hear Lillie speak, her soft melodic voice soothed their ears putting smiles on their faces.

Lula, quite the opposite, was the loud mouth. "Here come Lula Mae," is what people would say, hearing her before actually seeing her. At six years-old, Lula would initiate conversation with any and everybody, making adults laugh, even though she didn't quite get the humor in her words. Lula played hard, spoke her mind like Beatrice, and aimed to master everything like Leroy. Whatever Lula did, it had to be to the best of her ability—whenever she helped cook, it had to taste great; whenever she did Lillie or Mary's hair, it had to look like perfection. If it wasn't to her liking, Lula started over again until she got it right.

Lula and Lillie were best friends. Their bond was so tight, one couldn't be seen without the other. They spent many nights up talking, and Lula's loud mouth would always send Leroy or Beatrice in their room to hush them up, and when the door closed, Lillie and Lula covered their mouths bursting into laughter underneath the sheet.

Heading to the store, Lula let go of Lillie's hand and started running ahead.

Lillie yelled, "Come back here, Lula Mae! Yah kno' we gotta stay together."

Lula turned around putting her hands up, dancing and singing, "Na Na Na Boo Boo, stick yah head in Pu Pu."

Mary pointed, "Eww, I'm tellin', you said a nasty word."

"Hush up nah, nobody ain't tellin' on nobody. Lula Mae, please stop playin', we gotta stay together!" Lillie yelled, moving faster to catch up to Lula.

"Can't get me," Lula said, ready to run.

Lillie couldn't help herself after hearing those words. She took off running with Mary and they both chased after Lula, who ran up the road and behind a tree in front of the store. Mary and Lillie chased Lula around the tree and caught her, screaming and laughing as they tickled Lula's neck. Lillie finally stopped and brushed Lula and Mary off before brushing herself off. Lula fixed their hair, making sure they all were presentable, following Beatrice's motto: "Cleanliness is next to godliness."

They entered Mr. Pete's store which was full of candy, snacks, soda water, fruit preserves, tobacco, ice, fresh crackling, warm boudin, and smoked barbeque meat cooked out back on a grill pit. A Zydeco record was playing when they entered the store. Lillie took hold of Lula and Mary's hand, noticing they were the only ones in the store that early in the morning. Lula and Mary moved closer to Lillie as they crept into the store, stepping over each other's feet.

Lillie yelled, "Hello," hoping to find Mr. Pete's wife rather than Mr. Pete himself.

Mr. Pete popped up from behind the counter, leaning forward. "Nah I kno' y'all ain't gonna past ole Uncle Pete without speakin'," he said, scaring the girls half to death. Lula and Mary held tighter to Lillie's arm. Their hearts beating fast.

Lillie spoke, "No, sir. We didn't see yah. Hello, sir."

"Hello Mr. Pete," Lula and Mary flatly said in unison, looking everywhere but at him.

"Weather must've got y'all feverish."

Lillie swallowed hard, "No, sir! We didn't see yah, sir."

"Aw alright, Sha, I believe yah. Y'all ain't no bigger than fleas, can't see over dis here counter. I bet I look like King Kong to y'all, huh?" Mr. Pete laughed, slapping his knee. The girls forced a fake laugh, squeezing each other's hand. Mr. Pete was known for his bad jokes and having a few loose marbles. His missing tooth and lazy eye didn't help this theory. Beatrice, Leroy, and Big Ma weren't too fond of Mr. Pete and never allowed the girls to go to his store by themselves. If one wanted to go, they all went.

Mr. Pete came from around the counter and offered them Mary Jane's in a bowl to calm the rigidity down. They all declined even though that was their favorite candy.

Mr. Pete sat the bowl down. "So what bring y'all pretty young things here t'day? Louverta send y'all down here fo' somethin'?"

Lillie answered, "Yes, sir."

"What she need? I heard bout yah mama. Hope she feel betta soon."

"Thank yah, sir. She needs ice."

"Y'all sho' y'all can carry it back there? Y'all ain't nothin' but skin and bones. Look like skeletons in dresses," he roared an unnecessary laughter. This time, the girls just stared at him. Mr. Pete stopped laughing, clearing his throat in embarrassment.

Lillie spoke fast, eager to get back home. "We can carry it, sir."

"Yah sho'?"

"Yes, sir."

"Alrighty then." Mr. Pete went in the back and came back out with a block of ice in a paper bag.

"Y'all need dis here chopped, Sha?"

"No, sir. Big Ma got an ice pick."

He handed the ice over for Lula and Lillie to hold.

Lillie told Mary, "Look in my pocket and get the coin Big Ma gave us."

Mary's little hands dug in the side of Lillie's dress and pulled out a nickel. She walked it over to Mr. Pete, who took it from her, winking. Mary ran behind Lula.

"Anything else?" He chuckled, watching Mary peek from behind Lula.

Lula said, "Doublemint gum please, sir."

"I only got a nickel," Lillie said with her eyes telling Lula 'let's go'.

"Here, take dis fo' yah sister," Mr. Pete held out a pack of gum for Mary to grab. She ran over, snatched it, and ran back behind Lula.

"Thank you, sir," Mary said from behind Lula's back.

Lula added, "Thank you, sir."

They carefully headed towards the door.

"Hey!" Mr. Pete yelled. They stopped in their tracks looking back over at Mr. Pete. He pointed at his cheek and said, "Give me some suga'."

Lula and Mary looked at Lillie, and then followed her lead hurrying out the door, fast. Lula and Lillie tripped over the two steps outside while holding the ice, leaving Mr. Pete hysterically laughing and hitting his knee.

Lula stopped outside looking around. "Y'all see the Candy Lady anywhere?"

Lillie looked around. "No, don't see the Candy Lady t'day. Maybe she'll be here tomorrow."

Mary asked, "Who's the Candy Lady?"

Lula answered, "This lady gave me and Lillie Mae a whole lot of candy that time you stayed home. She's real nice."

Lillie said, "Com'on, dis here ice heavy. We'll look fo' her some other time."

On the walk home, Mary walked backwards playfully using her hands to guide Lula and Lillie, saying, "Wait. Stop. Slow down. Okay, com'on."

Lillie and Lula paced themselves carrying the ice through the yard with their arms hurting and fingers turning numb. Mary marched in front, guiding and encouraging them to keep moving until they all stopped in their tracks after hearing screams come from the house. Lillie and Lula sat the ice on the porch and shook out their arms while listening to the screams of their mother. Mary turned to Lillie with a worried look, waiting for an explanation. Lillie shrugged. They stood there motionless looking at their parent's bedroom window, listening to Beatrice yelling at the top of her lungs. Big Ma busted the screen door open and snatched up the bag of ice before running back into the house. She popped her head back outside and waved for Lillie to come to her. "Y'all stay out here fo' a while."

"Yes, ma'am."

Big Ma went back in the house and closed the front door, which they rarely closed during the day. The girls stared at the door for a moment with long faces before taking a seat on the porch. Lula opened her pack of Doublemint gum and gave Lillie and Mary a piece, listening to the commotion inside the house. Church member's voices were heard praying and reading scriptures from the bible while Beatrice screamed for everyone to leave her house.

An hour later, Doc walked out the house wearing faded pants with suspenders holding them up, a white t-shirt, and hat. The girls sat up fast folding their hands and holding their breath to perfect their posture. Doc nodded at them and left to go back home, allowing the girls to exhale and slump back down in their chairs.

Doc was a stern man who was quick to get a switch. He never gave any warnings, interrogations, or chances when a child was in trouble. The switch did the talking for him. Even though the girls rarely got in trouble with Doc, the stories Leroy told about getting beat as a child for no reason was all the girls needed to fear Doc. "Doc so mean, he'd scare a stick straight," they'd hear Leroy say on more than one occasion.

"Watermelon...Watermelon...Watermelon..." Watermelon man Bue rang his bell as he came down the road in his watermelon truck. The girls jumped out their chairs with their mouths watering for fresh watermelon. Big Ma came outside digging in her purse for a quarter. Watermelon man Bue stopped in front of their house, tilting his hat to greet them, and jumped out of his truck using a rag to dry the sweat off his face. Big Ma and the girls walked over to the wagon, getting first pick of the biggest, juiciest watermelon. Big Ma never knew why Watermelon man Bue started his route near her house all the time, but was thankful he did since she got first pick of the best watermelons. He pulled out the biggest watermelon and walked it over to the porch acting as if he didn't hear the screams coming from the house. The girls rubbed their palms ready to eat while Big Ma gave Watermelon man Bue a quarter. When he left, Big Ma lifted the watermelon without any struggle and went back in the house as Lillie held the door open for Big Ma. The girls waited by the door trying to peek in the house to see what was going on in there. They jumped back when Big Ma came out and handed Lillie a bowl full of watermelon chunks cut into huge squares.

Lula grabbed the first one and took a bite. "Mmm, Big Ma, dis taste just like yours. It's sweet."

Big Ma patted Lula's head and disappeared back into the house. Mary and Lula pulled their chairs near Lillie for easy access to the bowl, and they ate fast, trying to beat each other in getting the juiciest chunks.

"Where's daddy?" Lula asked Lillie in between chewing.

"At work."

"He never work dis much b'fore." Lula popped another watermelon square in her mouth, using the back of her hand to wipe the juice off her mouth.

"He workin' a double shift."

"What that mean?"

Lillie shrugged spitting seeds out into the yard. "Don't kno', heard daddy tell mama that."

When the girls finished, they sat in silence waving at the people passing by, hoping they didn't hear the screams from the house. Lula couldn't take hearing her mother screaming any longer. She got up from her chair and walked over to Lillie, whistling, looking around nonchalantly, and then quickly tapped Lillie on the head. "Tag, you're it," she said, running off the porch. Lillie and Mary jumped up chasing Lula around the house. When they caught her, they started a game of hide-and-go-seek, running around laughing and screaming until they heard the screen door fling open and saw Big Ma standing there with her hands on her hips. The girls froze. Big Ma looked at them for a moment, then relaxed her stance. She told them to be careful and went back inside, letting the girls resume their game.

***

Big Ma went inside the bedroom, walking around the bed, keeping a keen eye on Beatrice. Three of her church members held bibles in their hands while sitting at the corners of the bed worn out. Beatrice lay there quiet for the moment, breathing hard and crying in her pink gown and hair all over her head. Big Ma cautiously sat beside Beatrice, touching her head to feel if her fever went down. She flinched when Beatrice moved, but Beatrice remained calm. She looked up, recognizing Big Ma standing there and pointed at the water glass sitting on the night stand, smacking her dry mouth. Big Ma sat Beatrice up, placed the glass near her lips, and helped her take a sip of water with a shaky hand before laying Beatrice back down. One of Big Ma's friends mustered up enough energy to read another scripture out loud. Beatrice lay there listening and closed her eyes, taking in the blessed words of God. She felt at ease saying the Lord's Prayer to herself, thanking God for his everlasting mercy. Big Ma and her other friend got up and chimed in the prayer, placing a hand on Beatrice while waving their other hand in the air, shaking their heads feeling the Holy Spirit move in. The warmth of their hands soothed Beatrice, until she felt their hands turn cold and scaly. Beatrice opened her eyes to a snake wrapping around her arms. She screamed smacking the snake off her, falling out of the bed to get to the door. One of the strange people blocked the door while the other two strangers tried grabbing Beatrice's arms. Beatrice ran to the corner of the room, fell to her knees and told them to stay away. The women she had never met before stood there speaking in tongues, holding a book in their hand as Beatrice covered her ears to shield herself from the awful sounding dialect, closing her eyes screaming. When they stopped, Beatrice hesitantly opened her eyes, looking up at the woman staring at her. And then, right before her eyes, she saw the women's faces and bodies turn into green scaly creatures hissing with foaming mouths. Beatrice screamed in fear, crying as they closed in on her. When one touched her, Beatrice kicked and screamed trying to get away. Snakes began slithering out from underneath the door, bed, and window towards Beatrice's feet. Beatrice kicked wildly, throwing them off her while the three creatures moved in closer trying to touch her. Beatrice started screaming for God's mercy as she got outnumbered by snakes crawling up her gown. The biggest snake made its way to her neck, circling around it. The creatures closed in on Beatrice, showing their gruesome fangs, snipping at her face. Beatrice screamed hitting one in the face with all her might. She pulled the biggest snake from around her neck and threw it against the wall, and then jumped on one of the creatures, beating it all over its head, banging its head against the floor while the other creatures growled at Beatrice, snipping their sharp fangs, forcing her to fall back against the wall. The biggest snake slithered back over to Beatrice and lifted itself staring its black beady eyes at her, opening its mouth showing its fangs. It snipped at Beatrice, who screamed and put her hands over her face crying as she repeatedly screamed for God's help.

Then, at once, the hissing stopped.

Beatrice gradually lowered her hands cracking one eye open. The snakes and three creatures were gone. Opening both eyes wide, Beatrice saw Big Ma and her church friends breathing heavily, looking at her in fear. The one friend was on the ground holding her bleeding nose. Everyone stayed in their positions catching their breath, not knowing what to do next. Big Ma called Beatrice's name, asking if she was back. Beatrice wavered a bit and then nodded. Big Ma helped her church friend off the floor, examining her broken nose. Beatrice apologized, telling them everything she saw. Big Ma listened. She knew she had a long day of prayer ahead.

Chapter 2

Big Ma cooked smothered pork shanks with rice and gravy, mustard greens, fried okra, and baked sweet potatoes from her garden. For dessert, mashing butter into the frosting, melting it over the hot cake allowing the mixture to seep into the cake for a mouthwatering glaze, Big Ma prepared a homemade butter cake fresh out the oven.

Even with the delicious meal before them, Big Ma, Lillie, Lula, and Mary ate in silence after the ordeal with Beatrice; Doc's presence at the table didn't help any. Ever since Big Ma was spending more time at Leroy and Beatrice's house, Doc came by more often to eat or pick up a plate of food. He took care of Big Ma's garden back home, following her systematic instructions on the maintenance of the garden to ensure continued efficacy.

Lula noticed Big Ma avoiding eye contact with Doc at the table and wondered why Big Ma was upset with him, knowing this was the way Big Ma reacted towards people she was mad at. When Doc asked Big Ma to pass him the fried okra, she got up from the table and dropped the plate in front of Doc, leaving the plate whirling around before coming to a halt. Doc dished up okra on his plate, undaunted by Big Ma's abrasive manner.

She had pleaded with Doc before dinner to talk sense into Leroy, to make him come home and be with his ill wife. She wanted Doc to confront Leroy on the rumor of his alleged affair with another woman, knowing Doc was the only person who could get through to Leroy. But Doc didn't want to interfere and told Big Ma she needed to mind her business as well. Big Ma used the bible as a final attempt to convince Doc to talk to Leroy, preaching the word of God, stressing how adultery was a sin and Leroy was headed straight for hell if he continued. Doc was aloof to Big Ma's preaching. First and foremost, a man's manhood came before anything—a creed Doc adamantly stood by.

Underneath it all, Doc secretly was partial to Leroy finally taking a stand against Beatrice by finding another woman who treated Leroy like a real man and worshipped the ground he walked on. It served Beatrice right, in Doc's opinion, for treating his son like a boy and not a man. After hearing about Leroy's infidelities, Doc invited his son over when Big Ma was gone, pulled a chair out for him, gave him soda water, and did something for Leroy that Doc had never done before…cook a meal. This kind of attention from his father was something new for Leroy and a bit overwhelming, yet Leroy couldn't deny that he loved every bit of it, solidifying his decision to continue his affair with his mistress, Cordelia Butts.

Big Ma threw her hand towel in her plate and got up from the table. "I gotta check in on y'all mama. Y'all start clearin' dis here table off," Big Ma told the girls. They all wanted to run behind Big Ma to see about their mother too, and to get away from Doc, but they conceded and did as they were told. Lula and Mary stayed close to Lillie.

The plate of food on the nightstand was cold. Beatrice lay on her side looking over at the wall thinking about Leroy when Big Ma walked into the bedroom.

"Beatrice, yah gotta eat somethin', Sha. You ain't eat all day." Big Ma took a seat at the edge of the bed.

"Poison!"

Big Ma sighed, rolling her eyes. "Lord Jesus, help me. Ain't nobody tryin' to poison yah. I bought the rice and meat on that plate and the vegetables came straight from my garden. You always ate the vegetables from my garden, couldn't get enough of 'em."

Beatrice lay there biting at her thumb, still staring at the wall in a fresh pink gown Big Ma put on her after washing her with cool water to lower her fever.

Big Ma kept Beatrice's hair neat, frequently changed her gowns, kept layers of covers over Beatrice to stop the chills, and did everything in caution and in prayer. After Big Ma's friends left, Beatrice fell too ill to move.

"Poison," Beatrice blurted again.

Big Ma gave up trying to make Beatrice eat a home cooked meal and resorted to giving her the only thing she'd eat. "Yah want crackling, Sha?"

Beatrice perked up, nodding. Packaged food was the only food Beatrice ate.

Big Ma went to the kitchen and grabbed a bag of crackling and soda water from the pantry. She gave it to Beatrice who ripped the bag open, popped a bunch of pieces in her mouth, and opened the bottle of soda water to drink away her thirst.

"Dis here junk ain't healthy fo' yah, Bea. Yah gotta eat real food at sometime, Sha. At least vegetables or soup."

Beatrice ate a few more pieces of crackling, fearing the worse at the thought of eating any open food. Deep in her heart, she wanted to sit at the table and eat Big Ma's good food with her children, and be able to cook for them again. Beatrice's mouth watered for a taste of Big Ma's famous butter cake with a glass of cold milk, but the overwhelming sensation of death by poison consumed her. No one was to be trusted. The snakes, bugs, creatures, illnesses, and memory loss at any given time meant she could be poisoned at any given time, too. It was a burden for Beatrice to live in fear every second of the day and she took full blame for Leroy's growing absence.

Big Ma said, "I'll be back, Sha."

"Where are you going?"

"I gotta help the girls in the kitchen and get dem ready fo' bed," Big Ma said, leaving the room.

At the table, Doc helped himself and the girls to another slice of butter cake. He took a bite, sipped it down with coffee, and wiped his mouth. "How she doin'?" He asked. Big Ma motioned for Doc to follow her to the kitchen so that the girls wouldn't hear.

In the kitchen, Big Ma lowered her voice. "She's all there right nah. Fo' how long, Lord only knows. I got the sisters from church on alert if I need help. They'll be here tomorrow fo' prayer except for Sister Mattie. Her nose broke. But the rest of us gonna pray dem evil spirits away in the name of Jesus. We gonna save Bea's tortured soul and get her back to herself again. Yah kno' she's been eatin' package food fo' almost two weeks nah?"

"If Beatrice don't get betta soon, dem chillun comin' with us."

"No! Beatrice gonna be just fine and Leroy will back home soon. God's gonna make a way."

"Well, tell God to hurry up or else dem girls comin' with us!"

Big Ma squinted her eyes at Doc and went back into the dining room.

Lillie put a fork full of butter cake in her mouth and looked up at Big Ma, "Where's daddy?" She couldn't hold it in any longer. She needed to know where Leroy was for herself and for her sisters.

"Yah kno' betta than to get in grown folk business, Sha," Big Ma snapped. "Y'all get up and help me in dis here kitchen."

"Yes, ma'am!"

Lula and Mary rushed the rest of their cake in their mouths and got up with Lillie.

Doc grabbed Big Ma's arm. "How bout yah care fo' Beatrice in the day, then come back home at night."

"Leroy ain't here," Big Ma pointed her finger at the girls, "who gonna take care of dem when I'm gone?"

Doc pointed to himself. "That's why they should come live with us."

Lula and Lillie shot fearful looks at each other.

"That's not gonna happen. These chillun gonna stay here with they mama, even if I gotta be on bended knee every night in prayer to rid dem demons out of Bea!" Big Ma paused, regretting her words in front of the girls.

Doc walked over to Big Ma, slapped her face with the back of his hand and said in a stern tone, "Yah watch yah mouth, woman! I told yah bout back talkin' me. Do as I say, yah hear?"

Big Ma covered her mouth, embarrassed for being an elderly woman chastised in such a way in front of grandchildren who admired her. "Y'all go to bed."

Lillie, Mary, and Lula stood there, shocked. They weren't going to leave their grandmother alone.

"Go!" Doc yelled, taking off his belt.

The girls ran, pausing at the door, watching in terror at Big Ma holding onto the table bent over, trying to cover the blood seeping from her mouth.

She calmly said, "Go 'head, my babies, I'm alright."

They went into their room shutting the door behind them.

***

Lula slipped out of bed leaving Lillie and Mary there to sleep, and tiptoed past Big Ma, who was resting on the sofa with a swollen lip—Lula and her sisters didn't leave the room after Doc left. They wanted to come out to assist Big Ma, see if she was okay, but thought the better of it knowing it would break Big Ma's heart for them to see her after Doc hit her.

Lula sneaked into her parent's bedroom, pushing the door open slowly. She grabbed the hand towel from Beatrice's forehead and dipped it in the bowl of water on the nightstand, then squeezed the water out and dabbed the cool rag across her mother's forehead. She left the rag on Beatrice's forehead and went over to her feet, massaging them, squeezing the arch. Beatrice raised her head staring at Lula without saying a word. The lone candle burned on the dresser, providing enough light for Beatrice to see Lula looking back at her. This was first time Beatrice noticed her daughter in weeks. "Lula Mae?"

"Yes, ma'am! It's me," Lula perked up. "Dis what yah did fo' me when I was sick. You say 'we gotta get yah bones workin' again', so that's what I'm doin' fo' you. Yah gotta get betta soon. Grandpa Doc wants us to move in with him and I don't wanna stay with him."

"What did I tell you about your grammar? Pronounce your R's and your G's and do not say 'dis', it's 'this'. I haven't been sick that long, Miss Lula Mae Harrison."

Lula smiled, "Yes, ma'am."

"And there's nothing wrong with me, so don't believe anything that anyone is saying about me. I'm just seeing things that they can't see. They're just not listening to me."

"Then can you pick figs with us tomorrow?"

Beatrice lay back down on her pillow, taking a deep breath focusing in on the ceiling as she folded her hands across her chest. "I'm sorry, my baby. I can't right now."

Lula walked over to Beatrice's bedside, grabbed hold of her mother's pink night gown and started pulling at it. "I want some now. Com'on, mama!"

"Please stop, baby, I need more time. I have to make sure I'm safe first."

"Safe from what?"

Beatrice didn't answer.

Lula continued to pull, which wasn't working much, so she grabbed Beatrice's legs and pull them over to the floor, then started pulling her by the arms. Beatrice protested, but willingly sat up with every pull and heard bones cracking as she pushed herself up out of bed. Lula ran underneath Beatrice's arm helping her onto her feet. Beatrice winced in pain from the severe headache returning and knew the stomach aches, chills, and fatigue were soon to follow.

"Com'on, mama!" Lula encouraged, helping Beatrice take a few steps to the bedroom door. Lula opened the door quietly and walked Beatrice past Big Ma, who slept in an exhausted slumber. Beatrice's stomach turned as she opened the front door and took baby steps outside. Her pink gown danced in the night breeze. She had to hold it down to keep it from flying up. Shaking, Beatrice gripped Lula tighter going down the porch steps into the dark night. She held onto Lula so tight, her nails almost broke Lula's skin. They walked around back to the fig tree as Lula bored the pain of breaking skin, not wanting to startle her mother.

"We made it," Lula said, looking up at Beatrice.

Beatrice's hair blew in the wind as she shivered looking around hearing the leaves hitting against each other. She saw branches swaying in front of the moon lit sky.

Fear had been an illusion to Beatrice all of her life. It was something man made to distract and control people's minds as far as Beatrice saw it. She thought her phobia of snakes and bugs were long gone when she began to see them as God's creatures, only to be revisited by this same fear that was now attacking her relentlessly and worsening the more she got scared, realizing the fear never left, she just had been avoiding them all this time.

In the back of the house, red eyes formed on the leaves. The stiff fig tree branches started to wiggle. Sounds of hisses came closer to

Beatrice's ear. She got scared and pulled Lula behind her, standing strong, ready to fight to protect her child. Surrendering to her fears was not an option. It was either them or her.

Lula watched as Beatrice screamed and charged at the fig tree. She started breaking off limbs, ripping leaves off branches, and then climbed up in the fig tree and started snatching figs off, throwing them at the snakes with all her might, daring them to go near her child. "Come and get me," Beatrice screamed. Her head pounded, feverish body sweated, and stomach churned. Still, Beatrice fought off the beady eyed slithering snakes.

Lula backed away. This wasn't the proper woman who took her, Lillie, and Mary on nature walks to pick pecans, berries, figs, and apples from trees. This wasn't the beautiful woman who loved walking barefoot, stuffing her feet into the soil and mashing it between her toes. This wasn't the smart woman who taught them correct English and distained broken speech. This wasn't the courageous woman who didn't care if people called her crazy when she ate virgin soil, explaining that it was the highest source of nutrients which gave life to seeds that grew into fruits and vegetables to fuel people's bodies. This wasn't Beatrice Harrison.

Lula burst out in tears screaming for her mother to stop.

Beatrice stopped, panting out of breath, looking down at her frightened child. She got down from the tree, ran over and hugged Lula tight, apologizing. Big Ma came rushing towards them asking what happened.

Beatrice realized her aches were gone. She shook her head and tapped at her forehead. No pain. She didn't hesitate to look over her shoulder to find fallen figs, leaves, and branches everywhere. She smiled looking over at Big Ma. "They're gone, Big Ma. They're gone!" Beatrice reached for a fig off the tree and handed it to Lula. "There you go, my baby."

Lula smiled, admiring the fig in the moonlight.

Big Ma picked the leaves from Beatrice's hair wondering what went on out there. Beatrice collapsed to her knees and began regurgitating a weird liquid from her mouth.

Lula yelled, "Mama!"

Big Ma said, "Go to bed, Lula Mae!"

"But, Big Ma!"

"Nah, Lula Mae, go!" Big Ma bent down and rubbed Beatrice's back, waving Lula away.

Big Ma took Beatrice's arm and helped her up dusting her gown off.

She walked her back to the front of the house and Beatrice whispered under her breath, "I beat it."

Chapter 3

Lula woke up to a mouthwatering smell in the air, inhaling deeply as her taste buds aroused. She pushed Mary's foot off her face and crawled over her sisters to follow the smell wondering why Big Ma didn't wake them to help prepare Sunday's breakfast.

Entering the kitchen, Lula rubbed her eyes to make sure she wasn't dreaming. There in the kitchen was Beatrice, Leroy, and Big Ma preparing breakfast together. Lula hadn't seen Leroy in a week, and when he did come around, he didn't stay long. More surprisingly, Beatrice was full of vivacious energy cooking with hair rollers in her hair and wearing a pink robe as if the past few weeks had never happened.

Leroy knelt down holding his arms out for Lula, who ran into them grabbing hold tightly around her father's neck.

"Are you hungry, baby?" Beatrice said. "We got bacon, eggs, grits, biscuits, and cold milk for breakfast."

"Wow," is all Lula could say. She jumped down from Leroy's arms and ran over to Beatrice, hugging around her waist, feeling like she'd just awakened from a bad dream.

Big Ma said, "Go get yah sisters up fo' me, baby." She bent down for Lula to give her a kiss on the cheek.

Lula smiled. "We goin' to church t'day?"

"What did I tell you about your words?" Beatrice said with her hands on her hips.

"I mean, 'going'. Are we going to church today, Big Ma?"

"I'm goin', but y'all gonna stay here with yah mama fo' the day." Big Ma looked over her shoulder. "You ain't out the woods yet, Beatrice. Yah still gotta get yah strength back," she added, carrying a plate full of bacon to the dining room table.

"Ma'am," Beatrice answered, popping a piece of bacon in her mouth following with a pitcher of cold milk. Beatrice set it down on the table and felt a pair of hands wrap around her waist. Leroy kissed Beatrice on the cheek, thankful for her forgiving him after leaving her during a rough illness.

After the night outside fighting the snakes, Leroy sneaked into the house to get more belongings only to find Beatrice sitting there waiting, knowing he was coming. Beatrice gave him one last chance and Leroy assured Beatrice that he was going to stay home for good. His eye fluttering stopped for a moment when his eyes rested on Beatrice, the love of his life, and when she saw the love emanating from his eyes, she forgave him giving their marriage another chance.

At the table, Beatrice turned around and wrapped her arms around Leroy's neck, kissing her husband's lips. The two blushed while looking into each other's eyes like teenagers in love again. Lula stood by the door watching with a big grin on her face, happy to see her parents back to normal. She hurried to wake Lillie and Mary up.

"Get up, mama and daddy here cooking!"

"They are?" Lillie perked right up.

"No they not, daddy gone," Mary said, stretching her little arms out, yawning.

Lula ripped the covers off them. "Go see for yourself then."

Lillie and Mary inhaled the smell of food and jumped out of bed racing to see if Lula was telling the truth.

Big Ma led in grace thanking the Lord for performing a miracle on Beatrice's health and bringing Leroy back home, cracking one eye open to make sure the girl's eyes were closed. After her long-winded prayer, everyone started passing plates.

Leroy saturated his plate with hot sauce, shaking it all over his eggs, grits, bacon, and even the biscuits.

Beatrice said, "Leroy, that's enough."

"Nah it ain't, I need a lot of hot sauce. Help bring the taste out in food," he said, shoving a fork full of grits in his mouth. "Ain't that right girls?"

"Yes, sir!" They agreed in unison.

Beatrice said, "Alright, don't get mad at me when you get heart burn."

Lula pointed at the hot sauce. "Can I have some please?"

"That's my girl!" He laughed, handing the hot sauce over to her.

Beatrice protested, "Oh no, don't give her that!"

"Com'on nah, Bea, if the girl wants hot sauce, then give the girl some hot sauce. My grandfather gave me my first taste of hot sauce when I was bout her age."

They watched Lula shake the hot sauce over every inch of her plate just like Leroy did, showing that she could keep up with her father.

Big Ma finally said, "Alright nah, Lula Mae, that's enough!"

Leroy said, "Mama, let her put as much as she want on her food."

Big Ma shot a look over at Leroy, but relented.

Lula set the bottle down, picked up her fork and began eating her eggs, acting like it was no big deal. After a few bites, Lula paused, dropping her fork on the plate and started hollering, fanning her tongue hanging out her mouth. Leroy chuckled. Big Ma and Beatrice rushed to Lula's aid, taking her to the kitchen sink to rinse her mouth. Beatrice dried Lula's face with a hand towel asking if she was all right.

Going back to the table, Leroy was still chuckling.

Big Ma said, "Lord have mercy, why you laughin'? That ain't funny."

Beatrice added, "No it isn't."

Leroy said, "Aw com'on, calm down." He turned to Lula. "What I failed to add was, when my grandfather let me try the hot sauce, I ran screamin' thinking my mouth was on fire. And yah kno' what he said to me? He say 'Boy, think b'fore yah do. You knew that stuff was hot b'fore yah put it in yah mouth. Betta start usin' that God given brain of yours instead of following someone else'."

Beatrice reached over to wipe the tears off Lula's red face. Leroy got up and kissed Lula's cheek, "You okay, suga'?"

Lula nodded.

"I got yah nose!" He pretended like he took Lula's nose and pocketed it. She started laughing. He smiled rubbing her back and looked up at Big Ma, who was staring at him, unimpressed with his lesson for the day.

Big Ma continued eating breaking a wry smile. "You and yah lessons. Lord have mercy." She got up to prepare another plate of food for Lula and took the plate drenched in hot sauce, placing it in front of Leroy. "There, nah you eat it!"

Everyone burst in laughter, including Leroy, who took the plate and dumped everything on his own plate. "No problem. The hotter the betta!"

Chapter 4

Speeding down the back road, Cordelia Butts drove with fulminating emotions stirring. With a bottle of whiskey in hand, she drove fast past empty fields and farmhouses, accidently passing her house. Mashing on the brakes, she came to a screeching halt, put the car in reverse and screeched backwards, leaving the dirt trail twirling in the night air. Panting uncontrollably through her nose like a wild bull, Cordelia remained in the driver's seat to get her bearings, rubbing her forehead thinking of ways to counteract the image that kept wrecking her brain. She got out the car and shut the door, which flung back open, raising her anger to a new high. She slammed it closed with her foot for it to remain shut. "Humph!" She bragged to the car door daring it to open again, then staggered towards her house taking another swig from her whiskey bottle.

Cordelia Butts was a petite, square shaped woman who didn't hold her liquor well. Her nickname was "Redbone" because of the red undertones against her honey colored skin covered in acne bumps. Her bun failed miserably at holding her curly hair in place which she constantly had to brush back with no success. Heavy eyeliner outlined Cordelia's eyes, continuing in an upward slant to give her a more exotic look, which was countered by an enormous attention grabbing nose and gapped teeth. Sweat ran down Cordelia's face, underarms, back, and inner thighs as she rummaged through her purse for her door key and began hitting the screen door in a furious wrath when she couldn't find them. Exhausted, Cordelia fell to her knees huffing and puffing, smacking away the mosquitoes.

She took another swig from her whiskey bottle while wobbling back on her feet, digging in between her breasts, remembering where she put her house key last. She accidently pulled a boob out retrieving it and pushed it back in, cussing underneath her breath. She unlocked the front door and staggered into the house, finding her way in the dark. Turning a light on, Cordelia finished the rest of the whiskey bottle and screamed at it for being empty, shattering it against the wall. Without a flinch, Cordelia headed straight to her bedroom, falling to her knees next to the bed searching underneath it for a box.

Pulling her emergency stash out the box, Cordelia grabbed the half empty whiskey bottle, twisted the cap off and voraciously downed it to the last drop. She leaned up against the bed wiping sweat from her forehead with the back of her hand, and then sat motionless, allowing the alcohol to ease her jittery nerves.

"Why can't he just leave the bitch?" Cordelia screamed. "Just leave her!" She continued through tears, "WHY ME!" She screamed repeatedly, rocking back and forth. She pulled at her hair, growling through her teeth, and picked up the empty whiskey bottle, throwing it against her bedroom window, using her arm to shield her face from the glass flying everywhere. Quieting down after the sounds of the shattering glass bottle, and a now broken window, Cordelia whimpered pulling her hair out the untamed bun in a panic. Her soft cries grew louder turning into screams.

The memory of Leroy kissing Beatrice on the porch that morning replayed in Cordelia's mind, making her wish she had never driven by their house, and the thought of Leroy not noticing her riding by made Cordelia yank a lock of hair out in the mist of her fury. She circled the bald patch with her index finger feeling the smoothness of it, and then got up carefully to avoid the glass on the floor, staggering out of the room with her finger still touching the bald spot.

"It's time fo' a visit!" Cordelia slurred, stumbling back out the house. She studied the blurred car keys in her hand, then tossed them aside as she staggered up the dark road.

***

Knock knock knock. "Who is it?" *Knock knock knock.*

"God damnit, who is it knockin' at my door dis late at night!" Tauntadi took her shotgun from behind the door and swung the front door open, cocking the gun back pointing directly in Cordelia's face. Cordelia jumped back with her hands up.

"Cordelia," Tauntadi said, looking over her gun. "That you? The hell yah tryin' to do, break my goddamn door down! Why yah here at dis hour anyways?"

Cordelia's hands dropped when Tauntadi acknowledged her. She pushed the gun out her way and staggered into Tauntadi's house. Tauntadi slammed the front door and placed the shotgun back against the wall as Cordelia wobbled close in Tauntadi's face slurring her words, "Got some liquor?"

Tauntadi stepped back waving away the foul odor omitting from Cordelia's mouth. "Look like you had yah fair share already, Sha."

"So, where yah been? I came here earlier and yah was gone," Cordelia said, plopping on Tauntadi's dusty sofa covered in thick faded plastic. Cordelia waved away the dust coughing, "Why don't yah clean dis ole dusty place?"

"You act like yah never been here b'fore. Besides, don't worry bout my whereabouts. What's your business here anyways and it betta be good?"

Cordelia gave Tauntadi an evil look.

Tauntadi said, "Well, if yah got somethin' to say, say it! I ain't got all night!"

Cordelia burst out laughing.

Tauntadi shook her head. "You one crazy woman, Cordelia."

Cordelia stopped laughing and got up, looking around the room full of junk. Through her drunkenness, she saw different altars covered in dried blood, an opaque mirror in the hall, and windows covered in decade-old dust. Hideous antiques around the room didn't help enhance the place and the furniture, which seemed to be of high quality, was covered in thick dusty plastic that took away from its finesse. The living room and everything in it was dusty except for the green chair Tauntadi sat on. Even the peppermints clumped together in the candy dish was old and full of dust.

"Ugh," Cordelia muttered looking at it. The place reeked of mothballs, cedarwood, and some other unidentifiable odors. Her house gave Cordelia an eerie feeling and the dim lights made it look haunted. Even through her drunken haze, Cordelia felt unseen eyes on her making the hairs on her neck rise. Even though this wasn't Cordelia's first visit to Tauntadi's house, she noticed more with a high level of alcohol in her system.

Tauntadi tapped her foot. Her arms were crossed. She had grey hairs sticking out the edges of the black wrap on her head, and her thin tight lips hid a gold front tooth while the rest of her teeth held on for dear life. Tauntadi's eyes were cold as ice. Her stone face made her a hard read, always appearing emotionless. She was biracial, mistaken for white all her life. She would cornrow, tie, or tease her hair so that people wouldn't get confused.

Tapping her foot harder, Tauntadi's patience ran thin watching Cordelia sit there looking around the house "ewwing" and "ughing". She finally yelled, "Cordelia!"

Cordelia jumped out of her daze, "What!"

Tauntadi's screamed, "WHAT DA HELL DO YAH WANT!"

Cordelia held her hands together, begging, "I need yah help, Sha."

"I already helped you."

Cordelia shook her head no like a little school girl.

"I did exactly what you paid me fo' and it worked, so what's the problem?"

"You did a crappy job of it, that's the problem!" The alcohol made Cordelia forget about the haunted house she was in. She walked close into Tauntadi's face. "I paid you to do a job and it didn't work. I want my money back!"

"Yah want yah money back?"

"Yes! I want my money back! Why else would I be here? It's not like we're friends, hell, I don't even like you. I'm 'pose to be in marital bliss right nah, but NO, I'm not. Why? B'cause I hired an idiot! A phony. A fake. So give me my money back!" Cordelia stood there miffed, meeting Tauntadi eye-to-eye. Tauntadi didn't back down from Cordelia's intimidation. Standing at 4'11", Tauntadi learned at an early age never to back down.

She got closer in Cordelia's face and said, "I kno' it worked. My stuff always works b'cause I'm the best. And how do I kno' you not tryin' to take *my* money back?"

Cordelia yelled. "Oh please, Tauntadi, don't you dare turn dis back on me. I know fo' a fact it didn't work b'cause she's betta!"

Tauntadi strained her eyes looking at Cordelia full of vehemence. "Hold on nah, wait just one minute. I kno' you drunk right nah, but if you dare raise yah voice at me again, yah won't see the light of day ever again. I'll make sho' of it!"

Cordelia backed down remembering the line of work Tauntadi was in and was a person that stuck by her word. In addition to this, Cordelia still needed Tauntadi's help. She recoiled back on the couch and rested an elbow on her knee, leaning to the side, looking up at Tauntadi, asking for a silent truce as she said in a mere whisper, "Beatrice, she's betta nah and Leroy back with her." Cordelia's voice lowered, "He's spendin' more time with her than with me. When I passed by they house, I saw him and her sittin' there holding hands, and then I seen dem 'round town with dem girls and Beatrice kissin' on my Leroy," Cordelia began crying in the palms of her hands. "I don't understand, Beatrice was gone. People thought she lost her marbles," she laughed through her tears. "And dem church fools thought she was possessed." Cordelia continued laughing wiping away tears.

Tauntadi didn't crack a smile. "And yah think that's funny?"

"Hell yeah it's funny! But all jokes aside, Sha, I just want Leroy back. Whatever you *did,* did work at first…it just didn't last. I need it to last forever."

Tauntadi yanked at a few curly hairs on her chin saying, "Ah, I see." She took a seat in her big green chair across from Cordelia, picked up her pipe from a copper ashtray and began digging out the old tobacco, replacing it with more fresh tobacco. She lit her pipe, took a few hefty puffs to get the tobacco lit and said, "Sometimes a hex can be broken."

"How?"

"Willpower is greater than anything I can ever do, Sha. It can break through anything. And love, well love conquers all, including fears. The hex can only play into people's fears and someway, somehow, Beatrice beat 'em. One cannot fear what they no longer scared of."

"Then what's the point of your job, Tauntadi? And what's the point of me payin' fo' a job that ain't givin' me what I want? You guaranteed me Beatrice would be sick in the head and body long enough fo' me and Leroy to be together and all I see is the complete opposite."

"With anything there's chance, Sha, even with dis. I did my job. How's he been actin' with yah lately?"

"Quite frankly, I don't kno' what's wrong with him. I followed him to Mr. Pete's when he broke free of *her*, and he brushed me off. But I just think he didn't wanna be seen talkin' to me b'cause he don't want anyone gossiping. I kno' he still wants me and I want him, too. Beatrice is in the way again and I want her out fo' good. I'm willin' to do whatever it takes to become Mrs. Leroy Harrison. I always win! Cordelia Butts never lose!"

Tauntadi hesitated. "So what is it you want me to do, Cordelia?"

An ominous look came over Cordelia's face as she looked at Tauntadi through the cloudy haze of pipe smoke. She leaned over and said, "I want you to get rid of Beatrice once and fo' all!"

"You need to stop while yah ahead, Cordelia. Look at you, you're young, got long curly hair and, well, yah face is okay. There's plenty of men out there that would love to be with a drunken mess of a woman like you," Tauntadi laughed.

Cordelia rolled her eyes. "You so funny. At least I don't look like a walkin' corpse."

"Oh hush up, Sha. Relax. I'm just toyin' with yah. Why don't yah just leave Leroy and his wife alone. They have chillun fo' Christ sake."

"Don't care."

"Why yah want dis man so bad anyway? Leroy Harrison use to be one of the most arrogant bastards in Eunice."

"So…"

"So, it took a woman like Beatrice Redeaux to push him off that high horse of his. That gal there's a pistol. When I was livin' over there on Happy Hill, I remember one time when she was a teenager, these girls were teasin' her walking home every day from school, calling her 'white girl' b'cause she talk proper and they kept on 'til one day Beatrice snapped! That gal dropped her books and took the ringleader by the hair and threw her in a ditch, then picked up a can and almost sliced that girl ear off. She did two days in jail fo' that too, but they ain't never mess with Beatrice again."

"Why yah tellin' me dis? I don't care."

"B'cause I don't wanna find you layin' in a ditch if Beatrice get wind that yah tryin' to take her husband away from her," Tauntadi said, laughing while taking another puff on her pipe.

"Yah just tryin' to find a reason not to do it."

"Maybe so. Or maybe it's my righteous duty to give yah a chance to reconsider things first. Or maybe I like Beatrice and Leroy together," Tauntadi grinned, "or maybe I just don't like you very much."

"I don't got time fo' yah games, Sha. I just want my Leroy."

"Look, Sha, I'm gonna give it to yah straight! Beatrice and Leroy fit. You and him don't. He's a lady's man that can have any woman he want, and had his fair share of women, too. It's a miracle he even married Beatrice, so why waste your time? Yah hands would be full dealin' with a man like Leroy."

"You answered yah own question."

"So it's the challenge?" Tauntadi sat back. "Y'all young girls always want what yah can't have and it's usually somebody else's man. What bout their chillun then, they need they mama?"

"No they don't. You didn't have a mother and look how you turned out, then again, you probably not the best example."

"Yah can get the hell up out of my house, that's what yah can do!"

"Oh no, no! I'm jokin'. Remember, 'lighten up'," Cordelia mocked and continued, "dem girls will be fine. I just want my Leroy."

Tauntadi screamed, "My mother didn't want me b'cause I reminded her of what happened to her and I still turned out great despite the hell I was born into. Yah got a lot of nerve tryin' to tell me how I turned out. I'm just fine."

"Alright, Tauntadi, I was just toyin' with yah."

"Hell, these are two different things. Beatrice wants her babies. My mother would've wanted me if I was conceived differently, so don't tell me bout why my mother didn't want me. She loved me, she just didn't like what happened to her! My mother loved me!"

"Did I hit a sore spot or somethin'? I didn't make any mention of why yah mother didn't want you. So can we get back to business please?"

"Leave, Cordelia. I didn't wanna do dis anyway and you know I don't!"

"I'll pay yah double!"

The sound of more money made Tauntadi regain composure. Usually an aloof person, any mention of her mother pushed Tauntadi over the edge. But Cordelia didn't have time for Tauntadi's issues. Any issue made Cordelia sober up too much. She rushed the process along by grabbing a handful of twenty dollar bills out of her purse smacking them flat on the table. Tauntadi got up from her chair, snatched a bill up, examined it by the light, and smelled the crispness of it, only having seen that much money one other time in her life.

"I thought you'd like that," Cordelia hiccupped. "I wanna make sho' Beatrice's mind is so far gone dis time that not even God could bring her back! Put a hurtin' on her dis time so it won't be any room for sanity or 'willpower'," Cordelia said, rolling her eyes at that word.

"Alright, I'll do it. But b'fore I do, it's still my duty to warn all my customers bout what I've witness over the years in dis here line of work. Usually in jobs like these, I try to stick to targeting a particular person only, but it never fails, no matter how much I try to aim specifically at that person, the family is affected by it, too. God's will is a dangerous thing to play with, Sha. The effects of it last long after the person's gone, falling on the heads of the chillun and their chillun's chillun. Me warning you of dis exempt me of any fault of my own. Dis here is business fo' me, and you now knowin' dis, it's in your hands and yah conscious nah."

Cordelia yawned, "Thanks fo' the sermon, nah get rid of her."

Tauntadi set her pipe down and finished examining the twenty dollar bills. "How'd yah get dis here money?"

Cordelia smiled, grabbing hold of her vagina, gyrating it out at Tauntadi. "A girl's gotta do what a girl's gotta do."

Tauntadi snarled her nose. "You're disgusting!"

Cordelia laughed stumbling towards the door in an elitist attitude. She had Tauntadi in the palm of her hands, enjoying the power of the *ole mighty dollar*. Cordelia turned before exiting, "Hey, I'll do whatever it takes. Nah bring me my Leroy back!"

Tauntadi folded the money, placed it in her bra, and forced the words, "As you wish."

Chapter 5

Lula, Mary, and Lillie sat on the porch outside of their house listening to family and church members inside. Empathic passers-by waved at the girls with consoling nods. Everyone in town took notice that this issue was no longer a joke, it was serious this time.

Leroy stuck to his word and was by Beatrice's side as the church women prayed and rubbed anointed oil across her forehead.

It hurt Leroy to subdue Beatrice during her outburst, pinning her arms and body down, having no choice but to keep her from hurting herself or anyone else.

Beatrice's mother, Grandma Emma Guy, came outside to sit with the girls for a while, exhausted from her early morning travel from Humble, Texas. She was working a long graveyard shift when she heard the news that Beatrice had fallen ill again, worst than before. She d stopped everything before her shift ended and took the next bus to Eunice.

Mary crawled on Grandma Emma's lap, burying her head in her grandmother's bosom craving the comfort. Grandma Emma patted Mary's neat cornrows and began rocking in the chair. Lula and Lillie went over and leaned against the chair, feeling Grandma Emma's hands embrace them as well. She eased their worries by humming gospel spirituals while admiring the neat cornrows Beatrice did on their hair before she fell ill again.

Grandma Emma was a tiny woman with wavy black hair braided in a single plait down her back. Her father and mother were full-blooded Washitaw Cherokee Native American. She was a spitting image of her mother with dark, reddish, deep brown skin and high cheekbones. She and Papa Top were sixteen when they got married, but separated when Beatrice was young. Grandma Emma moved back to Texas, leaving Papa Top in Happy Hill, which forced Beatrice to live between two households until she married Leroy and remained in Eunice, Louisiana.

Grandma Emma felt somewhat guilty for the condition Beatrice was in. She had allowed distance and work to keep her from being more available to Beatrice after she chose marriage over living in Texas to attend college.

In between humming, Grandma Emma saw a white petal on the ground from the flowers sent to Beatrice earlier, and asked the girls, "Did y'all find out who sent dem pretty flowers yet?"

Lillie shook her head no.

The dozen of pink and white carnations that Big Ma found on the porch in the early morning were already in a glass vase tied with white and pink ribbons, now placed on Beatrice's nightstand. It was the mere beauty in the bedroom that brought Beatrice solace in between episodes of her erratic behavior.

When Grandma Emma was called back into the house, Lula whispered in Lillie's ear and they both nodded. Lula gave Mary a piece of Doublemint gum to placate her for a bit, and then Lula jumped down from the porch and began treading up the road by herself, dipping her head inconspicuously while looking back at Lillie who stood guard in the yard waving her hand to let Lula know she was watching her.

Lula came up to an ostentatious, pink house with a flowerbed full of different shades of pink and purple Impatiens flowers and rose bushes surrounding the front. Lula waved her arms wide signaling to Lillie that she'd arrived at the destination safe and sound, at a place Big Ma forbid them to go.

Lula opened the screen door and walked into a flower-scented house with plants and fresh cut flowers placed in vases across the sunny living room. The wooden floors glistened from the reflection of the sunlight. The white couch with a pink quilt in the middle created a soft atmosphere for the room. A flower printed tea set sat on a wooden coffee table in front of the couch. On the mantle were antique bells, small porcelain dolls, and pink and white candles shaped into womanlike figures with the wicks poking out of the hats. The dining room table was set with gold trimmed China dishes on top of a pink and white printed tablecloth.

Lula had been in her Aunt Samantha's house many times, yet each time always felt like the first. This was Lula's second home. She sat down on a pink chair, twirling her gum around her index finger and called out for her aunt. Samantha came from her bedroom startled to see Lula sitting there after hearing about Beatrice. She gave Lula a hug, kissing the top of Lula's forehead over and over, and then hurried to the kitchen to put water on the stove for Chamomile tea and heated the oven to warm teacakes. She sashayed around the kitchen, enthused that Lula had come to visit since few family members acknowledged Samantha as family. So when Lula or Lillie sneaked over for a visit, it was more of a celebration for Samantha. Thus, thinking about Beatrice's illness lessened the tone for festivities for this particular visit.

The town's women, primarily church women, ostracized Samantha years ago due to her relations with men. She gladly accepted the label as 'black sheep' of the family after going against Big Ma's religious beliefs, and dispensing herself from all religion in exchange for spiritual independence and freedom. Big Ma gave up on saving Samantha's soul long ago and no one spoke of Samantha in Big Ma's presence. All Big Ma could do was continue praying for her child.

Samantha considered herself a man's lady, contrary to popular belief amongst the town folks. Her curvaceous frame and feminine grace seduced any man without any effort. Her confidence peaked at its fullest capacity and she had a walk that put Mae West to shame, making the town pause when Samantha sashayed down the road, causing husbands to get slapped and children's eyes to be covered. Whistles and cat calls greeted Samantha as men removed their hats, nearly breaking their necks to open doors for her. She was often the topic of the daily gossip: who bought what for Samantha, who's Samantha dating now, who's trying to date Samantha, did you see what Samantha wore, look how she walks, talks, or dresses. Although the women in the town despised Samantha, they never dared cross her, and if a woman stepped out of line with Samantha, they paid the ultimate price...their man. Not only would Samantha fight back, she also stole their men and when she was done with them, she sent the men back home to their wives, leaving them yearning for Samantha to take them back. The few women who did cross Samantha fell victim to her wrath and were forced to perform the 'walk of shame' to Samantha's house to beg her to leave their man alone and apologize for whatever they'd said or done to Samantha.

Samantha realized in her early teenage years that she was damned if she do and damned if she don't, regardless of her kind actions. She used to overcompensate by being nice and generous towards jealous women; consequently, they took her kindness for weakness and eventually used or stabbed her in the back. After noticing how her friendliness got her nowhere, and that the women were going to hate her regardless, Samantha decided to have fun and *really* give them something to talk about. Unbeknownst to the women, gossip added fuel to Samantha's fire whenever they made mention of her name, turning her into an attention junky. She found pleasure in hearing daily updates about herself, even though most were fabricated or misconstrued.

Samantha placed the teacakes on a flower ridged plate and poured hot water in a matching tea kettle from a dish set which included plates, saucers, teacups and a sugar dish. She bought everything in sets, adding to the floral décor of her home.

Samantha set the tea and teacakes neatly on a tray and brought it into the living room where Lula sat. Lula smiled at the regal display before her, taking the handkerchief from the tray and tracing the embroidered initials with her finger before laying it over her lap feeling privileged. Samantha's carefree spirit and warm demeanor brought a sense of comfort to Lula—no religion, no rules, or no restrictions in Samantha's home. The only thing required of Lula was to let her hair down, be free, and relax. More than anything, Lula admired her aunt's independence, being one of the few women in town who owned her own produce business.

Assisting Big Ma in her garden as a child, Samantha learned how to grow fresh fruits, vegetables, and peanuts. Watermelons were Samantha's favorite and she became skilled at growing the largest and sweetest watermelons possible. By the time Big Ma kicked Samantha out the house at age sixteen for back talking and sinful behavior, Samantha moved in with a cousin and found work as a seamstress in a small clothing boutique store in Mamou, Louisiana, where she adopted her style and fashion. She saved enough money to buy land to grow watermelons to harvest and sell. Nobody, except for Lula and Lillie, knew that Watermelon man Bue worked for Samantha and she paid him generously for his work, and to keep his mouth shut since the women in Eunice wouldn't support Samantha if they knew they were eating watermelons she had harvested. Her watermelons became high in demand to where the markets in Crowley, Opelousas, Lake Charles, and Lafayette bought and sold

"Watermelon man Bue's" watermelons, making Samantha's profits triple in less than five years. Everyone in Eunice, including Samantha's family, assumed Samantha got her money from men—a lie that Samantha happily perpetuated to keep her business afloat.

Samantha poured hot tea, a little milk, and a tablespoon of honey in a teacup, placed it on a saucer and carefully handed it to Lula while humming, *This Little Light of Mine,* still harboring some of her church upbringing. Lula sat up holding the saucer, crossing her legs as she took a sip without slurping. Samantha grinned watching Lula imitate well.

Samantha said, "I wish I would've known you was comin' earlier, I would've ran yah a bath in my new tub, Sha."

"What's goin' on with my mama, auntie?" Lula wouldn't dare ask Big Ma such a question. Kids understood their place. There was no tolerance for kids meddling in grown folk business, but this rule didn't apply to Samantha.

"I don't kno', Sha," Samantha sighed. "All you can do is keep yah mama in prayer and you and yah sisters' help out where ever y'all can. I reckon God throw monkey wrenches in our lives to see how well we learn, that's if we learn anything at all."

Lula slouched staring at her tea. Samantha squeezed Lula's knee to comfort her. It was rare for Lula to hear Samantha use "God" in a sentence, making Lula realize the seriousness of the situation.

Lula asked, "What do you do when bad things happen to yah since yah don't believe in God?"

Samantha laughed. "I believe in God, Sha. I just don't believe in the God these religions portray *him* to be. I think certain people use religion to control others and say it's God that said it, but I highly doubt God personally appointed these hypocrites to tell us what to wear or how to act. So 'til my judgment day, I'm gonna live my life doing things that make me happy. And when bad things happen, I try to find the good in the situation. But people, mainly women 'round here, make it hard sometimes. But still, I try to turn the bad into the good by looking on the brighter side of things that will put a smile on my face," Samantha smiled and winked.

A man came out of Samantha's bedroom adjusting his work uniform. He looked surprised when he saw Lula sitting in the living room.

"Oh, hello," he said. Before Lula could greet him, Samantha sat her cup down and started shoving him towards the door.

He turned around saying, "I thought we were gonna go get somethin' to eat, Sam?"

Samantha kept pushing. "Later. I'm spendin' quality time with my niece."

"But wait! What bout me? I wanna spend some quality time with you, too!"

Samantha pushed him out the screen door, locking it.

He yelled, "Wait! My wallet's in there."

Samantha ran back in the bedroom and came back out with his wallet and threw it outside, shutting the screen door again.

He yelled, "When I'm gonna see yah again?"

"I'll contact yah later, Garson," Samantha said and walked back over to the couch taking a seat. "I tell yah," she said underneath her breath taking a bite of her teacake, nodding in approval of her baking skills. Samantha wiped the excess crumbs from the side of her mouth and said, "Yah kno' me and Big Ma use to make these when I was little. I imagine her bakin' with me every time I make these." Her face went blank, lost in thought.

Lula broke Samantha's muse. "Who that man?"

Samantha smiled wryly, hoping Lula wouldn't ask that question. "A friend. Com'on, follow me, I gotta get ready."

Lula followed Samantha into the bedroom and jumped up on Samantha's highly elevated bed, which was propped up on cement blocks.

Satin sheets, a pink quilt, and full-feathered pillows covered the bed Lula bounced on. She watched Samantha swing into action slipping out her robe, exposing a cream fitted slip that accented her wide hips and round buttocks as she stood in front of the closet twisting her mouth, chewing the inside of her cheek, looking for a dress to wear.

Samantha spotted her red dress, the one men lost their minds over, and pulled it off the hanger laying it out on the bed. After examining the dress, Samantha went over and sat in front of her vanity area full of make-up, perfume, scented powders and lotions, and began applying red lipstick in front of her oval-shaped mirror, positioning herself so that she could see Lula.

Samantha asked, "So how Bea schooling you on men?"

Lula covered her face laughing, embarrassed by the question. "Stay away from dem," she muttered behind her hands.

"That's right! Stay as far away from dem as possible. Education first! Study hard and get good grades, Sha. We need a college graduate in dis here family."

"I can't go to college."

"Take 'can't' out yah vocabulary. Especially when 'I' is before it. Don't ever doubt yah self, Lula Mae. Doubt only brings fear and fear takes away the ability to see yah full potential. Take me fo' instance, what happened if I said 'I can't' sell watermelons or 'I can't' own a business with a third grade education. I wouldn't be sittin' here t'day in *my* own house that *I* bought with *my* own money."

Lula listened to Samantha's every word.

Samantha's expression changed as she turned around, nervously looking down at her feet with a somber look on her face. "How my mama doin'?"

Lula was taken aback by Samantha's sudden childlike disposition when making mention of Big Ma.

"Big Ma doin' good, auntie."

Samantha twisted her mouth, chewing at the inside of her cheek still looking down at her feet. In her muse, she noticed chipped polish on her big toe nail and bent over to rub her finger across it, regretting working out in her watermelon fields barefoot. Priding herself in being a lady first, Samantha still couldn't stop the joy of getting her feet dirty while working her crops, as she did in Big Ma's garden when she was younger. Making a mental note to polish her toenails later, Samantha sat up with thought-provoking eyes, blurting, "I want you and yah sisters to come stay with me until Bea gets betta. I'll teach y'all how to grow the most delicious watermelons in Louisiana."

Lula sat quietly. She didn't know if Samantha was asking or just talking in the moment.

Samantha continued, "I don't want y'all to stay over there with Doc. He's a mean man and…I just don't want y'all over there with him. Y'all be safe here with me."

"My mama gonna get betta like she did the last time."

Samantha smiled, "That's right, Sha, she will." She turned back around trying to disguise her ambiguity on Beatrice's condition and continued applying make-up on her face. She batted her eyes making sure the mascara was applied evenly and smiled at the reflection of the new face she created.

Samantha motioned her head for Lula to come closer. "Come see."

Lula slid off the bed and went over to Samantha, who opened the drawer of her vanity area and said, "Which color yah like?"

Looking through different shades of lipstick, Lula said, "Red," the majority of all the colors.

"That's my baby!" Samantha took her red lipstick and applied it on Lula's tiny lips. Lula looked in the mirror and started posing.

Samantha laughed. "Go on girl. Watch out nah!" She laughed. Samantha joined in posing with Lula in the mirror until Lula fell on the bed, giggling. Samantha laughed sitting back down to finish the final touches on her face. Lula bounced on the bed dangling her feet, and for the moment, Lula forgot about the mayhem going on a block away. She quickly wiped the lipstick off her lips before Samantha could see her, but Samantha caught her and smiled, knowing Big Ma's influence was registering fast.

Samantha had a knack for putting a smile on children's faces, whenever a child was allowed to get close enough to her. She enjoyed the company of children and refused to give into the fact that she was unable to birth a child of her own. Big Ma told her it was God's way of punishing Samantha for her sins, but Samantha ignored that notion.

Lula sat at the end of the bed dangling her feet. "I don't think I'm gonna wear make-up when I'm older. Big Ma says it's not good to wear it."

"Then don't wear it if that's yah choice. But don't 'not' wear it just b'cause Big Ma said so. She told me the same thing when I was little and look at me." She pouted her lip. "When yah get older, the best thing you can do fo' yah self is be yah self. Don't live yah life fo' others, Lula Mae, that's a prison within itself."

Samantha moisturized her hairless legs and then lifted them, pointing her foot to slide the sheer stockings up. She stopped and snatched them off saying, "No, it's too hot fo' that."

Lula asked, "Why do people call yah names?"

"What kind of names?"

"Sometimes they call yah mean names and say yah make money the ungodly way." Lula frowned crossing her arms, displaying her anger for the people talking about her Aunt Samantha. Even though Lula didn't know what they meant most of the time, their tone depicted it wasn't good.

"Sometimes? Humph, I must be losing my touch if they ain't talkin' all the time," Samantha laughed. "But I don't care. What they say shouldn't bother you either, alright?"

"Yes, ma'am."

Samantha went over and gave Lula a big hug and a kiss on the cheek. She wiped her lipstick print off Lula's cheek and went back to her vanity area to squirt perfume on her neck and wrist.

Lula blurted, "But, I heard Big Ma say no man gonna marry you."

"Correction, I don't wanna marry dem!" Samantha said, pointing at her ring finger. "If I wanted to get married, trust me, there's a long line of men waiting fo' that chance. Marriage, oh no! It ain't fo' me."

Lula asked, "So yah not mad what people think bout you?"

"Why should I be? B'cause I'm not married or b'cause people runnin' they mouth bout me? Please, Sha. I have no shame with being Samantha Harrison. I like to sing, smoke my cigarettes, drink my liquor, and most of all," she stepped into her dress, "shake my porkchop."

Samantha bent down for Lula to zip her up, and then she turned to the mirror admiring the silhouette of her figure, snapping her fingers and popping her hip to the side loving how good she looked. She turned to Lula and started dancing, snapping her fingers and moving her hips. She went over to the record player to put on Zydeco music and pulled Lula off the bed and told her to shake her porkchop. Lula started jumping and shaking to the accordions in the music. Samantha clapped and hollered encouraging Lula, and took her hand doing steps together.

"Shake that porkchop, gal," Samantha laughed. "Let me tell yah, Sha," Samantha said clapping and stomping her feet. "I don't worry bout what people say bout me. Only one can judge me and it ain't dem. So don't worry yah cute little self bout me. What I want yah to do is have fun, and when yah get mad, find the good in the situation to make yah happy. That's how auntie keeps a smile on her face, alright, Sha?"

Lula nodded, "Yes, ma'am."

Samantha stopped dancing and looked at the time, "Yah should be headin' home soon. Don't want Big Ma comin' down here lookin' fo' yah."

Lula hugged Samantha around her waist. "Love yah, auntie."

"I love yah too, baby."

Samantha held on to Lula, glad that she was able to take the worries off Lula's mind about Beatrice for the moment. She kissed Lula's forehead and walked over to the record player screeching it to end. When she slipped into her three-inch heels, she raised her hands up high posing like a movie star and asked, "How do I look?"

"Beautiful!"

Samantha warmly smiled at Lula. She looked over at the mirror, "Yup, I think you right!" Samantha laughed, winking at Lula.

Knock! Knock! Knock!

They froze.

"Oh no," Samantha said, rushing to open the door.

She ran out to the front room and opened it putting her hand over her chest exhaling in relief, "Thank goodness it's only you."

The man stood at the door holding a boutique of roses. "Who'd yah think it was?"

"My mama."

"Oh."

Lula came from the bedroom.

Samantha told the man, "I'll be back, I'm gonna see my niece home."

Lula interjected, "Lillie watchin' me from the yard." Lula was ashamed that she didn't want to be seen with Samantha out of fear that word would get back to Big Ma.

Samantha peeked her head out the doorway, squinting to see Lillie sitting against the tree. Samantha bent down and whispered to Lula, "Yah gonna be alright, baby. I hope yah mama like dem flowers I sent."

Lula looked up, surprised. Samantha winked and put a finger to her mouth to keep quiet, and then said, "You be safe and tell Lillie Mae and Mary Lee I said hello. Kiss yah mama fo' me too, and tell Big Ma that I love her and my door's always open!"

"Yes, ma'am." Lula was reluctant to return home, and hearing the desperation in Samantha's voice for Big Ma to visit her saddened Lula. She hugged Samantha tight, and then hung her head as she walked down the road while Samantha watched until she saw Lula join Lillie back in the yard.

Samantha's attention went back to the tall, thick-framed man grinning like a little schoolboy.

She asked, "Fo' me?"

"Yes, ma'am."

"You shouldn't have," she said, flashing a flirtatious smile while leaning in to smell the flowers, giving the man a better view of her cleavage. His eyes widened. Samantha turned around giving a standing ovation performance of a walk, switching her round behind. The man followed sitting next to her on the sofa, trembling as he took out a pack of cigarettes offering her one. Samantha slowly pulled one from the pack while batting her eye and put the cigarette in her mouth. He leaned over to light it. She took a puff blowing the smoke from the side of her mouth, looking at him seductively while crossing her legs. "So, what we gonna do t'night, daddy?"

"Well, um, I, well, um, whatever, um."

Samantha got up and sashayed to the window, moving the white curtains apart. "How bout we take a ride in that fine car of yours."

"Of course! Yeah, um, yeah, we can do that, yeah, we can go right nah!"

Samantha smiled switching her hips over to the front door. He jumped up and raced ahead to open the door for her, and as Samantha swayed her hips outside to his car, the man's eyes locked to the rhythm of her killer walk. He rushed to open the passenger door for Samantha, then closed it and ran over to the driver's side nearly falling into the seat. He took one more glimpse of Samantha's luscious body before settling on her pretty face, mumbling, "Lord have mercy," and then he drove off.

***

Leroy sat at the edge of the bed staring at the mirror he had covered with a sheet, unable to look at his own reflection. Sitting there leaning his face on his hand with his eyes closed to stop the fluttering, Leroy battled against the image of Cordelia taking over his mind. He'd already ended things with her and returned back to his family, vowing to Beatrice that he would do right by her and their children. He didn't want to go back on his word, yet overwhelming emotions didn't leave him any choice. Beatrice was ill again and Cordelia bombarded Leroy's thoughts, in which she became his main focus. He contemplated his next move while rubbing the bruises and scratches left by Beatrice during one of her temper outbursts.

Beatrice and the girls were asleep.

Looking at the clock, Leroy was surprised that it was only eight o'clock at night. He was glad the house was quiet. No church folk traffic using his front door as a revolving entrance anymore. Leroy wanted them to leave his family in peace for the time being. Everyone needed their rest. Even Big Ma followed Doc's command to return home and tend to their own household, which was an offer she couldn't refuse. She was too exhausted.

Leroy went outside avoiding any reflections of himself, leaving Beatrice and the girls asleep in their beds. Lula woke up when she heard the front door open and ran out her bedroom just when the door was shutting behind Leroy. She ran over to the window in her tiny undershirt and panties and peeked out at Leroy, who was standing outside with his hands in his pocket. A white man pulled up in a car alongside the yard and got out. He walked over to Leroy. He was wearing an olive green suit and had a transparent hair comb over. Leroy recognized the man, but still seemed surprised to see him.

The man said, "Hey, how you doing there, Leroy? Sorry to stop by at dis hour, but I just wanted to stop before leaving back to Lafayette."

"How are you doing, Mr. Coleman?" Leroy asked, shaking Mr. Coleman's hand, changing his dialect to a more conservative speech.

"Doing just fine, Leroy, thanks for asking. I just came through to get some of that andouille sausage. They don't make it like that in Lafayette."

"Yeah, I use that andouille sausage in my sausage stew."

"Oh yeah, good stuff there. Went by my in-laws house, too." Mr. Coleman shook his head in annoyance. "Boy I tell you, if wasn't for my wife, them bastards would never see me."

"Where's Mrs. Coleman, sir?"

"Left her over there with them parents of hers to get me some sausage. Too bad these stores closed already. Gotta ride back out here some other time. But off the subject, yah know I heard you left

Pierre's." He chuckled and said, "You done made that man change his whole menu around because them new cooks couldn't make them dishes like you. Word has it, Pierre's business plummeted something serious after you left."

"Well, sir, if he'd paid me what I was worth, maybe I'd still be there."

"Yah find a new job yet, son?"

"I have places interested in me, I just ain't decided on which one yet," Leroy said, scratching the top of his head looking away hoping Mr. Coleman would change the topic. Quitting his job to care for Beatrice wasn't a subject Leroy liked to discuss.

When Beatrice got better from her illness, she and Leroy were inseparable like old times. The only time Leroy was separated from Beatrice was when he went to work. In between cooking, Leroy thought about Beatrice, counting the hours for his shift to end so that he could race back home to his family. Leroy never gave Cordelia a second thought after their affair ended and he ignored Cordelia's car riding past the house numerous times.

But on one particular afternoon, the thought of Cordelia sent chills down Leroy's spine, igniting a sudden urge to see her.

He wanted Mr. Coleman to leave, given that Cordelia had agreed to meet Leroy at a certain time.

Mr. Coleman said, "I'm sure you're not going to have any problems choosing a restaurant to work for, Leroy. You're one of the best chef's we got down in these parts."

"Why thank you, sir. That's awfully nice of you."

"An humble man. That's what I like about you, Leroy." Mr. Coleman pulled at his chin. "I'm not gonna stand here and waste any more of your time, I'm just gonna cut to the chase. I came to see about Beatrice. I heard she's sick and wanted to know how she was doing. Is she okay? Was she unhappy with her pay? Because if it's the money, I can pay whatever she wants at this point? I just need her back."

"You paid her well. She just wanted to spend more time raising the girls, that's all. She fell ill afterwards, but she'll get betta soon, sir."

"You know, it's a running joke at my firm that Beatrice spoiled me. See this here crease?" Mr. Coleman held out his leg. "Look at them wrinkles! I went through three housekeepers and none of them can starch clothes as well as Beatrice did. I'm a lawyer. I can't afford to look like this. I need Beatrice back, so when she gets better, can you see if she'll reconsider working for me again? I'll work out something so she can spend more time with y'all children. Maybe even have your girls stay with us during Beatrice's shift. Whatever it takes, I'm flexible. My grandchildren still ask about her, so I figure I'd just try my luck after hearing you left your job. No offense."

"None taken, sir," Leroy said, lying through his teeth.

A car pulled up in the driveway flashing headlights on Leroy and Mr. Coleman. Leroy put his hand up for the person to wait. Mr. Coleman waved smiling at the car, happy to see Beatrice driving now. He was ready to use his litigation skills to convince her to come back to work. He bent down still waving his hand looking into the car, then his face went flat. He stopped waving and quickly stood up straight clearing his throat.

Leroy said, "I will let her know, sir."

"Can you, um, tell your wife I stopped by please?"

"Will do, sir."

Mr. Coleman saluted Leroy good-bye and walked over to his car, whistling as if the car with the beaming headlights wasn't there. He almost tripped over his feet getting into his vehicle and screeched off without looking in Cordelia's direction.

Lula pushed her face into the glass window for a better view. She watched Leroy get into the passenger seat, but couldn't get a clear view of the mysterious person in the driver's seat, only seeing a woman's hand grab hold of the steering wheel. Lula backed away from the window holding her stomach from knots forming and ran into the bedroom. She jumped in the bed with Beatrice, who was still asleep, and cuddled close to her mother.

***

The girls did their morning chores in silence. Without Big Ma there, they felt alone, stricken with a sense of uncertainty. Beatrice's behavior and Leroy's disappearing acts again made the girls feel like they were being revisited by a living nightmare they'd thought was long gone, only to come back worse.

They witnessed Beatrice throwing food in the trash, screaming "It's tainted" or "It's poisoned" at Leroy. He argued with Beatrice to stop and eventually had to pick her up and carry her to the bedroom kicking and screaming. When Beatrice got loose and ran down the street screaming that Leroy was trying to kill her, town people stopped what they were doing to help Leroy chase Beatrice down before she hurt herself. And when Beatrice wasn't screaming or fighting unseen objects, she'd rock back and forth in the corner, mumbling with an occasional outbursts screaming, "GET AWAY FROM ME! SNAKES! THEY'RE EVERYWHERE!"

Leroy would give Beatrice two sedative pills for her to sleep. He'd sit on the bed squeezing his eyes to stop them from fluttering. And then, out of nowhere, his eyes would widen. The fluttering would stop. All he could think about was a perfect time to make his escape so that he could be comfortable leaving the girls alone with Beatrice while he visited Cordelia.

Doc gave Big Ma permission to return back to Leroy and Beatrice's house after numerous people reported the struggles Leroy was having with Beatrice. Doc usually would tell Big Ma to let Leroy and Beatrice deal with their issues alone. But he too began to fear for Leroy and their granddaughter's safety after hearing the horror stories taking place in Big Ma's absence.

Beatrice's parents, Grandma Emma and Papa Top, heard the news as well, which compelled them to visit, too.

Grandma Emma, Big Ma, and Papa Top began taking shifts caring for Beatrice and the girls, doing whatever was needed for the household in Leroy's absence. It was no longer a secret that Leroy quit his job, and now that Beatrice's parents and Big Ma were present, Leroy acted like a thief in the night leaving in and out the house, unseen at times. When Papa Top did catch Leroy, one look posed many threats, warning Leroy to cease his nonsense or else. But Leroy didn't care. His addiction to Cordelia began to consume his every move.

One night while Leroy was sneaking in the house in the early morning, he froze when he saw a gun resting on the table with Papa Top sitting on the couch waiting up for Leroy. Leroy swallowed hard, stepping back, hoping Papa Top didn't smell the perfume reeking from his shirt. Papa Top picked up the gun and held it in his hand, then looked Leroy dead in his eye and calmly said, "You ever meet my lady friend, Leroy? Her name is Miss Colt 1911 .45 Caliber Pistol. I call her 'Miss Colt 45' fo' short. She don't take too kindly to cheating husbands or deadbeat fathers so, keep on. We're watchin' you!"

Leroy stayed home for the rest of that day as well as the following two weeks, assisting Big Ma and Grandma Emma with Beatrice and the girls. When Papa Top's visits decreased due to him having to return back to Happy Hill to work in his shop, Leroy reverted back to his old ways knowing Papa Top would be too busy with backlogged work.

Big Ma and Grandma Emma's constant bickering and Papa Top's threats wasn't enough to keep Leroy away from Cordelia.

***

When everyone was asleep, Leroy sat on the edge of the bed, positioning himself so that he could avoid the mirror in the bedroom since Big Ma took the sheets off all of them. His head pounded in pain as he grabbed at his eyes, trying to stop them from twitching. He got up out of bed moving steadfast to change his clothes. When fully dressed, Leroy quietly bent down for his shoes underneath the bed. Holding in a sneeze, he reached for his other shoe and was unable to hold it, sneezing louder than ever.

Beatrice woke up startled, "Leroy!"

"Yeah, baby?"

"What are you doing?"

"Nothin', baby, go back to sleep."

"Come see."

Leroy walked over to Beatrice's bed side taking extra precaution in each step. Beatrice sat up waving for him to come closer. He knelt down beside her, flinching when Beatrice tried touching his face. Seeing the pain in Beatrice's eye, Leroy moved in closer again, cringing at his own actions toward her. She rubbed along the side of his face, the same way she used to before they went to sleep. Leroy closed his eye taking Beatrice's hand kissing it, remembering how sweet her embrace felt.

The first time in weeks, Beatrice saw Leroy. Even though she heard Leroy's voice inside a scaly lizard man chasing her down the road, or stopping her from throwing away food infested with snake's venom to poison her family, Beatrice wasn't taking any chances with any creatures who took on the voices of her loved ones.

Beatrice missed Leroy and was happy to see him sitting there on the bed. She pulled his face close for a kiss. He kissed Beatrice back, squeezing her shoulders, craving the tender love with the same intensity felt during their first kiss.

Coming up for air and looking into Beatrice's eyes, Leroy's heart raced with his body temperature rising. His precious Bea, whom he fell in love with the first day he saw her, stared back at him with the same warm smile that was so innocent. So sweet.

Beatrice whispered, "Please be patient with me. Help me stay here. Here is where I want to be."

"Stay where?"

"Here," Beatrice said, pointing at her head. She lay back down curling into a ball, ashamed of the condition she was in, aware of her unruly behavior, yet she couldn't control it. Her fist balled, her teeth clinched as she trembled, fighting to stay coherent, fearing what would become of her if she didn't get well soon.

Leroy took a deep breath still staring at the love of his life. He kicked his shoes to the side, took off his clothes and got in the bed next to Beatrice, wrapping his arm tightly around her. Scratching at the top of his head, Beatrice pulled Leroy's hand away from it and said, "Stop, you're going to flake up your scalp. You don't want to go bald up there, do you?"

Leroy chuckled and kissed Beatrice's lips, falling asleep in each other arms.

***

The following night, Cordelia sat under the moonlight on her porch sipping on red wine, patiently awaiting Leroy's arrival. She leaped out of her chair grinning when she saw Leroy hastily walking up towards her from the road. Before she could say a word, Leroy leaped up the porch steps and yanked Cordelia by the arm making the wine glass fall out of her hand and splatter onto the porch.

She screamed, "What's wrong with yah! That was perfectly good wine!"

"Get in here!" Leroy said. His grip tightened around Cordelia's arm as he shoved her in the house, slamming the door behind them.

"What the hell's wrong with yah? Let me go!" Cordelia tried yanking her arm away, but Leroy squeezed tighter, pushing her up against the wall.

Rubbing at her arm and frowning, Cordelia asked, "What's wrong with yah?"

Leroy pointed his finger in her face. "Make it stop now!"

"Make what stop?"

"Make it stop! I can't do dis anymore!"

Leroy released Cordelia and began pacing the floor back and forth, rubbing the top of his head.

"Would you stop moving, Leroy, yah makin' me nervous."

He stopped, looked around, and found a seat on Cordelia's couch to get his thoughts together.

"I want my life back. I want my family. I want my Bea back. And don't tell me you didn't do nothin' b'cause I kno' you been visiting that damn Tauntadi! What kind of name is that anyways?"

"Oh no yah don't! Nah uh, you my man!" Cordelia yelled, standing over Leroy, pointing at herself. "I loved you since the first day I laid eyes on yah and I ain't lettin' yah go that easy! What we have is real and I ain't gonna let Beatrice or nobody else stand in the way of us being together. I kno' yah love me too b'cause no one put a gun to yah head to be with me. Yah just followin' your heart and your heart's with me. We'll make it through dis madness, but yah gotta be able to trust me, baby. I'd *never* go to that crazy Tauntadi fo' that ole voodoo stuff. I'm a God fearing Christian woman!" Her voice started quivering, "And fo' you to think I'd do such a thing hurts my heart. I only went to the ole woman's house to preach the word of God to her and save her soul from that devilish work she do, so stop listenin' to these nosy people 'round here b'cause all they do is talk and you kno' that! I would never harm Beatrice and I pray every night that she gets betta. It kills me to see her like that and it hurts more to see you hurt by it. I love you so much and I'm so sorry your goin' through dis. Trust me, baby, if I could take your pain away, I'd do it in a heartbeat, Sha."

Cordelia sat down next to Leroy and rubbed his hand against her face. He snatched his hand away and got up pacing the floor again, rubbing at his head to stop his thoughts from racing a hundred miles per hour. He cringed holding the temples of his head, grunting at the images of Beatrice and Cordelia flashing faster than a speeding bullet through his mind. Images of Beatrice followed guilt for his betrayal. Dignity and pride for being a man of his word was long gone. He didn't like the man he'd become, yet he yearned for the physical benefits from Cordelia along with the pampering, adulating, sex, and her submissive behavior towards him—Doc wanted this for him as well.

Leroy paced the floor remembering how he brushed Cordelia's advances off at first—as he did all women who knew he was married and still pursued him. Usually disgusted by that type of behavior from women, Cordelia suddenly became the exception. She was persistent to the point that Leroy woke up one day and couldn't get Cordelia off his mind.

Looking over at Cordelia sitting on the couch, Leroy just stared at her. She wasn't his type and there wasn't anything extraordinary about her. Digging deeper, he thought Cordelia was rather annoying more than anything. In spite of this, there was something keeping him intrigued.

His love for Beatrice was undeniable. No woman compared to her class, beauty, smarts, and grace. He knew he would soon hit a crossroad where a decision had to be made and he shuddered at the thought of burning in hell for his adulterous sins, a visual that Big

Ma assisted in creating. Leroy scratched at his head and immediately stopped so that it wouldn't flake his scalp. A decision had to be made and it was now or never.

Cordelia's patience ran thin waiting for Leroy to say something. She got up and went over to him, put her arms around his waist and pulled him close to her. Leroy took Cordelia's arms off of him, but she fought them back around his waist to get Leroy to look into her eyes. He broke away again, but she took hold again telling Leroy to look at her. A short battle took place until Cordelia locked her hands on his face and made Leroy look at her. When their eyes locked, Leroy's eyes fluttered as he stared at Cordelia. He could no longer resist.

"It's you and me against the world, baby. Nothin, not even God, can stand between us!" Cordelia said, standing on her toes to give him a quick peck on the mouth. "Fo' great love to blossom, great measures gotta be taken, baby. We gotta do what we gotta do!" Cordelia started kissing Leroy's neck, whispering sexual pleasures in his ear, stopping to lick his earlobe between words.

Beatrice shot through Leroy's mind making him try to break free of Cordelia's arms one last time, but Cordelia wasn't backing down. They went back and forth again until Leroy's resistance grew tenuous looking into Cordelia's eyes, listening to her talk dirty. Without anymore tussle, Leroy picked Cordelia up and carried her to the bedroom.

Chapter 6

Screams permeated every inch of the house. Beatrice trembled, crying from the excruciating pain in her head, which felt like knives sawing at her skull. Lula, Mary, and Lillie continued playing outside, content with Big Ma's explanation of it just being a phase. Big Ma and Grandma Emma sat outside watching them play. The changing, feeding, cleaning, bathing, tussling, chasing, and praying took its toll on them both. Neighbors, family, and church members assisted Big Ma and Grandma Emma from afar by running errands, bringing food, and taking the girls for the day. No one stepped forth to care exclusively for Beatrice anymore due to her unpredictable, volatile state of mind, and no doctor or medicine helped. She didn't know her own name and the snakes, bugs, and creatures were relentless. Beatrice had no peace.

Grandma Emma placed flowers from an anonymous sender by Beatrice's bedside, which helped ground her for the moment with the beautiful colors and patterns, creating a short relief from the horrors inflicted upon Beatrice every second of the day.

***

Leroy spent the majority of his time at Cordelia's house. Doc threatened Big Ma to leave Leroy alone. His son was a grown man and didn't need Big Ma chastising him. She kept her mouth shut in Leroy's presence, allowing the silence to measure the disgrace she felt toward Leroy, which spoke more volumes than words could ever do. Grandma Emma, on the other hand, gave Leroy a mouthful, speaking for both her and Big Ma. Unfortunately, Grandma Emma's words fell on deaf ears. As long as Leroy knew he had Doc in his corner, he proceeded in action disregarding any objection. His only worry was Papa Top, whom Leroy kept tabs on through friends so that he'd know when it was safe to go home.

Leroy's finances dwindled as he took on Cordelia's household expenses along with his own. Living between two households, facing Big Ma, in-laws, and Beatrice's incomprehensible mental state, Leroy reached his breaking point. His life was in a whirlwind. He needed peace and consistency back in his life and knew Cordelia was right. A choice had to be made or else the stress of the situation was going to take him under financially, physically, and mentally. Either he stayed with Beatrice in hopes of her health improving, or take Cordelia's offer to move in with her.

After two week, Grandma Emma caught an early bus back to Texas to go back to work. Papa Top stayed in Happy Hill to run his shop, but periodically checked the house for Leroy, who stayed gone most of the time.

When the coast was clear of Beatrice's parents, Leroy had to make his move fast. He promised Big Ma he'd take over caring for Beatrice, and with assistance from Doc telling Big Ma to return home to tend to her wifely duties, she finally complied.

On Big Ma's last day there, Leroy assured her that everything was going to be fine and if he cared for Beatrice and the girls before, he could do it again. Big Ma nodded, wanting to believe and trust her son again. She spent many nights praying for Leroy to repent for his sins and be saved, sanctified, and full of the Holy Ghost so that he could revert back to being a great father and husband to his family. Big Ma ignored whispers circulating amongst the town folks that Beatrice had been rooted since, as a warrior for Christ, Big Ma trusted Jesus would rid Beatrice of all demons. The devil was at work and Big Ma was going to use her time away to spiritually regroup through fasting and prayer so that she could be strong enough to proceed in her anointed work of saving Beatrice's soul.

Leroy walked Big Ma outside as she softened up towards him, convincing herself that she was witnessing God already at work. Throwing caution to the wind, Big Ma rested on the notion that Leroy would come to his senses soon enough. It was hard for her to remain angry at Leroy for too long. He was her favorite child.

"Whose car is that?" Big Ma said, pointing at a dusty black Chevy parked in the yard.

"A friend loaned it to me in case I gotta make an errand fo' Beatrice."

"It sho' is nice!" Big Ma said, trying to register where she'd seen that car before.

"Yeah, it's a beauty. Need a ride home."

"No thank yah, my baby. I'm not far. Go take care of yah family."

"Alright, be careful."

"And make sho' dem girls eat and get 'em in bed at a decent hour. Try to get Beatrice to eat, too. She needs to get her strength back."

"Yes, ma'am. I'm gonna make sho' Bea is okay so don't worry, mama."

"I'll stop by tomorrow evenin' after church."

Leroy escorted Big Ma to the road, and passing by the car, she glanced over it now able to place a face with the owner, furthering legitimacy to the rumors. Big Ma didn't bother to confront Leroy about having Cordelia's car. She gave the situation to God in hopes that her prayers would be answered in its entirety soon.

Leroy stuck to his word. He bathed Beatrice, dressed her in a pink button down sweater, off-white skirt, and black shoes for a special family dinner. Beatrice managed to brush her hair into a neat ponytail, wanting to be presentable in front of her children and husband while still in a somewhat coherent state. Lula, Lillie, and

Mary hadn't seen Beatrice out of the room in weeks. Big Ma and Grandma Emma purposely kept them away from their mother to avoid them witnessing Beatrice in such a condition.

Beatrice sat at the table forcing herself to eat the food Leroy had prepared and fought to keep her mind steadfast. Seeing snakes lurking in the corner of her eyes, Beatrice banged on the table for them to go away as she chewed fast and swallowed hard before getting the urge to spit the food out.

Beatrice managed to speak, looking away grunting through words to prevent an outburst from the eating utensils turning scaly with beady red eyes.

Remaining calm, she grunted, "Girls, I'm feeling better now. Time is my medicine. I just need time to heal myself. God is going to help me." She spoke to the unfamiliar girls that were supposedly her children, and even though she never met them, there was a deep undeniable connection in which Beatrice felt obligated to comfort them with an explanation.

The girls grinned at their mother's statement, overlooking her struggles at the table. They knew God was going to cure their mother in due time, and like Big Ma said, it was just a phase.

Beatrice trembled balling her hands in an attempt to stay even-tempered. But, Leroy had enough. He didn't want them to see Beatrice in this state any longer, so he got up from the table saying, "Tell yah mama good night and give her a hug. It's time to go to bed."

Lillie, Lula, and Mary ran over to Beatrice and held on to her, not wanting to let go. Instead of having them help clean the kitchen, Leroy sent the girls to bed. Beatrice got up shivering and started gathering the plates off the table, moving her hand quickly to avoid the snakes snipping at her.

Leroy stopped her, "Com'on, time fo' you to get some rest, too."

"I'm not leaving these dishes messy."

"We can clean it up in the mornin', com'on. Yah still not strong enough to do all dis anyway. Yah need your rest."

Beatrice didn't protest. She was feeling weaker as the night waned and the hammer in her head banged harder by the minute.

Leroy lay down in the bed with Beatrice, who was fully dressed for their trip in the early morning.

Three o'clock in the morning came and everyone was sleep. Leroy dozed off for a moment, but woke up in time to get ready. He looked down at Beatrice and saw how neat her hair was holding up in the ponytail while she slept. Sitting bedside Beatrice, he kissed her cheek, flabbergasted about how thin her face felt. Already a thin woman, Beatrice had shed pounds during her mental breakdown. Leroy had to shrug it off and get ready for the day ahead. With his elbows on his knees deep in thought, he waited for the clock to strike four.

Four o'clock hit and Leroy sprang into action. He had formulated the plans for this day many times over to ascertain that this was the best decision.

He packed Beatrice's clothes putting their wedding picture between them, and then wrapped her up in a blanket while she was still sleep and carried her outside with the suitcase. When Beatrice was safe in the car, Leroy ran back to lock and secure the girls inside the house.

Jumping in the driver's seat turning the ignition, Leroy looked up and froze! Lula was in the window staring at him with a blank look on her face. There were no tears, no blinking, or no movement. Lula just stared. Leroy hung his head to evade Lula's subtle defiant stance. Nervously gripping the stirring wheel tight, he looked over at Beatrice sleeping, and then back up at Lula. He shook his head covering his face, unsure of what to do next, wondering why he was doing this in the first place.

The images of Cordelia flooded his mind.

His eyes fluttered.

Leroy put the car in drive and lifted his head to find Lula gone from the window. He screeched out the yard fast and headed down the road.

***

Beatrice woke up surprised to find herself in a car riding with Leroy alongside acres of grassland. She checked the car to make sure the snakes and bugs weren't following them, and then turned toward Leroy and asked, "You bought a car?"

"No, a friend let me borrow it."

Beatrice yawned, sitting up in her seat, peering outside the window at the green scenery in awe of the never-ending acres of land. "Where are we going?"

"I'm taking you to a place that can help you. Yah know, get yah head examined."

"Get my head examined? Why? I'm fine?"

"I kno', but we need to make sho' there ain't nothin' wrong with yah medically. No bleeding of the brain or somethin' of that sort."

"Oh, okay. This is good then."

They drove in silence.

Beatrice was relieved to finally get the medical attention she needed so that she could go back to living a normal life. Hanging her head out the window catching the breeze, feeling good to be outside in the fresh air again, Beatrice smiled up at the sun beaming on her face, taking in the soothing warmth to revitalize her spirit.

After five hours of driving, Leroy entered the open gates to Stolden House Penitentiary. The architectural design of the building looked as if it was once a castle secluded from the world. Metal bars locked in the windows with silver padlocks. Barbed wire lined the building and front gates. The parking lot was full of cop vehicles, regular cars, and buses. The grass was the only thing adding color to the dull building located in the middle of nowhere. The last sign of life was a few miles back at a gas station where Leroy stopped to fill the tank and used the 'Colored only' bathroom, which he refused to use due to the poor plumbing and filth, leaving him to empty his bladder in the bushes.

Leroy opened the car door for Beatrice. She peacefully got out clenching onto her purse. She didn't notice Leroy grabbing a suitcase out of the trunk since she was too busy looking over the massive building. Leroy took hold of Beatrice's hand and they walked up to the twelve foot high brown door that Leroy pushed open. He walked into a waiting area with a long, wooden bench up against the wall. A buzzing noise came from the dim florescent lights that flickered, adding to the noise coming from behind two dingy yellow doors down the hall. Leroy told Beatrice to have a seat on the bench, and then he walked over to a thick square glass window and knocked on it. Beatrice noticed the suitcase in Leroy's hand and lifted her head to see whose attention he was trying to get.

A short white man wearing a gray security uniform got up from a desk, went over to a circular opening in the middle of the thick glass, and asked, "Name?"

"Leroy Harrison, sir."

The man looked at the list and picked up the phone to make a call. He quickly hung up after a few words and motioned Leroy to take a seat. "Someone will be with you shortly."

Leroy went over and sat by Beatrice's side. He fixed the collar on her pink buttoned down blouse, avoiding eye contact with her as he grabbed her hand.

Beatrice asked, "Are you sure this is the right place?"

"Yeah, I'm sho'."

"How long do I have to stay here?"

"I'm gonna pick yah up later on t'night."

"What's the suitcase for?"

"That's just in case you have to stay overnight so I don't have to make another trip back out here."

"Please don't leave me here overnight, Leroy. Just wait for them to check me out and then we can go back home."

"If yah gotta stay fo' a day or two, then you should go 'head and stay. We gotta find out what's wrong with yah, baby. I'll pick yah up as soon as they contact me."

Beatrice hesitated and took a deep breath knowing this was for the best. If this was the sacrifice she had to make for her family, then so be it. She said, "Alright," holding tighter to Leroy's hand.

A short, gray haired man came from behind the yellow doors walking towards Beatrice and Leroy while pushing his glasses up that slid back on his nose. The doctor extended his hand, "Leroy, right?"

"Yes, sir. Leroy Harrison, sir." Leroy stood up to shake his hand.

"I heard bout dis place and decided to give it a try. You're Doctor Foster?"

"Yes I am and you made the best decision indeed. Our intake has a limited amount of colored women displaying psychological disorders. We're looking to open a colored division soon."

Doctor Foster looked over at Beatrice, and then motioned Leroy to follow him to speak in private.

Beatrice sat alone trying to read Leroy and Doctor Foster's lips and body language, but was interrupted by the aggravating buzz coming from the lights. She covered her ears to block out the noise while still trying to decipher their verbal exchange.

Doctor Foster looked over at Beatrice and back at Leroy. "I already can see signs of paranoia."

Beatrice could only make out the last words Leroy said as he told the doctor there was no need for a twenty-five lbs bag of rice and beans for admission.

Doctor Foster disappeared back through the yellow doors and Leroy went back over to Beatrice. "I'll see you a little later, baby." He kissed Beatrice's forehead and rushed toward the front doors.

"Wait, Leroy! Wait!" She screamed, but Leroy was already out the door.

The security guard behind the thick glass counter came over to Beatrice and picked up her suitcase saying, "On your feet."

Beatrice held tightly to her purse and followed the man down the hall behind the yellow doors. She turned around to see if Leroy had come back before the yellow door fully closed. The security guard yelled for her to continue following him. She walked down a dark hall with a cement floor, passing by empty jail cells until they got to the last one. He opened the jail cell and told her to go inside. Beatrice did as she was told and watched the cell bars close her in. She listened to the security guard's footsteps walk away, then she sat on the single mattress bed hoping the procedure would start and end soon so that she could go home.

Beatrice sat for a while and began to realize she'd had no headache or snakes sightings all day. Her stomach rumbled in hunger, making her urge to go home even stronger since she was now ready for a home cooked meal. She huddled into a ball on the thin bed mattress with her shoes and clothes still on and fell asleep.

A couple of hours later, a voice called for Beatrice to wake up. She jumped back scooting toward the end of the bed, clutching onto her purse while looking over at Doctor Foster and a hefty prison guard standing outside the jail cell.

Doctor Foster said, "Hello, Mrs. Beatrice Harrison. We will be transporting you to Pineville tomorrow morning. The guard will bring your supper in a bit. Any questions?"

"When is my husband going to pick me up?"

"You're going to be transferred to Pineville in the morning. Any questions?"

"Yes, when is Leroy going to pick me up?"

"You're the property of the state now, Mrs. Harrison. You've shown to be a threat to yourself and others and no longer can live amongst the community without proper supervision and treatment. Any questions?"

Beatrice was quiet.

Doctor Foster said, "Good, now there are some rules and regulations at Pineville that you will have to abide by to avoid any disciplinary action: First, you must understand that you will have to work for your stay. Patients have daily chores and duties and no one is exempt from them under any circumstances. Second, all medications must be taken at a set time and location. Failure to be at your designated location will cost you privileges and subject you to be reprimanded. In other words, don't make us hunt you down! Lastly, psychological treatment is given once a week. If you bother to fight, kick, scream, or holler, you'll only make matters worse for yourself, so it's your choice. Any questions?"

"When is Leroy going to pick me up?"

Doctor Foster cut his eyes at the guard. They both retreated without saying another word.

Beatrice looked around at the small cell with a tiny bed and small, dirty toilet. She started panting heavily pulling at her hair trying to convince herself that this was all just a dream. A tiny drip of water from the ceiling fell on her forehead. Wiping it off, she looked up at the ceiling as another drop splattered on her nose. She dabbed the drip of water realizing this was all real.

She dropped her purse rushing over to the bars screaming, "Leroy! Leroy! Leroy! Get me out of here!" Beatrice pulled at the bars, kicking and hitting them to break free. She took off one of her shoes and beat the lock with it. "I don't want the treatment, I wanna go home! Leroy! Leroy!" She screamed.

The short security guard came over to the cell yelling, "Shut your mouth!"

"Please, there must be a mistake. I'm only supposed to be tested. My husband is coming to get me soon! Please, just let me out, I want to go home!" She pleaded, "Where's my husband! Leroy, Leroy!"

The security guard pointed and said, "That's it!" He left and came back with two other guards and Doctor Foster.

Doctor Foster said, "Mrs. Harrison, I'm going to give you one chance and one chance only to settle down."

Beatrice ignored Doctor Foster, screaming for Leroy to come help her.

Doctor Foster said, "Last chance, Mrs. Harrison."

She continued to scream pulling at the bars.

Doctor Foster nodded his head at the guards. They opened the cell, tackling Beatrice to the ground pinning her against the floor, dirtying up her pink button-down blouse and off-white skirt.

"Leroy, please, help! Help! Leroy!" She screamed, fighting the men off her, freeing a hand to hit them with her purse. It took both guards to subdue Beatrice on the ground by holding her arms and legs against the floor.

Doctor Foster squirted liquid out of a needle, bent down, and pulled up her sleeve. He stuck the needle in the middle of her arm.

Beatrice cried, "Leroy! My babies! I wanna go home to my babies!"

All of a sudden, the room blurred and her body went limp. The men turned into distant shadows as her eyes lowered and she passed out.

Clothes dirty, hair messy, and barefoot, Beatrice lay there alone, surrounded by things scattered across the floor from her purse.

Doctor Foster and the guards waited until there was no sign of movement and then left, leaving Beatrice on the cold, damp, cement floor.

In the car, Leroy scratched at the top of his head during the somber ride back to Eunice going seventy miles per hour, feeling his heart drop deeper to the pit of his stomach in each mile he drove. He pulled over on the dirt road and stopped the car still gripping the steering wheel, swallowing hard to hold back his tears. He got out the car holding his stomach from the deep pain he felt and leaned against the car, sliding down to sit.

Beatrice was back in a prison waiting to be transferred to a mental institution, and there he sat in the middle of nowhere. In the blistering heat, Leroy picked up a few rocks and threw them as far as he could. He was unable to get the love of his life, the mother of his children, and the woman he married in Holy Matrimony out of his mind. Leroy cringed at the thought of Beatrice being in the jail cell alone. He balled a fist squeezing at his temples in shame. The question of why he was sending Beatrice away could not be answered. He couldn't deny the depth of love for Beatrice and the need for her to be by his side.

Getting up from the ground, he dusted himself off and jumped back into the car holding onto the stirring wheel. He leaned his head back, tilting the rearview window to avoid seeing himself, while thinking about the first time he saw Beatrice sitting in church, so prim and proper. It put a smile on his face. Then Doc and male family member's speaking ill of Beatrice angered Leroy. They had no business meddling in his marriage, and Leroy realized how taking advice from miserable men had caused him to lose touch with what was most important in his life. Putting the car in drive, Leroy screeched making a U-turn and slammed on the gas pedal heading back to Stolden House Penitentiary to get his wife. Beatrice's disturbing behavior wasn't going to stop Leroy from loving her. She could see a million snakes for all Leroy cared. It was a battle worth fighting for his beloved Beatrice. He wasn't going to give up on her. Not now. Not ever. If Doc or anybody else had something to say, they'd have to deal with Leroy's fist. Nobody was going to stand in the way of his love for Beatrice again!

At eighty miles per hour, the car couldn't go fast enough to reach Stolden House Penitentiary so Leroy could get his wife. The shame Leroy felt made his foot mash harder on the pedal. But then, Leroy's eyes fluttered making it hard for him to see the road. He slowed down pulling over on the side of the road to rub his eyes clear. The fluttering didn't stop. He stopped rubbing them hoping to wait out this eye problem.

His eyes fluttered uncontrollably, then stopped, leaving Leroy's eyes wide open looking straight ahead in a daze. He screeched the car making another U-turn back in the opposite direction without thinking twice about Beatrice. Going forty miles per hour, Leroy never blinked once while driving down the road to Eunice, back to Cordelia.

***

Leroy hid from the family in Cordelia's house for a few weeks after dropping Beatrice off at the prison. He feared for his life if Papa Top got hold of him.

Leroy drove down Beulah Road with a hat on, leaning far back as possible so that nobody could recognize him from the porches. His plan was to go to his house, get his belongings, explain everything to Big Ma, and deter any confrontation.

When Leroy pulled up to his house, he was in for a shock. There sat Papa Top. Leroy wanted to drive away, but thought the better of it. He had to face the family sooner or later.

Papa Top patiently sat watching Leroy get out of the car and walk up slowly toward the porch, looking everywhere but at Papa Top, while scratching the top of his head and dramatically waving away gnats as if that was the biggest issue for the moment. Papa Top's glare was strong enough to make Leroy flinch at any little thing.

In a deep commanding voice, Papa Top finally said, "You betta start talkin', boy!"

Leroy remained silent. He took off his hat, squinting his eyes to keep the sun from beaming directly on them, still waving the pesky bugs away.

Papa Top got up from his chair and calmly walked over to Leroy, and before Leroy knew it, a hard jab hit him across the head knocking him to the ground. Leroy grabbed his head looking up through blurry red vision at Papa Top holding a thick wooden cane.

In a deep, stern tone Papa Top said, "I'm gonna ask you one last time. WHERE'S MY DAUGHTER?"

When Papa Top didn't get a response, he lifted his cane examining it first, then hit Leroy across the head again breaking the cane in two.

Doc came out the house and hustled down the porch stairs saying, "Hold on nah, Oscar, hold on!" He wrestled Papa Top away from Leroy, who was lying on the ground holding his bleeding head. It was a struggle for Doc being only 5'8", almost a foot shorter than Papa Top who stood 6'7", to detain Papa Top from hurting Leroy.

Papa Top was a man of few words. An older Creole man, tall with great strength he rarely exerted. When he got the news that Beatrice was missing, Papa Top waited on their porch every day praying for Beatrice's safety and begging God to keep his lady friend, Miss Colt .45, from having a conversation with Leroy. The worst-case scenarios on Beatrice's whereabouts overwhelmed Papa Top, instigating Miss Colt .45 to do all the speaking if Leroy didn't cooperate. He waited for days with a cane in one hand and his gun in the other, and sent the girls away to family members' houses knowing things could get ugly between him and their father.

Doc tussled with Papa Top trying to take the two halves of a cane away from him, but Papa Top got loose and rushed over to Leroy and struck him again across his back. Leroy hollered out grabbing his back and rolling around on the ground begging for mercy. In all his pain, Leroy refused to fight back out of respect for his elders.

Once Papa Top was content with the last blow, he settled himself down throwing the two pieces of wood aside, and then waited for an explanation now that Leroy got some sense knocked into him.

Doc ran over to Leroy to help him on his feet, but Leroy angrily waved Doc away, especially since he felt Doc was part of the reason why he was in this situation. Leroy sat up on his own holding his back while wiping blood off his forehead.

Rubbing blood out of his eyes, Leroy said, "She okay, sir. Trust me, she's alright. I took her to get some medical help." He stood up on his feet and bent over huffing and puffing, trying to focus his double-vision.

Big Ma and Grandma Emma came outside. Big Ma rushed over to Leroy asking if he was okay.

Doc pleaded, "Son, just tell dem where Beatrice is at?"

"Don't worry bout where Bea's at. I'm her husband and all y'all need to kno' is that she's safe." Leroy put his hands up for Big Ma to stop checking the wounds on his head.

Doc pulled Big Ma away by her apron, upset at Leroy for refusing help. Doc backed himself and Big Ma away leaving Leroy prone to whatever Papa Top had in store next. Leroy balanced himself, taking a defensive stance when he saw Doc move back.

Papa Top, along with everyone else, waited for a more detailed explanation. When Leroy didn't speak, Papa Top had enough. He pulled out Miss Colt .45, cocked her back and pointed at Leroy's groin. Grandma Emma jolted over to Papa Top and pulled at his arm trying to grab the gun yelling in Creole, "No, Oscar, don't!" She tussled with Papa Top as he pointed the gun in the air out of her reach. Moving Grandma Emma behind him, Papa Top lowered the gun again, now pointing at Leroy's head.

Papa Top said, "Let's try dis again, where's my daughter?"

Doc didn't stop Big Ma from running in front of Leroy, holding her hands up saying, "In the name of Jesus, you ain't shootin' my boy, Oscar."

Still pointing the gun, Papa Top said, "Move, Louverta!"

"You think I'm just gonna sit here and let you shoot my boy! You must've lost yah mind." Her arms reached out wider. "In the name of the Lord Jesus Christ, the devil is at work. I rebuke you devil in the name of Jesus. Leave dis here family alone!"

"Leroy, if yah don't start talkin' on my daughter's whereabouts," Papa Top said, pointing a clear shot at Leroy's head above Big Ma.

Leroy gently moved Big Ma out of harm's way and looked Papa Top in the eye. "I'll tell you everythin', sir. All I ask is that yah put the gun down!"

Papa Top waited for a minute, never taking his eye off Leroy, and dropped his arm holding Miss Colt .45. Leroy took a deep breath and wiped away more blood from his forehead.

"Why don't we all go inside," Doc said, looking around. "Louverta can clean yah head up and you can explain everythin'," he told Leroy.

Everyone moved cautiously into the house, looking at Leroy and Papa Top for any false moves. Papa Top held onto his gun keeping a keen eye on Leroy as they all took a seat at the table. Big Ma got a towel and bowl of water and began cleaning Leroy's face, applying pressure to his head wound to stop the blood. Leroy took over holding the towel against his head as everyone watched in silence. Squinting in pain, no one displayed any remorse for Leroy. He tried to lighten the dense air in the room. "I feel like I'm on trial here," Leroy chuckled. Straight faces showed no amusement.

Doc said, "Boy, yah betta tell dis man where Bea at!"

Leroy shot an exasperated look at Doc.

Dressing Leroy's head with bandages, Big Ma was torn between wrapping her son's wounds carefully or mashing down on them. She turned away ignoring Leroy's pleading eyes, hoping God would have mercy for her son's sins, yet welcoming the punishment for Leroy to change his ways soon.

"Can I get some clothes first?" Leroy asked, "It's fo' Bea."

"Boy!" Papa Top got up from the table ready to attack. Grandma Emma and Doc grabbed Papa Top calming him down.

Grandma Emma said, "Look, let him go 'head and get whatever he needs to get fo' Beatrice, then he can come back in here and tell us where she is." She wanted to keep the tension at a minimum to prevent that awful Miss Colt .45 from pointing at Leroy's head again.

Papa Top fell back in his seat, giving room for everyone to relax.

Leroy stood up, "I'll be just a minute, then I'll fill y'all in on everythin' that's goin' on." He threw the bloody towel on the table and got up slouched over holding his back like a crippled old man walking to his bedroom, closing the door behind him. He took two white pillow cases, threw his clothes in them, and then pulled out a white envelope full of their life savings from in between the bed mattress and pocketed it. He stopped to grab at his throbbing head before finishing packing up his belongings.

Standing in the hallway bent over with two full pillow cases in hand, Leroy looked over at Doc, Big Ma, Papa Top, and Grandma Emma, all patiently waiting for Leroy to join them back at the table.

"I need help…my back! These clothes are fo' Beatrice. Can you put these in the car fo' me, pops?" Leroy asked, holding his back.

Doc got up and took the two pillow cases lifting them high. "These ain't that heavy."

Leroy told Doc the pain was unbearable and he couldn't carry a flea right about now. Doc shook his head and took the keys from Leroy to put the pillow cases in the car.

Grandma Emma asked, "So those are fo' Beatrice?"

"Yes, ma'am," Leroy answered.

Papa Top interjected, "Explain now!'"

Leroy hesitated. He waited for the car door to shut and for Doc to come back with the keys. "Beatrice asked me to take her to dis place to get her head examined." When Doc handed Leroy the keys, Leroy squinted in the pain holding his back and muttered, "She's in a good place to help her mind get betta. She begged me to take her there b'cause she didn't want the girls to see her like that anymore," Leroy said, taking a few steps back.

"Lord Jesus, where is she?" Big Ma asked, putting a hand on her hip losing her patience as well.

"Bea, she, she's at,—" Leroy said, before bolting out the house slamming the door shut, leaping off the porch and running over to the driver's seat of the car. Papa Top jumped up from his chair and ran after Leroy, but got stuck scrambling at the broken latch on the shut door. Papa Top kicked the door to the ground and ran out into the road shooting at dust the car left behind.

***

Cordelia banged at Tauntadi's door screaming, "Open up, Sha!" She banged, "Leroy moved in. He's here to stay!"

Tauntadi smacked the door open, livid that her afternoon nap was interrupted. Ready to cuss Cordelia out, Tauntadi stopped when Cordelia raised her left hand up showing a tiny diamond ring on her finger. Cordelia giggled clapping in joy, walking past Tauntadi into the house.

Giggling, she said, "I came here to thank you fo' workin' a miracle. He packed Beatrice's bags and sent her straight to the nut house. I can just kiss yah right nah!"

"Please don't," Tauntadi said, still standing in the doorway showing no sign of enthusiasm. "And don't thank me fo' the mess you made," she said, closing the door. She took a seat in her green chair and picked up her pipe and box full of wooden match sticks. "I was just doin' my job."

"Fine then, I won't. But at least accept my 'thank you' gift." Dust flew when Cordelia threw a stack of dollars on the coffee table.

Tauntadi looked up with a puzzled expression.

Cordelia added, "Fifty dollars right there from tips, and don't worry, I'm done makin' money *that way* anymore. I gotta man with a job to take care of me nah!"

Tauntadi said, "I didn't kno' workin' girls get tips, Sha. Learn somethin' new every day!"

Cordelia rolled her eyes. "I don't have to give you dis here money nah."

"Actually, I don't want no more of yah money," Tauntadi said, putting tobacco in her pipe.

"Why not?"

"B'cause, I just don't. I did my job. Doesn't mean I like it, but business is business and I gotta eat, Sha. Yah paid me fo' the job and it's done. I don't need no extra money or reward."

"Nah I kno' if I leave dis here money on the table, yah ain't just gonna let it sit there and collect dust, so I'll just leave it there 'til yah come to yah senses, okay?"

Tauntadi puffed on her pipe, gazing into the smoky air, drifting into her own world ignoring Cordelia.

Cordelia got the picture. She turned around to leave without picking the money up from the coffee table. She opened the front door and stopped in mid-step, turned around, and walked back into the room throwing another roll of dollar bills on the coffee table. Tauntadi's mouth fell open allowing the smoke to escape on its own.

Cordelia bent down and whispered, "You did a good job on Beatrice," she said and leaned in closer. "And a GREAT job you did on Leroy. He can't keep his hands off me! Leroy's finally mine! Funny what a little hair from a brush can do. Thanks, Sha," Cordelia winked then left.

Part 2

Chapter 7

It was 1951. Six years had passed since Lillie, Lula, and Mary had seen their parents. Leroy rented their home out to a cousin and moved out of Eunice with Cordelia, leaving Big Ma and Doc to raise the girls.

Lula blossomed into a beautiful, yet awkward adolescent girl. It took time for her to adjust into her newly developed body. At twelve years-old, she followed behind Lillie's footsteps as one of the first girls to graduate from the eighth grade in the family. Big Ma made sure they never missed a day of school.

Lula set her goals high and looked forward to furthering her education to become a teacher. Lula and Lillie helped each other with homework and taught Mary and older family members how to read since most of them weren't privileged to get an education.

Lula was excellent at English, thanks to Beatrice, and excelled in all of her other subjects including mathematics, history, and social studies. When Lillie or Lula needed some assistance for themselves, they turned to their older cousin, Junior Harrison, who at fourteen years-old, surpassed his teacher's academic level. He often visited from New Orleans to help Lula and younger family members with their work so that more family could follow him to college where he planned to study medicine to become a doctor.

The older Lula became, the more she looked like Beatrice, with almond shaped eyes, sugar brown complexion, angular face, and bright white teeth. With her body maturing faster than her mind, Lula camouflaged her curves with loose fitting dresses and long skirts that Big Ma made. Men still watched from afar, but kept their hands off, conscious of Big Ma ringing their necks if they dared look twice at any of her granddaughters.

Five years into moving in with Big Ma and Doc, Lillie began to change. She became more distant and disobedient, sneaking out the house in the middle of the night leaving Lula to cover for her. One morning, Lillie got caught coming through the window and was welcomed by Big Ma standing there with a switch. Lula pleaded for Big Ma to spare Lillie the spanking, and when Lillie fell over screaming and crying in fear, Big Ma left Lillie alone because deep down, she knew why Lillie was leaving.

Instead of chastising Lillie with a switch, Big Ma prayed and decided to keep the girls in church more to keep them in accordance to the way a God fearing Christian woman behaved. From three times a week, to now every day in church, the long hours were brutal at first for the girls. Nonetheless, they were already accustomed to spending the majority of their time in church, so a few more days was an easy adaption if they wanted to keep their reserved spot in heaven.

Lillie was almost fourteen years-old when she noticed a young man named, Bernard. Blossoming into an attractive young lady, she started spending more time with Bernard than at home, sneaking out at night, ready to face the consequences for her new found love. When Lillie was home, she was withdrawn and quiet to the point that Big Ma would forget Lillie was in the room, and when Lillie did speak, it was a near whisper. She'd sit on the porch step rocking for hours in a daze. The only thing that put a smile on her face was the thought of meeting up with Bernard later that night. The one person privileged to still encounter the "old" Lillie was Lula, who pressed and curled Lillie's hair, pinning it up on top of her head for her late night dates with Bernard.

For Lillie, Bernard was a safe haven personified into a man, saving her from a household she hated to call home. Lillie confiding in Lula made their bond tighter, appreciating Lula for keeping Bernard a secret. An already protective sister, Lillie watched over Lula to save her from the atrocities Lillie was enduring at home. Mary was still too young, but Lillie still kept a watchful eye on her as well.

Lillie, being the oldest, surrendered herself to Doc's harsh beatings to spare Lula and Mary whenever they got in trouble for little things. Doc was brutal to Lillie. He'd yell, call her names, and belittle her every chance he got. Doc gladly took the chance to beat Lillie for miniscule things like eating with her mouth open or not responding fast enough. Big Ma attempted to step in between the spankings, which only led to her getting a blackened eye or busted lip. Depending on her level of energy, Big Ma took the painful blows for Lillie, but at times, she was unable to sacrifice her elderly body and weak heart.

On the contrary, Lillie welcomed the beatings as opposed to "the snake" that caused mental, physical, and emotional confusion for Lillie.

Lillie and Lula were up talking one night and in between conversation, Lillie asked Lula, "Have yah ever seen a snake b'fore?"

"Yeah, they come in after storms and Big Ma swooshes them outside with the broom."

"I'm not talkin' bout those snakes, Lula Mae. I'm talkin' bout Grandpa Doc's snake."

"He got a snake? He doesn't like 'em either."

"No, Lula! It's a part of his body."

"Oh yeah?"

"Yeah, it look nasty and it grows, too!"

"Yuck! He needs to go see a doctor bout that. Garlic get rid of worms, so maybe it'll work fo' snakes, too."

"It's different. I don't think garlic can get rid of it. It's a part of his body."

"I'm tellin' Big Ma," Lula got up from the bed and started marching towards the bedroom door.

Lillie jumped up and pulled Lula's arm saying, "No, Lula Mae, please don't! You can't tell Big Ma. You can't tell nobody!"

"Why not?"

"B'cause he'll beat me. He said so if I tell anybody."

"Then I'll tell him I told Big Ma," Lula shrugged, walking back to the door. She was willing to take the punishment for her big sister.

Lillie ran over frantically pulling Lula by the arm. "Please don't, Lula Mae, I don't want him beatin' you either, and if I disobey him, he said I'm gonna go to hell. I'm scared!" Lillie sat on the bed folding her arms and rocked back and forth. She grabbed a pillow, put it over her face and screamed a gut wrenching cry into it while Lula sat there at a loss for words watching Lillie's hysteria.

Lula knelt down putting her hand on Lillie's back and waited.

Lillie calmed down and lifted her head off the pillow drenched in tears, saliva, and mucus. Lula ran to get a towel and wiped Lillie's face telling her to blow into the towel. When she was done, Lillie swallowed hard between short breaths.

Lula whispered, "I won't tell nobody. I'll pray extra fo' Jesus to protect you from that snake."

"I've been prayin'," Lillie said. Tears trickled from Lillie's eyes. "I prayed every night so I don't have to see that thang again. I hate it. It makes my private hurt!" Lillie blew her nose and sniffled, "That's why God sent me Bernard. He's a man. He'll save me. He makes me feel normal again."

"Why yah private hurt?"

"That snake hurt it. I hate snakes. I kno' the devil sent it, but I never heard bout it in the sermon, so I tried askin' my teacher bout it and she gave me an evil look and got away from me, so I kno' I'm doin' somethin' wrong. That's why I can't tell nobody. I just don't wanna go to hell fo' it."

"How the snake hurt yah?"

Lillie covered her mouth gagging in the towel.

Lula ran and got another towel for Lillie to wipe herself off and asked, "Yah want some water?"

"No thanks." Lillie looked up with sincere eyes. "You think I'm a good Christian girl…You think Jesus will forgive me?"

"I think yah a great Christian girl and Jesus loves you."

Lillie looked down and played with the thread hanging off the towel. "I wish everyone felt the same way you do. When I see people look at me, especially in church, I think they kno'. It makes me feel so bad. I just wanna crawl under a rock and die! I gotta leave dis house soon!"

Lillie cried in the towel. Lula hugged Lillie and started combing her sister's hair with her fingers.

Lula said, "It's too late to leave t'night. Here, give me your hands." Lula took the towel and wiped Lillie's hands off.

"I meant leave dis here house fo' good."

Lula stopped wiping and looked up at Lillie with a concerned look.

Lillie said, "Don't worry, when I leave, you and Mary can come with me. I'm gonna go with Bernard. He'll keep us all safe. Jesus sent him to protect us."

"Do Bernard know bout 'the snake'?"

"No! And he'll never kno'." Lillie looked down picking at her nail. "If I tell him, he might not wanna be with me. He kissed me yesterday!"

"Fo' real, Sha?"

"Yeah," Lillie bashfully giggled turning away, "I got my first kiss."

***

Sunday came and the girls were ready for church. Big Ma feared for Lillie, hoping what plagued Beatrice wasn't getting into Lillie, too. However, Lillie's condition turned her more solemn and introverted. Big Ma knew Doc's beatings were harsh for Lillie, so she tried talking to Lillie, but couldn't get through to her. It only made Lillie withdraw into herself even more. The mere thing that kept Lillie holding on was the prospect of leaving with Bernard for good.

Big Ma did notice the way Lillie left the room when Doc entered, and how she never acknowledged Doc's presence at the dinner table and vice versa. Big Ma found it odd for Doc to allow Lillie to act in such a dismissive manner without chastising her blatant disrespect toward an elder. And then, out of nowhere, he'd find foolish reasons to beat Lillie mercilessly. That was enough for Big Ma to know she did the right thing by keeping them in church.

When church Sunday arrived, the girls walked barefoot side-by-side with Big Ma, wearing freshly sewn dresses to church. Lula got up at five a.m. to press and curl Big Ma, Lillie, and Mary's hair using a hot comb and curlers on the stove. Everyone gloated on their dresses and the magnificent job Lula did with their hair.

In the red brick church, they sat in the third row aisles on the left-hand side. Lula made sure to sit near the end of the aisle to get a good view of the new members joining the congregation that day. This was the highlight of Lula's time in church, breaking up the monotony of Sunday service.

Mary sat to the left of Lula, followed by Lillie and then Big Ma. Mary nudged Lula to adjust her posture—slouching wasn't proper etiquette in church and because people followed body language closely, kids got popped if their posture wasn't correct.

This third Sunday was a highly anticipated day. No time was wasted for the new members to be called up front, coming from different areas of the church aisles to gather in the front of the congregation. Everyone mumbled amongst themselves, filling each other in on the new members. Lula intently watched the new members join together in the front, and she did a double-look at two young men in their late teens or early twenties standing in the front facing the church.

One of the young men captured Lula's eye. Butterflies cramped her stomach as her heart raced making her more nervous by the minute. Lula examined the young man from head-to-toe. Standing at 5'7" with a medium build, his reddish brown skin, mysterious eyes, full lips, and enigmatic presence made Lula bite at her lip anxiously waiting for his introduction. When his turn came to introduce himself, he stepped out from the line, cleared his throat, and situated his pose to exude confidence to say, "My name is, Bervick Frank, and I'm here t'day to show my devotion to my Lord and savior Jesus Christ. I'm honored to join dis here congregation and—" Lula didn't hear another word. All she saw was a mouth moving on the most handsome man she'd ever seen. Hearing that he was a devoted Christian man full of the Holy Ghost was all she needed to hear. Everything about him was charming: the way he talked, walked, stood, and his overall demeanor. Lula smiled gazing at him, enjoying the sight. *His name is Bervick, Bervick Frank,* Lula thought.

"That boy there, Bervick Frank, he a mess," Lula heard a voice whisper from behind.

No, not him! Lula thought lost in reverie.

The church members dissolved into thin air, leaving Lula and Bervick alone looking at each other. Time stood still. Bervick walked over to Lula and took her by the hand, gently pulling her into his arms as he kissed her lips whispering, "I love you."

A knock upside the back of Lula's head shook her out of the daydream. She grabbed the back of her head turning to find Big Ma staring dead in her eye with a "don't you dare" look. Lula rubbed the back of her head wondering how Big Ma managed to reach over Lillie and Mary to pop her, and furthermore, how did Big Ma know. Lula put her head down folding her hands in her lap without looking up for the rest of the church service.

When church was over, Lula got up with her head still down to avoid another surprise smack. When she was about to exit the double doors, Lula couldn't resist. She lifted her head to get one more glance at Bervick, and quickly flinched. Standing across the room, Bervick was staring right at her. Lula turned away blushing.

He had noticed her, too.

***

Bervick and his brother, Curley Frank, walked home together from church. Bervick was elated after seeing the most beautiful girl he'd ever seen seated in the third aisle on the left. When Bervick spoke in front of the church, he'd struggled to keep his nerves intact by looking straight ahead concentrating on an elderly woman who was less intimidating.

"Say, Curley, yah see that pretty girl sittin' at the end of the pew? She had on the white dress and curls in—" Curley interrupted Bervick's question with a quick "Yes!"

Curley said, "That's Doc Harrison's granddaughter."

"She a Harrison?"

"Yeah!"

"Dem Harrison girls sho' is pretty. What's her name?"

"Lula Mae."

"Lula Mae, hmm humph, pretty name fo' a pretty lady." Bervick pictured her in his mind. "I gotta meet her. Maybe you can take me 'round there after yah get off work some time dis week?"

Curley nodded as they walked on home.

Chapter 8

Lula cried hugging Lillie outside of their home. Lillie had eloped with Bernard and gotten married, unbeknownst to Lula, who had not seen this coming since she and Lillie shared everything with each other. Lula was disappointed and sad at the same time. Bernard wanted Lillie to move in with him right away and she jumped at the chance to do so since she was head over heels for Bernard, and most of all, Lillie couldn't wait to pack up and get away from Doc.

Lillie prayed a prayer of thanks to Jesus for paving the way to escape hell and fall into the hands of the man she loved and cherished so much. Just turning fourteen years-old, Lillie was ready to create a new life for herself. She regretted leaving Big Ma, Lula, and Mary, but had to put her feelings aside for now and do what was best for herself. She promised to be back for her sisters once she settled into her new home.

Outside the house, Lillie decided to delay their good-byes by inviting Lula over to the new house and Lula agreed, leaving without telling Big Ma, who was inside cooking and fuming at the fact that Lillie got married without her knowledge or consent.

Around the corner from where they grew up, Lula and Lillie walked into a small single room home that used to be a vacant shack. Lula played up her enthusiasm for the house well. She looked up at the sun shining through the roof. The decaying wooden floors, holes in the roof, and overgrown grass outside left nothing to be desired. Lula took heed of Lillie's efforts at cleaning and fixing up the house, but didn't like her sister moving into such a place. Thinking Lillie could do better than what Bernard had to offer, Lula felt sorry for Lillie, who seemed proud of her new home.

After a one minute tour around the entire home, Lula burst into tears as reality set in. This would be the first time she was going to be apart from Lillie. Lillie went over to hug Lula, rubbing her back, assuring her that they weren't that far apart.

Lillie said, "Once we get settled and fix things up a bit, yah gonna come live here with me. In the meantime, yah welcome to come over here at anytime!"

"Yeah, but it won't be the same without you. I need you," Lula cried in Lillie's arms. Lillie wiped away Lula's tears and rocked her back and forth.

"Listen to me, Lula Mae, I need you to stay in church as late as yah can and go home only when you kno' Doc's sleep, alright?" Lillie said, trying her best to disguise the urgency in her words.

"Don't yah think Big Ma keep us there long enough?"

"Stay longer!"

"Why?"

"I don't want you meetin' 'the snake'."

"I'll just tell him I don't wanna meet 'the snake' then."

"Just promise me you'll stay in church."

"I promise. You still gonna go too, right?"

"No. Me and Bernard goin' to another church."

"Aww no, you gotta go to church with us!"

Lillie's head dropped. "Please don't make dis harder on me, Lula Mae. I'm married nah and I gotta go where my husband tells me. Jesus is in all churches."

"I'm not gonna see much of yah anymore, am I?"

"Not as much, that's why I say just visit me 'til I get dis here house ready fo' yah to move in. I'll teach yah how to make some more dishes so you can get that 'Best Cook' title you want so bad," Lillie joked. "I'm still a betta cook than yah."

"I kno'," Lula laughed to pacify her sister's attempt to lighten the mood.

"Come over some time and cook with me. I'll help yah master some mo' dishes. I kno' a few secrets to make that gumbo, boudin, and cornbread dressin' sang."

"Alright, Sis."

Lula hugged Lillie, not wanting to let her go. Lula felt a piece of her heart being stolen away thanks to Bernard. They held on tight until Bernard walked through the door. Lula let go stepping back, wanting to grab Lillie by the arm and run away with her. Instead, Lula greeted Bernard, hugged Lillie one last time, and ran back to Big Ma's house before Big Ma noticed Lula was gone.

***

Four months passed since Lillie moved out and it wasn't long before "the snake" struck again. Unfortunately, this time came with unfavorable results.

Lula was lying on the bed, curled in a ball, sobbing. Big Ma sat across from her in a wooden chair praying for God to forgive them both while staring at Lula's swollen red face. Looking over Lula's small, pre-developed thirteen year-old body, Big Ma asked God why.

After witnessing the change in Lillie, Big Ma's heart sank when Lula presented the same change in behavior not long after Lillie moved out. Never discussing the matter, Big Ma took the proper measures to bring Lula back to herself by keeping her in church and sleeping in the bed with Lula and Mary to protect them. The beatings Big Ma endured because of this became unbearable to the point, Big Ma had no other choice but to let go and pray for God to protect them. Regrettably, Big Ma didn't expect in a million years what came next.

Looking down at Lula, who was lying on a pillow soaked in tears, Big Ma felt that she was an accomplice to Lula's sorrow given that it was she who left Lula alone with a man that had a track record with the young women of the family. Big Ma felt guilty for believing that Doc was finally saved due to him receiving the Holy Ghost in church many years ago. His sinful past was something Big Ma had happily forgotten, and felt her granddaughters was safe to move in with a born again Christian man full of the Holy Ghost. That part of Doc was so exempt from Big Ma's memory that when she got an inkling something was wrong with Lillie, Big Ma blamed the beatings and didn't look any deeper; however, those inklings still propelled Big Ma to keep the girls protected in the Lord's house. Ignoring the signs with Lillie only magnified the outcome for Lula, which Big Ma now had to face front and center.

An ominous cloud accumulated above the Harrison household, creating a series of unfortunate events that Big Ma prayed for light to be shed upon soon.

In the bedroom, Big Ma found the strength to stand her numb body up and sit beside Lula, who rested her head in Big Ma's lap. She stroked Lula's cotton soft hair, listening to sorrowful sounds from Lula that made Big Ma cringe. Lula whimpered raising her hand out, reaching for unattainable relief. Big Ma felt Lula slipping away and began rocking harder in an attempt to keep a grip on Lula's fragile state of mind. The joint pain between them sent Big Ma into her own mental frenzy, rocking Lula as the only antidote for grief. She knew it was time to leave and get things over with before Lula's mind was too far gone.

Big Ma helped Lula to her feet and walked her toward the screen door holding her close. Opening it, Lillie and Mary stood by the side of the steps, each holding a bag in their hand watching Big Ma help their sister down the steps. When Lillie heard what was about to take place, she flew over to Big Ma's house to see about Lula and stayed by her side until it was time. Lillie got Mary out the house by taking her to Mr. Petes for some goodies, but came back fast to see their sister off.

Lillie gasped in tears wanting to run up and hug Lula, but her legs stood frozen. She dropped her bag. Her chest got heavy from watching Big Ma walk Lula down the road until they were out of sight. Lillie and Mary sat on the porch hanging their heads, unable to wave back at the people passing by.

Big Ma knocked on the door of a small home while holding Lula close to her, kissing her forehead, rubbing her back, and resting her head on top of Lula's. A small, scary lady opened the door. They walked into an old foul smelling place with a cloud of smoke lingering in the air. Big Ma sat Lula on the couch and went to the back room with the woman.

Lula's eyes examined the room, observing antique statues, disgusting old candy covered in dust on the coffee table, and furniture older than dirt. She made noises on the plastic covered couch while scooting away from the creepy statues that were looking back at her. Lula bent over and hugged her knees as chills ran down her spine from having the feeling that she was being watched. She closed her eyes praying nothing bothered her in there.

Big Ma walked back in the front room with the scary woman following, and lifted an elephant man statue's head putting a twenty dollar bill in it. Lula was astounded at how familiar Big Ma was in the creepy place and jumped when she saw the frightful woman looking at her. The woman chuckled and carefully helped Lula off the sofa and began walking her into the backroom. Lula stopped to look back at Big Ma, who calmly nodded, telling Lula it was okay to go.

When the backroom door closed, Big Ma fell to her knees in prayer begging the Lord for forgiveness. In her mist of streaming tears, she stopped, realizing she'd been down this road before with Samantha and didn't deserve the Lord's mercy this time.

Lula lay down on a flat, narrow, long table in the back room. She trembled in fear covering her nose from a weird smell and started coughing from the smoke. She asked the woman's name to break the tension in the air and the elderly woman smiled showing her gold front tooth and yucky teeth, and said, "Tauntadi," and then poured hot water in a cup full of herbs and told Lula to drink it down slow.

When Lula finished drinking, Tauntadi put the pipe she was smoking to Lula's mouth, but Lula backed her head away giving Tauntadi a doubtful look.

Tauntadi said, "Relax, child, dis will help you."

Hesitant, Lula took a few puffs and started coughing, waving the repulsive odor away from her nose. Tauntadi held the pipe to Lula's mouth without budging, scaring Lula into taking a few more puffs.

Tauntadi said, "Take it in, Sha. Take in the smoke."

Lula did as she was told, inhaling and exhaling. She did so repeatedly until Tauntadi nodded and pulled the pipe away from Lula's mouth, then laid her down. Lula turned her head settling her eyes on a flickering candle. She grabbed hold of both sides of the table wondering why she started floating up. Her head moved side-to-side, up-and-down, feeling each movement in slow motion. Lula waved her hands in the air watching the colorful patterns to the music playing without an actual record player in the room.

Now nervous, Lula put her hands over her face closing her eyes hoping the feeling went away soon. She didn't feel her legs being pulled closer to the edge of the table, or her knees separating. Other than the cold steel object yanking her a bit, Lula was in her own world as Tauntadi worked fast.

Big Ma opened the door to see if Lula was okay and gasped holding her racing heart.

Tauntadi didn't look Big Ma's way saying, "She's in good hands, Louverta. Go on back to the other room."

Big Ma closed the door scurrying back to try prayer again.

Lula was intrigued by the colors circulating in the air and started painting shapes with them, not noticing the tug at her insides. The abdomen cramps felt more like marbles rolling around, tickling Lula making her laugh. She inhaled the sweet perfume-like odor in the air, incapable of realizing the wonderful scent was the scent of her own blood.

Time passed and Big Ma sat on the couch clinging to a bible she found underneath the coffee table. She stood up fast after hearing the backroom door open and saw Tauntadi helping Lula walk out. Big Ma postponed her cry to stay strong for Lula.

Tauntadi said, "She's still out of it so take her home and let her rest. She may suffer a headache, so get some BC's fo' that, and down there," she said, gently placing Lula in Big Ma's arms.

Lula could hardly stand, falling in and out of consciousness. She leaned into Big Ma as she struggled to keep Lula on her feet.

Big Ma turned to Tauntadi and said, "Dis here's our secret, right, Sha?"

"Don't worry, Louverta, yah situation ain't gonna get back to yah church folk. Y'all *secrets* are safe with me."

Big Ma managed to get Lula to the door. Tauntadi ran to grab a small towel to dab the drool escaping Lula's mouth. "Here, take that fo' her."

Big Ma took the towel. "Thank yah, Sha."

They made it down the porch stairs as Lula struggled to hold her body up. Big Ma turned around to Tauntadi and asked, "How yah do dis here line of work and sleep at night, Sha?"

Tauntadi chuckled, "Somebody's gotta help these poor baby girls. What I don't understand is how y'all church folk call *me* the devil when y'all the ones livin' under the roof with 'em."

Big Ma stood holding Lula and said. "You tell me where we go then, Sha? All we got is the good Lord and that's all we need."

Tauntadi bowed her head. Point taken.

Big Ma turned back around inching Lula away one step at a time while saying, "I'm gonna have a rough time with these sins of mine, but I welcome Hell, Fire and Brimstone over havin' dis child birth her own aunt or uncle."

Tauntadi looked away, unable to bear that notion herself. Seeing the state Lula was in, Tauntadi hung her head in shame, aware of her business transaction with Cordelia, which had a role in this terrible mishap.

Tauntadi walked up to Big Ma, who was holding Lula on the side of the road, and spoke in a whisper, "I have my own regrets, Sha. Could yah remember me in yah prayers?"

Big Ma nodded and continued down the road with Lula.

The next morning, Big Ma sat in her garden in a daze still recalling the event, shaking her head still in disbelief. Walking back to the front porch to sit and rest her aching joints, she almost tripped over Doc's footprint trail he had left from walking around the house.

Doc opened the screen door just before Big Ma took her seat and said, "I'm hungry! Cook me some dinner," and then he closed the screen door. Doc came back out adding, "Sorry bout the trail I left last night again. Yah gonna cover it back over fo' me, wont yah?"

Big Ma stood there just looking at him.

Chapter 9

Big Ma and a couple of neighbors were out on the porch catching up on the latest gossip while Mary and Lula were in the house lounging on a fair weather Saturday afternoon. Big Ma proudly bragged about Lula's upcoming graduation from the eighth grade.

"Lula Mae, come get these sheets off the line. I smell rain comin'," Big Ma yelled, happy to see Lula back to her old self after the ordeal that took place a couple months back. She was somewhat surprised at how quickly Lula bounced back. Lula got more into church, working hard to be the most devoted Christian child full of the Holy Ghost, reading the bible every day and studying the word of God more than ever before.

Lula came out on the porch with a basket in her hand, greeted everyone, and went to the side of the house to start taking the sheets off the line. Before she finished, Lula heard a familiar voice greeting Big Ma, and turned around to find Bervick standing in the yard. Lula was mortified. Her hair was full of paper bag curlers wrapped in a hair tie and she had on an old house dress. Yanking the last sheet off the line, Lula covered her face with the basket and ran to the back of the house to go inside. She scuffled around the house with her hands trembling as she snatched the wrap off her head and pulled out the paper bag curlers to fix her hair and changed into her Sunday church dress.

After checking herself over, Lula ran over to the window waiting for Big Ma to ask her to get lemonade for Bervick since all guests got a fresh cold glass of homemade lemonade or water.

Lula heard Big Ma tell Bervick, "Just a minute."

Lula fixed her clothes and patted her hair.

"Mary Lee!" Big Ma called out.

Mary came out the bedroom passing Lula to see what Big Ma needed.

Lula sucked her teeth. She peeked outside and ran over to the window to press her ear against the window screen.

"Please get dis young man somethin' to drink," Lula heard Big Ma say. Mary ran back in the house passing Lula, who was frowning with her hands folded. She stuck a piece of Doublemint gum in her mouth, chewing with her mouth closed while contemplating how to go outside without being too obvious.

Lula stopped chewing when she heard Bervick saying his good-byes. She began pacing the floor feeling her pulse speed up, ready to burst outside to greet him.

She perked up when she heard her name called. Lula ran over to the door, pausing to take a deep breath before opening it.

Big Ma looked over Lula's transformation, and then handed Lula a glass, "Take his glass fo' him please." Lula took her sweet time taking the empty glass while shyly grinning over at Bervick and waving before going back into the house. He smiled back, quickly straightening up when he saw Big Ma's piercing eyes on him. Startled by Big Ma's pungent look, Bervick cleared his throat and straightened his posture.

"Let's talk!" Big Ma said, getting up from her chair, excusing herself from her guest to walk with Bervick toward the road. Lula watched from the window, focusing in on Big Ma's body language. Big Ma turned to the window catching Lula, who almost fell over backing away. Big Ma turned back to Bervick and had a few words with him before he left.

***

Lula was so excited, she could barely sit still. Big Ma happily hummed while finishing Lula's hair, shuffling about in the kitchen like a kid in a candy store, smiling and chuckling to herself. She was proud of Lula for graduating from the eighth grade that day. An event the entire family cherished—a family member excelling academically.

Putting the finishing touches on Lula's hair, Big Ma loosely curled the sides so that they could fall from underneath her graduation cap. When Big Ma finished, Lula ran to the mirror grinning from ear-to-ear at the perfected finger waves and curls on her head. It turned out better than what she had expected.

Big Ma walked from behind smiling at Lula's approval, whispering, "You look beautiful."

Mary entered the room and said, "Wow, look at you!"

Lillie snuck up from behind Lula and playfully popped her neck, surprising Lula, for she didn't expect Lillie to be present at her graduation.

"Aww, look at my sister, you look beautiful, Sha!" Lillie said, thankful for Bernard allowing her to attend Lula's graduation—one of the few times Bernard let Lillie out of his sight; he didn't want the family to think ill of him.

The excitement of the day tickled the girls. They rarely saw Big Ma happy and smiling. She clapped her hand. "Alright, com'on. Help yah sister get dress, we don't want to be late."

Lillie took Lula's hand and ran into the bedroom with Mary following, and they both carefully put Lula's dress over her head making sure they didn't mess up her hair. Lillie stopped by Samantha's house to pick up pearls she wanted Lula to wear for her graduation and gently placed them around Lula's neck as she touched the pearls in awe.

Although it was three hours until the ceremony, Big Ma wanted to make sure Lula was ready, and the food was prepared for the graduation party. Adrenaline kept Big Ma from getting a wink of sleep. She was up all night cooking, baking, and cleaning, making sure everything was set and prepared. By morning, Big Ma had cooked fried Buffalo fish, okra stew, fried chicken, seafood gumbo, black-eyed peas and rice, and cornbread dressing. For dessert, Big Ma picked fresh pecans, apples, figs, and peaches from the trees out back, and pulled sweet potatoes from her garden to bake her famous sweet dough pies.

Mr. Pete delivered blocks of ice for the lemonade and soda water, and Watermelon man Bue dropped off three huge watermelons, refusing Big Ma's seventy-five cents.

Family and church members trickled in bringing all sorts of food that added to Big Ma's already full menu. The living room table was soon full of more sweet dough pies, spicy seasoned crawfish, chitterlings, hog malls, homemade sweet butter biscuits, dirty rice, greens, buttermilk cake, potato salad, and more fried chicken. Lula's uncles, Paul Robert and Willie Ray, slaughtered two hefty hogs to smoke and barbeque the meat.

Time passed faster than any regular day in Eunice, Louisiana. Doc called out for everyone to load up in a car he had borrowed from a friend. The immediate family crowded in the vehicle as other family members were already making their way to the school on foot. The rest of the family stayed behind at the house to prepare and wait for the graduation party since there wasn't enough room for everyone to attend.

This day was a special celebration for the family. Some came from as far as Texas, Washington, and California. Other members came from different parts of Louisiana such as Lafayette, Opelousas,

Mamou, New Orleans, and Churchpoint. The only two people missing were Beatrice and Leroy.

Nevertheless, all worries, troubles, and anguish were put aside for another day. Lula's family embraced the bright sun, blue skies and crisp air, looking forward to enjoying each other's company in celebrating a young family member's progression in education.

After the graduation ceremony, everyone went back to Big Ma's house to eat. Paul Robert and Willie Ray were outside still barbequing ribs, pork chops, shanks, and loin cutlets.

Taking her graduation gown off, Lula went outside to greet everyone, hugging and thanking people for coming while receiving envelopes full of money or cards from some folks. Tables and chairs were brought outside for card games and dominoes as Zydeco music played, which Big Ma opposed, but Doc overruled her opposition, leaving her to say a silent prayer of forgiveness for playing such ungodly music.

Lillie sat at the table beating male relatives at dominoes, smacking pieces down like a champ with Lula by her side cheering her on, happy to see Lillie in her glory, despite Bernard watching quietly from afar by himself. Mary sat on the porch listening to the church women and watching out for the younger children playing in the yard. Everyone else were laughing and talking while eating plates of food, dessert, or cuts of watermelon.

Hours into the graduation party, Samantha sashayed into Big Ma's yard unannounced and uninvited, holding flowers and a beautifully wrapped gift. Even though she hadn't been welcomed at Big Ma's house since sixteen years-old, Samantha took it upon herself to personally congratulate Lula.

The card games, music, laughter, talking, and eating stopped. The men fixated their eyes on Samantha's tightly fitted orange dress that outlined her full breasts, hourglass shape, and round behind. A flowery fragrance radiated from Samantha. Her facial features were accented by an orange-red colored lipstick, black eyeliner, and mascara. Women crossed their arms sucking their teeth, looking at each other in agreement with their disdain for Samantha, who didn't pay them any attention as she switched her hips harder to put on a good show. The children waved at Samantha, despite their parent's reaction towards her. One little boy made the mistake of running up to greet her and was promptly yanked away by his mother, who reinforced never to go near Samantha. The rest of the parents gave their children looks telling them stay put or else…

Samantha waved back blowing kisses to acknowledge their innocent efforts, and then walked up to the porch looking for Lula. None of the church women answered Samantha when she kindly greeted them asking where Lula was, so Samantha stood there waiting and wasn't going to leave until she gave Lula her gift. To save Samantha from the scrutiny and humiliation, Lillie got up from the domino table and went over to her aunt, greeting Samantha with a big hug and kiss while Big Ma and Lula came outside with more trays of sliced sweet dough pie and cake. Lula's face lit up when she saw Samantha. She handed the tray over to Lillie and was about to run up to Samantha, but Big Ma pulled Lula back by the arm.

Samantha took a step up on the porch and said, "Mama, I'm sorry fo' showin' up here like dis, I just wanted to give Lula Mae her gift and congratulate her." She reached out to hand Lula her gift. Big Ma stepped in front of Lula, blocking her off from Samantha.

Big Ma said, "Sam, you kno' betta than to step foot on my property."

"Trust me, mama, it's no picnic fo' me either," Samantha wryly chuckled, looking around at everyone staring at her. "But with all due respect, ma'am, I just wanna give my niece her graduation gift, then I'll be on my way."

"You can leave it on dis here porch, and then, yah can be on your way. Yah cannot talk to Lula Mae. You ain't taintin' my baby with dem ole devil ways."

"Mama, I'm not leaving nothin' here 'til I at least congratulate and hug my niece." Samantha turned towards the folks sitting and watching. "And ain't nobody here gonna make me leave either." Everyone looked at each other to see if anyone had the nerve to say something back. Samantha proudly smiled at their silence and turned back to Big Ma, who wasn't the least bit threatened.

Big Ma said, "Leave it and go, Sam."

"Please don't start with me, mama. What yah think, I'm gonna bite Lula Mae's head off? Yah treat me like I'm some type of animal. I just wanna congratulate her. I'm proud of my niece just as much as you are and everyone else out here. Why can't I stay here and celebrate, too?" Samantha shot a look from the corner of her eyes at the church women snarling their noses at her. She wryly grinned shifting her eye to see more church women at the other end of the porch with the same disgusted stares.

One church woman said, "Louverta, if dis child stay, I'm leavin' dis instant, Sha."

Another church woman said, "Amen, the devil is at work right nah, Lord have mercy."

Samantha said, "I come here to see my niece and dis what I get?"

Another church woman said, "You a sinner and like living in sin with yah men and clothes and that make-up. Look at yah, yah look like a cheap tramp. I just pray the Lord have mercy on your poor soul. "

Samantha looked up at Big Ma. "Yah gonna let dem sit here and talk to me like dis, mama? I'm yah daughter fo' Christ sake."

"It's yah ways they don't like, Sam."

"Ways?" Samantha laughed to herself, placing the flowers and present on the porch. Lula heard that laughter once before, a laughter that came right before a wrath unleashed.

Samantha backed away staring down every church woman on the porch and yelled, "Ways! Ways! What ways? All y'all do is talk and make up lies bout me to add a little spice to y'all drab lives." Samantha pointed at the church women, "Especially y'all fun killers! Fo' holly rollers, y'all are the *worst* bunch of women I *ever* met! Ain't God bout love, b'cause all I see is hate comin' from y'all! Y'all wanna judge me, holdin' a bible, prayin' to yah God thinkin' y'all saved b'cause y'all said a few 'praise Gods' and 'Halleluiahs' in church. 'Judge not, lest ye not be judged'. Ha! Didn't think I knew that one, Matthew 7:1. Y'all need to read that passage every day yah damn hypocrites! Hidin' behind God to cover y'all own skeletons in the closet, then wanna sit with yah damn noses in the air and judge me! Y'all need 'the bad person' to look down upon to feel betta bout what y'all done did. I highly doubt God appointed y'all to speak fo' *him*, so 'til my judgment day, to hell with yah all!"

Samantha waited, looking closely to see if anyone dared to respond. The church women were furious, pursing their lips, dropping jaws, and frowning faces, looking over at Big Ma to settle the score with Samantha on their behalf.

Big Ma was shocked and appalled herself, and said in a dismissive voice, "You get off my property now!"

"No! Not 'til you TALK TO ME!" Samantha shouted with all her might. Then her tone softened, "I wanna stay here and talk and laugh and make teacakes with yah in the mornin' like we use to, mama. Why can't yah defend me? I'm still your baby and no one can change that."

Before Big Ma could respond, Doc came out of the house. He wasn't too fond of socializing, spending most of time out back walking around Big Ma's garden in circles and smoking his pipe.

"What yah doin' here, Sam?" Doc said in a deep, intimidating voice. Samantha stared at him as if she had seen a ghost. She pointed at the gifts and flowers whispering congratulations to Lula, and then backed away while Doc stood there waiting for her to leave. Samantha turned around and sashayed out the yard as fast as she could. When she was gone, the music, games, and chatter resumed. Doc retreated back to the garden.

Lula picked up her gifts looking over at Big Ma without saying a word, now understanding why Samantha stayed away.

Lillie put her arm around Mary and Lula saying, "Com'on y'all, let's go in and see what she got yah. I kno' it's somethin' nice." They went inside the house while Big Ma stood frozen on the porch, rubbing her palpitating heart, convincing herself that she did the right thing. As a God fearing Christian woman, there was no tolerance for any child of hers to live the sinful lifestyle Samantha chose, and until Samantha abided by the word of God, Big Ma had no choice but to leave her daughter in God's hands.

Samantha was always a rebellious child who didn't respect Big Ma's house as far as Big Ma saw it. As much as Big Ma tried, Samantha questioned the bible and did the complete opposite of what she was taught, despite the harsh beatings from Doc to get Samantha to be more obedient.

One church woman said, "Good riddens to that devil in flesh woman. Lord, thank yah Jesus."

Another one added, "Indeed, Sha. That girl there is somethin' else."

Big Ma looked over at them with a blank look. "Y'all hush up!" She looked out into the road. "Sinner and all, that's still my daughter y'all talkin' bout."

Half way down the block, Samantha took her high heels off and ran the rest of the way home trying to fight back tears. Entering her home, Samantha threw her shoes against the wall and started stomping, kicking, screaming, and throwing anything in her way. For all the years it took her to build her self-confidence, it all went crumbling down at the sight of Doc. The child she had buried within long ago, surfaced like the Phoenix rising from its ashes—never gone, never going astray, bringing back the same bag of fear with it.

Settling on the couch, Samantha chanted affirmations on how weakness is an inhibitor. When she finally calmed down, she went into the bedroom and plopped down in front of her vanity area to apply more lipstick, eye liner, and mascara on her face to make that child disappear, and on no account, never to get loose again.

Long ago, Doc broke that little girl, making her a slave to his tyranny, but Samantha "the woman" wasn't going to allow him to break her.

She smiled when all traces of the child was gone. It had been so long since Samantha visited her family, she'd almost forgotten the reason she stayed away in the first place.

***

Lula was all smiles parading around like a queen for the day. She was grateful for the folks who came to celebrate her graduation, and had a fun time, minus the ordeal with Samantha and Big Ma.

Nighttime fell too soon. Lula's family and friends started leaving. Those who travelled far made arrangements to sleep at relative's homes and a few remained at Big Ma's for the night.

Big Ma packed plenty of food and soda water for Lillie to take home. It took a while for Lillie and Lula to part ways again, and before Lillie left, she pulled Lula aside near the road to ask how she was feeling—a camouflaged question for what Lillie really wanted to ask.

Lula forced a smile and told Lillie everything was fine, except Lillie wasn't convinced when she noticed the shame in Lula's face and how she was looking down moving rocks with her foot. Lillie wanted to offer Lula a place to stay, but knew that was out of the question. Bernard had already said no.

"Find a man that will protect yah soon, Lula Mae. 'The snake' don't bother married women," was the lone advice Lillie could give Lula. They hugged and Lillie walked away with the bags of food in her hand, not looking back, feeling ashamed that she failed to protect her baby sister.

Lula, Big Ma, Mary, and a few relatives who were staying the night cleaned up the remaining trash outside. Doc was doing his nightly stroll around the house smoking his pipe in a trance. No one paid him any attention, growing accustomed to his frequent routine. When Doc turned the corner strolling towards the back of the house, it couldn't have been perfect timing for Lula to be startled by a visitor walking into the yard, causing her heart to beat out her chest. There stood Bervick Frank holding flowers in his hand. Lula looked over at Big Ma who nodded, consenting to his arrival. Lula smiled at her, and then turned to Bervick.

He held out the flowers and asked, "Would yah like to go fo' a walk?"

"Sure!"

"Wait, wait, wait," Big Ma said, stepping down the porch stairs, shuffling over to Bervick. She took him aside and whispered in Bervick's ear. The few words Lula read from Big Ma lips were "or" and "hurt you". Big Ma smacked Bervick's back making sure he heard her well, and then smiled telling them to have a nice time. Bervick stood there with his eyes wide. He pulled his shirt collar out, shook off the threat and focused back on Lula. Taking her by the hand, they began walking, turning around to wave back at Big Ma, who squinted her eyes menacingly at Bervick, pointing at her wrist. Bervick nodded.

"These are fo' yah." Bervick handed Lula the flowers.

"Thank you!" She smelled them and accidently swallowed her gum, choking on it. Bervick patted her back asking if she was okay. Once the gum went down, Lula laughed embarrassingly looking down at her feet until she realized Bervick's hand was still on her back. She blushed looking up at him.

"Congratulations! Yah look very pretty t'day. I like yah dress, too. Yah folks must be rich," Bervick said, taking his hand off her back as they continued to walk.

"No, we far from rich. My aunt gave dis to me as a graduation gift t'day, so I changed into it. She kno' I like blue."

"Blue looks nice on yah."

"Thank you."

They walked in silence for a while, neither one sure of what to say next. Bervick grabbed hold of Lula's hand and smiled at her saying, "Yah kno', one day you're gonna be my wife."

Lula smiled.

He put his arm around Lula's shoulders bringing her closer to him and said, "Yeah, I knew from the first time I saw yah in church, lookin' so pretty, that yah were gonna be my wife one day. Yah wanna kno' how I kno'?"

"How?"

"God whispered it to me. He told me you a God fearing virtuous woman and yah the one I'm gonna wed."

Lula looked up at the stars smiling, thanking God for providing such enlightenment.

Chapter 10

Lula put pillows over her ears to mute the sound of hard thumps of rain smacking against the window. She tossed and turned from the thunder, lightning, and rain keeping her awake. She sat up annoyed at the storm's fury and tucked Mary in, wishing she was in Mary's dream state.

Lula flinched at how loud the rain was pounding and was suddenly startled by a shadow knocking on the window. She got out of bed, backed away, and grabbed a broom, unsure of what to do next. A face pressed against the window glass. Lula looked closer recognizing the face. "Oh my Lord," she grasped at her chest, hopping over Mary to lift the window up. She helped Lillie out of the rain, pulling her in the bedroom. Lillie carefully crawled over Mary to not wake her. Dripping wet, Lillie stood there barefoot wearing a slip that clung to her body, exposing her white underwear and bra.

Lula covered her mouth mumbling, "Oh my Jesus," and hugged Lillie tight. Lillie winced in pain. Lula took a quilt off the bed and threw it around Lillie's shoulders and whispered, "How long were yah out there?"

"Not long," Lillie whisper back. "Sorry to wake yah."

"No, don't worry bout that."

Lula felt her way to a chair in the corner of the dark room to grab a folded towel for Lillie. Lightning struck, giving enough light for Lula to see blood on the front of Lillie's slip. Lillie took the towel and stripped out of her clinging slip, panties, and bra to dry herself. She shivered as she put on the dry clothes Lula gave, and quickly wrapped up in the quilt.

Lula asked, "What happened?"

Lillie didn't respond. She sat on the edge of the bed wrapped in the quilt, hanging her head with rain still dripping from her hair. Lula sat beside Lillie, putting her arm around Lillie's shoulders as they sat listening to the rain pouring down with occasional cracks of lightning and thunder.

Lillie broke the silence. "You can't tell nobody."

"Tell nobody what?"

Lillie lifted her head to completely expose her face.

Lula gasped. She ran over to the small drawer, pulled out a white candle and lit it, putting it up near Lillie's face, examining the blood coming from her mouth, nose, and swollen shut eye. Lula dropped the candle on the floor, which quickly blew out. Still starring at Lillie's face, Lula didn't bother picking the candle up. She grabbed Lillie's shoulders asking, "Who did dis to you?"

"Shh, lower your voice." Lillie pointed at Mary, who slightly stirred in the bed. Lillie picked up the towel and dabbed at her face, spitting excess blood into it, feeling a loose tooth on the side of her mouth.

Lula bent down near Lillie's knee, looking up at her and repeated the question.

Lillie said, "Don't worry. I'll be just fine. The good Lord will make sho' of it."

"Bernard did dis, didn't he?"

"He's a good man, Lula Mae. Don't worry, he won't do dis no more."

Lillie's tooth came loose in her mouth. She hurried up and swallowed it, pressing her tongue against her gums to stop it from bleeding so that Lula wouldn't be more alarmed than what she already was.

Lula said, "Aww, Lillie Mae, why didn't yah tell me? How long dis been goin' on? Y'all still newlyweds."

"But I'm alright. I'm handling everythin' just fine, Sha."

"We gotta tell somebody. That man can't pound on yah like that. Look at yah face!"

"I'm gonna be just fine. Please, just leave it alone."

"No you not! We gotta tell somebody to make sho' he won't do dis again."

"And who am I gonna tell, Lula Mae? Who's gonna do somethin'? Huh? Who?"

"The pastor."

Lillie spit more blood in the towel and folded it over to wipe her mouth. "I'm sho' he knows already. Church members across the street saw Bernard pushin' me into the house last week and they just went bout they business like they didn't see nothin'. I'm sho' they heard us sometimes too b'cause I see the way they look at me and I see the difference in the way they treat me 'round there! So I'm sho' it got to the pastor already."

"What bout Papa Top? Yah heard what he did to daddy!"

"Yeah but that's different. Mama was missing, I'm not. He ain't gonna come between a man and his wife. Granddaughter, no granddaughter!"

"Big Ma can do somethin' then, if they don't!"

"So she can get a black eye, too! Com'on, Sha, please don't be like dis right nah, yah hurtin' my head. Just let it be!" Lillie sighed, "Even if Big Ma wanted to do somethin', I don't want Doc puttin' his hands on her fo' gettin' in married folk's business. Dis here between me and Bernard. God showin' me the way and I kno' exactly what to do. If I love my husband more, then he'll stop. That's it."

"And what if he don't?"

"Trust me, Sha, he will. I just gotta be a betta wife and show how much I love him and everythin' will be okay."

"I just don't like him hittin' you like dis."

"Dis is the last time, Lula Mae, trust me. I'm a God fearin' woman and I'm gonna honor, cherish, and obey my husband! I love Bernard so much. He's a good man. I'll never leave him. That's not how us Christian gals do."

"What's gonna happen if you do leave?"

"Hell, Fire and Brimstone. I can never break my vow with my husband. Never! I just have to do as he say and everythin' will be okay. Just promise me yah won't tell nobody?"

"You said everybody knows anyway, so who cares if I tell," Lula shrugged.

"Lula Mae, when you get married, you'll understand that no one comes between a man and his wife. If yah tell someone, all you gonna do is put that person in a bad situation b'cause they kno' they can't do nothin'."

"I wish mama and daddy were here right nah, they'd do somethin'."

"Please don't bring dem up right nah, Lula Mae. I got too much on my plate right nah."

"So you not gonna do nothin' if it happen again?"

Lillie was silent.

Lula picked up the candle and dug the wick out, lighting it again.

Lillie blew it back out and whispered, "I told yah, if I cook betta and do what I'm 'pose to do as his wife, there won't be a next time. The reason he did dis in the first place is b'cause I gave him leftovers fo' dinner. I should've known betta than to give him that after workin' hard all day. He needs a home cook meal every night."

"He still shouldn't hit yah like that."

"You'll understand one day. When you a wife, yah honor and obey yah husband. That's God talkin', not me. I messed up givin' him leftovers when I kno' he need his food cooked fresh. I'll get it right tho'. I'm gonna be the best wife to where he won't ever have to punish me again. I deserved it."

"But he still could've told yah nicely, he didn't have to hit you. Daddy never hit mama."

"He didn't mean it tho'. Like I said, I just gotta do a betta job as his wife."

"Yeah, but what happens if yah do everythin' right and he still hit yah?"

"I'll just continue tryin' 'til I get it right. Nah please stop with the questions bout that. Are you okay?"

"Yeah, I'm okay."

Lillie stared at Lula, waiting for the answer Lula knew Lillie was asking.

"Big Ma sleeps in here with us as much as she can. But 'the snake' hasn't bothered me after, well, you kno'." Lula stopped talking about it. The thought made her feel disgusted and nauseous. She quickly thought about Bervick Frank to take her mind off it.

Lillie shook her head putting her hand over her face. She grabbed Lula's arm pulling her closer and said, "Listen to me, I'm married nah and I'm here to tell yah, that ain't no snake!" Lillie quieted down when Mary stirred. "Yah gotta get outta here and I mean soon! It won't be long b'fore he strikes again. I thought yah could come live with me, but our place is too small." Lillie couldn't bring herself to say that Bernard didn't want Lula there.

"What bout Big Ma and Mary Lee?"

"Just do as I say!" Lillie squeezed Lula's arm harder. "Stay as far away from Grandpa Doc as yah can. I'm not here to protect y'all anymore and Big Ma can't sleep in here with y'all every night, he won't let her. Mary Lee will be fine, she's still too young. But yah gotta get outta here b'fore somethin' really bad happens again."

Lula was quiet.

Lillie asked, "Yah hear me?"

"Yeah I hear yah." Lula pulled from Lillie's tight grip, rubbing her arm.

"I'm sorry, Sha."

"It's okay," Lula smiled, "I love you."

"I love you, too."

Lillie dabbed at her wounds and dried her hair with the end of the towel, then lay down tucking the covers over Mary. She pulled Lula close as they snuggled up listening to the rain thrash against the window.

The next morning, Lula woke up from the breeze coming from the cracked window and saw that Lillie was gone.

Chapter 11

Lula was on cloud nine during her courtship with Bervick, whom she'd been seeing for months since her graduation. He was everything she could ever ask for and more. At thirteen years-old, Lula was in love, keeping her new found romance a secret out of fear that Big Ma would find out. Big Ma wanted Lula to continue her education and stressed to Lula that Bervick should be no more than a friend. After witnessing Lula getting a little too engrossed in him, Big Ma kept a watchful eye on Lula, but not close enough. Even though Doc was ten years Big Ma's senior, she felt Bervick, being twenty-three years-old, was too old for Lula. Nonetheless, Big Ma's continuous preaching and expressing her concerns about the age gap didn't stop Lula from seeing him. She caught glimpses of Bervick in church and met up with him by going to the corner store or friends' houses, making sure she saw Bervick at least a couple days out of the week.

Bervick was in love with Lula as well. His love was overpowering his every thought throughout the day, making his heart sing an enchanting tune as it rendered an obsession for him to have Lula all to himself. He was aware of her family's expectations for Lula to further her education, but Bervick wanted to be a part of Lula's future plan, too.

As their courtship slipped through the cracks, compliments of Bervick sharing his secret with the town gossips, Big Ma and the family took turns speaking to Bervick about their concerns with his intentions and how he needed to let Lula finish school first. Unfortunately, their words fell on deaf ears, in contrast, boosting Bervick's ego.

Sneaking around with Lula was getting tiresome for Bervick. After letting the goose out the bag, he wanted to love Lula freely without any objections from her family. He figured the best way to emancipate their relationship was by taking Lula's hand in marriage—a union the family would be forced to honor. Bervick knew the Lord chose Lula to be his wife and he was done being patient waiting for her family's approval.

***

One Friday afternoon, Mary pranced around the outhouse screaming, "Com'on, Lula Mae, open up!" Squeezing her legs together, hopping around in one place in front of the outhouse, she yelled, "I gotta go, I gotta go!"

Lula was in the outhouse leaning against the wall out of breath from regurgitating all morning, her stomach hurting from dry heaves. She fought hard to stop her stomach from turning so that Mary could use the bathroom. She finally opened the door, crawling out in pain. Mary flew in the outhouse already peeing down her leg.

Lula made it to her bed to lie down. A few moments later, Mary joined Lula in the bedroom. Mary wiped her legs clean and changed her underwear looking over her shoulder at Lula sprawled out on the bed. She went over to Lula, examining the discoloration in Lula's face and became alarmed and ran out the room. Lula lay there recollecting everything she ate that day to figure out what could've caused her stomach's squeamishness.

Big Ma came into the room with Mary peeking from behind with a concerned look on her face.

"Leave girl!" Big Ma told Mary without turning around. Mary disappeared fast.

Placing her hands on her hips, Big Ma walked over to Lula, scanning her from head-to-toe. She moved Lula's hands from in front of her stomach and pressed gently feeling the firmness at the bottom while Lula moaned from each touch. Blood rushed to Big Ma's head, rapidly changing her sugar brown skin to red. Her breaths shortened, lips pursed, and nostrils flared. She looked down at Lula without saying a word. Lula was afraid watching Big Ma morph into an embodiment of rage. Lula remained frozen in fear with only her lips quivering. Big Ma's tense body relaxed when she saw a tear fall from Lula's eye. Sitting down next to her, Big Ma embraced Lula and kissed her cheek repeatedly, rocking her back and forth, "Lord have mercy, not again. I stay up all night watchin' out fo' y'all."

Lula quietly said, "I kno', that's why it's not who yah thinking, Big Ma."

Big Ma looked puzzled at Lula's stomach, then back at Lula. Putting two-and-two together, Big Ma closed her eyes sighing, "You been seeing Bervick behind my back?" She shook her head, "Com'on, my baby, get up, we goin' to church."

After wiping Lula's tears away, Big Ma got up and left the room to get ready for church. Feeling sick and ashamed, Lula dragged out of bed to get ready for the long night in church.

***

The Pastor's sermons flooded Lula's mind, turning the word of God into a creed she declared to live by. When she experienced the Holy Ghost for the first time, the euphoric energy of bliss made Lula adhere to the word of God and vow to be a God fearing Christian woman. Hell, Fire and Brimstone created an unsavory visual during sermons, forcing Lula to continue reading her bible daily and dragging her pregnant body to attend church every day.

Being pregnant and unwed in church folk's perspective was equivalent to murder in the first degree. Big Ma knew how unbelievably nosy the women in church were and didn't want them to find out about her granddaughter's secret. She helped Lula hide her bulge under layers of clothes, despite the hot weather, to attend church as if nothing changed.

Lula's body went through an extreme transformation, which was uncomfortable for her during pregnancy. Her young body wasn't fully developed enough to carry a baby, triggering her body to expedite the developmental process to carry an unborn child. Her hips rapidly rounded, her breasts grew three sizes larger, her ankles and fingers swelled, and she had obsessive weight gain in her thighs, going from a skinny pubescent teen to a fully developed woman in months.

Church folks already were speculating Lula's pregnancy after months of observing her layered attire, and her distant behavior was opposite from her usual talkative manner. When church members tried to conversate with Lula, her response was a slight nod, then a quick retreat. When word got out that Lula didn't attend high school, rumors sprouted like wild flower. The mere thing Lula and Big Ma used to their advantage was that no one had the courage to ask them directly if the rumor was true.

When she entered her sixth month in pregnancy, Lula hunched over carrying the bible in front of her belly. She knew people would figure it out sooner or later, and it would get back to Bervick, but trepidation made her prolong the wait as long as possible. She was indecisive on when to inform Bervick about her pregnancy, fearing his reaction. The only relief out of the situation was that Doc left Lula alone, and she now believed there was some truth to what Lillie said.

As time passed, Lula rarely saw Bervick in church. Big Ma made sure of it, scheduling their church arrival time after the sermon began to seat Lula in the back and to make a quick exit when church was over. Conversely, unbeknownst to Big Ma, Lula still saw Bervick during her trips to the store, or "just because" walks.

One Afternoon, Curley called Lula from the porch and whispered an urgent message that Bervick wanted to meet with her. She gave Big Ma and Doc one of her "just because" excuses and left. She had on fewer layers of clothes walking with her arms crossed, rehearsing the way she was going to break the news to Bervick. The gig was up. It was now or never.

Lula met him at their usual spot, down the road from Mr. Pete's store, and Bervick guided Lula to the train tracks, away from possible town snitches.

During their love tussles, Bervick immediately stopped.

Lula asked, "What's wrong?"

"Are yah puttin' on weight?"

"Why, does it look like I am?" Lula said, looking at herself self-consciously.

"Hmm, not really. Well, maybe a little but ain't nothin' wrong with a lil' meat on my woman's bones," he laughed, running up to tickle her.

"I'm pregnant!" Lula blurted.

Bervick paused.

"Pregnant?"

Lula slowly nodded looking down. Bervick rubbed at his chin deep in thought. She waited for a response.

He said, "Yah ready to be my wife?"

Lula's pearly whites beamed from ear-to-ear. She rubbed away goose bumps prickling up on her arm, loving every moment with Bervick, hoping the feeling lasted forever.

"Yes!" She jumped into Bervick's arms.

"Hold on nah, don't hurt the baby," he said rubbing Lula's stomach. He looked up noticing an inquisitive look on Lula's face and asked, "What's wrong?"

"Why me?"

"The Lord told me so."

She smiled and hugged him again.

"Finally!" He muttered underneath his breath.

"What was that, Bervick?"

"Oh nothin', baby," Bervick said, hugging Lula again. He sighed a breath of relief that Lula found the courage to tell him, feeling bad watching her go through so many changes to be furtive with him. She was miserable in the heat wearing layers of clothes, but Bervick wanted Lula to suffer in order for her to learn never to keep secrets from him. He had tried for months to impregnate Lula and finally succeeded. Ready more than ever now to tell Big Ma in her face that he was going to marry her unwed *pregnant* granddaughter, Bervick smirked at the thought of Big Ma's face being forced to condone this marriage.

***

Big Ma approved Lula's absences from church on Sunday, giving Lula a well-deserved break. When Doc, Big Ma, and Mary left, Lula got dressed and made a trip to Mr. Pete's store. Lula could no longer hide her nine month pregnancy from the town, now wearing a maternity dress Big Ma made. She bought a pack of Doublemint gum, and then wobbled down the road to Samantha's house.

Samantha came to the door and led Lula to the bedroom to lie down so she could rest comfortably on a queen size mattress. Lula's own mattress was too hard to relax, but she wasn't about to hurt Big Ma's feelings.

Lula rose from her nap a few hours later feeling refreshed. She went into the living room and found Samantha chatting with her cousin, Edmonia, sipping on chamomile tea. Cuts of pound cake sat on a decorative plate next to the floral tea set and short stout tea kettle still omitting steam. Samantha had paper bag rollers in her hair, wearing a white robe with feathers around the neck, and light coat of lipstick on her lips. Edmonia was completely dressed in a beige skirt and white short-sleeve blouse. Lula was surprised to see Edmonia sitting there since Edmonia was ashamed of Samantha's lifestyle and seldom visited her. They grew up together, and as much as Edmonia didn't care for how Samantha turned out, she couldn't stay away from her favorite cousin for too long. Edmonia enjoyed Samantha's company, despite her biased views against Samantha.

Samantha said, "Good mornin' or should I say good afternoon, Sha?"

Lula kissed and hugged them both.

Edmonia said, "Hey, baby, look like you ready to drop any minute now, huh?"

Lula rarely saw Edmonia after she moved to Lake Charles ten years ago. Edmonia rarely visited Eunice, having moved to Lake Charles to escape the gossip stricken town, and to live a more luxurious lifestyle with her now ex-husband. After two divorces, Edmonia married another professional man who started his own insurance company. She considered herself an upper class woman, valuing the finer things in life. Prim and proper, Edmonia always crossed her legs when seated and kept a straight posture. Her wardrobe consisted of beiges and whites, comparable to her tea party colleagues, always dressed to impress to discuss the latest topics and sip tea while diplomatically bragging on how their husbands were better than the others—each woman hating the other women's guts behind a smile.

Edmonia and Samantha had been opposites since childhood, rarely seeing eye-to-eye, ironically making them the best of friends.

Most of their conversation ended in agreeing to disagree, the mere topic they respected each other's opinion on was men.

Samantha said, "Come see." Lula went over and sat down next to Samantha on the couch, opposite Edmonia, who was sitting in the love seat across from them.

Samantha asked, "Yah talk to yah fiancé lately?"

"Who, Bervick?"

Samantha raised a brow.

Lula looked away almost forgetting who she was talking to. "Yeah, I did. How yah kno' we gettin' married?"

Samantha and Edmonia laughed in unison. Lula had to laugh herself at that question.

Edmonia asked, "So y'all getting married, huh?"

"Yes, ma'am."

Samantha said, "That bastard been plottin' on her since day one…Oh, I'm sorry, Lula Mae, I didn't mean to call your fiancé out his name like that. I kno' how y'all young girls get over y'all men," she chuckled. "How my mama dealin'?"

"She doesn't kno' yet. I reckon she smell somethin bout to happen tho'. Did yah ever meet Bervick?"

"Humph! Ole Bervick Frank. Yeah, I've seen him 'round a few times. He's a little too old fo' yah if yah ask me. It's somethin' bout that boy that rub me the wrong way, humph." Samantha took a sip of her tea looking up at Edmonia to chime in at any time. Edmonia sat back, folded her hands in her lap, and grinned. It pleasured her to watch Samantha at a loss for words, which were few and far between.

Samantha rolled her eyes at Edmonia and looked back at Lula. "Love is a beautiful thing when it's with the right person, Sha. Nah, I kno' yah probably don't care to hear my opinion, but yah kno' I'm gonna give it anyways. I don't like that Bervick Frank. That boy head ain't wrapped too tight, and if there's one thing I kno' best, it's men! I kno' men so well, I can sum dem up in one glance. Uh huh, yes ma'am, it took years of me datin' to get dis here type of instinct," Samantha confidently boasted.

Edmonia mumbled underneath her breath, "That ain't no mess I'd be proud of."

"Yeah, well havin' dis here knowledge might've saved yah ass from two failed marriages!"

Edmonia's mouth fell open. She put her hand over her chest looking around in shock.

"Oh stop, Edmonia, yah such an actress. You start it, I always finish it, Sha." Samantha rolled her eyes and focused her attention back on Lula.

Looking in Lula's beautiful almond shaped eyes, Samantha searched for advice to give while remaining objective after completing her own investigation on Bervick, asking male companions about his character, in which their responses weren't favorable. Putting the pieces together from the men's feedback, and using her own intuitive perception, Samantha concluded one simple fact about Bervick Frank…he was an unequivocal lunatic.

Samantha wanted to share this revelation with Lula without hurting her, but got tongue-tied figuring out how. When the words made it to the tip of Samantha's tongue, she held back forcing a smile, convincing herself to be happy for her niece. If Bervick made Lula happy, then so be it. Samantha wasn't going to rob Lula of her happiness.

But in a split second, Samantha reneged on holding back, saying, "I'm gonna tell yah bout your fiancé, Lula Mae, and you can take it as yah wish. Bervick is a charmer and a strong believer in God. But his belief is to the point where it's damn near crazy. That fool, I mean Bervick, think he's one of God's prophets. Nah, whatever that man thinks bout himself is his business, hell, he can be Santa Clause fo' all I care, but," Samantha scratched the side of her head, "ask yourself dis, what is goin' on in that man head fo' him to think such a nutty thing? What does dis Prophet of God, he claims to be, consist of? What types of belief come with such a title? You followin' me, Sha?"

Lula shook her head no.

Samantha took a sip of her tea looking up at Edmonia for some assistance again. Edmonia sat back, took a sip of tea, and crossed her legs and arms grinning. Samantha sucked her teeth at Edmonia and looked back at Lula. "I reckon he's a man that believes he's above the average man, meanin' he can do *more* than the average man. Yah followin'?"

Edmonia raised her hand as if she was in class and asked, "Umm, 'cuse me, Mizz Samantha, but I don't understand what you talking about either. Could you elaborate a little more please?"

Samantha rolled her eyes, flagging her hand at Edmonia.

Lula sat motionless taking in the questions Samantha was asking. Bervick's words about God choosing her as his wife came into question until the baby kicked in Lula's stomach. She smiled rubbing her belly. Bervick was her savior, the salvation to an unsavory situation, the man she fell in love with. She felt the need to negate Samantha's doubts.

Lula said, "Him being a prophet may sound strange to some people, but to me, I think he's just closer to God, like God's chosen and anointed."

Samantha sat back realizing what she had already predicted: Lula was going to defend her man. Bervick was her ticket out of Big Ma and Doc's house. Away from the abuse, away from it all. Samantha knew all too well and grew sympathetic towards Lula's forced decision to marry when she wasn't ready. But her marrying wasn't the problem for Samantha, the problem was, out of all the men in Eunice, Lula fell in love with Bervick Frank.

From that point on, Samantha knew there was nothing she could say to convince Lula to think twice about marrying him. She put her arm around Lula's shoulder and whispered, "Congratulations, Sha."

Samantha maliciously glanced over at Edmonia to say thanks for nothing. Edmonia shrugged and finished the rest of her tea.

Samantha asked, "When yah gonna break the news to Big Ma?"

Lula lowered her head, picking at her nail.

Samantha twisted her mouth chewing on the inside of her cheek waiting for an answer, and decided to leave the question alone and go on to the next topic.

***

Bervick took great pride in conquering obstacles standing in the way of what he wanted. He felt it was a challenge from God to see how well he rose to the occasion to claim his prize. Victorious in winning Lula's hand in marriage, against the apprehension of her family, every move he made was a strategic plan like knocking another piece off a chess board, and checkmate was soon to happen on the walk to Big Ma's house.

Big Ma waited for Bervick to step foot in her yard for a meeting she had scheduled with him in church. "My house, two o'clock, Saturday," was the lone words she spoke to Bervick after service.

When Bervick arrived, Big Ma got up from her rocking chair and rushed down the steps towards him. She got so close in Bervick's face, he could feel the breath from Big Ma's nose when yelling, "Over my dead body!"

She stood there waiting for a response and added, "Her education is first!"

Bervick wasn't shocked that Big Ma found out. Rather ecstatic to say the least. He turned and walked away to avoid any confrontation, leaving Big Ma standing there.

Big Ma's hand trembled. Lips tightened. A tear ran down her face. Bervick disappeared out of sight along with the hopes and dreams Big Ma had for Lula. She took a deep breath and went back on the porch to sit, massaging her palpitating heart. Doc came from out back whistling his way into the house. Big Ma's heart picked up speed hurting her chest more. She picked up her bible and hugged it against her chest. A disturbing notion overwhelmed Big Ma that she was fighting an already lost battle.

***

Lula woke up at four o'clock in the morning. She slipped on the white knitted dress that Big Ma made which stretched around Lula's large belly, and moved around the room quietly so that Mary wouldn't wake up.

She had a difficult time untying her freshly curled hair. Jittery nerves caused her hands to shake.

Fully dressed and ready to go, Lula tiptoed her way to the front door, slowly twisted the knob, stopping the door in intervals to prevent it from squeaking as she opened it. Shutting the door behind her, Lula was excited at her successful escape. Her enthusiasm soon diminished when she looked up at the house where her loving grandmother and dear sister lay asleep. She wished the circumstance were different, but following her heart and Lillie's blessed advice, this was for the best.

At his home, Bervick dabbed cologne on which he stole from his father, fixed his three-piece suit he borrowed from a cousin, and slipped his feet into newly polished shoes loaned to him from Curley.

Curley also lent Bervick a tie, helping him tie it around his neck saying, "I don't kno' bout dis, Bervick. You sho' yah wanna go through with dis without her grandmother's blessin'?"

"God gave me the 'okay' and that's all I need."

Curley tightened the tie around Bervick's neck and smoothed it down. He stepped back to capture a full view of Bervick and said, "Yah look nice."

"Thank you, brother."

Curley stood quiet, not accepting Bervick's thanks. He couldn't bring himself to approve of Bervick's actions. The same height as Bervick, Curley had a more slender build with the same deep reddish tan complexion. A handsome, yet self-effacing man, Curley was a good provider to his growing family and was hands on in raising his two toddlers. At twenty-one years-old, a couple years younger than Bervick, Curley worked at an oil refinery, waking up before the break of dawn to walk six miles to get to work every day. He took his job seriously and was never late or absent. Management praised Curley's performance, which secured him a permanent position and decent salary.

Curley allowed Bervick to move in after he moved from Lake Charles to Eunice, and tried to help Bervick get on his feet.

Curley said, "Maybe nah that yah startin' a family, yah might wanna come work at my job. I can put in a good word in fo' yah."

"I don't do that type of work."

"What are yah gonna do fo' work then? Those odd jobs yah doin' ain't gonna be enough money. You got a baby on the way and need steady work to provide fo' yah family."

"I don't do that kind of work, Curley. God's gonna make a way fo' me. He always do."

"God help those who help themselves."

"I'm 'The Chosen One'."

"You claimin' yourself to be a Prophet don't make yah the exception, Bervick. You gotta work, too."

"I've got everythin' already figured out."

"And what's that?"

"I'm gonna preach the word of God. Everyone will soon follow me."

"How's that gonna feed yah baby and Lula Mae?"

"You'll see. I trust in my God."

Curley handed Bervick the wedding bands and watched him leave out the front door, hoping Lula knew what she was getting herself into marrying his brother.

***

Bervick stood near the train track waiting for Lula. He looked out at the sky changing color from the sun rising and listened to the crickets breaking the stillness in the air. Two multicolored butterflies tussled with each other, flying close to Bervick's head. He smiled and said to himself, "Must be mating season." The butterflies flew around him nearly missing his head. He gently waved them away to prevent hurting the delicate species. The smaller butterfly dropped on Bervick's shoes while the other one flew away. He lifted the front of his shoe looking at the dead butterfly slide off, staring down at it wondering what happened. Lula called out to him, snatching his attention away from the butterfly. She raced over, smiling and waving.

Bervick said, "Slow down, Sha, don't hurt the baby. Yah ready?"

"I'm a little scared."

"You wanna be my wife, don't yah?"

"Yeah but—"

"But?"

"Will I still be able to go back to school? I gotta finish school," she said looking around nervously.

"Of course yah gonna finish school. I wouldn't want it any other way. And, I got good news! Curley gonna get me a job at the refinery he works at. I'm gonna save my earnings to buy us a house. God is blessin' us."

"Really!" Lula said, seeing the sign from God she had prayed for—Bervick having a good job lined up.

"Yeah, so don't worry, everythin' gonna be fine. Yah ready to become, Mrs. Bervick Frank?"

"I'm ready!"

Bervick put his arm out for Lula and they made their way to the courthouse.

***

The two newlyweds walked hand-in-hand to Big Ma's house. Lillie, who was given permission by Bernard to visit, and Mary stood up from the porch, sighing in relief that Lula was safe. Mary's eyes lowered, upset that both her sisters went behind Big Ma's back, vowing to herself that she wouldn't break Big Ma's heart the way they did. Lillie waved and ran up to Lula, feeling on her stomach while Mary ran to the back of the house to get Big Ma. Lillie and Lula laughed and spoke fast trying to catch up with each other all at once. Bervick stepped back to let the sisters have their happy reunion.

Big Ma came from the back of the house. Her hands were covered in soil and she was wearing her gardening apron. She used the back of her hand to wipe the sweat off her forehead, and then stared a burning fire of distain at Bervick. She looked down at their ring fingers and back up at Bervick. She was relieved to see Lula was okay, but as far as Bervick was concerned, he was the devil in sheep's clothing. A man that assisted a woman in betrayal of her family was no man of God. Big Ma thanked God for Lula's safe return, then retreated inside the house without saying a word to Bervick or Lula.

Lillie tugged on Lula's arm after Big Ma exited, trying to keep Lula's mind preoccupied before she reacted to Big Ma's reaction. Lula and Bervick sat down on the porch with Lillie for a while. Lillie and Lula did all the talking until Lillie looked up and saw she was due back home.

She kissed Lula on the cheek and said, "I gotta go, don't worry, she'll get over it soon. I love yah so much," and gave Lula a hug.

"No, don't go."

"I got to, Lula Mae. I don't want any trouble if I'm not back in time. You kno' I'm expectin' too, right?"

"Really? Congratulations. How far along are yah?"

"Four months."

"Wow, I can't even tell the difference."

"Yeah, but I feel different. I gotta go and don't worry bout Big Ma, Sha. She just need a little time. She'll come around."

Lillie and Lula hugged each other and said their good-byes.

In the house, Big Ma shut her bedroom door and fell to her knees crying, wishing Lula would've given God some time to wash the sins in the household away. She rocked away the tide of anger, sorrow, and guilt building inside, and reached her hands high in prayer begging for Jesus' mercy. Big Ma stayed on her knees in prayer as time floated by without her attendance. When she finally got up, she sat on the bed grabbing the bible, searching for a must read verse to pacify her soul. After reading it, Big Ma shut the bible and thanked Jesus for the passage that always confirmed that God was with her and there was nothing she couldn't handle. She muttered, "Ole devil, you's a lie. Nah, let me go see what dis pint size of a man want with my grandbaby," as she got up, heading for the kitchen to wash her hands while humming, *This Little Light Of Mine*.

Lula and Bervick sat outside waiting for nothing in particular. Bervick tried to convince Lula to go inside and talk to Big Ma, but

Lula knew it was best to leave Big Ma alone when she was upset, banking on the notion that Big Ma would get over it soon, like Lillie said.

When they were about to walk off, Big Ma came out the house in a cleaner dress and soil-free hands, holding a ball of yarn and a needle still humming *This Little Light of Mine*. Mary followed behind Big Ma and they both sat on the porch. Mary copied Big Ma's mute stance waiting for what was to come next. Lula walked up towards them, motioning Bervick to wait. He reluctantly conceded. She continued on walking toward Mary and Big Ma.

Big Ma said, "Go inside, Mary Lee."

Mary sucked her teeth getting up.

"I kno' I don't see attitude, little girl."

"No, ma'am!" Mary went inside the house suppressing her anger. She was tired of people treating her like a child. At twelve years-old, Mary felt she was entitled to know what was going on in the family instead of Big Ma sending her away whenever something took place. Whatever the case may have been, Mary was on Big Ma's side one hundred percent.

Lula took cautious steps towards Big Ma, with her head hanging down, biting at the bottom of her lip. She kissed Big Ma on the forehead and pulled a chair up watching Big Ma knit. Lula clasped her hands together at a loss for words, feeling her heart pounding hard.

Big Ma said, "I'm ashamed of you, Lula Mae Harrison. I expected more from yah. All I asked is that you finished high school first so you could go away to college. First yah get pregnant, then yah go marry a man against my wishes knowin' how I felt bout it. You completely disobeyed me just like Lillie Mae did. I just don't understand you two. I didn't raise y'all to behave like dis. I have nothin' more to say." Big Ma looked up at Bervick standing in the yard, without moving her head still knitting. "Yah done jumped from the skillet into the fryin' pan, Sha."

"I'm followin' my heart. I love Bervick and dis here is what God wants fo' me."

"What God wants? Humph! Lord have mercy, I wonder who's feeding yah dis garbage."

Big Ma kept her eye on Bervick. Hand knitting fast and furious. He looked away rubbing the back of his head. Big Ma watched him while knitting so fast, Lula saw double the hands.

Never taking her eyes off Bervick, Big Ma added, "And what kind of man takes a woman's hand in marriage without her family's consent? A selfish man, that's who!"

"Ma'am, he's the man in my life nah. He's gonna protect and take care of me and my child. I don't have a father or mother anymore."

Big Ma stopped knitting and looked over at Lula, "That's a slap in my face, Lula Mae! I've been your mother and father fo' years and God knows I did my best to protect yah. I kept yah in church, I slept in the bed with yah, and even stayed up all night makin' sho Doc ain't leave our bedroom. I kept a watchful eye on yah after that happened. I made sho' nothin' happened after that and yah see it didn't. I got a wink of sleep, but dis the sacrifice I made fo' yah. All I asked is that yah finish school first, and then you'd be free and the world would've been yours with an education. That's all I wanted fo' yah!" She started knitting again, gaining her composer to stop her heart from palpitating.

Lula started crying. She had never heard Big Ma raise her voice at her before. She got up to hug Big Ma, but Big Ma put her hand up stopping Lula in her tracks, not wanting Lula near her. Lula froze. It was as if Big Ma had slapped Lula dead in the face. Lula sat back down and wiped her tears away. This was worse than she had ever imagined.

Lula said, "I kno' you been there fo' me, but I can't live like dis anymore. I want my freedom. Livin' here with Grandpa Doc is like walking on egg shells. I'm not blamin' yah fo' anything, I just wanna be able to come home without being scared anymore. I wanna free you from being on guard all the time, too. I have to save myself nah, and if that means marryin' a man that brings peace in my life, then that's what I'm gonna do."

Before Lula could finish, Doc walked up from the road with his pipe in hand, feeling a somber mood in the air. "Everythin' alright out here?"

Lula wiped her eyes.

"Sir," Lula said, acknowledging him. Doc didn't hear Lula. He was too busy watching Bervick.

Doc said, "It's best yah leave, Sha," he pointed, "him too."

Doc pulled at his suspenders waiting for Lula to adhere to his demand. Lula looked over at Big Ma who was engrossed in her knitting, waiting for Big Ma to embrace her, be happy for her, and tell her everything was going to be okay.

Big Ma continued knitting.

Bervick walked up and took Lula by the hand with Doc never taking his eyes off Bervick. Bervick began walking Lula away and turned around to salute Big Ma with a cynical grin on his face. Big Ma smacked her needle and yarn on the ground and retreated to her garden. The evil gesture Bervick made told Big Ma that she had a lot of praying to do that night.

Chapter 12

Lula screamed, panting heavily. Her hair was matted full of sweat. Alice, a midwife, brought hot water and towels into the tiny bedroom of her house. Samantha was by Lula's side, squeezing her hand when she felt a contraction. Alice rolled her eyes at Samantha, looking her up and down, blatant with her dislike for Samantha and her attire, which consisted of high heels, a pink fitted dress, and pancake make-up.

Samantha was immune to this type of treatment and blurted to Alice, "Why don't yah get one of dem camera things and take a picture of me? Then yah can look at dis here beauty all day long, Sha," Samantha said and winked. She laughed to herself, and then refocused her attention back on Lula, wiping her forehead and holding her hand.

Alice ignored Samantha and said, "On the count of three, I need yah to push, Lula Mae. One...two...three...push!"

Lula pushed with all her might, squeezing Samantha's hand, causing the tips of her fingers to turn blue. Samantha yelled, "Oh Lord, child!"

Lula took a few deep breaths and pushed again.

Alice guided Lula, "One more good push, yah can do it, Sha!"

Lula screamed, straining through her teeth in unison with Samantha yelling for mercy on her hand.

At last, cries could be heard. Alice lifted the baby up. Lula lay back down panting, looking at the little person in amazement.

Alice cut the umbilical cord, cleaned the baby off, and wrapped it in a blanket singing, "It's a boy, Sha." She placed the baby in Lula's arms while Samantha hovered over in admiration of new born baby boy.

"Hi," Lula repeated, looking into the eyes of her newborn baby.

Samantha asked, "What yah gonna name him?"

"Bervick. Bervick Junior."

Samantha asked, "Where's Bervick Senior at anyways?"

Alice answered, "Somewhere outside hidin'. Yah kno' how men get when a baby being born."

"I'll go get him. Let him kno' his son, Bervick Junior here," Samantha said exiting the room.

Alice said, "Lula Mae, yah gotta take care of yah self. Drink dis here tonic with plenty water. No greasy or spicy foods either. It might give the baby gas. And no funny business with yah husband fo' at least eight weeks, yah hear? No funny business! I kno' how men can get, but yah body's still very young and it need time to heal."

Bervick came into the room with Samantha, who was behind him acting like she was kicking him from the back.

Lula and Alice laughed.

"Don't give my wife that tonic with that herb stuff, Miss Alice. The Lord will heal her," Bervick said, taking the canning jar full of liquid from the dresser and handing it back to Alice.

Alice took the tonic back in silence, but was going to slip it to Lula after Bervick left. She encountered all types of men folk and ignored most of them to look out for the women's health after giving birth.

Bervick kissed Lula on the lips and looked down at his newborn son.

Lula asked, "Wanna hold him?"

"No!" Bervick curtly said.

Lula put her pinky finger out for Bervick Jr. to take hold of, blinking away tears forming in her eyes from Bervick's brusqueness.

Bervick turned and left out the room without a word.

Samantha rubbed the side of Lula's face whispering, "Don't worry, they like that sometimes. He'll come around, Sha."

Alice smiled at what Samantha said, realizing she wasn't so bad after all.

Bervick made it to the back of Alice's house falling against a pecan tree, hyperventilating. Nuts fell off hitting the top of his head. On his knees, Bervick bent over holding his stomach, regurgitating all over the fallen nuts. His knees weakened. He couldn't keep his balance, feeling faint. Bervick couldn't believe he had a son. A son name Bervick. A son named after him.

A father…I'm a father, Bervick thought. It wasn't long ago when he was a child. A child named Bervick, too. The memories of his childhood overwhelmed his conscious...

Bervick's mother, Christina Miles, yelled in Creole from the door, "Bervick, wash your hands, it's time to eat."

Bervick ran to the back where his brothers were already cleaning themselves up, washing their faces and hands, making sure every speck of dirt was gone. Christina set the table. She wore a long, yellow and white polka dot dress with an apron over it. Her hair was pinned in a bun on top of her head. She was a short, light-skinned Creole woman with high cheekbones and soft eyes. She had a gentle demeanor, which caused people to often underestimate her. Her primary language was Creole, only learning a few simple words in English.

Bervick's father, Joseph Frank, yelled in Creole, "Today," for his boys to hurry to the dinner table. They all ran trying to out run each other to be the first at the table. Bervick tripped over his own two feet, falling to the floor in front of the table, grabbing his foot. He bellowed in pain crying, reaching out for his mother. Christina got up from the table to rush over and help.

Even though at nine years-old, the middle child of five boys, Bervick was the shortest, slowest, and weakest.

"No!" Joe yelled, putting his hand up for Christina to stop. "Let him get up on his own." He told Christina in Creole, their primary language in the household. She obeyed and sat back down. Joe turned back to Bervick, who was in pain crying on the floor.

Joe said in a deep voice, "Get up!"

"I can't, papa."

"Yes you can, boy! Get up! And stop crying. No room for a man to cry."

Bervick sucked up his tears and tried to get up. His foot throbbed with every move. Joe watched Bervick with intense eyes, scaring Bervick back on his feet. Underneath the stern glare, Joe's heart cringed at the sight of his son in pain, but he was a master of disguise.

Weakness had no place for a black man in the south and Joe knew this all too well. No one will show his sons any pity, respect, or compassion, and at any given moment, his precious children could be called 'nigger'. From birth, they were already marked a target for harassment, beatings, rapes, and lynchings. Therefore, Joe was going to make sure his boys didn't break under any of these circumstances. Show no visible sign of weakness because if one happened to fall victim to exploitation, humiliation, or injustice, their unbreakable stance was their only armor against racism; ready to die still believing in themselves as true men, despite the extreme efforts put into stripping their manhood away. Emotions ran deep for black fathers during and after slavery. Wounds from loved ones being killed, kids taken away, wives raped before their eyes, and forced strenuous labor without compensation left untreated scars in black fathers, passing from generation to generation. The way black fathers survived and maintained their sanity was to distance themselves from those whom they loved most—their wives and children. Especially their sons, who were the number one enemy from birth. The less display of love exchanged between father and child helped save them from future heartache and pain from the silent stigma of being black.

Being a darker-skinned short man, Joe was mistreated by blacks and whites growing up, causing a block of ice to form around his heart for protection. The last sign of emotion Joe displayed was when his father went missing before being discovered hanging from a tree. This agonizing experience demolished whatever sentiment was left in Joe, who knew justice would never be served for the murder of his beloved father. Joe missed him terribly, cringing at the thought of his father's final hours. At age fifteen, that incident closed Joe's heart for good. Therefore, the way Joe showed love to his sons was through preparing them for their fate as black men in America.

Bervick lifted his little body up in agony and limped his way to the dinner table as Joe, Christina, and his brothers watched. He wiped away his tears and ignored his throbbing foot, pretending to be unaffected by his injury to preclude a beating.

Joe pointed and said in Creole, "I don't want to see them tears again, you hear me, boy?"

"Yes, sir."

Now, in back of Alice's house, Bervick got up from the tree brushing his clothes off. He crept near Alice's front door, placed his hand on the knob, and heard Lula talking to Samantha. Knots formed in Bervick's stomach upon hearing his baby boy cry. Everything Joe taught Bervick did not prepare him for this.

He released the knob and walked away from the house. Putting his hands in his pocket, Bervick walked up the road to Curley's house. When he arrived, Curley was already outside watching his two kids play in the yard. Bervick sat down beside Curley on the porch.

Curley asked, "So is it a boy or girl?"

"It's a boy. A boy named Bervick Junior."

Curley nodded.

The two sat in silence on the porch for the rest of the day.

Chapter 13

In 1955, Bervick and Lula lived in Curley's house, where they stayed until their church's elders assisted in purchasing a small house for them as a thanks for their hard work and service to the church. Bervick was making a name for himself in church as one of the most devoted evangelists, endlessly preaching the word of God. He worked various jobs making little money. For food, Bervick grew a garden in their back yard growing fresh tomatoes, okra, corn, watermelon, mustard and turnip greens, snap peas, sweet potatoes, lima beans, peppers, onions, garlic, herbs, and peanuts, making it easy for Lula to pick fresh vegetables for meals. They maintained a chicken coop for meat and eggs, and slaughtered a hog once in a while, using every bit of the meat it provided.

Bervick also went fishing, catching mounds of fish, crawfish, shrimp, and crabs. Perishable produce was canned, and the meat was dried or smoked for andouille sausage, ham, bacon, hocks, or fried crackling. The hog head, or any leftover hog meat was used to make boudin, and its feet were pickled and given away since neither Lula nor Bervick ate it.

Lula became estranged from her family soon after she married Bervick. Even though she saw them in church every Sunday, few words were exchanged. Lula and Bervick would have outdoor meals for neighbors and friends to bring bowls for gumbo and rice—a furtive attempt on Lula's part for her family to visit.

Starting the meals in the early morning, Bervick arranged a fire out front of their house and sat a steel tube full of water over it. Lula would cut up bell peppers, tomatoes, chunks of corn, and onions in it, then add seafood, smoked pork, chicken, andouille sausage, and gumbo fillet to thicken the texture. Everyone stopped by to eat and mingle, listening to Lula talk and laugh in her glory.

A sociable person, Lula took every chance she got to talk and laugh with people, yearning to socialize rather than be stuck in the house alone, cooking, cleaning, and raising a child. She always waited for Big Ma or other family members to come with their bowls. Much to her regret, they never showed up.

Now sixteen years-old, Lula was six months pregnant with her second child.

One Saturday afternoon, she was outside hanging sheets on the line, barely walking due to swollen ankles. Bervick was gone spreading the word of God, leaving Lula to her daily chores. The hot sun drained her energy, slowing her usual fast pace, but in spite of this, Lula tended to her wifely duties.

Peering down the road between blowing sheets, Lula saw a tall figure walking in her direction. She squinted, putting her hand above her eyes to block the sun, focusing pass the waves of heat.

She waved yelling, "Hey there!" She clipped the last sheet on the line and came from behind them yelling, "Papa Top!"

"How yah doin', baby girl? Got somethin' fo' yah." Papa Top gave Lula a paper bag.

She opened it and smiled. "Boudin! Thanks, Papa Top. Who made it?"

"I did, Sha."

"Oh, I kno' it's gonna be good then."

Papa Top smiled and embraced Lula. He missed seeing his granddaughter and made it a point to travel from Happy Hill to see her on occasions, being one of the few family members who still spoke to her.

Lula was beside herself. She tugged at Papa Top's arm to follow her inside the house.

Papa Top looked around at the tiny brick home, no bigger than 18′ by 20′ square feet with a bedroom sectioned off by a wooden partition. One couldn't differentiate the division between the kitchen and living room; it was more like four walls and a floor, and there was no furniture except for a second-hand worn chair and a single mattress in the middle of the floor. Near the potbelly stove were two wooden chairs placed underneath a miniature round wooden table.

Papa Top pulled out both chairs for him and Lula to sit on. She took a piece of boudin out of the bag and motioned for him to take a piece, but he declined.

Lula bit into one saying, "Hmm, dis here some good stuff! Yah sho' yah don't wanna piece?"

"No thanks, sweetie. When I cook, it's hard to eat my food."

"You too, sir?" She laughed. "It's hard fo' me to enjoy my own food when tastin' all the time to get the flavor right."

"Yeah, Sha. Where's Bervick Jr.?"

"With Aunt Samantha. I had chores to do so she agreed to watch him fo' me. It's too hot fo' him to be outside with me t'day."

"Samantha got your baby! Pigs must be flying right bout nah."

"She's actually good with him. If yah ask me, she's pretty good with kids."

"Really! I reckon, no matter how a woman behaves, yah can't take that nurturing part out of dem. So, how you doin', Lula Mae?" Papa Top lit his pipe, quickly putting it out looking over at Lula's belly.

He shifted in the hard uncomfortable chair.

"I'm doin' fine. How's everyone? Care fo' some water? Do yah need a pillow or somethin'? I kno' dem chairs are pretty hard."

"No need fo' that, Sha. Everyone doin' just fine. Mary Lee growing like a weed and Lillie Mae, I haven't seen her since she moved to Texas."

"I miss her so much."

"We all do, Sha."

Both sat in silence. Lula finished eating her warm piece of boudin and reached in the bag for another one. Papa Top struggled to stay neutral when observing the condition of the house, but anger seeped through slowly after seeing Lula's living situation. His lady friend, Miss Colt .45, nudged him to have a one-on-one with Bervick. Papa Top had to pat her to ease up a bit.

He had spent so many years chasing down Leroy and searching for Beatrice, until the soles of his shoes had worn away. Papa Top wasn't going to give up on finding Beatrice. However, his old age and arthritis in both knees slowed down his search.

Papa Top asked, "How yah really doin', Lula Mae?"

"I'm fine. Me and Bervick gettin' ready fo' the new addition to the family," Lula said, patting her belly.

Papa Top nodded, "Did Bervick find a job yet?"

"He fill in fo' dem construction workers from time-to-time and do railroad work when they need an extra hand. "

"How does he find time to work when he busy preachin' all day, Sha?"

"Once we get on our feet, we'll be just fine. God always makes a way, Sir."

Papa Top didn't entertain that statement, knowing those words came from Bervick. Instead, he asked, "Are yah returnin' back to school?"

"I plan to after dis here baby born."

Lula got up, wiped her hands off and threw the skin of the boudin away. She poured Papa Top a glass of water as he watched Lula wobble on swollen ankles around the pathetic looking kitchen, wishing she was in a better situation. To give peace a chance, Papa Top kept the boiling rage building for Bervick at a minimum and outwardly displayed a fictitious smile while taking the glass of water from Lula.

Lula sat back down across from him, smiling back and said, "Wanna a piece of pecan candy? Made 'em fresh dis mornin'."

"No thank you, Sha." Papa Top pointed at his cheek where his teeth were missing in the back. He took a sip of water and cleared his throat, pointing at Lula's stomach. "What yah think, girl or boy?"

"Doesn't matter. As long as he or she is healthy."

He nodded in agreement taking another gulp of water.

"How's the family, sir?" Lula repeated her initial question, unable to drop the subject of the people she terribly missed.

Papa Top chuckled, "Everyone's doin' fine, Lula Mae."

He wasn't going to reveal that the family was still in an uproar about her marrying Bervick against Big Ma's approval, or that Doc and Big Ma vowed to renounce Lula from their lives in good faith that, if she lay in the bed she made, she would soon learn and see Bervick's true self. Lula was aware of the resentment they had towards her, but wasn't conscious to the degree of it.

Papa Top learned at a young age that some things were better left unsaid.

Lula said, "I'm happy to hear everyone's doin' good." Sorrow surfaced from underneath her faint smile.

Papa Top finished the rest of his water trying to overlook the sadness in Lula's eyes. "I'm gonna be on my way, Sha. Got work to do in my shop." He examined the outside of the empty glass and handed it over to Lula. She walked him outside to say good-bye.

"When yah comin' back to visit me, Papa Top?"

"I'll be checkin' on yah again, Sha."

"Alright, I'll be here waitin', sir. I'll have pork chops smotherin' fo' yah, or maybe some beans and rice. You can bring more of that boudin, too!"

Papa Top nodded and gave Lula a hug. She watched her grandfather slightly limp down the road on his cane until he was no longer in sight. Lula went back into the house. Feeling alone, she put her feet up and picked up the bible to take her mind off the visit with Papa Top. She felt he was holding back information, and wished he had spoken more about the family so that she could weigh the odds of getting back in good with them, especially Big Ma.

Unable to concentrate on the bible, Lula sat it down on her lap and took a deep breath reassuring herself that everything was going to be okay and back to normal soon. She mulled over a way to rectify her relationship with Big Ma sooner, but kept hitting a brick wall with every idea.

In her pondering state, the baby kicked, redirecting Lula's attention to what was now important in her life. She got up to share another piece of boudin with her unborn child and noticed the money left on the chair Papa Top had sat in. Lula picked it up counting twenty-five dollars, kissing and holding the money over her chest, thanking God for Papa Top.

Sunday in church, Lula clapped in the front pew, singing and praising God along with other church members. Bervick was in the front leading the church in song. He worked his way into becoming the lead evangelist through his efforts of preaching the gospel of the Lord from house-to-house, business-to-business, and was finally banned from Juke Joints and French La La's for stirring up trouble, calling Zydeco music the devil's music and informing the patrons that they were all going to hell. Bervick's primary goal was to solidify the open position for assistant pastor, which was a baby step towards his dream to take over the church one day.

Pastor Evans was looking for a devoted evangelist to preach every other Sunday and ultimately become his assistant. Bervick marveled at the opportunity, going to great lengths to impress Pastor Evans. Curley sought out the position as well, causing Bervick to compete with his own brother for the title. Curley, on the other hand, believed whoever was meant for the position would earn it fair and square. He stayed steadfast as an evangelist and remained low-key to prevent animosity between him and Bervick. Inevitably, a strain on their relationship occurred since there was only room for one assistant pastor. It took years for a decision like this to occur, giving Bervick and Curley ample time to prove themselves.

The choosing of the assistant pastor was going to be a pivotal moment for Big Ma. Whoever attained the title of assistant pastor determined whether she was going to remain a member of the church or leave for good. Therefore, Big Ma moved in silence, letting it be known to Pastor Evans that Bervick was not the candidate for the position.

During church, Big Ma sat in church while watching Lula's every move, wanting to call out her name, picturing herself hugging her sweet grandbaby. The sound of Bervick's obnoxious voice screaming, "I'm saved, sanctified, baptized and filled with the Holy Spirit," broke Big Ma's daydream, bringing her back into her living nightmare.

The evangelists were seated in the front of the church, alongside the church mother and visiting elders and bishops. Bervick achieved an award winning performance by singing the loudest, clapping the hardest, and leading the church in the longest prayers ever, silently infuriating the members.

During Pastor Evans' sermon, Bervick rallied the people up yelling, "I am saved, sanctified, baptized, and filled with the Holy Ghost," followed by his signature scream and slap on the knee.

Bervick eventually caught the Holy Ghost, which happened often, bringing the church members to their feet, singing and praising while he hopped up and down the aisle, falling over screaming and praising God as people surrounded him trying to assist in keeping him safe.

Big Ma remained seated with her arms crossed, unimpressed.

After he settled down, Bervick sat down with someone feeding him water while another person fanned him. He turned and winked at Lula, making her smile bashfully. This furthered Big Ma's irritation watching the romantic gestures between Lula and the devil's idiot.

Pastor Evans said, "Let us pray."

Everyone quieted and bowed their heads.

"Heavenly Father," Pastor Evans went into prayer and stumbled across words when he heard a baby start crying. Lula comforted Bervick Jr. to quiet him down. She got up to carry him out the church so the prayer wouldn't be disrupted. Just when she was making her way out the door, Big Ma lifted her head to catch a glimpse of her grandson for the first time. She clutched hold of her chest when she saw Lula's pregnant belly. Big Ma quickly bowed her head back down closing her eyes. Oblivious to the prayer, she rubbed at her chest, rocking, shaking her head side-to-side in disbelief.

Mama Deavia, Big Ma's friend and informant, peeked up from prayer and saw the anguish across Big Ma's face and whispered, "What's wrong, Sha?"

Big Ma formed her lips to say, "Lord Jesus help me. I didn't wanna believe yah, but seein' is believing. That poor child *is* pregnant again. Lord have mercy. I thought she'd come to her senses by nah."

"I told yah so, Sha," Mama Deavia said. "Bervick hardly take care of the child he got nah."

"I kno', Sha. I kno'. Jesus, have mercy on my baby."

Prayer finished and Mama Deavia fanned Big Ma when they sat down, relieved that Big Ma saw it for herself in the house of the Lord where she had no choice but to remain calm.

Bervick got up to lead the congregation in another song. Big Ma closed her eyes, squeezing her bible against her chest to stop her tempted hand from throwing it at Bervick's head. She chuckled at the thought of the bible hitting him during one of his "Holy Ghost" moments, quickly rebuking that notion while in the house of the Lord.

As Bervick sang, a stinging sensation forced him to turn and find Big Ma looking at him with an irked look on her face. He ignored her and continued singing and clapping louder.

***

Lula did her regular daily chores, humming and singing to Bervick Jr. as he watched her work. She smiled over at him as he stared at Lula with inquisitive eyes with his finger in his mouth. After the chores were done, Lula took Bervick Jr. around the block visiting friends and Bervick's side of the family to chat and show off her baby.

"Look how cute he is" or "look at all that pretty hair he got" is what people said, gloating on Bervick Junior. Lula was proud to have such a cute baby boy and enjoyed being away from the house for the day.

"Gurl, yah figure came back nicely. Why yah go and get pregnant again?" Mable Victoria, Bervick's first cousin, asked Lula when she stopped by. "If I got my figure back that quick, I wouldn't have any more kids!" She'd laughed, sharing homemade peach cobbler and lemonade with them.

Lula said, "We have to be fruitful and multiply, Sha."

"That sound like Bervick right there, Sha."

"We don't live fo' ourselves, Sha, we live fo' God and what he wants fo' us."

Mable just smiled and continued on laughing and talking.

The next day, Lula suffered from walking too much the day before, falling ill and bedbound for a few days. Grandma Emma travelled to Eunice to assist Lula for a week and care for Bervick Jr. while Lula was down. Grandma Emma was uncomfortable sleeping in the small house, appalled at how Bervick was gone preaching the word of God instead of finding permanent work to maintain a stable household. Yet, Grandma Emma didn't want to burden Lula with these feelings due to enough family members in Eunice dismissing Lula as kin. She traveled back to Texas when Lula appeared well enough, but promised she would return around the baby's due date.

Bervick worked odd jobs, knowing it wasn't enough money to fix up and maintain his house, but his mind was preoccupied with obtaining the assistant pastor position; that's all what mattered. His focus was on spreading the word of God and impressing Pastor Evans.

After her health improved, Lula took it upon herself to make sweet dough pies in her final months of pregnancy, baking and selling out quickly, bringing in enough money to purchase household necessities and clothes for the baby. She baked when money was tight, even during times she felt weak. But Lula didn't mind. She loved making pies, feeling the sweet dough between her fingers reminded her of the good old days baking with Big Ma.

People in Eunice were putting in orders whenever they saw Lula, or went by her house to see if any were made or when she was going to bake them. Her pies became so popular that she could hardly keep up with the orders. A few church friends helped her bake, splitting the profits, and Samantha put up the money for Lula to buy the supplies and ingredients needed. When Lula sold the first few batches, she'd give Samantha back the money with a little extra in the envelope, only to find it tucked away in the kitchen, untouched.

Bervick would come home and watch Lula in action without assisting with the baking or tending to Bervick Jr., hoping she'd tire herself out. Every day he'd return home from church or preaching the word of God, thinking Lula's pregnancy finally slowed her down. But found the complete opposite. She'd still be in the kitchen working harder, faster, and more efficient with swollen ankles and caring for Bervick Jr. at the same time. Although Bervick believed God blessed him with the most virtuous woman he'd ever met, he felt Lula's pie selling was done in vain, given that she was supposed to use those talents for him and him only.

The more Lula baked her sweet dough pies, the better she became at organizing and maintaining efficiency. In a short period of time, Lula's profits bought baby clothes, drapes for the windows, a rug, a lamp, and other items to spruce up their small dwelling, making it more inviting and cozy. Bervick wasn't too pleased about Lula becoming the main breadwinner in the house. Feeling his manhood threatened and the town people watching, Bervick had to put an end to the pie making business because Lula's pregnancy was taking too long to stop her. God put man in charge of households; therefore, biding his time, Bervick waited for an answer from God on how to deal with Lula. Being deliberate with Lula would come across as jealousy, and envy was a deadly sin that Bervick rebuked. So instead, God bestowed the perfect answer to Bervick.

He sat Lula down and expressed his dissatisfaction with how she was caring for Bervick Junior. He told Lula that she needed to tend to their son more, reminding Lula that she must remain a virtuous woman and not worry about making pies, assuring her that God was going to help him find a permanent job soon, so the money made from pie selling was no longer needed. He preached the word of

God, stating that money wasn't a spiritual necessity and chasing money was trickery from the devil to make people worship money instead of God. Bervick acted concerned for Lula's immortal soul, as well as the health of their unborn child, telling her that a pregnant woman should rest or else the baby could fall ill.

Lula was reluctant at first, but she trusted Bervick's heartfelt words and wanted to continue being the God fearing Christian woman who obeyed her husband wishes. She didn't want to be fooled by the devil nor hurt her unborn child. Hell, Fire and Brimstone wasn't about to be her fate, so Lula finished the last of the orders, and that was the end of her pie selling for the time being.

Selling her last pie made Lula despondent. Baking was in her heart and even though quitting was the best thing for the baby, selling pies didn't seem as bad as how Bervick portrayed it to be.

Nostalgia kicked in.

Lula missed Big Ma and Lillie more than ever. They would've helped her discern her internal conflicts. Lula didn't understand why Bervick rejected the increase in cash flow when he too sought after a good paying job for the same reason.

Lula took to the bible for refuge to denounce the disturbing inkling of Bervick having the wrong intentions for her. Bervick was her husband and he had to be correct—she was about to have a baby soon and needed her rest, Bervick Jr. needed her undivided attention, and her children and husband must always come first, thus said the Lord.

Lula graciously stepped down for Bervick to take care of the finances, realizing he was the God fearing man of the house.

Reflecting on the money made and work accomplished from selling pies in such a short period of time, Lula envisioned herself opening a restaurant to do what she loved most, cooking and baking. Confident that it would be a profitable business, the idea sparked a new endeavor to consider pursuing in the near future. She decided against sharing this with Bervick, ashamed for doing so. Yet, Lula's heart wouldn't allow her to expose her new idea. This was an inspirational dream belonging to her only. A future plan with Big Ma, Samantha, Lillie, and Mary included, working together side-by-side, showing the town what they were made of in the cooking department. As much as Lula tried, she needed something to call her own without Bervick's counteraction and dissuasion. She needed an outlet for breathing room in their marriage. She abided by all of Bervick's rules, but still yearned to have some semblance of independence and free thinking of her own.

Content with the restaurant revelation, Lula felt more at ease. Her future looked brighter with an idea that would bring the family together again.

Lula grabbed her bible asking for the Lord's forgiveness for not disclosing this notion to her husband.

***

Bervick paced the room listening to Lula's cries coming out of the bedroom until he couldn't take it anymore. He swiftly left the house and went down the road, strolling to no particular destination.

Grandma Emma was by Lula's side holding her hand as Alice told Lula to push, keeping Lula's legs from trembling in pain. In labor for twenty-two hours, Lula was terribly weak, her skin color was bleak, and her lips were turning a grayish hue.

Alice and Grandma Emma begged Bervick earlier to take Lula to a hospital, but he refused, dismissing conventional medicine, telling them that God heals the sick and weak and will take care of Lula and their baby. He figured, regardless of the outcome, it was God's will.

Grandma Emma and Alice attempted to take Lula to the hospital when Bervick left the first time, despite his wishes. Unluckily, they needed a husband's signature for admission.

Lula continued to push.

Alice screamed when she saw a head and said, "Com'on nah child, push!"

Grandma Emma shouted, "Push, Lula Mae! Push, Sha!"

Lula gathered the last bit of strength in her body, pushing with all her might as her face turned beet red. She collapsed back into the bed when done. A faint cry could be heard. Grandma Emma and Alice exhaled in relief and Lula caught her own breath, feeling drained.

Grandma Emma dabbed the sweat off Lula's forehead, removing pieces of hair out Lula's face. Lula had been ill a week prior to delivery, and since the baby was a couple of weeks early, Grandma Emma took the first bus to Eunice to be by Lula's side when Samantha got stuck in Lafayette, working to expand her watermelon profits at local markets.

Grandma Emma stood by Lula's side holding her hand while asking Alice, "Is the baby alright? She sounds weak."

Alice felt around the baby's chest checking its heart beat. The body temperature was high and breaths were faint. A premature baby with a high fever was a perilous combination.

Alice wrapped the baby up in a blanket and handed it over to Grandma Emma.

"It's a girl!" Grandma Emma said, placing the baby in Lula's arms. Lula's weak face muscles struggled to smile, taking hold of her new born baby, admiring the new addition to the family.

Alice hesitated before whispering to Grandma Emma, "Dis baby might not make it."

Grandma Emma yelled out, "What yah mean 'might not make it', Miss Alice?"

Alice pursed her lips at Grandma Emma, who now realized why Alice was quiet about it. Lula gasped, looking at the both of them for answers.

Alice started cleaning Lula up, knowing the news she was about to share wasn't good. She warily looked up at Grandma Emma, then at Lula, "I gotta be honest, Sha, that baby's burnin' up with fever. One of the hottest lil' bodies I ever felt, and if I can't break dis here fever soon, the baby may…let's just say the chances of dis baby makin' it is slim. I'll do my best tho', Sha."

Lula felt the baby's forehead with the back of her hand. Chills ran down her spine. Her eyes swelled up. "Oh Lord have mercy, she is hot! She is hot!" Lula looked up at Grandma Emma for answers, but even she was at a loss for words, covering her mouth with her hand. Lula started praying out loud through quivering parched lips.

Grandma Emma pulled Alice aside and said, "You betta tell me somethin' and it betta be somethin' good, Miss Alice!"

Alice tried loosening Grandma Emma's grip. Grandma Emma held on tighter.

Alice said, "That baby ain't gonna last by t'night, Sha."

Grandma Emma twisted Alice's arm. "I said say somethin' good! You the midwife, DO SOMETHIN'!"

"Let me go, Emma! Yah hurtin' me."

Grandma Emma let go, backing away holding her chest, feeling faint. Lula stopped praying, looking back and forth at them. Alice helped Grandma Emma over to the chair next to the bed, and then went over smiling, staring at Lula and the baby, putting her pinky out for the baby to grip it. The tiny hand was limp and couldn't grip.

Alice stood there pondering ways to help the premature baby's temperature reduce, and also mentally preparing herself for the inevitable and the best way to assist the family in coping after the death. A premature baby had zero to no chance of living with a fever that high.

Alice asked, "Watcha gonna name her, Sha?"

"Miss Alice, I want yah to be honest with me, do you think her fever gonna break?"

Alice took a deep breath, debating whether to tell Lula the truth or lie so that Lula could be at peace during the time the infant was still alive. Then eyeing Grandma Emma, Alice thought the better of it. "I think it's best if yah say yah good-byes soon, Sha." Alice turned away to avoid Lula's reaction. In her many years as a midwife, Alice still was never prepared for moments like these. Resting on the fact that God was in control now, Alice pulled herself together and went to Lula's side to console her.

Lula's breath grew rapid. She bellowed out the most gut wrenching cry screaming, "No, no, no! Not my baby! Oh God, please Lord no!"

Lula hugged the baby closer, kissing her forehead repeatedly, rocking back and forth. "No God, please no!" She repeated through quivering lips.

Grandma Emma sat in the chair still dumbfounded, and then, she perked up, getting out of the chair rubbing tears off her face.

Grandma Emma said, "I'll be back, Sha," and darted out the room before Lula could ask any questions.

Grandma Emma bolted out the front door and sprinted down the road, slightly lifting her long green skirt to free her legs so she could run faster. People stopped conversations on porches, taking heed of Grandma Emma running by, now alarmed that something major must've taken place for a tiny old woman to run that fast.

Grandma Emma ran into a yard, nearly leaping up the porch stairs, and banged hysterically on the door. She peeked in the window and saw no one, so she ran to the back of the house, tripping over the trail Doc imprinted during one of his strolls around the house.

Big Ma was on her knees pulling weeds out of her garden when she saw Grandma Emma running up behind her and stopping, bending over out of breath.

Grandma Emma muttered between breaths, "Lord, I'm too old to be doin' all dis here." She bent over pressing her hands on her knees, sucking up as much oxygen as she could in her overworked lungs.

"What's wrong, Sha?"

Grandma Emma sucked in more air to help her speak. Big Ma stood up, dusted dirt off her knee, and went over to Grandma Emma putting an arm around her back. "Breathe, Emma. Breathe, Sha. Let me get yah some water!"

"No, Sha. She needs yah nah!"

"She who?"

"Lula Mae! She just had the baby, a baby girl, and it came too early and got a fever so high that Miss Alice told us to say our final good-byes b'cause the baby ain't gonna make it through the night!"

Enough said.

Big Ma ran inside the house, leaving the back door wide open, grabbing various herbs, cure all tonic, and anointed oils from the pantry and met Grandma Emma out front in less than a minute, carrying a bag over her shoulder with shoes flopping off her feet.

Big Ma and Grandma Emma strutted up the road like soldiers marching to battle. "In the name of Jesus, death ain't gonna be dis baby fate t'day," Big Ma declared treading along. She prayed the Twenty-Third psalm out loud in a commanding tone as people nudged each other and pointed at Big Ma and Grandma Emma. Cars stopped in place with passengers' heads hanging out. Kids pulled parents out of homes to witness Big Ma and Grandma Emma's steadfast stride, serious temperament, and convergence on the way to Lula's house. Whispers rose amongst the growing spectators, offering their own supposition on what was happening.

When they made it to Lula's house, Big Ma pushed the door open heading straight behind the partition to the tiny bedroom with

Grandma Emma behind her. Alice had finished cleaning up and was startled to find Big Ma standing there.

Big Ma said, "Lula Mae?"

Lula looked up, "Big Ma?"

Big Ma dropped her bag, ran over to hug and kiss Lula's forehead, and then went over to Alice. "I'll take over from here, Sha."

Alice nodded, eager to move aside with a new found hope. She handed the baby over to Big Ma.

Grandma Emma said, "Thank yah fo' all of yah help, Miss Alice, you a blessin' to us and sorry bout earlier."

Alice put her hand up to say no need for an apology and began packing her things, moving aside to watch Big Ma in action. It wasn't every day Alice got to see Eunice's oldest midwife come out of retirement.

Big Ma held the newborn in her arms. "You gonna live my baby, I kno' God won't have it any other way." She smiled at the frail baby in her arms and told Grandma Emma to set up everything and make coffee because it was going to be a long night.

In a tin pail, Big Ma concocted a cap full of alcohol, peppermint and eucalyptus leaves in warm water. She held the infant over her arm and began washing her fragile body down. Grandma Emma held Lula close, rubbing her back as they watched Big Ma pray out loud while washing the baby. She hummed spiritual hymns and said prayer after prayer.

Alice decided to stay and continued heating more water whenever Big Ma called for it.

Big Ma prayed over the baby non-stop, falling into a trance-like state with her eyes closed. In every wash, she imagined Jesus lifting the sickness out of the baby's body, dissipating the sickness into thin air, and then transporting *his* healing energy from her hands into the infant, letting it revitalize the baby's organs one at a time. Big Ma whispered to the baby, constantly telling it to stay put, it wasn't her time to leave this earth. God said so.

Early morning hours hit and Grandma Emma stayed by Lula's side, stroking her head to comfort her. Alice couldn't bring herself to leave and remained in the bedroom, making coffee for Grandma Emma, as well as answering the knocks at the door from different town folk and relatives offering their services. Alice told them to stay near and pray for Lula and the baby.

Big Ma's prayers were the only sound coming from the room. Lula said silent prayers to herself, letting the soft touch of Grandma Emma's hand relax on her face. Lula refused to look over at her baby and Big Ma, fearing that if she saw the sight of her lifeless baby, it would stain her memory for life. All Lula could do was repeat prayers in unison with Big Ma, listening to the holy drips of water wash upon her baby girl.

Everyone was up all night repeating the same rituals, except for Lula who nodded off in Grandma Emma's arms from exhaustion. Grandma Emma lay Lula slowly down on the pillow, and then sat her sore legs down in the corner chair, waiting for Big Ma to signal for more warm water.

Prayers and songs could be heard from outside as friends, neighbors, relatives, and church folks surrounded the house, bringing support within the bedroom.

Lights stayed on in the church that night, along with porch lamps outside of homes.

In the morning, the sun beamed down on Lula's waking face. She blinked her eyes open, furious with herself that she had accidently fallen asleep. She sat up in a panic, moaning in pain from jerking her body to hard. Big Ma, Grandma Emma, Alice, and her baby weren't there. Lula lost control. She felt no pain at this point yelling, "Oh, Lord, no, please no! Big Ma…Grandma Emma…Alice…Bervick…Big Ma…!"

Bervick peeked in, "Yah up?"

"No Bervick, I'm sleep," Lula said sarcastically. "Where's everyone at? Lord, where's my baby at?" Her lips quivered.

Bervick pulled the wooden partition back for Big Ma to enter, carrying a bundle in her arms. Lula's mind raced. *Am I saying good-bye or hello, Lord Jesus help me,* she thought. Big Ma placed the baby in Lula's arms. Tears poured down Lula's face looking down at the tiny baby girl who was yawning.

Lula said, "Yeah, it's been a long night fo' us, too."

Big Ma and Bervick laughed.

Lula put her pinky finger out and the baby grabbed hold of it. The grip was weak, but she was alive and looked healthier.

Lula chanted, "Thank yah, God. All praises to my Lord and Savior Jesus Christ."

Bervick led everyone in prayer, giving thanks for the miracle performed. When finished, Lula looked around and said, "Where's Grandma Emma and Miss Alice?"

Big Ma said, "Alice went home and Emma over my house cookin' breakfast."

"Bless their heart." Lula smiled. "Big Ma, is my baby gonna be okay?"

"Her fever broke in the early hours, which is a good thing, but her body's still very weak. I'm gonna stick 'round here to make sho' she's strong enough to feed. I'll kno' she's okay if she's able to feed on her own. But the worst is over, Sha. Thank yah Jesus. Wasn't nothin' but the good Lord's work."

"Thank you God and thank you, Big Ma. I love you!"

Big Ma bowed her head, humbly accepting Lula's appreciation. It pleased Lula to see Big Ma and Bervick being civil to one another even though Big Ma hardly spoke or looked his way.

A knock at the front door startled everyone out of the moment. Bervick went to open it and came back with Samantha following behind, holding Bervick Jr. in her arms. Big Ma's lips tightened looking at Samantha in her tight yellow dress, white hat, high heels, white gloves, and pounds of make-up on her face.

Bervick didn't bother to look Samantha's way either. No sinners were allowed in his home. He was going to inform Lula later that Samantha was not welcome in their home anymore, and forbidden to care for Bervick Junior.

Samantha went over to Lula's side and said, "Oh my goodness, look Bervick Jr., there goes yah lil' sister. Say hello. Aww, Lula Mae, she's adorable. I'm glad to see you and the baby doin' well, Sha. Yah sho' nuff gave us all a scare there."

Samantha waved Bervick Jr.'s hands at the newborn, then looked over at Big Ma and smiled. "Hi there, mama. Heard yah were up in here workin' a miracle with dem healing hands of yours, huh?"

Big Ma turned to Lula and said, "Lord have mercy, Lula Mae, you let her watch yah baby boy?"

Before Lula could answer, Samantha interjected, "I don't see no other family members helpin' her out, so why not? I just took him to Lafayette with me and he enjoyed himself, too. When she needs her rest, I take him fo' her."

Big Ma shot a look over at Lula, who quickly looked down at the baby, feeling lucky to have the newborn in her arms.

Big Ma put a hand on her hip and looked back over at Samantha, shaking her head at the sight of her sinner daughter. "Look at all that make-up on yah face. Clothes so tight, I don't kno' how blood flow to that brain of yours."

Bervick added, "She looks like a clown with all that devil make-up on."

Samantha snapped, "Shut yah mouth, Bervick! Stop tryin' to get in my mama's good graces, b'cause I got news fo' yah, she ain't never gonna like you!" Samantha turned to Lula, shifting Bervick Jr. to her other side, "Anyway, Lula Mae, what's baby girl name?"

"I don't have a name fo' her yet."

"Well, thank goodness she's okay. I hurried on the first bus back to Eunice when I heard bout the baby havin' a high fever. Shit, that ain't nothin' but God's work there." Samantha paused, putting her hand over her mouth saying, "Oh my God, mama, I'm sorry. It slipped out."

Big Ma snatched Bervick Jr. out Samantha's arms, rebuking the foul language coming from Samantha's mouth and using God's name in the same sentence. Big Ma lowered her eyes heatedly at Samantha and looked down at Bervick Jr., giving him a kiss on the cheek, realizing this was the first time meeting him. She glanced back up at Samantha. "You get out of here nah!"

Samantha stood frozen with an apologetic expression on her face. "Ma'am, I didn't mean to—" Samantha said, getting choked up in mid-sentence.

"Leave nah!"

Samantha glanced over at Bervick and rolled her eyes at the grimace on his face. She bent down to kiss Lula's forehead, then lifted her head looking over at Big Ma. Samantha stepped back taking off her hat. She pulled her gloves off and held her arms out for Big Ma. Big Ma didn't flinch. Her daughter's make-up, tight dress, and cleavage hanging out disgusted Big Ma. Samantha stretched her arms out wider, asking for a hug. She finally dropped them when she realized that Big Ma wasn't moving an inch. Samantha blew a kiss to Lula and the babies, rolled her eyes at Bervick one last time, and said in a low tone to Big Ma before walking out, "You still love me, mama?"

Big Ma ignored Samantha and bypassed her over to Lula. "You got beautiful babies, Lula Mae," and then cut her eyes at Bervick, "you too."

Lula watched Samantha's head drop as she backed away leaving out. She listened to her aunt's heels step its way to the front door and out the house. Lula wanted to speak on Big Ma's actions toward Samantha, but saw how indifferent Big Ma was about it. Lula didn't want to make matters worse since she too wasn't on the best of terms with Big Ma, so Lula decided to leave the situation alone, saving it for a later date.

Big Ma tested the baby to see if she was strong enough to feed on Lula's breast. At first, the baby's mouth was weak and wasn't gripping, but after a few more tries, it finally gripped, sucking with a ferocious appetite.

Big Ma waved a hand above her head saying, "Glory be to God, thank yah Jesus!" The appetite was a sign that the baby was going to be all right.

Bervick said, "Glory, Glory, Gloria, Gloria Jean. The glory God gave us from heaven. Dis here child was blessed comin' into the world, so I'm gonna name her, Gloria Jean."

"Gloria Jean, I like that," Lula agreed, admiring Bervick's God given gift of wisdom. Lula chuckled, thankful that God blessed her with such an anointed husband. It was Bervick who prophesized that the baby was going to get sick if Lula kept working too hard, and if she had followed Bervick's orders in the beginning, Gloria Jean may not have fallen ill. Thanking God for another chance, Lula vowed to obey her husband's wishes and respect his prophetic views.

***

The first few weeks after the birth of baby Gloria Jean, Big Ma visited Lula every day, making sure her and the baby's health was improving. Big Ma would enter their home, hold Gloria Jean, play with Bervick Junior, cook, clean, and then return back home with Mary Lee before Doc came home from work. The more Big Ma visited, the more she knew her intuition about Bervick was correct. He wasn't the godly man he pretended to be. His behavior was rather unnerving. Bervick had no steady work to provide for his family, never lifted a finger to show he cared for Lula or his children, and made ridiculous prophecies of having God's powers while Lula sat back in admiration of her spiritual husband. He'd rejoice, screaming, "Halleluiah, thank yah Jesus," out of nowhere, creating an obstacle for Big Ma to remain cordial and hold her tongue. All Big Ma could do was turn the other cheek and pray that Lula would soon see that her husband wasn't mentally stable, and in the meantime, put her precious Lula and her blessed children in God's hands.

The one question Big Ma asked Lula was if she was returning to school, offering assistance in caring for her two babies if Lula agreed to go back. Lula stated that she still wanted to continue her education and planned to go back the following school year if the good Lord said the same.

Big Ma's civilly towards Bervick waned thin. Her dismissive attitude returned, causing tension thick enough to cut with a knife. Lula attempted to offset the rising hostility by starting conversations, including Bervick and Big Ma in them. Nonetheless, all attempts failed. Big Ma didn't like Bervick and he wasn't quite fond of Big Ma. Once Gloria Jean was strong enough, Big Ma's visits lessened until they ceased altogether.

On her last visit there, Big Ma put her and Bervick's differences aside to have a heart-to-heart talk. She pleaded with Bervick to wait on having more children and to allow Lula to complete her schooling, offering any assistance needed to make it a reality. Big Ma expressed to Bervick that Lula's body was still very young and needed time to heal after having two babies back-to-back. Bervick listened, nodding his head in hopes that Big Ma would stop talking. This was his family. He could do anything he pleased. Being fruitful and multiply was Bervick's Godly creed.

When Big Ma finished talking to Bervick, she went into the bedroom and kissed Lula and the babies good-bye. Lula melted, feeling her grandmother's touch again, only to have her heart break yet again watching Big Ma walk out of the room and out of Lula's life for a second time. Big Ma's presence brought a sense of familiarity and fullness back in Lula's life in a way only Big Ma could do. Nevertheless, a person of her word, Big Ma stuck around until Lula and Gloria Jean's health improved, and then, like a puff of smoke, she was gone. Big Ma promised herself that as long as Bervick was there, she had to remove herself from Lula's life, resting on the fact that Lula was in God's hands now and when the time arrived when Lula come to her senses, she'd be there with open arms for Lula.

Big Ma's last day there was a glorious day for Bervick—she would then stop interrupting his home with her presence. He didn't like the way Big Ma looked at him, as if she were looking right through him, making Bervick feel unsettled in his own home. *Good riddance, another devil gone,* he thought.

***

Lula missed Big Ma and Lillie sorely, but managed to move forward and be happy with her two children and Bervick. After being bedridden for weeks and caring for Gloria Jean and Bervick Jr. around the clock, Lula felt well enough to leave the house to get some air and visit neighbors to laugh and talk and introduce them to Gloria Jean.

Given that money was low and Bervick was devoting all of his time at church and doing evangelical work, he agreed to allow Lula to bake sweet dough pies for extra money, allotting him more free time to reach wayward souls and preach the word of God to them.

Lula was able to join Bervick for Sunday's service again after having Gloria Jean. Church folks swarmed to see the new baby after the ordeal around the birth. Lula caught glimpses of Big Ma sitting a few pews in front, but Big Ma never turned around once. At the end of service, Lula tracked down Mary to get updates about Lillie and send messages back to Lillie through Mary.

Things were back to normal. The town's people were happy to see Lula attending church service again, back to her old self with an alive and healthy baby. Neighbors and friends rarely visited Lula anymore. They were turned off by Bervick's long sermons that eventually ended with him portraying them as sinners, giving him more reason to continue preaching when they only stopped by to visit Lula or pick up their sweet dough pie.

Their house got busy with people coming to buy sweet dough pies, sometimes eating at the house when Bervick wasn't there. He'd stop by for afternoon supper, observe Lula filling orders and the traffic going in and out his house, then leave back out to preach. As much as they needed the money, Bervick didn't like Lula socializing and felt she made enough money, but the longer and harder she worked, the more difficult it became for him to tell Lula it was time to stop. It enraged Bervick when Lula added giant molasses cookies to sell. Furthermore, when he wasn't home, friends and neighbors stayed longer, eating dinner that Lula cooked, praising her food. They'd beg Lula to give up the secret in her food and she always responded saying, "Love," followed by her contagious laughter. When Bervick returned home, everyone suddenly forgot to do something, needed to be somewhere, or had to get home to their children. Whatever the case was, they got out of dodge when Bervick arrived.

Bervick was not pleased at people's reaction towards him, opposite of how they treated Lula, or how Lula's income from selling pies was increasing, and he hated when people praised her cooking and baking. Lula was his wife and must adhere to her wifely duties and tend to his needs only. Her baking started interfering with her being the wife God intended her to be for Bervick—at home cooking, cleaning, and having his babies. Bervick felt at age sixteen years-old, Lula was old enough to understand her role as a wife. Hence, there was no reason to discuss a matter she should already recognize.

Instead of speaking on the issue, Bervick sought out his God for an answer to force Lula to be the virtuous wife God intended her to be. God blessed them with more money from the baking, and indeed made it easier for Bervick to spread "the word" and save lost souls, but it was time for Lula to stop before she got too greedy. If her baking caused neglect to her wifely duties, it must come to end and Bervick prayed for an answer on how to make the baking cease altogether, again.

A feeling of bliss came over Bervick when the answer soon hit him. One hot afternoon, Lula left the house with Gloria Jean and Bervick Jr., holding a back pack she made by hand to deliver sweet dough pecan pies and molasses cookies to different friends and neighbors' houses. Bervick left as if he was going to go to church, and circled the block, hiding and waiting for Lula to disappear down the road. When she was no longer in sight, he sneaked back into the house, took all of Lula's dresses, grabbed a knife, and went in back of the house. He dropped the dresses on the ground and shredded each one, then bagged the shredded garments and carried them to the back of Mr. Pete's store, ducking and dodging his way to throw the bag over other trash bags.

Walking swiftly to church, Bervick felt elated.

Part 3

Chapter 14

By 1961, more babies joined Lula and Bervick's growing family. Sadly, a set of twin girls died at birth. Lula couldn't mourn the loss of her twins for long because at age twenty-two, she had six other children depending on her. Town people spoke amongst themselves about Lula and Bervick having children, one after the other, without enough income to support their growing family.

Money was tight for everyone in Eunice. As a community, people helped each other by sharing, bartering, or putting together resources.

Unluckily, Lula and Bervick were on their own with six children, which Bervick never seemed to mind. Church members, family, neighbors, and friends took turns stressing their concerns to Bervick on having too many children so close in age. When Big Ma saw Bervick in church, she pulled him aside, begging Bervick to let Lula heal every time she delivered another baby. Big Ma's wishes fell on deaf ears, as they always did. She would've gotten a better response from a rock than an obstinate man like Bervick. He'd quietly listened to the advice and complaints, allowing the information to juggle around in his head, then flee out his ear. God was in control of his and Lula's lives. Big Ma and everyone else's opinions were of no relevance to Bervick. As more town folks distanced themselves from Bervick, and by association, Lula too, Bervick came to understand what the Lord meant by the term: "Wolves in sheep's clothing." Bervick would rather walk alone with his family than to answer to ungodly heathens.

Contrary to people's opinions on Bervick, Lula continued to be the virtuous woman that God commanded wives to be, and a good mother to her children. Lula wanted to create the family she always wanted. The family she once had before the age of six. When she looked at her children, they represented her answered prayers of having a family unit again. Lula's biggest fear was for her children to endure the same fate she encountered—losing both parents at a young age. Lula envisioned her children raised by both parents who guided them through the journey of life, seeing them graduate from college, get married, and have children of their own while being saved Christians filled with the Holy Ghost.

Lula regretted eloping to marry Bervick against Big Ma's wishes, so to balance the shame with some dignity, Lula strived to be a good wife and great mother, despite their unfavorable financial circumstances. She wanted to prove to Big Ma that she wasn't a sinner and that she still was the devoted Christian girl Big Ma raised her to be.

Lula cooked for the church, attended church service every Sunday, and cleaned houses for the sick and elderly without payment—God's services to people in need was done without compensation. Lula involved herself in becoming a servant to God by serving the people in need along with caring for her children and Bervick. Every good deed was a step closer to heaven.

Lula delayed her return back to school, and dreams of starting a restaurant dwindled as time passed. She had children, a husband, church, and Christian duties to tend to. School had to wait. But her business idea didn't stray afar. It just took back seat, only to resurface when Lula cooked her favorite Creole dishes for dinner, imagining herself in a big kitchen preparing food for the people waiting to eat in her restaurant.

People still saw Lula as the sweet, friendly, and talkative woman they had grown to love, holding a special place in all their hearts.

Thus, they tolerated Bervick at times because of Lula. Neighbors and friends were forced to interact with him during times Lula fell ill before and after pregnancy. They'd washed clothes, cooked, cleaned, and cared for their children. When Lula got better, she didn't see much of them, except for in church or when she visited them without Bervick.

To take the feeling of abandonment away, Lula wanted to start doing what she loved most, baking and selling her sweet dough pies. It was now a need. Money was tight again. She stopped for a long period of time after most of her dresses went missing, but Lula wanted to bake pies again in hopes that Bervick would allow her to sell them. When she did ask, the question enraged Bervick. He thought the babies were enough to keep Lula preoccupied. Without much of a wardrobe and many infants to care for, Lula still yearned to do the very thing Bervick wanted to keep her from accomplishing. He told Lula he was going to give it some thought before making a decision, and stayed on his knees praying to calm his spirit and asked for the strength to get rid of Lula's irritating desire to sell pies. God provided enough for the family. Lula didn't need to sell any more pies.

In the meantime, Lula continued to rely on the food from their garden and chicken coop to feed their children, as well as the meat Bervick brought home from catching fish, shrimp, crab, or crawfish. Men from the church offered Bervick work in construction, loading docks, and slaughter houses to financially help him, aware of the situation at his home, but Bervick refused them all.

Bervick devoted his time and energy towards his future position in church, staying under Pastor Evans on a daily basis, working overtime to prove that he was the right man for the assistant pastor position. Bervick saw God's plan clearly. The assistant pastor position was going to endow him with abundance and give Bervick the opportunity to lead all sinners on the path of righteousness. This position was in accordance to what God wanted, shedding light on why he and Lula must crawl before they walk, proving there was light at the end of the tunnel. This made Bervick focus more on securing the sacrosanct position.

Bervick trained for the assistant pastor position by staying close to Pastor Evans, following Pastor Evans home every night, and knocking on his front door at the break of dawn every morning. Unexpected visits to Pastor Evans' house were the norm in Bervick's daily routine, and if the pastor wasn't there, Bervick waited outside. His determination flirted with obsession to the point that Pastor Evans had to forcefully shove Bervick out of the church to go home to his family.

Six years had passed since Pastor Evans' announced the opening for the assistant pastor position, and ever since then, Bervick revolved his entire life around attaining this position. His brother Curley worked for the position as well, except, he called it quits in the early evening to return back home to his family and rest for work the next morning.

Curley and Bervick hadn't spoken in years, except for in Pastor Evans' presence. Curley gave up on trying to mend their relationship years ago, concealing his pain by reciprocating the same cold vibe Bervick omitted towards him. Bervick didn't care. He was going to get that position at any and all cost.

One early morning, Bervick received a letter in the mail. He took it to a cousin to read out loud, and learned that an attorney in Lake Charles wanted to see him. He didn't understand why the attorney contacted him until the words "your" and "money" were mentioned. Bervick rushed to the bus station on foot, taking the first bus leaving to Lake Charles without telling anybody where he was headed. An hour later, Bervick arrived at the attorney's office in Lake Charles and was greeted with open arms.

Listening to the attorney speak, Bervick didn't understand a single word the attorney said as the attorney tried to explain Bervick's inheritance from property sold after his grandfather died, and that Bervick and his brothers were next to kin to receive the property after Christina, who passed away years ago. Because manufactures had no luck buying the property from his grandfather in Lake Charles, they waited until his death to buy the land from whomever the inheritor's were, which were Bervick and his siblings. They never authorized the sale, and with legal documents written in incomprehensible language, they didn't realize the sale took place without their consent.

Bervick looked at the papers and signed the agreement with an "X". The lawyer paused at the big "X", then proceeded in handing Bervick an envelope with a check inside. Bervick took the envelope wondering if a transaction such as this took so little time.

Looking at the attorney in his three piece suit, spit shined shoes, and white hair, tapping his fingers on the table and sweating bullets down his red face, Bervick figured it must be legit. Bervick did sense nervousness coming from the attorney. Nevertheless, all suspicions flew out the window when Bervick opened the envelope to find zero's next to his name. His eyes lit up. This was the most money he'd ever received in his life.

Thanking the attorney repeatedly, Bervick got up, shook the attorney's hand, and made his way to the door before the attorney could renege on the offer.

Bervick turned around before walking out and said, "Thank yah, sir."

"Call me, George."

Bervick bowed with every word. "Thank you, Mr. George. Thank yah, sir!"

"No, thank you."

Bervick strolled down the road, blowing kisses to the sky with his hands raised high, giving thanks to God all the way to the bus station. The two hour wait for the bus to Eunice felt like an eternity. Bervick could hardly sit still. He knew the Lord had provided him with a chance to change his life for the better. For the first time in Bervick's life, he could tell Lula that everything was going to be all right and mean it this time. A new beginning for his family had arrived. "Halleluiah," Bervick yelled.

***

When Bervick got off the bus, the first stop he made was to Big Ma's house. No one was home, so Bervick decided to pay Curley a visit. Bervick knocked on Curley's door and waited, rocking back and forth on the heels of his feet with his hands behind his back. When Curley opened the door, he put his hand out to embrace Bervick, glad to see Bervick wanted to make amends after too many years apart. Bervick kept his hands behind his back, leaving Curley standing in an embracing position. Curley's hands dropped, wondering why Bervick was there if not for that reason.

Bervick said, "Get ready," and walked off without looking back.

Curley was confused. Watching Bervick whistling, prancing down the road, made Curley know for certain that something was wrong with his brother and hoped the good Lord would watch over Bervick's poor wife and children.

Bervick went back to Big Ma's house, snapping his fingers in disappointment that she was still gone, taking away his chance to gloat. Bervick calmed his anger with the notion that it was better she wasn't home. The shock factor on what was to come was enough to make Big Ma have a heart attack. Bervick smiled at the visual and thanked God for Big Ma's soon to be absence.

Bervick's last stop was the church. He whistled his way there, waving at passers-by, going out of his way to greet everyone. When he arrived at the church, Bervick whistled up the steps, patting his pants pocket with the check in it. He found Pastor Evans sweeping the front church area.

Bervick said, "Pastor Evans, beautiful day t'day isn't it, sir?"

Pastor Evans cringed at the sound of the voice behind him and turned around forcing a polite greeting. "I reckon," he muttered.

Pastor Evans was shocked to see a rarity on Bervick's face—a smile. He was used to Bervick being a serious man, always on a mission.

"Can we talk in private, sir?"

Before Pastor Evans could decline, Bervick was already walking towards the back of the church to Pastor Evans' office.

"Lord Jesus, help me!" Pastor Evans mumbled through his teeth, smacking the broom on the floor, looking up at the ceiling shaking his head. He moved slowly to his back office and took a seat behind his desk.

The office had a wooden desk taking up most of the space in the room, and a leather seat that wasn't enough to compliment the worn wooden chairs for visitors to sit. On the desk were pictures of the pastor's wife and two kids in wooden frames, an agenda book with his initials engraved on it, and a small plant with small dark leaves. Religious ornaments he collected through the years surrounded the room creating a cluttered display.

Bervick pointed to the candy dish full of Mary Jane's on the desk. "May I, sir?"

Pastor Evans motioned Bervick to help himself. Curiosity built on the reason for Bervick's visit. He did not eat candy. But for Bervick, today was a day to celebrate with something sweet.

Pastor Evans leaned back in his black leather chair, crossing his hands over his stomach. "What brings you here today, Bervick?"

Bervick put his finger up for Pastor Evans to wait, he was still chewing. Pastor Evans scratched at his eyebrow, blinking fast in irritation.

Bervick began, "So yah need a new assistant pastor?"

"I do, Bervick," Pastor Evans said, as if he were talking to a child.

"And yah makin' the announcement at dis Sunday's service, correct?"

"Bervick, I told you once, I'm not telling you again, I'm not giving you any information. You're gonna have to find out this Sunday like everyone else."

"No, sir, that's not what I'm here for...unless you care to give me a hint since, in all due respect, sir, it's been six years."

Pastor Evans looked stone faced.

Bervick laughed, "It was worth a shot, sir. Halleluiah!"

Pastor Evans' stone face didn't change. Bervick quickly stopped laughing and straightened up.

Bervick said, "I just wanna say, it was an honor to work and learn from yah, sir. I want dis position more than anything in life. Dis is what God put me on dis here earth fo'. Dis is my life purpose! So that being said, I have a gift fo' yah from the Lord, Jesus Christ."

Bervick pulled out the envelope and handed it to Pastor Evans, who sat up in his chair and put on his glasses to open it.

He looked up at Bervick. "Bervick, this is a check for fifteen hundred dollars. What you want me to do with this?"

"That check shows how much I'm indebted to you, sir. I'll sign it over to yah in the name of our father, Jesus Christ. Halleluiah!"

Pastor Evans leaned back in his chair folding his hands over his stomach, shaking his head at Bervick. He said, "What are you doing, son?"

"Nothin', sir. I'm just doin' what God told me to do. Dis here check was given to me by God to give back to my church."

"Bervick, I can't—"

"Yes you can! Yah can't say no to the will of God, sir. I'm his faithful servant. All I ask is that you remember dis here gift b'fore yah make your decision," Bervick said, and before Pastor Evans could speak, Bervick got up and rushed out the office.

It was dark outside when Bervick finally made it home. He was tired from the long travel to and from Lake Charles. Time waned as anticipation ate at Bervick's conscious.

Lula was in the kitchen cooking a light snack while the kids ran around playing. When Bervick walked in, Lula ran over kissing his lips. "How was yah trip dis mornin'? You hungry?"

"How yah kno' I took a trip?"

"We in Eunice. Eyes are everywhere."

"It was good. No, I'm not hungry."

"How yah brother's doin out there, Sha?"

"Good."

"You visit Papa Joe?"

"Yeah."

"How's he doin'?"

"Good."

Bervick's short responses signaled Lula to stop asking questions. His one word answers meant he didn't feel like talking. Lula went back to seasoning and buttering the baked sweet potatoes and asked, "Yah got any money? I need to buy somethin' fo' the baby to chew on. She's teethin' and I don't wanna ask Aunt Samantha fo' any more money."

"I'm sho' Samantha wouldn't mind you askin' fo' money, Sha."

"I kno' she won't mind, but I'm shame every time I ask her. Did yah get the construction job that man offered yah?"

"I didn't get that job, but everything's gonna be okay. Trust me, Lula Mae. Trust God."

***

Easter Sunday was a day every member of the church had been waiting for: the announcement of the new assistant pastor for the church. Everyone anticipated this day for so long, even non-members came out for this special occasion.

Big Ma led the church women in preparation for Easter Sunday's feast, working hard all week, cleaning, cooking, and prepping. They made homemade rolls, fried chicken, greens, dirty rice, red beans and rice, crackling, chitterlings, barbeque pork, stewed chicken, andouille sausage stew, cornbread dressing, sauce piquant with crawfish, fried buffalo fish, fried okra, and seafood gumbo. Lula made sweet dough apple, sweet potato, and peach pies along with molasses pecan candy and teacakes. Other members brought pies, cakes, fruit, and side dishes. Countless watermelons were donated from Watermelon man Bue's truck and Mr. Pete supplied the ice. The food alone was an incentive for everyone to attend. Pastor Evans put up the money to finance the cost for the food. The rest of the food came from church members dropping off necessities at Big Ma's house such as flour, eggs, sugar, live chickens, and rice.

Bervick was eager to go to church this Easter Sunday morning, unable to eat or sleep a wink. He paced around outside all night, praying and chanting praises to his Lord Jesus Christ. When dawn broke, Bervick ran inside to find Lula up already ironing everyone's church clothes. He saw his special suit freshly pressed hanging neatly up against the door. Bervick kissed Lula's cheek and got dressed, thanking his Lord for his virtuous wife. She hid her pain while finishing the ironing, laying all the clothes out neatly across the bed, working in silence so the children didn't wake.

Lula dragged her feet, weak from her last delivery and felt sharp pains in her stomach, distracting her from concentrating fully on ironing. She had worked hard all week, preparing sweet dough pies for Easter Sunday, and did it with a smile even though she was delirious from pain and fatigue.

Lula felt lethargic caring for her children when Bervick was gone. Samantha assisted Lula with the children prior to Easter Sunday, after Bervick allowed Samantha back in the house if it meant he didn't have to bother tending to his children's needs. That was a woman's job. It was either going to be him or Samantha, and Bervick wasn't about to let anything stand in the way of his goals by assisting in a woman's duty.

Samantha was concerned about Lula. It was taking Lula longer to get back on her feet after each pregnancy. Every time Samantha saw Bervick, she wanted to kick him in the rear. She'd tell Lula that if Bervick wasn't outside pestering people, he would have more time to get a job and take care of his family.

Lula was thankful for Samantha's help, given that she was one of the few family members left in Lula's life after marrying Bervick.

Samantha knew all too well about standing one's ground on convictions and belief, and knew Lula was doing just that for her marriage. Samantha saw a lot of herself in Lula; consequently, minimizing her opposition on who Lula chose to love. All Samantha could do was support Lula by offering financial assistance, which Lula either declined or hesitantly accepted if she needed it bad enough. On many occasions, Samantha sent Bue to leave bags of food on Lula's porch to prevent Lula the shame and embarrassment of asking. Lula's pride and faith in Bervick caused unnecessary suffrage in their lives that angered Samantha, but she concealed it well.

Lula never asked Bervick for help knowing he was too busy securing the assistant pastor position in church. That position was going to change their lives for the better and Lula was going to stand by Bervick, assisting him in any and everything needed as the devoted God fearing Christian wife she strived to be.

Bervick walked out of the bedroom with his head high announcing, "T'day is the day that will change our lives forever. Get ready, Lula Mae, the time is now! Halleluiah, thank yah Jesus!"

Easter Sunday's weather was neither hot nor cold; it was just right for the occasion. Bervick and Lula walked to church with their children. Gloria Jean held her little sister, Sandra Dee. Lula held her newborn, Deborah, in her arms. The three toddlers, Joseph, little Leroy, and Luvicy held on to their big brother Bervick Jr.'s hand.

Bervick walked in front, dusting unseen dirt off his tailor made white suit loaned to him on his wedding, which Bervick never returned to his cousin. He saved the suit for another special occasion.

Joe sent Bervick a pair of brand new white shoes when Bervick told his father he was about to become assistant pastor of a church.

Lula wore white as well, except her dress wasn't new. After her dress collection vanished years ago, Lula resorted to wearing a few old dresses Big Ma made years ago. She altered two dresses into one, and walking barefoot, Lula overcompensated her shabby attire by doing her hair in fancy curls.

The children were dressed in their best clothes and were barefoot, too. Lula pieced together their every day clothes, cleaned and starched them to make their clothes look fresh for Easter Sunday. She trimmed the boy's hair with scissors and did the girls' hair in cute ponytails with white ribbons and barrettes.

When they arrived at church, they were one of the first families there. Bervick went to the front and sat in the first pew. Lula sat with the children four pews behind him, pulling out a piece of Doublemint gum to keep from passing out. She rocked her baby in her arms, mentally preparing herself for the work that awaited after service. Lula's eyes closed humming a prayer to God, asking him to give her strength.

The children sat beside Lula playing games with their paper fans and some already falling asleep. They were obedient during service, molded since birth on how to behave. If one attempted to misbehave, another one was there to put them in check. Their ages were in consecutive steps, from one month old to seven years-old, except the gap between Joseph and baby Deborah where the twins were born.

Everyone trickled into church dressed in their best. Big hats, gloves, freshly pressed suits, dresses, and scarves were worn as if a fashion show was about to take place.

When church members greeted Lula or stopped by the pew for a quick chitchat, Lula noticed them looking down at her dress, then back at her with sympathetic smiles while adding extra emphasis on how great her hair looked. Taking their seats, the women whispered behind Lula's back, blaming Bervick for the way she was dressed. Some snickered at Lula's misfortune, resenting the fact that Lula was still an attractive young woman. Even in shabby garbs, Lula stood out from the rest.

Lula got up to change Deborah's diaper. Gloria Jean, who was about to turn seven years-old, followed her mother, wanting to help change her little sister. Lula walked past the church women, old and young, greeting them with warm smiles and nods of 'Praise the Lord'. They quickly smiled back, some disguising their jealousy when they saw how slim Lula was after having her last baby.

Lula quickly changed Deborah, and then they returned back to their seats in time for service, not wanting to miss a moment of this glorious day.

Pastor Evans spoke his sermon in haste, aware of the highly anticipated food, fun, and most of all, the announcement of the new assistant pastor. The congregation sang faster, shortened their prayers, and amazingly, no one caught the Holy Ghost, not even Bervick, much to everyone's relief.

Pastor Evans preached in front of his church for twenty-five years. Mindful of his age catching up with him, he sought out to find the most saved and sanctified assistance to become his apprentice, and eventually become pastor of the church one day.

Pastor Evans' retirement approached, and for six years, he dedicated a lot of his time in observing the candidates to find the best man for the position. Out of fifteen prospects, it came down to four men, including Bervick and Curley. These were the men who proved to be the most determined and dedicated men. Unbeknownst to the four men, Pastor Evans furtively received feedback from trustworthy missionaries and elders of the church to provide information to assist in his decision. Based on the feedback, and his own prayers and observations, Pastor Evans made a decision.

When service ended, Pastor Evans took time to speak on the men individually, giving backgrounds on how and why they stood before the church. He spoke on why this process took so long and finally informed his congregation that once the assistant pastor acclimated into the position, they would further their study to become pastor, in which Pastor Evans could retire.

People heard Pastor Evans' words and couldn't foresee the church without him. He was irreplaceable. He was loved by them all and would surely be missed.

At the end of Pastor Evans' speech, he got choked up, turning his attention back to the final four men. Bervick balled his fist, nervous and excited at the same time. This was the day he'd been waiting for, ever since the announcement six years ago. Bervick dreamed of himself standing in front of the church preaching the word of God. He didn't want his sacrifices to have been done in vein. Throughout Lula's sicknesses, the birth of their children, countless days in church, seldom jobs, and memorizing future sermons was soon about to pay off. Bervick sacrificed it all and would've done it again if need be. Nothing deterred him from his duty for the Lord. The people who doubted Bervick would soon have to bow down and kiss his feet because only he, God's prophet, could lead these heathens to salvation.

Pastor Evans asked everyone to stand. The four men upfront shook hands wishing each other luck.

Silence in the church.

Lula waved at Bervick, who winked back at her. Standing proud with his head held high full of confidence, Bervick was ready. Curley nudged Bervick, nodding his head to make a truce with his brother. Bervick nodded back in reconciliation as well.

Pastor Evans looked over the congregation, smiling at their curious and impatient faces. He turned to the four men, feeling confident in his decision.

He said, "It's been a long journey to get to this moment. It took a lot of time, prayer, and consideration. Now, we are finally here. Can the church say 'Amen'?"

"Amen."

"The men you see before you have proven themselves to be God fearing men worthy of this position in many ways. Unfortunately, there can only be one. Ladies and Gentlemen, I present to you, your new assistant pastor…"

Pastor Evans proudly walked from behind the pulpit, to a bishop who had come to partake in the ceremony. The bishop handed Pastor Evans a pendant and gave an approving nod. Pastor Evans walked over to the four men, going back and forth in front of them, heightening everyone's anticipation.

Bervick stuck his chest out ready to receive his victory. Pastor Evans stopped in front of Bervick and grinned. Bervick smiled back patting the left side of his chest for the pendant to be placed there. Pastor Evans smiled back at Bervick, took a deep breath, and went over to place the pendant on Curley. "Our new assistant pastor is, Brother Curley Frank!"

Everyone roared, cheering and applauding, rejoicing into a song. Curley Frank, their newly appointed assistant pastor and future pastor for the church. Curley hugged Pastor Evans, shook Bervick and the other two men's hands, and waved at his wife and children.

Lula's hand was over her mouth, astonished and horrified for Bervick. She waved her hand to get Bervick's attention, but he didn't look her way.

Rage permeated Bervick's heart, circulated through his veins, spreading throughout every inch of his body. His skin turned beet red as sweat struggled to cool Bervick's rising body temperature. His fist balled, jaws tightened, and breaths shortened as he struggled to mask a look of approval for Curley.

Bervick finally looked over at Lula, watching her wave and blow kisses at him. He rolled his eyes detesting Lula's levity at a time like this. *How dare she smile at me! To hell with her, Pastor Evans, Curley, this church. To hell with everyone. Damn them all to hell!* He thought. Bervick saw he was surrounded by devils that disobeyed God's order, Pastor Evans being the main heathen. The money given to him was a gift from God and Pastor Evans chose to ignore it. Bervick had to get away from that God forsaken church, and fast.

***

A couple of weeks had passed since Pastor Evans' announcement, and Bervick wasn't feeling any better than he was on that fretful Easter Sunday. His behavior was distant. He was docile toward everyone, especially Lula.

Bervick visited Pastor Evans a week after the announcement, asking for his money back. Pastor Evans informed him that the money was in the church's treasury. Bervick left Pastor Evans speaking in mid-sentence, not wanting to hear another word from him. He never looked back and planned on never attending that church again.

Bervick felt embarrassed, ashamed, and most of all, feared his secret will soon be exposed. The one thing he'd kept hidden for most of his life. The one thing he didn't want anyone to find out. The one thing he felt was his lone flaw as God's prophet. Living in a gossip stricken town such as Eunice, Louisiana, made it inevitable for his secret to soon emerge.

Lula took it upon herself to visit Pastor Evans to apologize for their sudden absence from church. She sat with him to get to the bottom of why Bervick wasn't chosen for the position. She thought maybe if Bervick heard a reasonable justification, he wouldn't be as upset and allow their family to return back to church.

Lula entered his office and didn't waste any time asking the question. Pastor Evans was shocked at her audacity. As a pastor, he wasn't a man to be questioned and never had to offer an explanation for his actions. However, he loved Lula dearly and excused her impudence.

The sight of Lula brought up old feelings for Beatrice that Pastor Evans thought was long gone, tucked away with a lock and key, never to open again. After Beatrice went missing years ago, Pastor Evans went on his own search for her, coming up short each time.

He looked away so he wouldn't see Beatrice's face.

Pastor Evans' wife, Dorotheanne Evans, became suspicious when she saw Pastor Evans constantly looking at Beatrice during sermons, and when he invited Beatrice to dinner, he acted as if Dorotheanne wasn't at the table. The day Pastor Evans built up the gumption to reveal his feelings to Beatrice in a letter, Leroy and Beatrice came into the church holding hands sitting next to each other. It broke Pastor Evans' heart watching Leroy court Beatrice, and to make matters worse, he had to marry the two love birds. But Pastor Evans' preferential treatment towards Beatrice didn't stop there. Leroy detected Pastor Evans' odd behavior with Beatrice, which only boosted Leroy's ego to have the pastor smitten on Beatrice. Dorotheanne, on the other hand, didn't take too kindly to it. After years of witnessing Pastor Evans treating Beatrice with preferential treatment, and finding the love letter he had written to her, Dorotheanne took matters into her own hands by introducing Leroy to her niece, Cordelia. Dorotheanne knew Cordelia had been infatuated with Leroy for a long time, but Cordelia didn't pursue Leroy, fearing Beatrice. Hence, Dorotheanne gave an address to Cordelia, informing her that this elderly woman named Tauntadi would make Cordelia's every dream come true with Leroy. Dorotheanne knew when it came to men, Cordelia was an obsessive lunatic, suiting Dorotheanne's purpose perfectly. It wasn't too long after that, Beatrice was gone for good, away from Dorotheanne's husband. When Pastor Evans heard that Leroy didn't tell Papa Top where Beatrice was, he took it upon himself to visit Leroy, telling him that neither he nor Cordelia were no longer welcome in his church and suggested they move away from Eunice.

Back in the office, Pastor Evans offered Lula a Mary Jane while popping one in his mouth.

"No, sir," she said politely, unwrapping a piece of Doublemint gum.

Pastor Evans said, "I reckon I do owe you an explanation."

"Sir, I just hope it's not b'cause of what I think it is."

"And what's that?"

Lula hesitated. She didn't want to disclose Bervick's secret to Pastor Evans in case he wasn't aware, yet she couldn't lie to the pastor.

"Pastor Evans, Bervick, he, well, sir, he can't read," Lula hung her head.

Pastor Evans sat back in his chair folding his hands over his stomach. "I already figured that. Bervick maneuvered around it very well!"

Lula looked up puzzled. "Sir?"

"I noticed when Bervick cited scriptures, he never once looked at his bible. I commend his dedication, but, it was a little odd to say the least. To memorize the bible, page-by-page," Pastor Evans shook his head. "I never called him out on it. To be perfectly honest with you, Lula Mae, that's not the reason why I didn't choose him. I need a man with integrity, honor, and compassion to lead my congregation one day. Your husband is not quite there yet."

Lula looked incomprehensively at Pastor Evans.

He said, "Let me put it this way, a man that cannot take care of his family cannot take care of a church. I judge a man based on character. It's not what he do in front of the church when all eyes are on him, it's what he does when nobody's looking. An honorable man takes care of his family first without seeking a reward or pat on the back. A man that can do this is the right man for my church. A true man of God!"

"But he does take care of us, Pastor Evans, he really does. We have issues with money at times, but who doesn't, sir."

"You're a beautiful woman, Lula Mae, and he's a very lucky man to have you as his wife." Pastor Evans was too disgusted to speak about Bervick any longer. He was somewhat ashamed of himself for taking the money from Bervick, and wanted to tell Lula about it, but couldn't go against the man of the house by discussing this matter with his wife.

Pastor Evans got up and fumbled with his keys to open the drawer to his desk, digging fifty dollars out a stack of money, then quickly closed it back up. "I don't want you to tell no one about this, you understand?"

"Yes, sir."

Dorotheanne peeked her head in. "You ready, honey?" She smiled, surprised to see Lula sitting there. "Hi there, Mrs. Lula Mae. Where have yah been? Haven't seen yah in church lately, Sha."

"I'll be there in just a minute," Pastor Evans said, rushing his wife away. Lula was thankful for the interruption because, for some unknown reason, she didn't care for Dorotheanne even though she was nice and always smiled.

"Alright, honey. See yah later, Mrs. Lula Mae," Dorotheanne said, closing the office door behind her.

"Put that somewhere safe for a rainy day and take care of yourself, Lula Mae." Pastor Evans led Lula to the door. "Everything is gonna be alright. As long as you trust in God and continue to be the devoted Holy Ghost filled Christian woman you are."

"I will, sir. Thank yah, sir."

Later that day, Lula was home with the children when she heard a knock on the door. She opened it and was shocked to see Lillie standing there with her two children. They hugged, jumping up and down screaming, unable to let each other go. Lillie was visiting from Humble, Texas, and was four months pregnant. Lula kept in contact with Lillie through Mary and letters since Bernard monitored Lillie's contact with family.

Lula smiled down at Lillie's children, meeting them for the first time. She bent down pinching their cheeks, asking if they were thirsty.

"Yes, ma'am," they answered. Lula gave them cups of water and told all the children to go play outside so she could put baby Deborah down for a nap.

Lillie's two children, Janice and Melvin, were well-mannered. Janice was a sweet child with round eyes, button nose, and small lips. Melvin was the outgoing one, a skinny boy with deep brown skin and gentle eyes. His lighthearted personality was contagious and he always stole the spotlight when dancing.

Lula and Lillie stood in the front door laughing at Melvin performing for his cousins, teaching them how to move.

Lillie and Lula laughed their way back to the kitchen. She gave Lillie a glass of water and heated the potbelly stove to cook while Lillie sat down exhausted from the long bus ride. She fanned herself after getting overheated in the muggy weather, wearing a white long-sleeve blouse, skirt below the knees, and closed toe sandals that she quickly kicked off. Her hair was loosely curled, turning thick from the sweat absorbing in it.

Lula heated the stove to cook eggs and rice and warmed tea cakes while laughing and talking with Lillie like old times. She updated Lillie on everything that happened since they last saw each other. Lillie quietly listened. When Lula stopped to catch her breath from talking, she asked for an update on Lillie, who wasn't too eager to speak about herself, giving one word answers. To take the spotlight off herself, Lillie knew Lula all too well and asked the right questions to get Lula running her mouth again.

Lula spoke, grabbing at Lillie's arm recollecting a fond memory.

Lillie winced pulling her arm back.

"What's wrong, Sha?" Lula asked, feeling bad that she hurt Lillie. "Did I grab yah too hard?" Before Lula said another word, her worries turned into anger. She took Lillie's arm and pushed the sleeve back, gasping at the black and blue marks on Lillie's arm. Lula looked up with her mouth open.

Lillie said, "Please don't."

Lula stood there looking Lillie in the eye.

"I beg you, please don't." The look in Lillie's eye scared Lula more than the bruise itself. She gently pulled Lillie's sleeve down and buttoned it back up.

Lula said, "You kno' yah always have a place to stay here. It ain't much, but we'll make a way, Sha."

Lillie took a sip of water and held the cup between her hands staring at it, lost in thought.

Lula said, "I still need that recipe fo' that butter cake."

That got Lillie's attention. She smiled and told Lula how to make it.

In between their discussion, Lillie asked, "Where's Bervick?"

"I don't kno'."

"I heard what happened. I'm sorry, Sha."

"I'm tryin' to forget that day, Lillie Mae. They cheated him. Pastor Evans told me that Bervick wasn't the man fo' the job b'cause he wasn't a family man, but if that's the sacrifice Bervick had to make, then so be it."

"There'll be brighter days. Jesus always makes a way. Yah just make sho' yah doin' your part no matter what."

"Oh I am. I'm honoring my vows, Sha. It's just that, I don't know."

"Yah don't kno' what?"

"It would be nice to have a steady income and a little help with the kids. How do I kno' he's doin' his part?"

"Doesn't matter what he doin', just make sho' yah being the wife God wants yah to be so dem pearly white gates can open to heaven. Hell, Fire and Brimstone won't be our fate, Sha."

"But don't yah think God wants you protected first?"

"To whom much is given, much is required. God won't put nothin' on me that I can't handle."

Lula nodded.

Lillie finished the rest of her water and sat it on the table, twirling the cup with one hand, falling deep in thought. Lula resumed cooking and they both were silent for the moment, listening to the movement of the cup.

Lillie asked in a low tone, "What else I'm gonna do?"

"What yah mean?"

"If I leave Bernard, what else am I gonna do? Where will me and my chillun go?"

"I told yah, you can come stay here."

Lillie looked around at the pint size space, already too small for Lula and her children. She smiled at Lula's offer.

Lillie searched the time and quickly said, "I gotta go."

"Why? Yah just got here. I'm not done cookin' yet."

"Can I take it with me fo' the bus ride? I gotta get back home soon. I can't be late!"

Lula flatly said, "Yah sho'?"

"Yeah, I'm sho'."

As Lula prepped the meal for Lillie to take on the bus, Lillie called Janice and Melvin into the house.

"Ma'am?" They answered.

"Com'on, get ready to go."

Chapter 15

Bervick was outside working in the garden. He spent most of his time pulling weeds, planting, and maintaining his vegetables while trying to keep his mind off Curley stealing the assistant pastor position away. The world no longer existed to Bervick. Lula would go outside and try to console him, but all Bervick did was continue working quietly in the garden, hours at a time, contemplating his next move.

Weeks passed. Bervick contacted his friend Cleve, who had moved out west to California a few years back. A lot of Bervick's family relocated to California from Lake Charles and Eunice, in search of a new life away from the south.

It didn't take much convincing from Cleve for Bervick to consider moving to California. His next step was to figure out how. Bervick returned to the garden to work and listen for God's voice and command.

At night when the children were asleep, Bervick lay down with Lula and said, "We're gettin' out of here!"

"Out of where?"

"Out of Eunice! Dis here town full of devils. I can't stand to look at their faces anymore."

"I kno' yah not serious! Where we gonna go?"

"As far away as possible. California."

"California! Bervick, we can't just up and leave like that. Our families here."

"My point exactly!"

Lula was quiet.

Bervick said, "I've already talked to Cleve and some cousins out there bout jobs and homes. Yah remember the last time they visited, tellin' us how great it was out there? I didn't realize back then that that's where we belonged in the first place. They got a big church out there and everythin'. We can start a new life out there and forget bout these heathens 'round here."

"Yah talk to Curley since Easter Sunday?"

Bervick gave Lula her answer with one look.

Lula grew frightened by the minute, biting at her bottom lip. She didn't want a bigger wedge between her and her family. They were distant enough as it was already. "I don't kno', I lived here all my life. Eunice is my home. It's all I kno'."

"And what have Eunice done fo' you? Fo' me? Fo' us or dis here family? Nothin'! Your kin stopped carin' bout yah the day yah married me and they act as if our chillun don't even exist. And quite frankly, Lula Mae, I'm tired of being surrounded by these heathens. All they do is talk bout us and laugh behind our back. I'm tired of it! No more! We gonna start a new life somewhere else where we can be appreciated."

"Aunt Samantha is there fo' me."

"Samantha's a whore. It's bad enough I allow that devil in my house."

"Please stop, that's not nice. Grandma Emma comes 'round sometimes and Papa Top do, too."

"Emma lives in Texas and Papa Top over on Happy Hill, too busy workin' in that shop."

"But Bervick—"

"We're leavin' and that's final! God showed me what to do and we're doin' it. He gave me a vision. A new start is what we need. All we need is the money and we're gone! I might have to go out there with Cleve fo' a while to find some work. I'll contact him to start makin' arrangements."

Lula had no choice but to concede. Her husband had spoken and usually when Bervick had his visions, they came to pass on many occasions.

Lula said, "I'll ask my family fo' money."

Bervick chuckled. His God was in control. Nobody else. Bervick was glad to hear Lula's efforts and insisted she do so since he knew it would be a cold day in hell before Lula's family gave her any money, but Bervick wanted Lula to find that out for herself.

In a way, Lula welcomed a change from Eunice. Word around town was that California was the land of milk and honey. Folks that moved out west reported back on how their lives changed for the better. She figured there would be available work for Bervick, better education for the children, and maybe a chance at continuing her own education.

Lula asked, "When yah tryin' to move out there?"

"As soon as possible, if the good Lord say the same. Cleve will help us. God told me so."

Lula smiled kissing Bervick on his cheek.

***

Bervick gladly watched their kids when Lula went to visit different family member's houses. Lula was confident that people would assist financially, as they always did for one another. People took collections for weddings, funerals, relocations, birthdays, graduations, and other events. Most were low income households, which impelled the town to work as a unit, putting money together, assisting each other in achieving their desired goals as a community.

Aware of this, and never being a person who asked for much, Lula knew she would be able to collect money to reach her desired goal to move.

Everyone welcomed Lula with open arms, thinking she had finally come to senses and left Bervick, but when Lula asked for financial assistance to help them move to California, her family turned cold and standoffish again. She tried to explain how moving would provide a fresh start for her family, with great jobs for Bervick and schooling for the kids. Still, everyone shunned Lula. They gave her an ultimatum: leave Bervick or no help. Some said "no" point blank. Samantha was the only one who gave Lula money, although it wasn't much. She didn't want Lula to leave.

As long as Lula was in Eunice, Samantha was able to keep a watchful eye on Bervick, making sure he didn't get out of line with Lula or their children. It bothered Samantha that she would no longer be Lula's secret protector if she moved to California.

Every time Lula set foot on a family member's porch, she cringed, embarrassed to ask for money, but she forced her pride aside and prayed for at least one family member to support her in the decision to move. Alas, Lula was devastated by how easily the family denied her, some with smiles on their faces. These were the same people who collected the little money Lula had for their own expenditures and needs.

It seemed the only family that would've cared to assist Lula were all out of reach. Grandma Emma and Lillie lived in Texas, and Papa Top was too busy working in his repair shop in Happy Hill.

Barefoot and sweating out curls, Lula walked up the road following a trail of smoke that carried a delicious aroma, perking up her taste buds. Lula inhaled deeply already tasting the yummy barbeque on her tongue.

Leroy's younger brother, Daniel Lee, stood in the heat manning the grill, looking through the smoke at a figure of a woman walking towards him. He put the grill lid over the meat to seal in the smoke flavor, and waved smoke away from his eyes to see who was coming. "Lula Mae, that you, Sha?"

"Hey unc!"

"Hey! What brings yah here t'day? Haven't seen yah in a month of Sundays."

Daniel Lee smiled. He hadn't seen much of Lula after she married Bervick.

Before Lula could answer, Leroy's older brother, Willie Ray, came out the house carrying a pan of more seasoned meat marinating in a special sauce. He sat the pan next to the grill, wiping the excess juice off his hand onto a towel hanging over his shoulder.

Willie Ray said, "Hey there, baby girl. What yah kno' good?" He put his hand up for Lula not to hug him, pointing at the sweat covering his shirt. He took the towel from his shoulder and wiped off his forehead. Between the scorching hot sun, humidity, and heat from the barbeque pit, it felt like a hundred degrees plus out there.

Lula asked, "What y'all doin' barbequing in all dis here heat? Y'all gonna mess 'round and have a stroke out here."

Daniel Lee said, "Yeah, but we gotta get these orders filled by t'night. Mrs. Dupont's daughter gettin' married tomorrow."

Willie Ray added, "Its bout time, too! That big ole gal almost thirty and still ain't married."

Daniel Lee laughed, "Yeah, that's a big gal there. That's why we gotta get dis here meat ready. That family sho' nuff can eat!" He lifted the grill lid, placed the marinating raw meat on the other side of the grill, and stirred their special barbeque sauce, dabbing it on the sizzling meat.

He picked a piece up with a fork. "Hmm, humph. Look at that there meat. Don't get no betta than that," he said, placing it back on the grill and continued stirring the rest of the sauce.

Lula and Willie Ray stood there watching Daniel Lee dab every piece of meat with their special barbeque sauce, listening to the sizzle. Lula's stomach growled. Daniel Lee heard it and picked up a piece of cooked meat and placed it on a slice of bread, "Here yah go, Sha."

Lula was shocked her uncle gave up a piece a meat. "Thanks, Uncle Lee, I'm starvin'!"

Willie Ray asked, "How's everythin' goin' with yah?"

"I'm fine and the kids are good."

"Heard yah been sick?"

"On and off, mainly during my pregnancies. Aunt Samantha helps me out a lot tho'."

"My sister? Takin' care of kids? Nah I done I heard it all."

They laughed.

Lula got quiet, realizing her uncles were aware of her being sick and never once bothered to see if she was okay. She couldn't believe these were the same uncles that watched her grow up playing with their children, and gave her a penny to buy treats at Mr. Pete's store. Her heart broke standing there.

Lula blurted, "I'm movin'," before she lost the gumption to ask them for money.

Willie Ray and Daniel Lee simultaneously looked up at Lula.

Daniel Lee placed the lid back on the grill.

Lula continued, "Me, Bervick, and the kids are movin' to California."

Willie Ray yanked the sauce stained towel, smacking at the air. "How the hell Bervick Frank movin' y'all to California when he hardly take care of y'all here in Eunice?"

Lula said, "Fo' a new start."

Daniel Lee said, "Is that so, Sha?"

"Yes, sir."

Willie Ray shook his head looking down at the ground with one hand on his hip. The gossip was true.

Daniel Lee and Willie Ray were both tall, muscular built men with dark brown skin, and similar features to Leroy. They were fairly handsome men and prosperous due to their lucrative barbeque pit business. Everyone in Eunice and the surrounding areas bought barbeque from them, loving the secret barbeque sauce. As much as people tried, no one could decipher what the ingredients in the sauce were that made it so incredibly tasty. The sauce was so delicious that on more than one occasion, people knocked on their door in the middle of the night to inquire if any barbeque meat was left. Willie Ray and Daniel Lee quickly learned to have extra cooked meat ready for those unexpected visits.

They went from working only weekends to every day, working long hours in the sun. Money was their motivation.

Lula would send Gloria Jean to get a barbeque sandwich as a treat. Aware of Lula and Bervick's tight budget, Daniel Lee still took every cent from Gloria Jean. Daniel Lee was a greedy man who hoarded money worse than Ebenezer Scrooge, living a meager lifestyle, and was just as cheap with himself as he was with his wife and children. He justified his tightfisted by claiming that it was he who slaved over the barbeque in the heat every day, therefore, he's the only one entitled to the money. When his wife challenged him about money, he'd beat her. The town folks witnessed Daniel Lee's wife wearing sunglasses, which still didn't hide the black bruises. In spite the obvious, everyone minded their own business. The unspoken creed amongst the community was to stay out of marital affairs, and if a wife challenged her husband, who ultimately had the final say, she deserved it. Daniel Lee beat his wife the same way he watched Doc beat on Big Ma. He hated Doc for beating on Big Ma, and vowed that he'd never be like Doc while watching helplessly as a little boy huddled together with Leroy, Willie Ray, and Samantha—all too young to rescue Big Ma. Daniel Lee grew resentful of Samantha when she found the guts to fight Doc off Big Ma. Unfortunately, Samantha's little body was no match for Doc's adult frame, and she ended up being muscled in a room with the door slamming behind them, leaving the boys to run by Big Ma's side huddling around her bruised body. Big Ma would grab hold of Leroy first, and they all prayed for the devil to leave their house as they listened to the screams of Samantha coming out of the room.

Near the barbeque pit, Lula was upset with Daniel Lee and Willie Ray's response. "I don't understand why y'all have such a problem with me movin'. Why can't y'all just support me? There's so much opportunity out there fo' us. All people do here is laugh and talk bout me and Bervick behind our backs. I can't take a breath without someone gossiping bout when, where, why, and how I did it. People joke bout me havin' all my babies. Family ain't talkin' to me. I can't live like dis anymore. We need a new beginnin'. Me and the kids, we need a fresh start! That's why I'm askin'. I supported y'all when y'all first started dis here pit. Cleaning and workin' fo' free. Never asked y'all fo' nothin' back. How can everyone help each other 'round here, but nobody can help me? I gave the little I had for collections down through the years, so why can't nobody help me nah?"

Daniel Lee wiped more sweat off his forehead with the back of his arm, lifting the lid back up. He looked over at Willie Ray, who had his arms folded deep in thought while stroking the hairs on his chin.

"Please, all I'm askin' fo' is a little money to help us move and get situated out there," Lula said, rubbing her sweaty palm on the side of her skirt while chewing her Doublemint gum and waiting for her uncles' response, watching their body language closely.

Willie Ray continued stroking his chin. Daniel Lee already knew his answer and it wasn't what Lula wanted to hear. "Lula Mae, baby girl, we love yah but," he scratched at the top of his head feeling new growth from neglect of not getting a haircut. He continued, "I'm sorry, were both sorry. We can't help you."

Lula said, "All that money y'all make and yah can't help me?"

Both uncles shook their head no.

Lula asked, "Why not?" She frowned. "Big Ma got to y'all, didn't she?"

Daniel Lee resumed cooking, turning his meat over and poking at it with a fork unnecessarily, avoiding eye contact with Lula. Lula turned to Willie Ray waiting for an explanation. Her almond shaped eyes threw darts in Willie Ray's direction.

She said, "So that's it? Dis how y'all gonna treat me?"

Willie Ray said, "We don't have it, Sha," and shrugged patting at his pockets looking for his pipe.

Lula said, "Com'on, unc! Y'all expect me to believe dis. Yah gonna boldly lie in my face?"

"Is that yah mouth gettin' sideways, Sha?"

"No, sir!" Lula rubbed at her arm. "Just need my uncles' help."

Lula felt her noble deeds toward the family throughout the years had gone unnoticed and unappreciated. On many accounts, she would get up before dawn to clean Willie Ray and Daniel Lee's grill, and then rung a dozen of chicken's necks to pluck, clean, and cut for barbequing. She added her own spices to their barbeque sauce that people now went crazy over, which helped Daniel Lee and Willie Ray's sales double. Lula didn't get the credit or money for discovering the sauce. Her only compensation was an extra piece of meat in her barbeque sandwiches, which she still had to pay for.

"Uncle Lee," Lula said trying to get him to look at her. "I'm not askin' fo' much. Anything will help. Anything. Please!"

Daniel Lee shook his head no while poking at the meat on the grill. He picked up the empty pan and placed the cooked meat in it. Willie Ray stuffed tobacco in his pipe.

Lula sorrowfully asked, "Why y'all doin' dis? Who cares if I married Bervick. It's still me here."

There was silence.

Daniel Lee was too busy examining pieces of meat while Willie Ray was having the toughest time getting his pipe lit—a task which usually came natural to him.

"Fine," Lula threw her hands up. "I'm leavin' anyway, with or without y'all help." Lula waited folding her arms and tapping her bare feet. Daniel Lee concentrated on the meat. Willie Ray couldn't seem to get his pipe lit for the life of him.

Lula turned and stomped away, sucking up her tears, muttering questions about how her family supposed to be God fearing Christians and still treat her in such a way. She flung the piece of meat Daniel Lee gave her in the bushes.

When Lula was out of sight, Daniel Lee looked up from the grill. Willie Ray lit his pipe without a problem and walked back into the house, making a mental note to shave the scruffy hairs off his chin. Daniel Lee took a bite of a juicy piece of rib, tasting the tender succulent meat that marinated in their famous special barbeque sauce.

***

Lula walked like a snail to Big Ma's house. Entering Big Ma's yard was bittersweet. Beads of sweat rolled down her face as the blue dress Samantha gave her flowed in the hot winds. Walking barefoot up the porch steps, Lula hesitated before knocking. She hadn't stepped foot near the house in years. She counted backwards, then knocked fast. Those few seconds waiting felt like an eternity. Big Ma opened the screen door shocked to see Lula standing there. Big Ma pulled at her blouse showing that they had the same colors on. Lula jumped in Big Ma's arms hugging her tight. They missed each other dreadfully and Lula had made several attempts to get back in Big Ma's good graces, except Big Ma didn't want anything to do with Lula after the birth of Gloria Jean. She made it clear, as long as Lula was married to Bervick, she wasn't speaking to them both, an assertion of the disapproval for their union.

Big Ma's embrace put Lula at ease. They sat on the porch and Big Ma said, "How yah doin', my baby? See yah got that blue dress Sam gave yah on. It looks so pretty on yah," she smiled, rocking in her chair.

Lula pulled a seat up closer to Big Ma, "Thank yah. You look nice, too."

"How dem chillun, Sha?"

"They doin' great. They gettin' so big."

They sat looking out at the road, waving at passers-by who took double takes at Lula sitting with Big Ma.

Big Ma rocked back and forth assessing Lula from the corner of her eyes. Lula's almond shaped eyes, deep brown skin, neatly pressed blue dress made Big Ma proud. For having little money, Big Ma saw that Lula maintained an elegant appearance, almost forgetting how beautiful Lula was up close. Her petite figure, after having so many babies, had no effect on her physical appearance. Made Big Ma reminisce on how easily she got her figure back after giving birth. Her thoughts turned sour thinking about Bervick stealing Lula away. She shook her head in disappointment asking God why. Her stone face returned.

Lula felt Big Ma's eyes on her, while staring out into road with her elbows resting on her thighs and her hands clamped together.

Big Ma broke the silence. "What is it, Lula Mae?"

Lula tensed up hearing the abrasive tone back in Big Ma's voice. She took a deep breath choosing her words wisely and spoke in a mere whisper. "We're leavin'."

"Come again, Sha?"

"We're movin'."

"Movin'? Movin' where?"

Big Ma leaned in closer to make sure she heard correctly to prove the gossips wrong.

"We're moving to California, ma'am."

"Movin' where?" Big Ma leaned in closer hoping old age was getting the best of her ears.

"California. Me, Bervick, and the kids are movin' to California soon."

"California! I thought y'all were goin' to Texas," Big Ma waved her hand annoyed that she even bothered to listen to the gossip. "Never mind that. California! What in God's name y'all movin' out there fo'? I kno' yah ain't doin' dis b'cause that fool ain't get his way in church, is it?" she said, now upset her ears weren't failing her.

"No, ma'am!"

"Humph," Big Ma said and crossed her arms. "He got nerve movin' y'all away just b'cause he ain't get his way. Somethin' really wrong with that boy! He 'pose to be a man of God. More of the devil if yah ask me."

"Please, Big Ma, don't blame him. I wanna leave, too. I think it'll be good fo' me and the kids. We can start a new life out there. There's nothin' here fo' us no more."

"Yah life and family is here."

"Family?"

Big Ma turned away rocking harder in her chair.

They sat in silence wondering what the other was going to say next.

Big Ma said, "Listen to me, Lula Mae, if he wanna go, let *him* go. You and the kids stay here. We'll take care of y'all. Hear me when I say, yah life will be so much betta. You and the kids can move back in with me. I'll make room!"

Lula looked at Big Ma as if the she said the most repulsive thing. Big Ma quickly re-tracked her angle of persuasion and said, "Okay not here, but if yah stay in Eunice, you'll have my full support, Sha. You ain't the problem. Lord knows yah not."

"With all due respect, ma'am, it seems I am the problem by the way y'all treat me. The whole family ignores me."

"We stay away from Bervick, not you, Sha! And no, I don't agree with the choices you've made creating' dis here problem in the first place. You eloping, gettin' married to that boy knowin' full well I disapproved of it. And out of all the men in Eunice, you pick Bervick Frank to marry." Big Ma shook her head, irritated.

"I love him. He's all I got nah. Where else am I gonna go? What else am I gonna do? Yah want me to move back in here with Grandpa Doc?"

"Betta here than with that boy. He do everythin' in his power to keep you away from us and he done run everyone away from you. Any husband that do that ain't got no good intention. Somethin' really wrong with that boy, sayin' he's the 'Anointed One' or 'Chosen One', and how God gave him special powers to heal the sick and how he's one of Jesus' disciples? Lord have mercy!"

"I understand what yah sayin', Big Ma, but I rather be free and married to a 'crazy' man rather than live my life sleepin' with one eye open. I wanna sleep in peace," Lula looked away, "Bervick take those memories away."

Lula's words stung Big Ma to the core of her soul.

Big Ma struggled through her words. "I did all I could fo' you and yah sisters. I kept y'all in church and worked overtime to make sho' y'all was safe. I love you. You my heart. I just don't wanna see yah make the biggest mistake in yah life movin' out there with that boy. Please, Sha, don't go!"

Lula bit at her thumb nail while weighing her options. Big Ma was giving an unreasonable ultimatum: stay in Eunice with a family not willing to love her for the man she married or go with Bervick to start a new life, in turn, losing Big Ma forever. For the first time, Lula was angry with Big Ma.

Lula said, "Yah think I don't kno' what y'all say bout me behind my back. Bout Bervick's back problems, and women at church laughin' at my clothes, or me having too many babies, or Bervick being crazy and y'all laughin' b'cause he ain't get that assistant pastor position. Movin' was Bervick's idea first, but God gave him a vision and I think it was the best idea he came up with thus far!" Lula looked down, "And you my grandmother. You should love me regardless, not toss me aside like a pair of old shoes when I don't do what yah want, Big Ma." Lula took a deep breath to calm herself, "California's got a lot more opportunity fo' us. And yeah, Bervick wasn't happy with Pastor Evans' decision, but that ain't no news. I believe us movin' was a great idea. All I ask is fo' once, you support my decision. I'm asking fo' yah help and support me. Can you please help me, Big Ma? Please?"

"Help how, Sha?"

"We need help movin' and might need money."

"Might?"

"We do need money, ma'am."

"So yah askin' me to help you move to California with dem chillun and that boy? Away from me? That's not gonna happen, Lula Mae Harrison."

"Frank, ma'am, Lula Mae Frank."

"Whatever, Sha."

"You act as if I don't exist anymore, so what's the difference?"

Big Ma didn't respond.

Lula continued, "I'm begging yah please! My mind is already made up and so is his. I need yah support and love right nah. Please! I'm beggin' you, please!"

Big Ma leaned in close so that Lula wouldn't miss a word. "If God is my witness, as long as yah with *that boy*, I can't help you. I'm sorry, baby!"

Lula sat back biting the inside of her cheek. "If I still go, where does that leave us?"

Big Ma stopped rocking and looked out into the road. "It's yah bed, you gotta lie in it." She turned to Lula and said, "Good-bye, Sha."

Lula's eye's swelled with tears. She said in a quivery voice, "Fine. That's just fine. Nah I kno' how Aunt Samantha feels."

"What was that, Sha?" Big Ma's voice rose with every word.

"Nothin', ma'am."

Lula sucked on her bottom lip and waited a few minutes before wiping her eyes and getting up, walking away without saying another word. Big Ma watched, feeling her heart drop to the pit of her stomach. Her stone face now grief stricken seeing Lula walk away. Big Ma rocked in her chair bumping it against the wall.

Being a respected member of the church, Big Ma had played a large part in Bervick not getting the assistant pastor position. Big Ma confided in Pastor Evans on her true feelings about Bervick, and how he wasn't taking care of Lula or their children. She made sure Pastor Evans had a firm understanding on the type of husband and father Bervick was to his family.

Rocking back and forth, Big Ma wondered if she had spoken positively about Bervick, would Lula still be leaving Eunice. She mulled over what could have been done differently to save Lula and Lillie from Doc, besides keeping them in church and sleeping in the bed to protect them.

Big Ma re-tracked herself and thought the better of it. A firm hand was what Lula needed and if it meant standing firm on cutting Lula off, Big Ma was going to do just that. Bervick's days were numbered in his marriage with Lula. Lula was smart. Big Ma knew Lula will soon see the forest for the trees, and when she did, Big Ma would be there ready for Lula and her children with open arms. God only knew how much she missed Lula. All Big Ma had to do was be patient and give it time, because in time, Lula would soon come to her senses.

Big Ma shuddered at the thought of a wife leaving her husband, but then again, Bervick wasn't the average husband, and because of this, God would wash away Lula's sin for not upholding her vows she had professed in their union in front of the Lord.

Big Ma rocked rubbing her heart and taking deep breaths to calm her irregular heart beat. Tough love didn't help the pain of losing another granddaughter.

The heaviness in her chest rose, coughing up from her throat, releasing itself, "Lord have mercy, Jesus! Oh my baby!" Big Ma screamed out.

***

Lula walked from Big Ma's house in a hurry. Hurt and disappointed, she still wasn't surprised. Once Big Ma made up her mind, she stuck to it. Lula had been resting on the notion that if she allowed time to pass, Big Ma and the family would come to accept Bervick. Instead, nobody budged in years. The more Lula stayed with him, the less anyone spoke to her. She and Bervick became so isolated from the town folks that Lula was in the dark about how much people in Eunice despised him. She wasn't aware that Bervick took it upon himself to confront pastors in the surrounding area, telling them they were headed straight to hell if they didn't listen to his sermon or allow him to preach the word in their churches, furthering everyone's belief that Bervick was touched in the head.

People began hiding when they saw Bervick Frank coming. The more they ran, the more Bervick felt it was time to depart as the Lord commanded. God wanted him to go where fresh souls waited to be saved, and California was the land of milk and honey that would enable him to do God's work.

The wedge between Lula and her family prompted a yearning to search for her parents before moving to California. After the episode with Big Ma, Lula longed for Leroy and Beatrice more than ever. It had been over a decade since Lula last saw them, and the more alone she felt, the more adamant she became about finding them.

Lula started piecing together information that Papa Top gave down through the years, which all led to dead ends. She asked town's people, including Cordelia's family, about Leroy's whereabouts, unsure if the people didn't have a clue or were intentionally withholding information. She suspected a little bit of both.

Lula visited house after house to find information every morning until her feet were sore. Still in pain, she woke up one final morning to make a last attempt at finding information. Dropping the children off at Samantha's house, Lula walked barefoot to Cordelia's distant cousin's house. This cousin was a person that Cordelia's family told Lula to stay clear of, compelling Lula to go find out why.

The cousin greeted Lula, already aware of whom Lula was and hurried her in the house. She offered cold lemonade and sat down across from Lula, smiling. Lula mentally conjured the physical appearances of Cordelia's family to gather what Cordelia might look like since Lula had never met her. The younger pictures of Cordelia in the cousin's photo albums didn't help any. Lula had to see Cordelia for herself. In person. She had to see the woman who Leroy fell madly in love with, the woman he gave up his children and wife for, and the lone question Lula had for him was 'why'.

In talking with the cousin, Lula learned that this Cordelia woman had slept with this cousin's husband for money. The cousin hated Cordelia and happily gave Lula their address, and even offered to go with Lula. Lula graciously declined. This trip was one she had to take alone.

The following week, Samantha bought Lula a roundtrip ticket to Lafayette, Louisiana, and babysat her children for the day without asking any questions. Bervick was off in Mamou preaching the word of God in unsavory places of business.

Lula dressed in Samantha's more Christian-like attire (few and far between in Samantha's closet) and borrowed a pair of new shoes. Samantha waved excitedly, thinking Lula was sneaking off to see another man. It never entered Samantha's mind that Lula was going to see Leroy.

During the bus ride to Lafayette, Lula thought about everything she was going to say, what to do, and how to act towards her father. Even though she loved Leroy dearly, Lula wanted to stand firm on finding out where Beatrice was and if she was okay.

Her mother's absence left a void in Lula's heart, having to push memories out of her mind when it did come into question. Lula prayed for her mother every day knowing the situation was out of her control.

She rode on the bus rubbing her now clammy hands together, knocking her knees against one another, unable to sit still. She hadn't seen Leroy in over a decade and pictured him the way she wanted to remember him—in his chef uniform, standing tall and handsome, waiting for her to fly into his open arms.

Staring out the window popping her Doublemint gum, Lula felt nostalgic thinking about the good times she had as a little girl with

Beatrice and Leroy. The family never explained what had happened to them. All Lula knew was that Leroy ran off with Cordelia, and he was the only person who knew where Beatrice was, dead or alive. Lula didn't mind Big Ma, Doc, Papa Top, Grandma Emma, or any other relatives keeping the situation from her. The state Beatrice was in before she had left made Lula not want to know for a long time. Many stories circulated around Eunice, and when the story made its way to Lula's ears, she heard that Papa Top aimed a gun at Leroy and accidently shot Beatrice, causing her to run away out of fear for her life. Lula ignored all stories after listening to that nonsense. She knew Beatrice would never leave her children, and the faint memory of Leroy driving off with Beatrice late at night solidified that notion.

Lula chewed her gum fast, wondering what Leroy's response would be. With every mile that passed, fear rose within her from awaiting this long overdue reunion. Anxiety reached a new high on the ride to Lafayette. Lula couldn't sit still. Excited, yet terrified. She prayed for Jesus to be with her during this life altering event that was about to take place. The depth of her heart needed answers that only Leroy could provide.

When the bus stopped in Lafayette, Lula got off and made her way across town on foot. She followed the directions Cordelia's cousin gave, and walked two hours to the destination in the hot humid heat.

The closer Lula got, the slower her stride became. The moment she dreamed about was finally going to happen. She wondered if Leroy would recognize her as his little girl, or as Lula Mae 'the woman'. A woman with a husband and seven children; a woman who was a God fearing Christian woman; a woman who learned how to bake the best sweet dough pies; a woman who fell out of Big Ma's good graces and thrown into the same boat as Samantha; a woman who wanted to ask her father if he ever loved her; a woman who needed her father to confide in and ask him what he thought about Bervick; a woman who needed to know if she should move to California with Bervick. Most of all, a woman who wanted to know if her mother was still alive.

Lula slowly walked up to a house. She froze on the sidewalk in front of the house while matching the address on the paper, wondering if she was doing the right thing or if some things were better left alone. But it was too late to turn back. There in front of Lula was the house of her estranged father, who abandoned her and her sisters. The father who knew where Beatrice was at.

Lula grabbed at her chest trying to calm the pressure rising in her chest. The sun beamed brighter and hotter. The air grew thicker. Her breaths got shorter. Lula backed away, ready to make a run for it thinking this was a bad idea. A plan not thoroughly thought out.

Just when Lula positioned her body to run, the front door opened, making Lula rush behind a big oak tree on the sidewalk and smack her back against it as she covered her mouth with both hands. Her eyes closed upon hearing a familiar male voice telling someone to hurry up. Lula peeked her head out from behind the tree and was stunned to see Leroy standing on the porch holding the screen door open. He weighed about forty pounds heavier from when Lula last saw him, and his pants and shirt were dingy and wrinkled. Even though it was Leroy's voice, his tone was abrasive, short-tempered, and full of curse words. Lula couldn't believe her ears. The sloppy man scratching the top of his balding head couldn't be her father.

Despite the physical change, Lula smiled. The same feeling she felt in his presence as a little girl came flooding back. Ready to jump from behind the tree and run into Leroy's arms as his little girl again, Lula stopped in her tracks when a woman came out the house with a baby and two other children. Lula hugged closer behind to the tree and squinted for a better view of the woman, trying to connect the familiarity. Lula's eyes widened. Her breath stopped.

In that moment, Lula realized the nice lady who bought candy for them outside Mr. Pete's store, asking questions about their family—primarily Beatrice—was the woman Cordelia. She'd make Lula, Mary, and Lillie promise not to tell anyone she was giving them candy, and they never did. They just wanted more candy.

Lula's jaw dropped. It fell lower upon seeing the children's strong resemblance to Leroy. She watched Leroy and his new family walk to the same car Lula had seen Leroy drive Beatrice away in. She quickly leaned back behind the tree and stood there listening to Leroy argue with Cordelia the whole time.

Lula slid to the other side of tree as the car pulled out the dirt driveway. It screeched off passing the big oak tree.

Leroy drove down the road, and out of nowhere, slammed on the breaks. The car jumped forward when he stopped. He slightly looked back over his shoulder in curiosity, but saw nothing but trees and houses. Leroy shook his head in disbelief at what he thought he had seen, and then drove off arguing with Cordelia.

***

Lula got off the bus in a somber mood. After witnessing Leroy with his new family, she wasn't quite sure what to do or how to feel. Lula felt numb and dejected, doubting if any of her family members had her best interest at heart. If her father could leave without a trace and start a new life with another woman, and if Big Ma along with other family members could dismiss Lula because of Bervick, did they really love her unconditionally? Even Papa Top and Grandma Emma stopped coming around as often.

The two family members left in Lula's corner were Lillie, who lived all the way in Texas, and Samantha, whose worldly views made it difficult for Lula to relate to now that she was an older Christian woman with a deeper understanding of her role as a saved Christian.

This heartbreaking realization made Lula anxious to leave Eunice once and for all. Bervick's vision was right again. It would be a cold day in hell before her family supported any decision she made, as long as she was married to Bervick Frank. God just confirmed that it was definitely time to leave Eunice.

Lula put a piece of Doublemint gum in her mouth, popping like a pro as she walked to Samantha's house trying to wrap her thoughts around her family as a whole. When she arrived, Lula changed her clothes, brushed her hair into a ponytail, and sat with Samantha, waiting for the children to finish eating their cornbread and milk.

Lula wasn't hungry. She held her sleeping baby, listening to Samantha laugh as she told stories about the children's silly antics while Lula was gone. Lula wryly smiled, followed by a flat "Um huh" or a bleak "Fo' real, Sha".

Samantha stopped with the stories after noticing that Lula's visit to Lafayette must not had gone well. It was unusual for Lula to never laugh or scarcely speak. All she did was answer in monotone words with her head tilted on baby Deborah, rocking while popping her gum.

When Lula made it home with the children, Bervick was sitting on the porch waiting for her to cook dinner. His hands and pants were covered in soil from working in the garden, pulling ripe greens and sweet potatoes after he returned home from Mamou. They all went inside the house and Bervick sat with the children waiting for a meal.

After eating dinner, Lula cleaned up and spent time singing and playing with her children, and then put them to bed.

In bed, Lula tried confiding in Bervick about her day in Lafayette, but in mid-sentence, she nudged Bervick when he started snoring.

Mumbling a bunch of gibberish, Bervick turned his back to her and starting snoring again. Lula smiled and tucked Bervick in, realizing he was all she had in this world, crazy or not, she was going to make the best of her life with her own growing family.

Lula laid down contemplating what life would be like in California. *Where would they live? How were the schools? Would Bervick find a job? Could she start a Creole restaurant out there? Was it too late for her to finish school?* So many unanswered questions wracked Lula's brain, leaving her to redirect her faith and trust in God. It was *he* who was in control and all of the signs were evident that it was time to leave Eunice.

Lula got up from the bed and went where her children were huddled together on a small mattress. She looked around the small room, then sat in a chair watching her children sleep, wondering what their future would be like in Eunice and if they'd be able to build a relationship with a family that hated their father and had ostracized their mother. This question made Lula fall more at ease with the decision to relocate to California.

***

Big Ma shouted, "Halleluiah, Thank yah Jesus," while looking out the window at Lula coming. After Lula's ordeal with her uncles, Leroy, and the rest of the family, she weighed out her options that left her no other choice but to try Big Ma one last time.

Big Ma went outside thanking Jesus for answering her prayers. She had prayed every day since Lula's last visit, visualizing Lula walking up into the yard. Big Ma was delighted that her tough method had not been done in vain.

Big Ma took a seat in her white rocking chair, holding the bible in her lap as Lula approached. Doc came outside to greet Lula as well, missing her dreadfully and hoping too that she was returning home. Lula nodded at Doc, avoiding eye contact with him. He stood there quiet and got the hint that Big Ma and Lula needed to talk. He went back in the house to escape "women's chatter".

Big Ma patted the bible in her lap ready to read inspiring scriptures to enlighten Lula. She was fairly convinced that Lula, being a saved child of God, wouldn't deny *his* words after hearing an earful of the Holy Spirit. She patted the seat next to her ready to pour the message on thick.

Lula sat next to Big Ma and began listening to her read highlighted scriptures. Lula knew better than to argue, fuss, or attempt any objection during Big Ma's preaching. She just sat and quietly listened.

Two hours passed and Big Ma was still reading about how God would help Lula make the right decisions in her life and forgive Lula for her sins if she left Bervick. When Big Ma set the bible down, she explained that she couldn't give Lula any money because the money would insinuate condoning Lula's marriage to Bervick, who was a part of the devil's work to break the family apart. Once Big Ma was done explaining, she pulled out a hanky to wipe the sweat off her forehead, now relieved to get everything off her chest.

Lula calmly stood up, kissed Big Ma on the cheek, and stepped down the porch stairs. Underneath her calm demeanor, anger was brewing, rising to a new high, leaving Lula numb before the emotional storm erupted.

Lula said, "Good-bye, Big Ma. I love you."

As Lula walked away, everything Big Ma had preached reiterated in Lula's mind, making each step weigh heavier than the last. She tried to get away before saying something she would regret, but it was too late.

Lula stopped in the middle of the road and turned to face Big Ma, yelling, "Dis the way y'all treat me! Y'all don't want me to go, but y'all ignore me when I'm here! Ignored me fo' years! Yah don't treat the people yah love like dis?" She marched on yelling over her shoulders, "I'm still leavin', and the only way I'm comin' back to Eunice is in a pine box!"

Big Ma stopped rocking and sat up astounded by what Lula said. She grabbed hold of her chest feeling her heart palpitate. Nonetheless, frequent palpations were the least of Big Ma's concerns. Her plan had backfired. Lula was still leaving.

The only thing Big Ma had to thank God for was time. She had to be patient. Her heart rate lessened, rising and falling in its natural rhythm due to the simple fact that her grandbaby will come to her senses in time, whether in Eunice or California.

***

Bervick thanked Lula for her attempts to seek financial help and decided it was best for them to leave the family out of their business once and for all. Lula agreed, accepting the terrible revelations about her family. Of all the people she'd helped in the past, not one person could spare a penny to help and support Lula's decision to move. It baffled her how easily the family accepted her help cooking, cleaning their houses, and free sweet dough pies. Lula used to challenge Bervick when he said her family was full of selfish sinful negroes, but after this eye opener, Lula was in agreement.

The following Saturday afternoon, Lula watched the children play in the yard while she and Gloria Jean washed clothes outside. Lula contemplated on how Bervick was going to raise the money to move them to California. He didn't have a job and the little income they did save was from her selling sweet dough pies again.

It was impossible to foresee having enough money to move anytime soon, so Lula decided to fast and pray for God to make a way, and once they were able to move, she knew one thing was for certain—she was never coming back.

Lula felt terrible saying those words to Big Ma, hoping God would forgive her for howling at her grandmother. Yet, she had to speak her truth which had been lurking below the surface of her mind. She wasn't going to stay in a town with a family who ostracized her and her children for years because of whom she chose to marry. What hurt Lula the most was that she knew Big Ma was leading the pack.

Chapter 16

Constant harassment from Bervick forced Pastor Evans to relent. He told Bervick where he could retrieve at least half of his money. Given the location of the man who had his money, Bervick discovered it was his cousin in Crowley.

Bervick didn't waste any time heading down the road to visit his cousin whom he hadn't seen in years. He wanted his money back!

He hitched a ride with an acquaintance in Eunice and was dropped off a block away from where his cousin resided, giving the driver a five dollar bill for them to meet in the same spot in a couple of hours.

He started up the road feeling more at ease. He walked, rubbing and clapping his hands together praising God in the scorching sun.

Seeing that the money didn't serve his original purpose, Bervick knew it would at least help move his family to California. He reckoned, the Lord worked in mysterious ways. It was meant for him to move to California in the first place.

Bervick approached Deacon Frank's big house in the middle of the block, taking two long strides up the porch stairs. He brushed himself off, straightened his clothes, patted his hair, and slicked both eyebrows back with his pinky finger. He took a handkerchief out of his back pocket, dabbed sweat off his face, and clamped his armpits tight to hide the sweat stains. After a deep breath, Bervick knocked. He alternated his demeanor from an anxious school boy to a distinguished gentleman.

The door opened.

Deacon Frank said, "Bervick, Bervick Frank."

He opened the door wide, surprised to see Bervick at his doorstep.

Deacon Frank was a short man with a stocky build, reddish complexion, and green eyes. He hadn't seen Bervick in years. Their only correspondence was through messages relayed by other relatives.

Deacon Frank hugged Bervick, patting him on the back. Bervick felt uncomfortable hugging another man and gently pushed Deacon Frank away. He nodded, stepping back to shake his hand. "Deacon Frank," Bervick said, giving a less invasive space of greeting. There was an awkward pause before Deacon Frank gestured for Bervick to come in. Bervick walked through the door poised and calm. He looked around at the extravagant house with expensive artwork hanging on milk white walls, gold trim vases filled with fresh flowers, area rugs on polished hard wood floors, crystal chandeliers, and a large marble table in the living room.

Bervick said, "Nice place yah got here, deacon."

"Oh yeah, oh yeah. Bettie Lou sho' kno' how to decorate. Women kno' how to do that kind of stuff."

Bervick looked around acting impressed with the décor of the house, when in actuality, the furthest thing from his mind was Bettie Lou's artistry. The house was full of devil objects symbolizing wealth.

Deacon Frank said, "Come, come see. Have a seat, have a seat. Can I get yah somethin' to drink, coffee, Scotch, coffee?"

Bervick noticed Deacon Frank repeating his words—a habit Deacon Frank had since they were children. He stuttered or repeated himself when nervous.

Bervick raised a brow, "No thank yah, deacon. I just wanna get to the reason I'm here."

"Okay, Okay."

They took a seat at the dining room table. Deacon Frank lit a cigar, took two long drags offering one to Bervick, who waved his hand no. Bervick coughed waving the smoke away, snarling his nose at the stinky smell.

Deacon Frank took two more healthy puffs and put the cigar out, chuckling, "Almost forgot yah don't like smoke. So, what's goin' on with yah?"

"Evans said yah got my money, so where is it?"

"Evans?"

"He's no pastor of mine."

Deacon Frank exhaled his aggravation, seeing not much has changed with Bervick. "I see. And 'Pastor' Evans told yah I got yah money?"

"Yes, sir."

Deacon Frank chuckled.

Bervick said, "Did I say somethin' funny, deacon?"

"No, no. I'm laughin' at what Pastor Evans said to yah."

"Excuse me?"

"I don't have yah money! It seems like the pastor done sent you on a wild goose chase!" Deacon Frank picked up his cigar and lit it again, taking a few puffs, blowing out the smoke, chuckling.

Bervick cleared his throat to interrupt Deacon Frank's amusement. "What yah talkin' bout? He told me to come here b'cause you have my money, and what's so funny?" Bervick coughed.

Deacon Frank smashed his cigar in a wooden ashtray. His behavior turned serious. "Let me be frank, like us Frank's like to do," he said, laughing at his own joke.

Bervick ignored his cousin's bad humor, "Where's my money?"

"What did Pastor Evans tell yah?"

"Evans said yah got it. At least half of it."

"That's all he said? 'I got it'?" Deacon Frank chuckled, shaking his head. "He playin' yah like a fiddle, Bervick. I ain't got yah money. Nah Pastor Evans paid me back the money he owed me and that's bout it."

Bervick's jaws clenched. He saw himself jumping across the table, shoving the cigars down Deacon Frank's throat, and then choking him to death.

Bervick said, "So yah tellin' me my money gone?"

"I'm afraid so." Deacon Frank folded his hands on the table, "What yah need it fo' anyways? Maybe I can help yah out? I heard something bout y'all movin'? Is that true?"

"Yeah, we're movin' to California."

"I can probably give yah a hundred dollars. It ain't much, but it's somethin'."

"I don't need yah help."

Bervick got up from the table and made his way to the door. As he walked away from the house, Deacon Frank yelled, "Somethin' small is betta than nothin' at all, Bervick. We all kno' yah options are limited. Lula Mae still helpin' yah memorize dem bible verses?"

Bervick froze in step. He balled his fist, slowly turned around, and walked back over to Deacon Frank.

Deacon Frank nonchalantly lit his cigar.

Bervick asked, "What yah mean by that?"

"We all kno' you miss one too many lessons in school. Do yah kno' how to write yah own name yet?"

Bervick felt the walls closing in on him. He turned away from Deacon Frank to get away fast, now remembering why he'd stopped talking to his snobbish cousin in the first place.

Deacon Frank yelled, "Awe, com'on, Bervick! Let me help you. I didn't mean nothin' by it."

Bervick kept walking, ignoring him.

Deacon Frank closed his door, regretting the words he'd spoken, yet laughing at the same time. Somebody had to bring his crazy cousin to his knees. Bervick was a disgrace to the Frank name.

***

Bervick made it back to Eunice, but didn't go home right away. He stood across the road from his house, hovering behind tree branches, watching his children play in the front yard while Lula hung clothes out on the line. When she got close to the end of the line, Bervick stepped back farther into the leaves so he wouldn't be seen.

Lula looked up, shielding the sun with her hand. "Bervick, that you?"

Bervick backed away and marched in the opposite direction, ignoring Lula's calls, cutting through a couple houses to get to another road.

Free and clear, Bervick's pace dawdled. He strolled, too upset to greet anyone. People who bothered to speak had to repeat themselves, surprised that Bervick didn't stop to acknowledge them. He wasn't bothering himself with any greets or preaching the word of God that day as he walked the walk of shame to a place he used to call home. He rubbed his palms together making his way to the bus station to buy a one-way ticket to Lake Charles to pay his father a visit.

***

Bervick's bowlegs legs buckled standing on Joe's porch. This was the first time Bervick had set foot in front of the house he had grew up in since his mother's death. Nostalgia took over. Memories of Christina came rushing in. Her golden skin, curly hair, gentle eyes, and angel face smiled at Bervick in his mind's eye. She had been his protector over his overbearing father. The one woman who loved him unconditionally, no matter what he did or how he behaved, Christina was there.

Bervick grunted away tears, wiping them off as if they were "the plague". But his grunts failed him. Seeing Christina's smile made Bervick's chest tighten, ready to explode. He balled his fist trembling, struggling to keep his self-control and manhood intact. "No tears Lord, no tears," he mumbled to himself followed by more grunts and a pounding of the chest.

Bervick paused.

A familiar scent besieged him. Bervick breathed in. He couldn't believe his nose. A hint of Christina's perfume surrounded him.

A tear broke loose. Bervick allowed it. He watched a tear drop fall on his shirt. Another one broke loose, streaming down his cheek, followed by another tear, aiding the lone tear in splashing on his shirt.

The perfume smell heightened.

One more tear escaped his eye. That was it for Bervick. He slapped it away fast and furious, hitting his face until all tears were gone, damning each one to hell for making him fall weak for that moment. Bervick grunted back any other tears daring to escape his eyes.

All tears were finally gone and the scent went with them. Bervick knew it was nothing but the devil's tricks on his manhood.

Bervick was a seventeen year-old when Christina died. He suspected foul play around her death, but never asked any questions. Tormented by his own belief, Bervick got up one day and walked away from home, never to look back or speak of Christina's name again. The thought of her brought despair unto his heart, the one thing in the world that had the emotional capacity to cripple his manhood. Thinking about Christina opened the door to another memory of what her brother had done to Bervick at age eight.

Bervick had altered his brain to believe the occurrences between him and his uncle were blessings in disguise, since it was during this time, he learned of his special powers from God. He learned how to separate himself from his body when alone with his uncle. Bervick transcended his body into a vehicle with no purpose, so when his uncle took him for the day, Bervick detached himself from the vehicle, leaving his uncle to have his way with the vehicle without Bervick's actual presence. When Bervick learned of these special gifts from God, he decided to stay put in his body to exert his power by preaching the word of God to his uncle.

"I am God's Prophet and he ordered you to stop!" he said. The command coming out the eight year-old boy startled his uncle, making him leery of Bervick's state of mind. After seeing the disturbing loath in Bervick's eyes, his uncle backed off, never to touch Bervick again. Witnessing his uncle back down empowered Bervick, and from that day forward, Bervick knew he embodied special powers over people given to him by God. He never breathed a word about this to his parents. Being God's chosen one brought enough solace in Bervick's life to obliterate those encounters for good.

On the porch, Joe stood in the doorway watching Bervick smack at his face and mumble underneath his breath about being a man of God.

Joe asked in Creole, "You alright there, son?"

Bervick jumped out of his fit when he heard his father's voice.

"Yes, sir."

Joe motioned for Bervick to come inside the house.

They walked inside and sat in the front room across from one another. Bervick noticed Joe was now walking with a cane and his salt and pepper hair had turned completely white.

"What were you doing out there on the porch?" Joe asked, still speaking in Creole.

"Sir?"

"You were out there acting crazy." Joe shook his head. "What be going on in that head of yours?"

"Nothin', sir," Bervick said in English. He hated speaking Creole over English.

Joe stared at Bervick, miffed that his son was still acting strange after all these years. He concluded long ago that Bervick was just an idiot—there was always one in the family, Joe reckoned.

Joe asked in Creole, "What brings you here, son? Before you answer that, I don't want you standing here, a grown man, asking for money."

"I didn't come here fo' money, sir."

Bervick sat with his elbows resting on his thighs, hands clamped together, looking around at the house seeing not much had changed, except for everything appearing much smaller from what he had remembered. Bervick looked over at Joe lighting his wooden pipe, which was still a show for Bervick ever since a little boy.

Joe stuffed tobacco in his pipe, lit it with a long wooden match, then took a few puffs and paused looking up at Bervick watching. "What? You never seen me light a pipe before?"

Bervick quickly turned away, annoyed at his father for speaking Creole.

After the tobacco was burning good, Joe sat back in his chair and looked Bervick over. "So, what's your business here, son? I know you didn't come here just to visit me." Joe knew his son very well. He blew smoke from the side of his mouth to avoid fogging his view of Bervick. Bervick sat quiet before answering his father, aware that Joe was the only person in the world he couldn't get one over on.

Joe sat twisting his mouth to the side blowing out smoke, waiting for an answer.

Bervick said, "I need a favor, sir?"

Joe chuckled. He wasn't surprised.

Bervick hesitated before continuing. "I kind of do need money. Money to help move me and my family to California."

"No."

Conversation over.

Joe got up from his chair, "Want something to eat? Got beans with pork meat and rice cooking."

"I'm not hungry, sir."

Joe turned giving Bervick 'the eye'.

Bervick quickly said, "I mean yes, sir!"

"Come on then," Joe said, motioning Bervick to follow him to the kitchen. He stopped and turned to face Bervick again. "Why you taking your wife and children to California?"

"I reckon, time fo' a change, sir."

Joe lowered his eyes, piercing them right through Bervick. Bervick swallowed hard.

"Humph," Joe muttered and continued to the kitchen. "You might as well stay the night. No more buses leaving town tonight."

"Yes, sir," Bervick finally answered in Creole.

The moon shone through the window. Bervick lay on his back staring up at the moon with his hands behind his head, listening to the silence in the room. He reminisced about happy memories with his siblings and how they laughed at Bervick being the most daring out of the bunch, frequently getting hurt during his escapades. Bervick felt proud after he discovered his powers from God and proved it to his family after jumping barefoot from a tree onto a rusty nail that jabbed into the middle of his left foot. Curley, who was ten years-old at the time, got down from the tree and ran to get help when he saw Bervick's foot leaking blood.

Bervick remembered the nail as a symbol of trusting in the powers God gave him. When he looked at the rusty nail halfway in his foot, Bervick ripped it out without flinching and watched the blood gush out. He squeezed the wound, moving his foot back and forth, craving every ounce of pain. He squeezed until there was no more pain and the blood receded, then hopped his way home, ducking behind a tree when he saw everyone being led by Curley to where Bervick fell. Once they were out of sight, Bervick went into the house, cleaned the blood off his foot and applied pig lard to it. He glared at his holy work, feeling different about himself. God told him exactly what to do and he succeeded in healing the pain away. He showed his holy work to his family and vowed to follow whatever God told him to do, even if his family had concerned expressions on their faces.

Bervick lay in bed smiling, remembering the feeling he'd felt when he healed his own foot. He turned on his side looking into the dark room, remembering games he'd play with his siblings such as shooting marbles, kick the can, and his all time favorite, hide-and-go-seek. Sometimes when his brothers were preoccupied with the games, Bervick would run off to see what Joe was doing while they played. Bervick hid in a tree to watch Joe sneak out the house and scurry off like a thief in the night. Bervick would get down from the tree and follow Joe, hiding behind trees, barely breathing, knowing if Joe heard him, his butt would soon be raw. Bervick peeked as Joe dug a hole in the dirt under a pecan tree near the barn. Joe dug and looked, looked and dug, making sure no one was present. Once Joe finished, he'd hurry back to the house before the boys returned. Bervick would wait, then run to the spot and start digging. When he felt something in the ground, Bervick dug up an old tin can with a thick stash of money from the store Joe owned.

After discovering this, Bervick frequently started up new games to preoccupy his brothers so that he could disappear in the mist of the fun to count how much money Joe had added.

The stash increased so much that Joe needed another can, and when Bervick saw Joe starting to throw money in the can without counting, he started taking a little for himself. After God revealed Joe's hiding spot, Bervick had an unspoken supremacy over his father, knowing that at any given time, he could destroy everything Joe worked for. The power of God soared throughout Bervick's psyche, causing his brothers and friends to stay clear of him, but Bervick didn't mind. The one person he needed in his life was God. God's chosen prophets walked alone, away from the earthly devil-filled heathens.

Bervick lay in the bed still staring up at the moonlight, grinning slyly. He got up and left out of the house quietly taking Joe's box of wooden matches. He lit a match outside and went to the spot under the pecan tree and started digging, pulling up three cans. Bervick paused when he heard a stir, and lit another match to find a squirrel running pass. He grabbed his chest exhaling, and then opened the can that was fuller than ever before. He shoved half the money into his pants pocket and put the rest back, placing the lid on top and burying it back in the ground. When Bervick stood up ready to walk away, he stopped for a moment and rubbed at the back of his neck. He knelt back down, dug up the same can, and took the rest of the money, stuffing it into his bulging pants pocket. He threw the empty can back in the hole and covered it up with dirt making sure his vandalism was indiscernible.

Bervick said a prayer thanking God for the gift, and then lit a match to make his way towards the road, happy his God never failed him. Bervick walked through the sleeping town of Lake Charles to the bus station and sat on a bench waiting for the sun to rise, relieved that he was now able to begin the process of moving to California.

"The Lord works in mysterious ways. Thank yah, Jesus," Bervick muttered in Creole in honor of his father Joe.

***

Cleve and Hattie Ann were previous neighbors who had already moved and settled in Pacoima, California, years ago. They loved their new home in the small community in the San Fernando Valley. Cleve visited Eunice often and met with Bervick to assist in laying out a plan for him and Lula to move.

Before returning back to California, Cleve went by Bervick's house to see how things were going with the moving process. They stood outside talking while Lula was inside feeding the children cornbread and milk.

Cleve said, "Yes, sir, you ain't never gonna have the same type of success down here in Eunice the way you'll have out west in the Valley."

"Do they got yards fo' gardens?"

"You don't gotta worry bout all that. They got grocery stores."

"What's a grocery store?"

"That's where they got all the food yah need. Vegetables, fruits, meats, diary, they got it all. You don't need no garden or chicken coop out there. Me and Hattie go there twice a month to stock up on everythin' we need."

Bervick nodded, impressed.

Cleve listened to the children in the house. "It does get sort of quiet out there tho'. I don't hear chillun runnin' 'round like they do here in Eunice. I sho' do miss the sounds of chillun." Cleve's head lowered. He looked down at the ground, leaning up against the house. "Too bad my ole lady broken. We would've been done had some babies by nah."

Bervick stood quiet empathizing with Cleve. Men had to be fruitful and multiply to spread their seed. A man wasn't a complete man without a child to carry on his name.

Bervick said, "Yeah, too bad she ain't no bearer." He refrained from saying a barren woman was a curse by God. Cleve was a good friend.

"Yeah, too bad."

Both nodded in agreement.

Cleve said, "We did come into somethin' new here, yeah."

"Oh yeah?"

"Oh yeah. We gonna get a child of our own soon!" Cleve's face perked up.

"How much a child cost these days?"

"Not sho'. It varies depending on the family you buyin' from. If the parents got good genes, yah kno', nice skin, hair, color. It can run pretty high. But I'm willin' to pay whatever, hell, I don't want no ugly kid. If the parents look good, the hell with it, I'm buyin'. Dis man in Opelousas scout families who tryin' to sell they kid, yah kno', if they got too many and can't take care of all dem. He do all the negotiating and get 'em sold to a couple lookin' to buy. They call him Mr. Jolivere. I hear he's good at what he do."

"How soon you want yah baby?"

"Very soon!" Cleve popped a cigarette in his mouth, patting himself down in search of matches.

Bervick said, "Halleluiah, God is good! Name yah price?"

Cleve looked up with a cigarette hanging out his open mouth. He broke out laughing, dropping the cigarette on the ground. He stopped when he noticed Bervick's straight face.

Cleve asked, "Wait a minute, yah ain't…you and Lula Mae?"

"How soon can I get the money?"

"Hell, I'll get it to yah tomorrow!"

"Don't kno' bout tomorrow. Gotta tell Lula Mae first."

"Boy or girl?"

"Girl."

"That's exactly what Hattie Ann wants, too."

Cleve picked up his cigarette, blew the dirt off, and popped it back in his mouth. He pictured Lula's pretty face and nice body while digging in his pocket for matches. He lit his cigarette, inhaling deeply and blew out the smoke away from where Bervick was standing. He checked out Bervick's skin, hair, and facial features, nodding in approval of Bervick's looks. Cleve couldn't smoke his cigarette fast enough, excited about the baby he was about to become a father to.

Cleve finished his cigarette and said, "Guess I gotta tell Mr. Jolivere there'll be no need for his services."

"I reckon so. Thank yah Lord, Jesus."

"I can't wait to tell Hattie Mae."

Bervick walked into the house late after waiting at the train station with Cleve, making plans before Cleve left back to California.

Everyone was asleep.

After falling on his knees and giving thanks, Bervick quietly slipped into bed next to Lula, kissing her on the cheek. Lula woke up yawning, "Where yah been, Sha?"

Bervick cuddled close to her, closing his eyes as she started stroking the top of his head.

"Out with Cleve. Found us a way to get mo' money. Told yah my God was gonna make a way."

"The money Papa Joe gave yah ain't enough?"

"It's enough to move us out there and put money down on a house, but we still need money to eat and live on 'til I find work. Cleve said they got a place out there called 'a grocery store' where we buy vegetables and fruits and chicken and stuff, so I found a way to get mo' money."

"And what way is that?"

"The Lord said we gonna have to sell Deborah."

"WHAT!" Lula yelled at the top of her lungs and abruptly sat up causing Bervick's head to fall in the bed.

"Yah tryin' to wake the chillun, Sha?" he said, sitting up rubbing the back of his head.

"What yah mean 'we're sellin' Deborah'? I'm not sellin' my child, Bervick. You must've gone and lost yah mind."

"God told me he was gonna make a way and he did. He blessed us with a lot of babies and nah we can be a blessin' to Hattie Ann and Cleve. Yah kno' Hattie Ann broken."

Lula crossed her arms sucking her teeth at Bervick's chauvinistic comment and said, "You kno' cotton picking' well she ain't the one with the problem. Cleve had a few women b'fore Hattie Ann and none of dem got pregnant."

"I'm gonna ignore what yah just said." He lay his head back down and said, "Nah, we needed a way to get to California and dis here is the way. I already got money fo' a down payment on a house and the rest of the money will pay fo' suitcases, tickets, furniture, and food to start. Dis move ain't gonna be cheap, Lula Mae, and I don't question God's work and you shouldn't either. We got a lot of kids and we always can have more. It would be a sin not to spread our blessings to others, especially when Cleve is helpin' us get out of Eunice. Remember, yah my God fearin' virtuous wife first and foremost."

"Dis is my baby, Bervick, not cattle! How yah gonna just take my baby?"

"Dis here is God's work and that's that. She'll have a good life with Cleve and Hattie Ann and we gonna have a good life living in California with the rest of our chillun. I don't question God and yah not gonna either. Nah I don't wanna hear another word bout dis. We're sellin' Deborah and that's final. It ain't like yah not gonna see her anymore."

"But—"

"Lula Mae, 'honor and obey'! That is the word of God. Remember that!"

Bervick fluffed his pillow and turned on his side with his back facing Lula.

Lula lay back down inching away from Bervick, crying in her pillow, sniffling loudly to be heard. She threw the covers off her body and flung them over Bervick, who didn't flinch. He was unaffected by her cries and antics, pretending like he had fallen asleep, snoring loud to prove how much he was unfazed by Lula's temper tantrum.

Lula's blood boiled listening to the snores. She grabbed her bible for refuge, holding it against her chest. The more she held on to it, the more Hell, Fire and Brimstone made her tense in trepidation, not wanting that to be her immortal fate if she went against her husband's wishes. She made a vow to love, honor, and obey Bervick and had to keep her oath to God.

Lula lay down holding the bible against her chest, sobbing herself to sleep.

Bervick lifted his head when Lula's sobs stopped and moved closer to her, wrapping his arm around.

Lula flicked Bervick's arm off and inched farther away. He shrugged and fell fast asleep.

Chapter 17

Big Ma was tired of Doc pushing everybody away. Distance between the two grew after Mary moved out. Their house was quiet. No children or grandchildren in sight. Visitors came by frequently to sit on the porch or eat with them, but after they left, silence again. Big Ma spent the majority of her time in church while Doc worked and came home in time for dinner, then smoked his pipe and strolled around the house until bed time. Big Ma knew not to bother Doc during his stroll. She had made the mistake of doing so when they were newlyweds, which led to Doc revealing just how mean he could get.

Big Ma would cook special dinners to lighten Doc's somber mood at times. A mood she was no stranger to since he often fell into these deep bouts of depression throughout their marriage. Big Ma never questioned why Doc never offered an explanation. His favorite food and dessert pacified him until his next despairing temperament.

Big Ma and Doc didn't discuss Lula moving to California. Doc found out through word of mouth without Big Ma having to break the news to him. His mood change, after hearing the news, quickly prompted Big Ma to cook his special dish.

After Doc finished eating dinner, Big Ma went to church leaving Doc to his business. He grabbed his pipe and started walking around the house, slightly bent forward looking down at his feet. He blinked slowly with every stride. His pipe dangling from his lip thinking about his father, which meant a deeper, more hollow trail...

Doc's father, Xavier Harrison, had pulled strings through church members to enroll Doc in a school across town. On his first day of school, eleven year-old Doc had a long ten mile walk ahead and had to get up at 4 a.m. with Xavier.

"Com'on son, get up! First day of school t'day," Xavier said over-joyed. Xavier had paced the porch in the dark most of the night with a pipe in his mouth, excited about Doc being the first man in the family to attend school and ecstatic that his son would soon be able to teach him how to read—something Xavier longed for his entire life.

Doc's mother, Anna Harrison, was in the kitchen packing his breakfast and lunch. She had been up since two-thirty a.m. baking and cooking for Doc's first day, making fresh teacakes and buttermilk for his breakfast; crackling, smoked hog malls, and cornbread for his lunch. She also put the finishing touches on a shirt she sewed for Doc to wear under his overall pants.

The church came together to provide everything Doc needed: a homemade school bag, wide straw hat, pencils, books, ruler, and a notebook.

Anna packed Doc's supplies and food in his school bag and gave him a jar of buttermilk. She fixed his clothes numerous times before he left the house.

On the porch, Anna squeezed Doc in her arms, unable to let go.

"Yah gonna snap that boy in two yah squeeze him any harder, Sha," Xavier laughed. Doc grinned, rarely hearing such a joyous sound of laughter come out his father's mouth.

Anna let Doc go, kissed Xavier good-bye, and waved at them as they left. She smiled at Doc walking in his overalls with a straw hat on, holding his school bag over his shoulder and buttermilk jar in hand. She grinned even harder when she saw Xavier put his arm around Doc.

It was dark outside, still too early for the rooster's crow as Xavier and Doc walked side-by-side talking in the dark. It was a rarity for Doc to have Xavier's undivided attention. Xavier rarely communicated with his children, period. He worked a fourteen hour shift six days a week, traveling by foot to local farms to harvest seasonal crops. Then when Xavier was home with Anna and their children, he hardly interacted with them, especially the boys.

Being a child of parents born into slavery, Xavier felt a relationship with his children was an emotional risk. Too many monstrosities took place with black men and their families, which Xavier found out all too well at an early age. Emotional separation was the only resort to maintain mental stability. Anna, in turn, imparted the nurturing to their children while Xavier kept a roof over their heads, clothes on their backs, and food in their bellies.

Doc was confident his bond with Xavier would strengthen since they would be walking together during the week, and he noticed a positive change in Xavier already. Doc marveled over school and how it was already helping him in more ways than one. He looked forward to becoming acquainted with this stranger he called "father". By far, the first day of school was becoming the best day of Doc's life, and he could tell by how exuberant Xavier was acting, it was his as well.

Dawn broke by the time Doc and Xavier reached Old Oak Road where they had to separate. Xavier had to go left and Doc was to keep straight.

Xavier leaned down on one knee fixing Doc's clothes and adjusted his hat. "Son, you a man nah and when yah get there, be polite to yah teacher and fellow schoolmates. Sit up straight, pay close attention and learn everythin' yah can b'cause yah not learning' just fo' you, yah learning fo' me, yah mama, yah younger siblings, and yah kinfolk, yah hear?"

"Yes, sir!" Doc stood up straight poking his chest out while looking directly into Xavier's eyes, ready to adhere to his duties. Xavier smiled and gave Doc a hug—the first embrace Doc had ever received from his father. He squeezed Xavier tight, trembling from the overwhelming yearn for Xavier's love. Doc tried to fight back tears, coughing to stop them from rolling down his face.

Xavier patted Doc's back saying, "Yah alright nah, son?"

"Yes, sir."

Xavier reached into his pocket and handed Doc a pocket knife. "Dis here fo' yah protection. Keep it in yah pocket at all times, yah hear?"

"Yes, sir."

"And put that jar in yah bag. Yah mama scarred it might break, but it's not," Xavier laughed.

Doc smiled and put it in his bag.

Xavier said, "Alright, go on nah. I'll see yah later on t'night."

"Yes, sir."

Xavier watched Doc walk down the road until he was no longer in sight, and then turned, smiling to himself as he began walking down the lone trail to work.

Doc marched down the road with his chest out like a little soldier. Head high and eyes steady, mentally preparing himself to absorb as much knowledge as possible so that he and his family could receive the education they'd been deprived of for far too long. Doc was honored, gracious, and humble to take on this duty that the good Lord set aside from him. On this very day, he became a man.

Doc was a couple of miles from where he separated from Xavier, still marching, giving thanks for his straw hat that protected him from the blazing sun. He took deep breaths inhaling the fresh air to clear his mind for what was in store for him, listening to the birds chirp in the grassland fields while taking in the scenic beauty of

Mother Nature. Taking another deep breath, Doc got a whiff of tobacco. He stopped before coming to a four-way intersection, listening to unfamiliar voices behind the long blades of grass.

First voice said, "How could yah miss that ole thing you asshole, it was right there!"

Second voice yelled back, "Would you shut up, I told yah a fly flew in my eye!"

A third voice said, "Why don't yah both shut the hell up? Who gives a shit what happened, let's just get on home b'fore it get too hot out here!"

Doc started running in the opposite direction and parted through long blades of grass to hide, dropping his hat. He ducked between the blades of grass covering his mouth.

First voice said, "What was that?"

Second voice said, "Com'on, we ain't goin' home empty handed!"

They ran up the road toward the sounds and saw a hat on the ground.

Third voice said, "Would yah look at here? I don't think we hunting animal anymore, fellas."

Doc started trudging through the grass, ducking, trying to cross over to the other road to get away, but the more he moved, the more noise he made. He figured he could out run them through the grass as long as he wasn't seen.

First voice said, "I hear it!"

They followed the sounds.

The first man took his shotgun and shot through the grass.

Doc screamed.

Third voice yelled, "Wait you idiot." He snatched the shot gun from the young man and yelled, "Who's there?"

Doc cried out, "Please don't shoot, sir!"

Third voice said, "Get out here and show yah self."

They stood in the road with their shotguns ready. Doc came out from the long blades of grass with his hands up.

The third voice chuckled, "My my my, look what we've got here, a nigger." The third voice was an older white man with a potbelly and white beard, and wore grease stained overalls and a straw hat. He held up the hat, "Dis yah hat, boy?"

"Yes, sir."

The second voice asked, "What you doin 'round here, nigger?" The second voice was a tall skinny man with blues eyes and dirty blonde hair. He had on a worn out t-shirt with tan colored paints and boots without laces.

"Nothin', sir."

The first voice said, "What you mean 'nothin'?" The first voice looked young in the face with dusty blonde hair, blue eyes, and sunburned skin. He constantly spit tobacco through his stained teeth showing the results of his habit. Doc could tell by the similarity of their eyes that they were all related.

Doc said, "Just goin' to school, sir." Doc cringed at what slipped out of his mouth, now wishing he had listened to Anna's advice about thinking before speaking.

The older man said, "School? Where yah live?"

Doc pointed in the opposite direction from where he was walking.

The old man said, "Well, I suggest you take yah coon ass back home then, boy."

Doc stared at the ground. Before he knew it, his legs broke out running in the direction to school.

One yelled, "Aye, get back here nigger!"

They all started chasing him.

Doc ran fast losing his shoes, still holding tight to his bag full of school supplies, breakfast, and lunch.

The tall skinny man yelled, "Nigger, we gonna shoot you!"

Doc kept running.

The tall skinny man shot his rifle in the air.

Doc stopped abruptly.

The three men caught up to him laughing.

The older man laughed, "Look at that, nigger done pissed himself."

After a good hearty laugh, the old man gained his composure and turned serious. "So, yah wanna learn somethin', huh? Well, I got somethin' to teach yah." He smiled with tobacco stained teeth, grabbed Doc by the arm and dragged him into a wooded area, pushing him against a tree. Doc dug in his pocket grabbing Xavier's pocket knife and held it out shaking uncontrollably, causing it to slip out his hand.

The tall skinny man ran up to Doc, gripping him around by the neck, whispering, "Yah think you gonna hurt somebody, boy," and then punched Doc to the ground.

Doc's vision blurred as he slipped unconscious.

Half an hour later, something warm pouring on his face woke Doc up. He looked up at two of the men relieving themselves, and quickly crawled backwards up against the tree. The men zipped their pants while Doc looked through his swollen eye at his torn school bag, empty jar, shredded notebook paper, broken pencils, and saw that his food was gone.

The older man said, "Nah we're gonna try dis again. Where yah goin', nigger?"

Doc closed his eyes releasing a stream of tears. He had a duty to uphold for his family and couldn't let them down. "School, sir."

The younger man punched Doc in the stomach, pulled him by his overall strap, and waved his fist with each syllable. "You breakin' the law, boy!"

The older man pulled the younger man off Doc and said, "Easy, son, easy," holding up his hands to calm the young man down. "There's more than one way to skin a cat."

The old man punched Doc in his swollen eye. Doc saw stars as tears squirted through open flesh. The old man started ripping Doc's overalls off.

Doc cried, "Stop! Please, sir!"

The old man punched Doc in the stomach, and then jumped behind him, choking him around the neck saying, "Be still, boy."

Doc's body went limp from lose of oxygen.

The old man released Doc to unsnap his own overalls.

The other two men stepped back watching their father sexually attack Doc. The tall skinny man turned away, massaging the back of his neck while the youngest man looked down at his feet. They stood there looking everywhere but at what was taking place, listening to Doc's screams and the loud heaves from their father, hoping nobody out yonder heard him.

It felt like eternity before the screams finally stopped. The old man got up sweating and pulled his dingy overalls back on. He spit at Doc and turned to his son out of breath, "Get over here, boy," he said, snapping his overalls back together. The youngest man didn't move. The old man grabbed his shot gun from against the tree and went over to the youngest man, pushing him down by the neck near Doc, who lay there still crying.

The youngest man didn't touch Doc.

The old man said, "What's yah problem, boy?" He pointed at Doc. "Dis here how you break these niggers."

The younger man said, "I don't wanna, pa." He got up and walked backwards away from Doc.

The old man yelled, "If you don't get yah ass over here, boy! I swear, yah weak just like yah mama!"

The tall skinny man said, "Pa, leave him alone."

The old man pointed. "Hush your goddamn mouth." He turned back to the youngest man and pointed at Doc again. "Get over there nah, boy!"

The youngest man shook his head no backing away and ran off.

The old man screamed, "You good fo' nothin' bastard." He looked at the tall skinny man and said, "Yah brother ain't shit. I'm gonna get him later! Okay, nah, it's your turn."

The tall skinny man said, "Com'on, pa, let's just go."

"Fine then," the old man looked around. "Damn, where's a rope when yah need one."

The old man took his shot gun and put it to Doc's head. Doc could hardly see the gun pointed between his eyes, but froze when he heard it cock back.

The old man said, "Kno' yah place, nigger! Education's for whites only," and then fired a blank.

"God damnit! I'm out of bullets. Give me your gun." The old man snatched the tall skinny man's gun and said, "Dis how yah break these wise guy niggers!" He cocked the gun back and shot another blank.

"Damnit," he said angrily, bashing Doc over the head with the end of the shot gun.

Doc moaned in pain.

The old man repeatedly beat Doc over the head with the end of the shot gun until he tired himself out and no more moans could be heard.

Out of breath wiping off sweat, the old man kicked at Doc's foot.

His lifeless body didn't move.

The old man bent down looking Doc over. "Yeah, he dead. Let's go."

Doc woke up in the dark. His eyes swollen shut. He lay there cold in a trance of confusion and worst of all, humiliation. His naked body felt numb until he tried to move, intensifying the aches and pain as he stumbled up. He limped passed his shredded book bag, broken pencils, pieces of notebook paper and an empty jar, then fell back down crying, holding onto his buttocks from the unbearable throbbing. Fear of the men returning forced Doc back on his feet.

Doc dragged his naked body to the road and collapsed in pain, unable to continue on. He screamed out loud, hoping he was using his last breath for God to hear so that the gates to heaven could open. Living was not an option anymore.

"Doc…Doc!"

Doc heard a faint voice calling from afar. A voice that sprung Doc up. A voice that brought Doc back to coherency helping him breathe again.

"Daddy!" He screamed out. "Daddy!" He screamed from the depths of his soul. "Daddy!" He screamed through the pain and tears.

Xavier and his two brothers ran fast following Doc's voice. They carried shotguns and burning oil lamps to guide them. They had left work early when they got word that Doc didn't return home from school, and trailed the dark roads for hours.

Xavier's brother pointed at a dark lump on the side of the road. They all ran over holding up their oil lamps.

Xavier gasped, "Oh dear God," as they stopped with their mouths open in front of Doc, observing his naked body covered in blood, urine, and semen. Xavier handed his shotgun and oil lamp over to his brother, and bent down lifting his son's swollen face. He swallowed hard picking Doc up slowly, listening to Doc scream in pain as Xavier's brother held the oil lamp up to examine Doc's body. His brother gasped when he stopped the oil lamp near the blood coming from Doc's buttocks. He looked up in horror at Xavier. Xavier scrunched his face shaking his head no at his brother's reaction. His two brothers sorrowfully turned away, unable to bear the sight of Doc or the look on Xavier's face.

They arrived back to the house, Xavier carefully carrying Doc in his arms, listening to his son moan the whole way home.

Anna, family, neighbors, and church members were on the porch waiting outside when they saw Xavier coming with Doc in his arms. Anna fell to her knees screaming, covering her mouth with trembling hands. The men outside stood in disbelief as the women screamed out crying over Doc's battered body. They helped Anna to her feet and followed Xavier into the house.

Xavier laid Doc on the bed, grabbing a sheet to cover his naked son's body, and then he backed away slowly while swallowing hard as he exited the room.

Xavier and the men waited outside while Anna and the women went into action washing Doc down, treating his wounds, crying in unison with Doc the entire time.

Uncles, brothers, male cousins, friends, and neighbors stood outside with Xavier for the rest of the night without anyone breathing a word. They smoked cigars, pipes, and cigarettes, supporting Doc and Xavier in silence. Most of the men stood closer to the road with Xavier to avoid hearing the cries from his house.

Doc never began school after the incident and that was the first and last day Doc and Xavier ever bonded. Xavier's distant behavior returned, worst than before, and he and Doc seldom spoke again...

Hours had passed and Doc was still outside smoking his pipe, blinking slow. He took dawdling strides around the house and didn't realize Big Ma had returned home from church and it was already bed time.

She came out the house and said, "Would yah please come in here and get some sleep, Doc? It's late."

"In a minute woman!" Doc replied.

Part 4

Chapter 18

In 1963, Bervick moved to California, three months prior to Lula, to put a down payment on their house and took baby Deborah with him. He stayed with Cleve and Hattie Ann until he found permanent housing, and then sent for Lula and their children.

Lula smiled down at her children's bewildered faces sitting on the train, too small to see outside the window. Bervick Jr., Luvicy, and little Leroy sat together. Gloria Jean and Joseph sat beside Lula who held Sandra in her lap. Lula was confident they would fall asleep soon after they ate.

The move to Pacoima, California, helped take Lula's mind off of losing her youngest baby girl and how the town was buzzing about what she and Bervick had done. She had already lost her twins at birth and to lose another child broke Lula's heart.

Bervick was long gone, leaving Lula to bear the brunt of the backlash from the family and community; but through a lot of prayer, Lula found solace in knowing that Hattie Ann and Cleve would be great parents, and looked at it as Deborah being a blessing to her dear friends. Lula knew she could see Deborah at any given time thanks to Bervick finding a home close to where Hattie Ann and Cleve lived. Lula imagined her visits with Deborah, wondering if her child would notice she was her birth mother. Hattie Ann made it clear in their adoption agreement that Deborah saw Hattie Ann and Cleve as her biological parents, not Lula and Bervick. Lula had no choice but to respect Hattie Ann's wishes.

On the train, a lady came by Lula's seat with a blue sailor cap, white blouse, blue skirt, stockings, and penny loafer shoes on. Her hair was pinned in a tight bun that accented her round eyes and high arched eyebrows, making her face appear to have a permanent surprised look.

The lady said, "Good afternoon, care to place an order?"

Lula smiled admiring her proper tone. This was the first time Lula encountered someone who sounded similar to the people she saw on neighbor's televisions.

Lula scooted up to look at the lady's nametag. "Hello, Miss Tammy?" Lula raised a brow.

"Yup, it's 'Miss' Tammy. Hopefully one day I'll be a Mrs., but for right now, you can call me Tammy, no Miss needed, honey."

Lula smiled and nodded.

Tammy passed Lula a plastic sealed paper with food listed for sale. Looking at how expensive the food was, Lula remembered seeing a vending machine with more reasonably priced food, plus she had fried chicken and teacakes she packed for their trip.

Lula said, "That's okay, I think I'm going to get some food out of the machines."

Gloria Jean and Joseph looked over at Lula, noticing a change in their mother's dialect. No southern lingo or tone used. Lula learned proper diction from Beatrice and knew when to turn it on and off. She didn't like speaking too country to people from up north.

Tammy asked, "Would you care for something to drink at least?"

"No thank you, ma'am." Lula smiled at the woman and handed her back the expensive menu.

"Alright. If you need anything, I'll be around," Tammy said and continued down the aisle.

Lula leaned over and tapped Bervick Jr.'s shoulder. "I need yah to watch out fo' yah siblings. I'll be right back. Don't anybody move."

She got up and put Sandra in Bervick Jr.'s lap and sat Joseph with the rest of them, then took Gloria Jean with her down the aisle to the vending machines.

Lula looked in the machine at the cheese, bologna, and tuna sandwiches. She turned to the beverage machine full of milk and different colored bottles of juices she had never seen before. She grabbed three cheese sandwiches and five small cartons of chocolate milk. Gloria Jean helped Lula carry the food back to their seats and Lula split the food up for everyone to eat. The oldest got their own chocolate milk while the youngest shared half a carton.

Lula opened her bag of food and gave everyone a piece of chicken after they ate their half of cheese sandwiches. By the looks on their faces and growing silence, Lula knew her babies were enjoying this strange new food and drink.

Tammy walked by accommodating passenger's needs and lifted up her nose to a delicious aroma that she hadn't smelled in years. She stopped where Lula and the children were sitting and looked down at the crumbs on their faces while Lula hurried to clean their mouths with a handkerchief. Tammy's professionalism vanished, licking her lips, looking down at the fried chicken in Lula's bag.

Lula picked up a piece, placed it on a paper bag, and handed it to Tammy. Tammy graciously thanked Lula and sat down on the edge of the seat, biting at the chicken with her eyes closed, humming and hitting her knee. She shook her head in disbelief at the great taste. "Nah dis here is some fried chicken. Dis how my mama cook it. They don't do it like dis up north."

Lula laughed listening to Tammy's native tone. "Where are you originally from?"

"New Orleans, but I moved to New Jersey ten years ago."

"Oh, so you a southern gal, too?"

"Born and raised. My mama moved us up north when I was a teen and I've been there ever since."

Two young men in uniforms walked up to Tammy, warning her to continue her job or else she was going to get caught by their supervisor. Tammy bit into her chicken ignoring them. She was in chicken heaven and almost forgot what good fried chicken can do to a person. The two men kept looking back and forth down the aisles hoping nobody noticed Tammy sitting on the job. Lula offered them a piece of chicken, and as tempting as it was, the two men declined seeing all the mouths Lula had to feed.

One of the men was taller than the other with a skinny built and honey colored skin. The other man was of average built and height with shiny, smooth, chocolate colored skin.

"If you need anything, let me know pretty lady," the shorter man said to Lula, flashing his milk white teeth.

Tammy said, "Give it a rest, Eddie," while chewing off chicken gristle. Eddie shrugged and looked back at Lula trying to catch her eye. He thought she was the most beautiful woman he'd ever seen and wanted her captivating eyes to lock with his.

Lula said, "Thank you, sir," while adjusting Sandra in her lap to display the wedding ring on her finger.

Eddie strained a fake smile before saying his goodbyes and swiftly disappeared down the aisle.

Tammy wiped the crumbs from her mouth chuckling at his speedy exit. "Eddie saw you when you first got on the train. Kids and all, that fool honestly thought he had a chance."

Tammy and the slim man laughed while Lula looked down at her children to avoid laughing at poor Eddie.

The slim man nudged Tammy to look up at their supervisor coming down the aisle and she quickly got up and whispered, "I'll be back," to Lula. Tammy and the slim man went back to work.

Lula sat with her children enjoying the rest of their meal together and cleaned their faces, clothes, and their area after they were finished.

Tammy kept her word and came back a few hours later to sit and chat with Lula for a moment during her break. As time progressed, they were still talking, laughing like best friends reuniting. Tammy was seated holding Joseph in her lap while the other children were asleep. She talked about growing up as an only child and being lonely most of her life. Her stories were heartfelt, yet amusing. Lula kept covering her mouth holding in laughter, playfully telling Tammy to stop with her sly remarks about her family and how crazy some of them were. Lula had to keep motioning Tammy to lower her voice when the children started stirring.

Tammy asked, "So where you headed?"

"Pacoima, California."

"Oh, so you getting out of the dirty south too, huh? Where you from?"

"Eunice, Louisiana."

"Wow, you're moving a world apart from home. Were you born and raised there, too?"

"Yes, ma'am. I don't kno' what to expect out in California tho'."

"I'll tell you one thing for sure, women got a hell of a lot more freedom than they do down south! California's a nice place, too. More modern. Upbeat. Why you leaving Eunice, if you don't mind me asking?"

"No, Sha, I don't mind. Family issues, I reckon. And the town's too small to keep our business to ourselves. I don't care too much for gossip, let alone be the person everybody talking bout."

"What they say?"

"A lot of the church women talked bout my clothes and how my husband wasn't taking care of us."

"You know you can't run from gossip, honey. Trust me when I tell you that. But what you mean when you say 'family issues'? And stop me if I'm getting to personal, honey, it's just so boring on these damn trains sometimes. Pay good though."

"Oh, it's no bother, Sha." Lula leaned her head back, shifting Sandra's sleeping body to the other side. "My family don't care fo' my husband, so they don't speak to me anymore. I understand their concerns, but they just don't understand the reasons fo' my decision and why I love him so much. I don't know why they just didn't accept him and let us be. I know he had a hard time finding work, but don't all men have that problem at some point in their life?"

"Well, hopefully he find work out west. You're too pretty of a lady to be living less than a queen. That's probably why your family is so upset."

Lula nodded even though she wasn't on the same accord as Tammy. As a saved Christian woman, Lula was content with her marriage, under any and all circumstances.

Lula felt a need to defend her religious beliefs and Bervick. "I pride myself in being a good wife, a great mother, and to serve my Lord, Jesus Christ. I am saved, baptized and filled with the Holy Ghost. In serving God, I have to serve my husband and that means through thick and thin, 'til death do us part. I've stuck by him through our toughest times and will continue to do so, and I'm honored to be with such a great anointed man of God. He is my savior and even tho' he isn't perfect, he is as close to God as I'm going to get."

Tammy laughed.

Lula smiled, "What's so funny, Sha?"

"I don't know," Tammy shook her head. "It seems like I'm not the one you're trying to convince, honey. I never met the man so I can't judge, but if you ask me, it seems like *you're* the prize! You're beautiful, hair look nice, got pretty white teeth, and cute little body for a woman with all these babies. And your children look nice and well-mannered, thank God. You should see some of these little monsters that be riding on here crying and screaming the whole ride." Tammy laughed, "But you have a beautiful family and your husband should work hard to bless y'all with the best life possible, honey."

"He does in his own way. He's the best Christian man I know and he can prophesize things before they happen."

"Really? Such as?"

"Well, he prophesized that my oldest girl was gonna get sick if I kept working, and she did, and by the grace of God, she's alive and well today. And he knew my family wasn't gonna help us move, although I wish he was wrong bout that one. And it's other stuff he prophesized that came to pass, too. He prays a lot, fast a lot, and he's very close to God."

"And so are you!"

Lula looked puzzled.

"Yes you, honey. Prophesizing don't take much if you ask me. All it is, is just good old fashion common sense."

"So I can prophesize like him?"

"Yes, honey."

"Women can't do no such a thing," Lula said, repeating the words chiseled in her brain since childhood.

Tammy smiled at Lula's naiveté and quickly changed the subject. "So, how your folks feel about you moving to California?"

"Hurt, I reckon. My grandmother didn't even say good-bye."

"What about your parents?"

"I have no parents."

"I'm sorry to hear that. So it was just you and your grandmother growing up?"

"No, it was me, my two sisters, my grandfather and grandmother. My older sister moved out first, then I left, thank the Lord. I didn't like living there."

"Why not?" Tammy laughed, "I love going to my granny's house."

"My grandmother was strict on us," Lula looked down and asked, "Can I be honest with you?"

"Sure, honey?"

"I loved church, but it was just too much sometimes. They'd have us in there praying 'til the early morning. I got problems with my knees today because of all that kneeling."

"Your grandfather didn't help balance your grandmother out with all that church. My grandfather was pretty easy going."

"No, I got tired of him the most!" Lula's eyes watered. She dabbed at her eyes with her finger and pulled Sandra closer, rocking, looking out the window.

Tammy sucked on her bottom lip watching Lula. She got up and laid Joseph next to Lula and said, "You and your kids have a safe and blessed trip, Mrs. Lula Mae, and if you need me, just wave a hand."

Lula smiled and said thank you with her lips. Tammy waved goodbye and left.

A couple of hours later, Lula woke to something wet seeping in her dress. She lifted Sandra and saw that she had wet her diaper through the plastic pants. Lula got up, stood Sandra in the seat, and grabbed their small suitcase from above which was full of extra clothes and a towel to wash and change Sandra. When pulling the suitcase down, Lula noticed it was heavier than when she had packed it. Opening it, she was shocked to find the suitcase full of cheese sandwiches and cartons of chocolate milk.

Lula smiled, "Aww, thanks Tammy," she said to herself.

Lula went to the bathroom and washed and changed Sandra. They returned back to their seat and Sandra fell back to sleep.

Lula sat chewing Doublemint gum while looking out the window. She thought about how Doc was so mean and aloof towards her, Big Ma, Lillie, Mary, and his own children. The stories Leroy told about Doc was playing back in Lula's head as she wondered how Doc could be so cruel to his own family. She couldn't bring herself to hating Doc, but was glad to be moving as far away from him as possible and hoped to never see him again.

After checking on each of her children and adjusting their sleeping bodies so that they didn't get any crooks in their necks, Lula fell asleep.

***

Lula and Bervick moved into a three bedroom, one bathroom house. The front of the house had a tiny porch with three steps in the front and a cemented walkway lining the grassless yard. The inside of their house had the basic appliances and was partly furnished. A long hallway led to the back two bedrooms, both positioned on the left, and the kitchen sat to the right of the front entrance hall. A garage was attached to the back of the house with color stained glass windows on the side walls.

Lula, Bervick, and the children settled in Pacoima, worlds apart from Eunice. The shape, structure, and style of their house were completely different. Lula had to now shop at a place called "a grocery store" since there were no signs of growing gardens in the neighborhood, and their own yard couldn't sustain grass. She had to walk six blocks to this foreign place that sold harvested vegetables, lifeless chickens, and de-shelled nuts already prepared for purchase. Lula was shocked at the packaged meat, picking packages up in amazement while wondering how meat stayed fresh for so long. She examined the vegetables and fruit laid out with the same shape, texture, and size. Vegetables from their garden in Eunice grew differently, all having their own unique sizes and shapes. It took some time for Lula to get used to the grocery store and the different tasting food in it.

She could only afford the bare essentials and walked back home carrying vegetables, eggs, corn meal, can milk, molasses, rice, beans, okra and toilette paper. Lula fed the kids more meatless dishes such as rice and eggs, rice and milk, cornbread and milk, teacakes with molasses, beans, and baked sweet potatoes. The kid's favorite dish was couscous with sugar, butter, and milk. Alas, the children ate less food. Bervick made it mandatory for everyone to fast on Tuesdays and Fridays, believing that food was a necessary evil to the body and weighed the spirit down causing a separation between them and God.

Months passed and Lula adjusted well to their new lifestyle. She got the kids ready for school in the morning, did their hair, ironed their clothes, and made their lunches. Once they were gone, Lula took the two youngest, Sandra and Joseph, and went across the street to a woman she befriended named Fran, who was a beautician that did hair from her house. When she saw Gloria Jean and Luvicy's hair one day, Fran offered Lula a chair to do hair.

Fran was a non-religious woman who didn't bite her tongue. A short round shaped woman with no kids, she lived alone ever since her divorce from her husband of eight years. She was ten years older than Lula, and took a liking to her fast, enjoying Lula and the children's company while doing hair.

Women came from all parts of the town to get their hair straightened and curled for church, work, school, or the man in their life. Lula was a master with a straightening comb and began having regular clients. They were patient with Lula having to stop to care for Sandra and Joseph, and were generous with tips because of it. When the work day ended, Lula put her two toddlers down for a nap and sat outside with Fran, talking before the rest of the kids came home from school.

Fran said, "Your kids fall asleep like clockwork."

"Yeah, I got dem on a good schedule."

"I wouldn't mind if they were up with us. You got some well-behaved children."

"Thanks, Sha. Yah kno' what's so funny, yah like the fifth person that told me that out here. I don't see kids behavin' any other way in Eunice."

"Southern children are more mellow than the ones out here. Watch, you'll see soon enough."

"Oh, okay."

Fran held up a cigarette, "You mind?"

"No, go 'head, Sha."

Fran lit her cigarette, took a drag, and then picked up a cold beer and asked, "Want one?"

"No thanks."

"I'm going in the house to get you one. Hell, you deserve one after a hard day of work and caring for them children, too? You need something to take the edge off a bit." She chuckled, "Not to mention that husband of yours, but I'm not going to discuss that right now."

Fran laughed going into the house to get a beer for Lula. She came back out taking another puff of cigarette while handing Lula a beer.

Lula said, "I don't understand why everyone say there's somethin' wrong with my Bervick. Yah only met him twice. I thought it was just the people down in Eunice."

"I'm not saying something wrong with him," Fran said, taking a huge swallow of beer, almost emptying the can in one gulp, then burped. "That's how you drink a beer," she said hitting her chest.

"Take it in fast! But anyhow, it's just something about your husband that give me the creeps. I don't understand how a pretty gal like you married such a creepy man. I guess you see something we don't. And all that fasting stuff he got y'all doing is insane. Those are growing children. They got to eat!"

Lula shook her head. "It's in the bible, Sha. Besides, only my oldest chillun fast."

"In the bible? Gal, can you imagine this world if everyone followed the bible verbatim? Them kids got to eat!"

Fran got up from her chair wearing her white shorts and a sleeveless top that exposed her big arms, and went back into the house finishing the little beer left in the can. Lula sat on the porch pondering what Fran said about the kids fasting, and agreed with Fran in a way. Lula knew she was a God fearing Christian woman, honoring and obeying her husband, and didn't want to go against Bervick's wishes. On the other hand, her growing kids had to eat regular meals every day.

Fran came back outside already drinking her second beer. When Fran belched taking a seat, Lula glanced over at Fran's sleeveless top and short pants, a more conducive attire for the warm weather. Lula looked down at her own clothing. The old buttoned up blouse and skirt below the knee covering her overheated body made that beer more enticing. It wouldn't hurt to take a little sip to cool off. Lula was a little curious to see what the fuss was all about. She opened the cold beer can and tasted it, frowning at the icky taste.

Fran said, "Don't worry. Just take a few more sips. It's an acquired taste. You'll get use to it."

Lula took a couple more gulps, cringing at the taste.

Fran said, "Slow down a bit. Let it get in that bloodstream."

Unbeknownst to Fran, Lula was already feeling a change from those few sips, causing her mind to dwell on Fran's previous words and how a total stranger, far away from Eunice folks, had the exact same views on Bervick. Lula took another swig and thought about how her children needed clothes, more food, and a car since she was getting tired of carrying heavy bags from the grocery store. Bervick forbade Lula from studying to get a driver's license, stating that God would always make a way for them to get to their desired destinations.

Lula thought about how their financial circumstances were ending up the same as when they were in Eunice. She did hair making more money than Bervick while he took low paying odd jobs. His excuse was that God blessed him with these jobs which paid for their bare essentials, and to ask God for more would be the deadly sin of greed.

Lula took another sip, provoking her thoughts to visit the issue she disagreed with the most—Bervick giving almost half their earnings to the new church they attended. She didn't object to their donations, but a feeling of dissatisfaction started growing within her knowing that an obstinate husband like Bervick would stand by his conviction to give a percentage of their income to the Lord's house.

Thinking over her first few months in California, Lula began to believe there may be some truth in what Big Ma and her family was saying about Bervick.

She quickly shook off that possibility.

The oath she had taken to honor and cherish Bervick to avoid Hell was enough to dismiss any third party perspectives on their marriage. Their children deserved a mother and father in a stable and happy household—something Lula was deprived of at an early age.

Lula lifted the can of beer, inspecting it in amazement.

Fran laughed, "That's a hell of a drink, huh?"

"It sho' is, Sha! I just hope the good Lord forgive me fo' dis one."

Fran rolled her eyes laughing.

***

Bervick, Lula, and their children joined First San Fernando Valley Church of God and Christ once they moved to Pacoima, California, and never missed a Sunday. They were devoted members alongside Cleve, Hattie Ann, Bervick's cousin Sis, and a few other distant relatives who relocated out west from Eunice. They also met an elderly couple, Brother and Mother Adams, whom they built a tight bond with.

Brother and Mother Adams were devoted members of the church. The eldest and most respected evangelist and missionary, it was an honor for Lula to have them at their house. The Adams was retired school teachers who never had children of their own. Church members allowed Brother and Mother Adams to watch their children and sent them home spoiled rotten. They'd watch Lula's children when she and Bervick sold barbeque hotdogs or sweet dough pies for the church. The children loved going over to the Adams' house, playing with their pet monkey, Jojo, and enjoyed fresh baked cookies, cakes, pies, and candy. Mother Adams took a preferential liking to Lula's kids. She saw Lula as a daughter and thought her children were cute, well-mannered, and neat, regardless of their old clothing. She loved to see how Lula did her girls' hair, and in turn, Mother Adams' referred the most clients to Lula. When Lula picked her children up in the evening, Mother Adams would give a bag of food for Lula to take home, aware that Bervick gave a lot of their income to the church. She wanted to make sure Lula's adjustment to California was smooth and stress-free.

Adjusting to a bigger church, with more than four hundred members, came easy for Lula and Bervick to get back into the rhythm of attending church again after their departure from the church in Eunice. Lula spent her free time raising money for the church by selling her famous sweet dough pies, which sold as quickly as they did in Eunice. The people out west had never tasted such a unique tasting pie and it rapidly became high in demand. Before Lula's pie stand was set, she would sell out of them.

Bervick used his special barbeque sauce on hotdogs to sell for twenty-five cents apiece, adding to his church contribution. Lula put her pie selling on hold at times to assist Bervick in selling the barbeque hotdogs. They were easier to make and sell.

It was difficult doing hair, taking care of children, attending church, and making pies all night and on weekends. Their household income took a loss since Bervick gave forty percent of their income to the church, not including the money spent to purchase the food they sold.

After returning home from a long day of selling hotdogs, Lula gave the her kids baths, warmed up beans and rice with cornbread for dinner, and put them down for the night while Bervick stayed at the church.

She went into her bedroom to find something to wear for the next day and saw the same two dresses, skirt, and blouse she wore often. She walked over to the mirror and stared herself down, looking at the white skirt with a flower print on it and same old blouse she wore almost every Sunday to church. Lula sneaked into her children's room, opening the door wide enough to let the hallway light shine upon her children who were sleeping on two mattresses on the floor, just like they did back in Eunice. She walked over to their closet to examine their clothes and was content with the effort she put into cleaning and ironing them to ensure her children looked fresh for school, except, they still needed more clothes. She smiled down at them sleeping, and then silently closed the door turning the hallway light off.

Lula sat on the edge of the bed feeling restless that night. She calculated the funds for the household and things weren't adding up.

Bervick recently found better odd jobs working forty hours a week, and still, she was making more money than him, which took care of the majority of their household expenses. She believed Bervick to be the man of the house who took care of the family finances, and never once questioned how he distributed their income; however, Lula felt some of the money Bervick gave to the church could be reallocated towards buying more clothes for their children.

Lula wept quietly at the edge of the bed feeling hopeless about discussing this issue with Bervick. He wasn't going to distribute funds from the church to buy new clothes for the children. Yet, she had to bring this issue up because now her babies were starting to suffer due to his financial decisions.

In the mist of her tears, Lula looked up at the clock. Bervick was late!

The next morning, Lula woke up and heard Bervick in the kitchen preparing coffee and toast. She got up out of bed, walked into the kitchen and gave Bervick a kiss on his cheek, saying, "Can we talk?"

Bervick grabbed his toast and coffee and followed Lula into the bedroom, closing the door behind them. Lula opened the drawers showing the empty spaces in them, and then went over to the closet and pulled out her two dresses, skirt, and blouse, throwing them on the bed next to Bervick.

"You see that," Lula pointed at the clothes, "That's what I wear all week long, and the amount of clothes the kids got should be a crime b'fore God. Me and the kids need clothes bad. I'm tired of wearin' the same ole skirt and blouse to church. I do my best to change up our clothes, spendin' extra hours cleanin' and ironin' dem to make 'em look betta. We need new clothes! You, too."

Bervick took a bite of his toast, dropping crumbs on Lula's dress. She picked up the dress and shook it out looking over at him with an annoyed look. Bervick shrugged and took a sip of his coffee to wash down his toast, then said, "Y'all don't need new clothes, Sha. God already gave us the clothes on our back, so there's no need fo' all that extra stuff. It's a waste. As long as y'all ain't walkin' 'round here naked, y'all be just fine. God gives us what we need, not what we want."

He took another bite of toast, now dropping crumbs on the floor. Lula put her hands on her hip looking at Bervick, then at the crumbs, and back up at Bervick. Bervick shrugged again. He brushed the crumbs off his shirt to the floor.

Lula said, "Why yah doin' that?"

"I'll get it later, Sha."

"Please listen to me! I kno' we can do without the extra clothes and I kno' God provides the basics in our life, but I wanna see my babies goin' to church and school lookin' nicer. I'm sho' it's not going against God to provide just a little bit more clothes, don't yah think?"

"Do yah got money fo' all these clothes yah wanna buy?"

"No, but I could if we use some of the money you been givin' the church to buy dem."

"Absolutely not! We ain't gonna do no such a thing and don't bring that devil talk into my house again. When yah hang 'round with devils, yah turn into one and that Fran woman is just that. Don't think I don't kno' bout you drinkin' that devil juice over there with her."

"One beer. That's all I had..." Lula scratched at her chin, "Wait a minute. How yah kno'?"

"My God told me."

"You been watchin' me?"

Bervick was quiet.

Lula threw her hands up. "Nevermind. Let's just stay on the subject right nah. Look at dis!" She picked up her dress and wiggled her finger through a hole underneath the arm of the dress. "See that? I can't even raise my arms high to praise his name without being self-conscious of someone seeing that." She threw the dress back on the bed and picked up her blouse. "And look here!" She slightly tore a piece of blouse off. "See how easily that came off! Dis here is worn out!" Lula threw the blouse back on the bed. "And have yah even bother to notice how the kids been lookin' lately? Their stuff is old and worn, too. I do my best to salvage the little clothes they got, but I can only iron and wash dem so many times."

"So yah say all dis to say what, Lula Mae?"

"We need clothes!"

Bervick was startled by Lula's tone. He had never heard Lula raise her voice. He took another sip of coffee to shake the rattle off.

She said, "And bout the beer yah *heard* me drinkin', yes I was drinkin' a beer. *One* can of beer. There ain't nothin' wrong with that. I stayed in prayer bout it and came to believe it wasn't as bad as I thought."

"I'm not gonna sit here and argue with yah, Lula Mae. I'm not buyin' no new clothes fo' you or the chillun. Y'all got clothes. The Lord's house gets all our extra money. And I don't want yah drinkin' that devil juice anymore with that woman, either! Nah, I'm done talkin'."

Bervick got up from the bed and exited the bedroom taking another bite of toast. Lula feared her urge to yell at him. She knew that would be wrong, so being a God fearing woman that honored and obeyed her husband, Lula remained silent. Still, the anger inside her was building, making it difficult to ignore.

She sat on the edge of the bed and picked up her bible. Pastor Evans' embedded sermons echoed in her mind. *Woman, you must honor and obey your husband's and know your place with your husband. If you take a vow in front of God, you must abide by the rules of our Lord and Savior Jesus Christ and not give into your selfish needs and worldly desires, or else suffer the consequences of your final resting place in Hell, Fire and Brimstone.* The thunderous applauds and loud "halleluiahs" from the congregation confirmed for eight year-old Lula that Pastor Evans' sermon was correct. The visual he depicted of Hell, Fire and Brimstone frightened Lula, and she kept that visual at the forefront of her interactions with Bervick.

With the bible in hand, Lula prayed away her selfish behavior toward Bervick. He worked hard all day, praised God in church all night, only to return home late and do everything all over again the next day. God chose this for Bervick. It wasn't his fault.

Lula prayed away her negative feelings towards Bervick and placed the bible down on the nightstand to go in the kitchen and make amends with her husband.

In the kitchen, she watched Bervick spread butter on toast for their children who were now up sitting at the table. She went over to Bervick, hugged him from behind, and whispered, "God did provide enough fo' us. I do apologize."

Bervick pulled away from Lula and walked over to the kids, placing a plate full of toast on the table. Lula smiled and playfully hit his arm while the children helped themselves to toast, watching. Bervick grabbed milk out of the refrigerator and cups out of the cupboard, ignoring Lula playing with him. He waved her away, but she laughed and kept playing to lighten him up. "Com'on Bervick," she said giving him love taps, "Let's see what yah got!"

He waved Lula away and poured another cup of black coffee.

"Look at daddy y'all, look at daddy," she said making faces, grabbing at him. The kids laughed chewing on their toast.

Bervick turned to Lula with a straight face. "Leave me alone, woman!"

Lula paused.

Bervick picked up his coffee, snatched another piece of toast from the plate and left out the kitchen to the bedroom, slamming the door behind him.

Lula stood in the middle of the kitchen staring at the bedroom door for a moment. She looked over at the kids staring at her with crumbs on their faces still holding their toast. She hurried to the stove putting on a pot of water to make oatmeal. One-by-one, they turned away from their mother, taking slower bites of their toast, quietly listening to Lula prepare the rest of their breakfast in silence.

Chapter 19

A year passed and Lula was pregnant with her eighth child. Like her previous pregnancies, she fell sick again. Fran and Bervick's cousin, Sis, went and helped take care of the children while Lula was bed-ridden. The kids spent most of their time playing outside after school. The oldest, Gloria Jean, Bervick Jr., and little Leroy watched over Luvicy, Sandra, and Joseph while outside.

Since Bervick's work hours increased, Fran and Sis kept Lula company during the day, feeding her homemade soup, and Fran combed Lula's hair while they sat and talked.

Sis said, "Lula Mae, you gotta go to the doctor, Sha."

Sis was a full-blooded Creole woman and spoke Creole as a first language before being introduced to English in school. She wore her hair curly and had reddish, light brown skin like Bervick. A petite woman, Sis had a loud mouth to compensate for her tiny size. She was a lot like Fran, except older and religious, never missing a Sunday service since a child.

Lula was in bed with Sis on one side lying down with a pillow underneath her arms and Fran on the other side doing Lula's hair.

Lula responded, "Dis ain't nothin' new fo' me. I get sick durin' my pregnancies. I'll be alright."

Fran said, "It's not healthy for you to be getting sick every time you get pregnant, Lula Mae. When a woman start having babies back-to-back so young, it wears on that young body."

"It ain't nothin' the Lord can't heal."

Sis laughed, "You soundin' more and more like Bervick, Sha."

Lula said, "And he's right. God always healed me after my babies were born."

"Yeah, 'til Bervick got yah pregnant again a month later. I love my cousin dearly, but he got to stop dis, Sha."

"He's my husband, Sis, what am I 'pose to do, tell him 'no'?"

Fran said, "YES! He need to stay off you, give you a break and let your body rest. Your body too young to be carrying baby after baby like that. Don't worry about his needs, it ain't like he gonna fall over and die. You need to enjoy *not* being pregnant for once."

Sis said, "Com'on nah, that's my cousin yah talkin' bout. Can't talk bout my blood."

Fran said, "Oh please, Sis, you feel the same way I do. As a friend, I choose to tell Lula Mae upfront instead of talking about her behind her back like y'all church folks do."

Sis gave Fran an evil look.

"Don't be mad at me." Fran circled her hand across her face, "You see only one face here. I see two faces with y'all holy rollers though." She chuckled.

Lula asked, "Ya'll been talkin' bout me?" She looked over at Sis.

"No, Sha, we been talkin' more bout my damn cousin. 'Cuse my language. Lord forgive me."

"Sis, yah kno' dis is one of the reasons I left Eunice."

"Can't run from talk, Sha. Especially married to him. I bet if you go out to the desert, you'll find gossip somewhere," Sis laughed. "Besides, our family been talkin' bout Bervick b'fore y'all married. He went from being a halfway decent kid to some crazed nut talkin' bout he God's prophet or somethin'. My daddy quit going with Bervick to Aunt Christina and Papa Joe's barn b'cause he said Bervick went mad. Told us to stay away from him, too."

Sis felt good letting that fact out. But what she didn't tell Lula was that their family spoke to Bervick on numerous occasions to stop having children, given that he barely took care of the ones he had.

Lula said, "Alright, I'll ask him to take me to the doctor so I can attend church soon. It's been four weeks. I miss everybody."

Lula enjoyed the unity of the church in Pacoima and how they welcomed their family with open arms. She felt bad that she couldn't cook or bake throughout the week to earn money for the church, and despised being bed bound alone in her room on Sundays. She prayed for strength to get well soon so that she could praise God with her family and friends.

Sis and Fran looked at each other, alarmed at hearing Lula wanting to return back to church. They looked away trying to act normal, but it was too late, Lula noticed.

Lula stopped Fran from brushing her hair and sat up looking back and forth at the both of them. "What is it?"

Sis said, "Nothin', Sha. I'm mindin' mine." She cleared her throat looking over at the wall.

Lula turned to Fran. "Talk to me, Fran."

Fran let out an exhausting breath, not wanting to bring up the subject. "You need to wait until you get better first. We're not going to tell you nothing while you're sick."

Lula's tone lowered, "Tell me."

Fran looked over at Sis whose head was turned to the wall. Fran shifted her body to look Lula in the face. "I can't say anything because I'm not a hundred percent sure about this. It's my own speculation without no facts to back it. Matter of fact, it's gossip and you know how that go. I don't wanna get you upset in anyway so please, Lula Mae, just relax for now."

Lula lay back down looking at Fran with inquisitive eyes, and then turned to Sis, who happened to be busy reading Lula's bible.

The queasiness in her stomach made Lula give up for now. She was too ill to interrogate them any further. She smiled at Fran, pointing at her hair for Fran to finish brushing it.

In between Fran's brushing, Lula said, "Sis, can you do me a favor and iron my cream skirt with the flower print hangin' in my closet please? I wanna make sho' it's pressed fo' Sunday's service. I need to be in the Lord's house again."

***

Lula convinced Bervick to take her to the doctor a couple days after speaking with Sis and Fran. She did so by telling Bervick that the church was talking about him neglecting to take her to the doctor. Bervick scheduled an appointment immediately. The last thing Bervick wanted was for this pastor's perception of him to be altered.

In the doctor's office, Lula and Bervick sat in a room waiting for the results of her physical. An old white man walked in wearing a long white coat, slacks, and dress shoes, holding a chart in his hand. "Mr. and Mrs. Frank, I have good news and bad news. The good news is, the baby seems to be doing just fine. It seems all you have is a urinary tract infection that can easily be cleared up. The bad news is, I highly recommend this be your last baby! Your body is very weak and eight babies has taken its toll on your body causing a slow break down, which will make you more susceptible to illness if you do not allow your body time to properly heal. I prescribed antibiotics for your urinary tract infection that won't affect the baby. You'll be pain-free in a few days. You're lucky to have come to me when you did, the infection would've gotten worse."

"Thank you doctor," Bervick said, getting up to shake the doctor's hand. Lula remained seated, wincing and holding her stomach, now free to show Bervick how much pain she was in without fearing him insisting that God was going to cure her.

The doctor said, "Get the antibiotics right away for her, Mr. Frank."

"Yes, sir. I surely will."

Lula smiled at the doctor, showing her gratitude for his help.

The doctor said, "You have a beautiful smile. What do you use on your teeth?"

Lula smiled bashfully covering her mouth, "Toothpaste."

The doctor laughed, "I mean which one?"

"Forgot the name of it."

"That's fine, Mrs. Frank."

Bervick said, "Good day, sir," and hurried Lula up to leave. He noticed the doctor treating Lula the same way other men treated her, even after Bervick's continuous efforts to keep her pregnant to show that she was already taken. *Can't he see her stomach,* Bervick thought when another man looked Lula's way.

Before Lula and Bervick exited the doctor's office, the doctor held out a form for Bervick to sign. "Excuse me, Mr. Frank, I need your John Hancock right here."

"My name's Bervick Frank, sir. Not John Hancock?"

The doctor said, "Oh no, I mean your signature, Mr. Frank. John Hancock signed the Declaration of Independence. That terminology came from how pronounced and legible his signature appeared on it."

"Oh, I see," Bervick laughed nervously. "If yah give me the form, I'll sign it when I get home and bring it back to you tomorrow mornin'."

"I do apologize, Mr. Frank, but we need this form for verification of your wife's visit."

Bervick took the clipboard from the doctor and signed it.

The doctor looked at the form, then back up at Bervick. "We can't accept this, Mr. Frank. It's only an 'X' here."

Bervick turned away rubbing the back of his neck. The doctor held the clipboard in front of Bervick, waiting for him to sign. He quickly pulled it away from in front of Bervick, now realizing the issue.

The doctor said in a low tone, "Can your wife sign for you, Mr. Frank?"

"No! No she can't!"

Lula looked down at her shoes trying not to hear the conversation.

The doctor said, "My apologies, Mr. Frank, but I need a signature before you both leave." He looked over at Lula, "Mrs. Frank, are you able to sign this form for your husband?"

Lula never looked up and whispered, "Yes, sir."

She hesitated before taking the form and signing it.

The doctor took a glimpse at it, "Thank you, Mrs. Frank. You're penmanship is superb."

Lula wryly smiled still focusing on her shoes.

When they left the doctor's office, Bervick promised himself never to step foot in a doctor's office again, no matter what condition Lula was in or what the church thought of him. The Lord was all the doctor she needed. If he would have obeyed God and allowed Lula to heal on her own, there wouldn't have been no need for a signature in the first place. Something bad happened every time Bervick went against God's wishes. Bervick knew this was God's way of paying him back for defying *him*. God was in control always.

***

Lula wasn't able to attend church the following Sunday due to Bervick refusing to buy the antibiotics she needed to get well. He left it up to God to heal her. When Fran visited, Lula was in so much pain, Fran had no choice but to take action. After Bervick left for work one day, Fran gave Lula a mixture of elder flowers, yarrow, and peppermint leaf tea to kill the infection without harming the baby.

Two weeks later, Lula was well enough to attend church with Bervick and their children. She did the girls' hair in curls, cut the boys' hair, and neatly ironed their clothes while she wore the same cream skirt with the flower print on the side that Sis ironed two weeks ago.

Church members were excited to see Lula back and she was glad to be back. She singed loud, clapped hard, and praised the Lord's name giving thanks for the healing. She didn't bother to mind Bervick turning his head looking back every five minutes.

When service ended, everyone went downstairs to eat and mingle. Lula, Bervick, their children, Sis, and Fran—which Lula thought was odd for Fran to attend church—sat at the same table eating. Bervick got up from the table and went to the other side of the room. Lula was too busy laughing and talking, that she didn't notice Bervick was gone, but did sense a change in Fran and Sis' disposition. They got quiet with a hint of agitation.

Lula asked, "Y'all alright?"

Fran and Sis stared at Lula with disturbed looks on their faces.

Lula said, "It's good to see your attendance in church, Fran. Thank the Lord fo' your presence here t'day, Sha."

"It's good to be here, better yet, it's great to see you up and well again."

"Thanks to you. You're a blessin' in my life, both of yah are."

"Likewise, sweetie. I had to get you back here in church," Fran said, nudging Sis.

"Oh yeah," Sis laughed nervously. "It's good to see yah back. Back listenin' to these wonderful sermons, and singin, and praisin', and watchin' over yah chillun, *and husband*."

Sis smiled turning her attention to Joseph, who was seated on a thick book next to her. "Look at those big ole cheeks!" She gave him quick kisses all over his cheeks. Joseph smacked at his cheek using both hands with a disgusted look on his face.

Everyone laughed.

Sis laughed, "You stop wipin' my kisses away, boy," and began tickling him.

Fran whispered, "Lula Mae, bring your baby girl Sandra by my house tomorrow so I can scrape her scalp and give her an oil treatment. Her scalp's dry."

Lula felt on Sandra's head, "I kno'. I wanted to take her to the doctor fo' it but…well, yah kno'."

Fran said, "Like hell I know," and quickly covered her mouth hoping no one heard her. "Damn, I forgot…oh my Lord help me!"

Lula laughed, "Girl, that's why yah butt need to be in church more. What brings yah hear t'day anyways? It ain't Easter Sunday."

"The food."

"Fran, yah kno' we eat dinner here every other Sunday."

Fran wiped her mouth and threw the napkin in her plate. She dug food out the sides of her mouth and asked, "Where Bervick go?"

Sis looked up to see Lula's response.

Lula shrugged getting up to clean her children's mouths.

Fran took a piece of uneaten chicken off little Sandra's plate and started eating it while Lula wiped Joseph's mouth. When she sat back down, Lula's posture straightened as if she had seen a ghost, now sensing where Fran was going with her question.

Lula stood on her toes searching for Bervick in the crowded room and spotted him sitting at a table with a couple that was new members of the church. "He's over there talkin'," she pointed, sitting back down to clean little Leroy's face.

Fran said, "You know them?"

"No."

"My point exactly. That's that damn Geneva Jo and her husband Ralph."

"Mind yah mouth, Fran. We're still in the Lord's house and in front of—" Lula pointed to her children.

Fran took another bite of fried chicken and said with a mouth full, "Sorry." She filled her mouth with greens from Sandra's plate and pointed over to where Bervick was sitting. "Why don't you go over there and introduce yourself?"

Sis leaned away from Fran, appalled at the question, and more so repulsed by the way Fran was dabbing a roll in the plate full of gravy, chewing with her mouth open. Sis said, "Can you be just a lil' bit more disgustin', Fran? These chillun eat betta than you."

Fran sipped on her soda water, belched, and wiped her mouth with the back of her hand. "If you don't like it, don't look!" She rolled her eyes turning to Lula, "Anyway, Lula Mae, like I was saying, it would be good for you to go over there and introduce yourself."

"Why should I?" Lula shrugged, "I'm too tired to go over there anyways." She took a bite of her potato salad.

Fran leaned back staring at Bervick and the couple. "Thought you'd like to meet them, that's all. Maybe next time."

Lula bit at her lip wondering what Fran was getting at, igniting her curiosity. "Okay," Lula said, getting up from the table to see what Fran was indirectly communicating. She walked over to where Bervick was seated while Fran and Sis watched intently from the table.

Bervick saw Lula walking up and got up from his chair. "Here yah are, honey."

Lula looked at Bervick for referring to her as "honey", and furthermore, pulling out his chair for her.

Bervick pulled another chair up for himself and sat down next to Lula, putting his arm around Lula's shoulder and kissing her cheek. Lula's body tensed from Bervick's unusual behavior.

Bervick said, "My darling, dis here is Ralph Waters and his wife Geneva Jo."

"Hi, pleased to meet you both." Lula shook their hands from across the table, smiling, and got nervous from Ralph's prolonged hand shake, gazing hard into her eyes. Lula pulled her hand away playing it off by scratching the back her neck. "I'm glad to see new members here."

Bervick said, "What new members? They been here fo' a few months nah. You were sick when they came." He turned to the couple. "Thank the Lord I took her to the doctor and got her dem autobiotics. She had a bad infection down there."

Lula gave Bervick a baffled look for the lie that came out his mouth followed by a phony laugh. If he was going to lie, at least get the word "antibiotic" right. Furthermore, Bervick disclosing her personal business humiliated Lula. She looked away pretending as if she didn't hear a word he said. She grew accustomed to Bervick's sly remarks in front of people. She always brushed it off like it was no big deal, he didn't mean any harm. However, sitting there feeling embarrassed in front of the couple, Lula began to wonder if Bervick knew what he was doing all along. She tried to keep an upbeat attitude toward Bervick's alter ego in front of the two strangers.

Listening to Bervick, Geneva Jo glared at Lula's pregnant stomach. Lula smiled back at the pale woman whom, without the African American features, could pass for white. She had jet black bushy hair, bluish gray eyes, medium sized nose, and large lips.

Geneva Jo said, "Your husband does you no justice, you're gorgeous! I hate you!" She laughed.

Lula smiled, "I'm gonna take that as a compliment."

Ralph said, "Oh, of course it is. You have to excuse my wife. She just don't know when to shut up sometimes."

Geneva Jo faked a smile at Ralph's comment, but was going to give him a mouthful later for it.

Ralph had a brawny build standing 6'5" inches tall with dark skin, smooth as velvet, which gave him the nickname 'Midnight'. He had deep set eyes and was a handsome man with an innocent face that few people took heed to due to his dark color and size, which often scared people away before he was given a chance to speak. He overcompensated with kindness to offset people's visual perception of him.

Lula got up from the table, unable to stomach Bervick's performance any longer. "It was very nice meeting you both, but I need to go back and tend to my kids. Welcome to our church family and I look forward to gettin' betta acquainted with yah both."

Ralph said grinning, "We look forward to it, too!"

Lula got up and hurried back over to the table where Fran and Sis were waiting.

Fran said, "So?"

"They seem like a very nice couple."

Lula got up and started cleaning the table so that Fran and Sis didn't see her disgruntled face. She felt uneasy witnessing Bervick act peculiar with the couple and wasn't sure what to make of the situation yet.

Fran and Sis watched Lula closely, glanced at one another, and then got up to help.

That night when everyone was asleep, Lula lay in bed looking down at Bervick sleeping. A God fearing man who was one of the most devoted Christians she knew. He stayed in church, prayed every day, fasted for God, spread the word of God, worked hard to support his family, and was the man she fell in love with when Pastor

Evans introduced the new members to the church back in Eunice. Keeping these positive attributes in the forefront of her mind, Lula tried to suppress the anger that revisited her conscious after the way Bervick behaved in front of the couple. The lies, character change, and subtle mocking of her health made Lula see another side of Bervick that she didn't like. God fearing, saved Christian man, Bervick Frank, told a blatant lie in the house of the Lord. This incident made Lula forget about excuses for the moment. Instead, it made her dissect the situation verbatim to figure out his clandestine motives for his actions. *Is he trying to sell another one of my babies? Were they part of an elite church group? Was the couple wealthy? Is it something Bervick wants from them?* Too many questions and no answers to appease Lula's unwelcomed anger toward him.

She took a deep breath and picked up her bible which was her guidance and strength during times like these. Reading a few scriptures soothed Lula's conscious as it reinforced God's good will. There was no need to contemplate on negative thoughts about her husband whom she loved and vowed to stand by despite his flaws. There was no need to question or discredit Bervick. As long as he was God's anointed one, Lula would continue to hold her stance in being the devoted wife she vowed to be, and forgive him for the lies and shame he had brought upon her. The situation earlier wasn't about to sway Lula's beliefs, or put her at risk of encountering eternal Hell.

Lula remembered, she did drink that can of beer, so everybody makes mistakes. God is a forgiving God. That's why Lula was thankful.

She kissed Bervick's forehead, turned off the light, and went to sleep.

***

Lula gave birth to a healthy baby boy that Bervick named after Cleve, in honor of his good friend. In no time, Lula was back doing hair, caring for her children, selling sweet dough pies for the church, and standing strong as a God fearing Christian wife to Bervick.

Back to the normal scheme of her daily activity, Lula woke up, got her children ready and off to school, kissed Bervick before he headed to work, and then went across the street to do hair with baby Cleve after Mother Adams picked up Joseph and Sandra to babysit them.

Baby Cleve was no problem for Lula while she did hair. He quietly watched Lula work and only cried when he was hungry. The women adored him. Tips flowed for Lula due to her remarkable hairstyles and the presence of her newborn.

Fran no longer took customers after three p.m., so when their last client left, Fran and Lula took a break on the porch after baby Cleve fell asleep.

Lula declined a cold beer from Fran. She just sat back relaxing, taking time for herself before Bervick and their kids returned home. At twenty-five years-old with seven children, Lula needed time for herself, if only for an hour.

Sitting on the porch, Fran sipped on a cold beer discussing the soap opera stories they watched with their customers, debating on what tomorrow's episode will bring. Fran got up to get another beer and came back outside sitting down, looking over at Lula's skirt with the flower print on the side. She turned away tired of Lula in that skirt. It angered Fran. The amount of money Lula brought in, without tips, was more than enough to buy a new skirt by now.

Fran, Sis, neighbors, and church members were disturbed by Lula and her children wearing the same clothes while Bervick seemed to have more options in his wardrobe. Seeing Lula's kids in the same clothes interchanged amongst themselves, and Lula's transparent results of washing and ironing in efforts to keep their clothes looking fresh, burned Fran up inside. But she chose to be a good friend by remaining silent along with everyone else who had noticed. They honored Lula and Bervick's marriage and opted not to interfere in their personal business. However, Fran's patience waned thin waiting for Lula to do something about it on her own, especially now that Bervick was spending an excessive amount of time at Ralph and Geneva Jo's house.

Fran's fortitude wavered after her third beer. It was time to wake Lula's slumber about her husband.

Fran drank the rest of her beer and mashed the can in one hand. "So, Bervick, he's been spending more time over there with Ralph and Geneva Jo lately, huh?"

Lula chuckled at Fran's sudden audacious question. "Yeah, Ralph's helping Bervick get a supervisor job. He don't wanna work the jobs he got now and I don't blame him. And just think, I didn't kno' why he was actin' weird in front of dem in church that day, but nah I kno'. He wanted to get a steady job from Ralph. Bervick's quiet with what he do, but he always has a reason."

Fran shook her head almost forgetting the naiveté in Lula's age and her sheltered country upbringing. "Sweetie, listen to me and listen to me good. Ralph worked his butt off for fifteen years, kissing a whole lot of white ass to get where he's at. Do you really think them white folks gonna let Bervick walk in there and get a supervisor position with no experience? Com'on now, Lula Mae."

"He's also helpin' Ralph rebuild his shed in the back. Maybe Bervick made up the supervisor job so I can think he gettin' somethin' betta than what Ralph offered him. You kno' men and they pride. I gotta let a man be a man tho'."

"Say's who?"

"God! I'm a God fearin' Christian wife and mother to my family. I'm in dis holy union with my husband fo' life and I'm makin' the best of it."

Fran shook her head, happy to be a non-religious woman. She looked up puzzled, now taking heed to Lula's previous statement. "Bervick's helping rebuild what?"

"A shed."

"What shed?"

"Ralph's shed in the back."

"Lula Mae, that man don't got no shed! Do you see any sheds around here?"

"Some people got dem, so maybe Ralph got one."

"And you believe all this stuff Bervick's feeding you? Do you think he's a prophet, too?"

"I kno' I didn't marry a perfect man, he has many flaws, but I trust him despite all dis. The little lies he tell and him sayin' he the 'Chosen one' or 'God's prophet' is just talk. He's harmless."

Fran took a deep breath and sat back in her chair shaking her head. Lula patted Fran's arm to lighten her up. Fran forced a smile and left the matter alone. Lula sat back humming a tune Big Ma use to hum. She thought about Big Ma and how she used to subtly warn her about Bervick. It was ironic that Fran, a woman who had never met Big Ma, had parallel suspicions about Bervick, too. Lula suddenly felt a need to know why.

Lula said, "I'm listenin', Sha."

Fran was thrown by Lula's question. She stared at Lula with a perplexed look.

Lula turned to Fran with serious eyes. "I'm listenin'."

"I don't wanna hurt you, Lula Mae. You're like a sister to me."

Hearing those words made Lula wait for more. Her silence gave Fran no other choice but to continue.

Damning her big mouth to hell, and the liquor that pried it open, Fran sucked her teeth and said in a monotone, "I know for a fact that Ralph gets off work at eight o'clock. Bervick gets off at five o'clock, so my question is, what is he doing over there when Ralph's still at work?"

Lula was taken aback by Fran's question. She traced her mind back to when she and Bervick were sitting at Ralph and Geneva Jo's table in church. The look on Geneva Jo's face and her malevolent joke about hating Lula rippled into another recollection of Bervick constantly looking over his shoulder in the direction where Geneva Jo was seated in church.

Lula blinded herself to the signs and discounted her hunches by hiding in her bible.

Blood rushed to Lula's head. Religious beliefs fought what she was concluding. Rage beat out any rational thinking. An explosion of anger mixed in sadness, betrayal, and humiliation took over. Her fist balled, shaking frenziedly.

Fran was startled by Lula's angry reaction, unsure of what to do next. When she saw the tears break free on Lula's red face, Fran knew it was safe to get up and hug her friend. "Let it out, child, just let it out. You've been through so much. You deserve to be angry, hell I'm angry, too. You got to release it at some time."

Lula cried in Fran's arms, asking repeatedly what she had done for Bervick to act in such a way. She worked hard to be the wife Bervick wanted her to be, and still, it wasn't enough.

Fran lifted Lula's head. "Don't you dare go blaming yourself for that man's issues. Don't ever base your worth on how he treats you, you hear me. Know yourself for being the great loving Christian woman you are."

Lula's tears poured like a faucet. Fran hugged Lula to calm her down, sympathizing with Lula since Fran too was in the same predicament with her ex-husband years back.

Shivering in Fran's arms, Lula said, "I wanted to believe him, but somethin' inside me already knew. I prayed fo' God to make things right. All I ever wanted was a happy family and fo' my kids to have a father and mother. Lord Jesus, why?"

Fran knelt down by Lula's side holding her hand, "What you gonna do?"

"I reckon pray and just ask God fo' strength. I just wanna keep my family together fo' the sake of my chillun. Please Lord, I don't want dem to grow up in a broken home." A mystified look came over Lula's face. "And no Hell fo' me! Please, God no."

Fran wiped a tear from Lula's face. "Whatever you do, I'm here for you."

"Thank you, Sha."

***

During church service, Bervick stood next to Lula singing out the same hymn book. He slightly looked over his shoulder winking his eye at Geneva Jo, and then turned back around before Ralph noticed. Lula sung louder, pushing the hymn book closer to Bervick's chest, aware that he couldn't read a word off the page, but had memorized most of the songs.

Bervick excused himself to the bathroom and went down the stairs to the first floor, passing the men's bathroom and going down another flight of stairs to the basement. It was dark in the basement with a single opaque window omitting a dim light shining upon minuscule particulars floating in the stuffy air that reeked of mothballs and mildew. Bervick avoided touching anything while waiting in the dusty cobweb infested area filled with old broken chairs, tables, worn bibles, and hymn books stacked against the wall. Geneva Jo came down moments later and followed Bervick into a tiny, out of order bathroom. He turned on a flickering light and closed the door. Less than ten minutes later, they came out fixing their clothes. Geneva Jo brushed her hair back with her fingers and left up stairs minutes before Bervick followed. He made his way back up the basement stairs to the first floor, passing the men's bathroom, wiping his face with a handkerchief. He froze at the bottom of the second staircase when he saw Brother Adams at the top, staring him dead in the eye. Brother Adams stepped down the staircase, never taking his eyes off Bervick. Neither said a word. He looked Bervick up and down, then pointed at Bervick's crotch. Bervick looked down and quickly zipped up his pants.

Brother and Mother Adams usually sat behind Lula and Bervick during church. They had witnessed the gestures Bervick was giving Geneva Jo and disapproved of it. Brother Adams had a problem with Bervick after observing how Lula and the children dressed for church while Bervick's attire looked as if he stepped out of a magazine.

In the staircase, Brother Adams' silence spoke volumes standing there face-to-face with Bervick in the staircase. Bervick gave Brother Adams a threatening look, jerked his collar back, and rushed back up the stairs leaving Brother Adams in the staircase. He sat down next to Lula, who was chewing her Doublemint gum fast. She pulled out a pack of gum offering Bervick a piece and he took one. Lula crossed her legs and arms, biting at the inside of her cheek, furious that Bervick took a piece. He never chewed gum, let alone, chewed during service. Smelling a whiff of cheap perfume made Lula's teeth clinch. She put the gum away and looked at Bervick, who was listening to the Pastor's sermon. She squeezed his hand. Bervick patted Lula's back and put his arm around her shoulder, something he rarely did. Lula got nauseated from the scent of another woman on Bervick and flicked his arm off her shoulder, scooting away closer to Gloria Jean who was holding baby Cleve. Lula turned away from Bervick as he sat watching Lula's dismissive attitude, and thought he heard a few grunts come from her mouth. He rebuked her devilish behavior and continued to listen to the sermon, now content with God's choice in finding him another anointed virtuous woman. A cough from behind interrupted Bervick's train of thought as he turned around to find Brother Adams clearing his throat watching him.

Brother and Mother Adams visited Lula and Bervick's house the following Saturday after Bervick got caught with his pants unzipped. They brought bags of fresh fruit, vegetables, bread, milk, eggs, cake, and candy for the household. Bervick took the bags from their hands and carried them to the kitchen while Lula thanked them for the amount of food they brought. Each of the children greeted the Adams' with hugs and kisses, collected their goodies, then ran outside to play. Mother Adams and Lula went outside with the kids, taking chairs with them to sit and talk. Brother Adams took a seat at the kitchen table and watched Bervick put the food away.

Bervick wasn't pleased with the junk food they brought into his home, shaking his head at the sweets. Brother Adams sat watching Bervick's blatant disapproval of the sweets, waiting for the right time to speak.

Brother Adams was a short, medium brown skinned man with a gray mustache and salt and pepper hair. Every day he wore a hat, three-piece suit, and shiny black shoes, despite the temperature outside.

Bervick asked, "Care fo' some coffee, Brother Adams?"

"Yes, thank you, Brother Bervick." Brother Adams sat his hat on the table. "Can we talk for a minute?"

"I'm listening, sir."

"Aren't you gonna sit down with me first?"

Bervick continued putting the food away with his back to Brother Adams. "No, sir, I can hear yah just fine."

"Alright then. There's been a lot of talk around church lately, and I'm not sure I like what I'm hearing...or seeing."

"Okay," Bervick said and turned around folding his arms, looking at the hat on his table, annoyed.

"You got to stop what you're doing, Bervick. I know you have more respect for the Lord's house than what you've shown it lately."

"Stop what?"

"I'm old, Brother Bervick, not dumb! You and Geneva Jo, that's what needs to stop. What you're doing goes against everything us God fearing Christian's stand for. God blessed you with a beautiful family. A great wife, lovely children...don't do this to them. You know, when I see your children, it's like looking God directly in the eye because only *he* can create something so precious. Why risk your blessings chasing tail that already got a husband? Have some respect for yourself and your family, Brother Bervick! I'm not a man that pries into another man's business, but I wouldn't be a man of God if I just sit back and watch this go on without intervening. God, Lula, and your children deserve better from you. You understand, son?"

"Like I said, sir, I don't kno' what yah talkin' bout."

"Why haven't you been able to look me in the eye since I got here, Brother Bervick."

Bervick turned around to finish putting away the food.

Brother Adams continued, "I'm going to leave you with this: I lived long enough to witness that no good can come out of lies and deceit. Don't allow your actions to cost you your family because, if there's one thing I want you to remember, the sins of the father falls upon his children. But if you're not willing to listen to this old eighty-five year-old man with arthritis in his hands," Brother Adams said massaging his knuckles, "then you're going to face your actions in front of God one day, and that's a day can't nobody evade. You can't lie, manipulate, or cover up in front of the Lord, Brother Bervick! So, on that note, where's that cup of coffee?"

Bervick poured Brother Adams a cup of coffee, placed sugar and crème on the table, and sat down across from Brother Adams.

Brother Adams asked, "Can you stir this for me, son? My hands are hurting pretty bad."

Bervick stirred sugar and crème in Brother Adams' coffee, making sure the sugar dissolved completely. He stopped stirring for a second and looked directly into Brother Adams eyes. "One thing you'll soon understand bout me, sir, I'm not yah average man and certain rules don't apply to me, in all due respect, sir." Bervick said and resumed to stirring the coffee.

***

Bervick hid behind a van across the street from Geneva Jo's house. He waited for Ralph to leave for his normal game night with the fellows across town, never missing a Saturday night. When Ralph's blue car pulled off, Bervick crept up to the front door and softly knocked. Geneva Jo opened it, jumping into Bervick's arms like a school girl greeting her first love.

"Hey baby!" Her hair was down and she had on a white robe with nothing underneath, pulling Bervick in her four bedrooms, two bathrooms house.

The home could've been a regal home if it weren't for Ralph and Geneva Jo's five children destroying it. The couch sat opposite a boarded fireplace and mantle with porcelain plates, out of the children's reach. A huge clay vase with a colorful imprint of an eagle sat in the corner of the living room with fake flowers hanging out of order due to child's play. The dining room had a scuffed up faux marble table with dirt spotted cream chairs surrounding it. The kitchen was next to the dining room with white and green tiled floors and hand-made cherry wood cabinets that Ralph constructed to Geneva Jo's liking.

Bervick loved their house and felt he should've been the owner of this palace, praying for God to bless him with that house one day.

Geneva Jo bought Bervick white clothes and shoes—his preferential color—to go to church in, getting the money from Ralph's wallet to supply Bervick's gifts. Ralph never asked any questions. This was the norm for her to take money to go clothes shopping.

Bervick felt like royalty in Ralph and Geneva Jo's home, and she treated Bervick as such, waiting on him hand and foot, showering him with gifts. The more Bervick made himself comfortable, the more he felt their house was a place built for him by God.

Bervick walked down the hall to the family room where Geneva Jo's rambunctious kids were playing. When they noticed Bervick standing there, they systematically ran to the back room and shut the door. Geneva Jo put the fear of God in them not to utter a word about Bervick to Ralph or else their butts would be raw. She had her children so frightened, they never discussed Bervick amongst themselves.

Bervick and Geneva Jo retreated to the bedroom, kissing and hugging every step of the way. Closing the door, they fell on the bed like two wild animals in the mist of mating season, unable to get their clothes off fast enough. Stopping their surge of lust, Bervick sat up and inched his way to the edge of the bed.

Geneva Jo sat up, "What's wrong, baby?"

"Do yah love me?"

"Of course! You're my world. My everything. You're the reason I breathe every day. I hate that our love gotta be a secret. I keep telling you I'm getting tired of sneaking around like this."

She got off the bed and knelt down in front of Bervick, taking his hands, kissing all over them.

Bervick jumped! "Yah hear that?"

Geneva Jo stopped and listened, then shook her head no.

"Thought I heard somethin'," he said looking around paranoid. He calmed down when there was no sound. "I love yah too and someway, somehow, yah gonna be my wife soon."

Geneva Jo stretched her face smiling and took the back of Bervick's hand, rubbing it alongside her face with a longing look. "How we gonna do it, baby?"

"Not sho' yet. The Lord's gonna make a way tho', he always do. Yah think you can handle raisin' my chillun, too?"

Geneva Jo got up from the floor and sat next to him on the bed, leaning her chin on Bervick's shoulder while rubbing his thigh. "I'll do whatever it takes for us to be together forever."

"God want us to start plannin' our future together. It might take some time fo' me to figure things out, but I kno' God's gonna lead me in what I need to do."

"God's anointing is all over you. You're a great prophet and anybody that thinks otherwise can go to Hell."

Bervick leaned in kissing on Geneva Jo's neck. The door swung open and her two eldest children fell on top of one another.

Geneva Jo got up screaming, "What the hell y'all doing?"

They got up pointing at one another to blame. She ran to her closet grabbing a shoe and yanked her ten year-old boy by the arm and started hitting his legs with it. The boy screamed out while the nine year-old boy grabbed at her arm to stop.

"You want some, too?" Geneva Jo screamed, beating him over the head with the shoe. The ten year-old boy wrestled the shoe out of Geneva Jo's hand and threw it out the bedroom door, tired of that shoe. He stood there breathing hard staring at Bervick.

Geneva Jo ran her hand over her face and went to grab her purse, pulling out change. "Here, take your brother and sisters to the candy store."

The oldest boy said, "But it's getting dark outside!"

"You better do as I say and go!" she yelled, pointing her finger at the door.

Bervick said, "That ain't nothin' but the devil in dem."

The oldest son's nostrils flared looking at Bervick, and then he and his brother left out the room. Geneva Jo waited to hear the front door close before taking her robe off completely and closing the bedroom door.

Chapter 20

Cleve sat on his sofa reading the paper when he heard a knock at the door. Hattie Ann was cooking in the kitchen with Deborah on the counter watching. Cleve opened the door and saw Bervick standing there with a sour look on his face. He hurried Bervick in the house and the two sat on the couch. Bervick didn't waste any time asking for money.

Unbeknownst to Lula, Bervick had lost his job doing various work at construction worksites five months after moving to Pacoima. He had been using Lula's profits to pay bills, although he told Lula most of their earnings were going to the church.

Cleve assisted them financially as well, giving more money each month until he was paying most of their bills and rent along with the money Lula brought in. Cleve did this in hopes that Bervick would find a job soon; however, the more Cleve gave, the more Bervick asked for more money, telling Cleve how God was going to bless him for helping a prophet who hurt his back on the job. Cleve ignored that notion and selflessly gave for Lula and the children to have a roof over their head.

Hattie Ann and Cleve constantly argued about the money he was giving. It was bad enough Hattie Ann was jealous of the way Cleve treated Lula while in her presence. She didn't want Lula nowhere near Cleve's money and felt Lula should suffer for choosing Bervick to marry in the first place.

On the couch, Cleve spoke low so that Hattie Ann wouldn't hear. "Bervick, why don't yah try and get yah old job back? You said yah left in good standin'. I haven't seen yah back hurtin' as much lately. Maybe yah strong enough nah to do the work. "

Bervick was quiet. What he failed to disclose was that he had been fired from all of his jobs due to him preaching the word of God during work, becoming a nuisance to other workers. The complaints forced management to take disciplinary action against Bervick. When his boss asked for an explanation, Bervick explained that he had to spread the word of God and adhere to his duties as a Prophet of God. The supervisor quickly showed Bervick the door.

Bervick figured if he couldn't preach in church, he was going to preach to whomever, wherever, whether they chose to listen or not. That was the least Bervick could do for the blessings God provided throughout his life, and him being "The Chosen One".

Cleve sat thinking about Lula and her children and contemplated if he should give Bervick a chance. After being an outstanding worker for many years at General Motors, Cleve landed a managerial position paying excellent money, and he knew of two positions open for hire on the assembly line.

Although he was losing his patience for Bervick, Cleve told him about the position and agreed to pull a few strings to get Bervick hired. Cleve figured the job would relieve him from carrying the burden of taking care of two households and enable Bervick to start supporting his own family.

Bervick felt a weight lift off his shoulders. He thanked Cleve and went by the kitchen to greet Hattie Ann, without acknowledging Deborah, and then left.

Leaving the house, Bervick walked to the sidewalk and stopped when he heard Hattie Ann calling from the door. She walked barefoot outside towards Bervick, wiping her hands on her apron. "How yah doin', Bervick?"

"Praise the Lord, I'm good."

"You're looking good," Hattie Ann smiled. "Got any scriptures fo' me t'day?"

"No, not t'day, Sha."

Bervick grew suspicious. Hattie Ann, the devil in the flesh, seldom spoke to him.

Hattie Ann said, "I need yah to do me a favor. I kno' Lula Mae doesn't mean any harm, but she's been comin' over here more often than what I'd like, bringin' dem kids with her, too. Deborah's gettin' older and I don't want her to kno' Lula Mae or y'all kids. I'm her momma and Cleve is her daddy, period."

"I thought y'all was friends?"

"We are, it's just Deborah need stability in her life and with her siblings and Lula Mae comin' 'round here, it ain't helpin' any. Cleve sit there waitin' on Lula Mae like a crazy man and...I shouldn't be sayin' all dis but when she come, he get dressed up and brush that nappy ass head of his, and fo' what? It makes me sick!"

"So dis here ain't bout Deborah then?" Bervick sucked his teeth, "My God, my God."

"Does it matter? I don't want her 'round my family anymore. If I didn't kno' any betta, I'd think somethin' goin' on between dem two."

"What time she be here?"

"Five or six, and I gotta fix *your* children food b'cause Lula Mae say they ain't eaten all day, and she cry bout you and Geneva Jo. Nah I ain't one to bud in anybody's business, and I can give a rat's ass bout you and that Geneva Jo, but dis here gotta stop!"

Bervick's eyes widened after hearing that Lula was aware of him and Geneva Jo, and worse, she had confided in Cleve about it.

Hattie Ann noticed Bervick's surprise. "The gig is up, Bervick, we all kno' bout you and that woman, and damnit, I don't care. Just keep Lula Mae away from my Deborah please?"

"I'll talk to her about it. Have a blessed day, Sha."

Bervick saw Deborah in the doorway with a finger in her mouth calling out for Hattie Ann.

Hattie Ann yelled, "Get back in the house b'fore I get my switch fo' dem legs!"

Cleve ran up behind Deborah and picked her up. "Yah don't have to yell at her like that!"

Hattie Ann turned back to Bervick. Her lips pressed tight, shaking her head, irritated. "See what I mean. Always taking *Lula Mae's* baby side."

"Maybe you shouldn't yell at her like that. Good day, Mrs. Hattie Ann."

Hattie Ann stomped back into the house slamming the door.

Bervick walked down the street, passing his house, headed straight to see Geneva Jo.

***

Four a.m. in the morning, Lula sat at the edge of the bed reading her bible, waiting for Bervick to return home. She found out Ralph was out of town, which was the last thing she wanted to hear. Her patience waned. Lula got up, put old clothes on, and went into the kitchen to mop the floor. She made the water extra hot, got on her knees, and started scrubbing, moving the table, chairs, and anything else in the way. She scrubbed the corners hard and fast, moved the refrigerator to scrub underneath it, and then poured more hot water in the bucket to mop over the floor twice. When she was done the floor, Lula emptied the cabinets and took out the bowls, pots, and pans to soak, and then wiped down the inside of the cabinets. Once that was done, Lula wiped down everything, from the table and chairs to the coffeepot and countertops. She went to the bathroom when there was nothing left to clean in the kitchen, and started scrubbing the toilette inside and out with an old toothbrush, getting every nook and crevice. She stepped into the tub and scrubbed the tiles up and down with both hands, and then bent down to scrub the tube, rinsing it repeatedly so that all germs were gone. She walked over to the already clean sink and wiped it down, then cleaned off the mirror and walls.

Looking around at the bathroom, Lula saw a speck of dirt on the floor and got on her knees to scrub and mop over the floor twice. After emptying the trash can next to the toilet, she let the floor dry and washed her hands before leaving out to her bedroom to check on baby Cleve. She checked on the other children asleep in their bedrooms, and then went back to her room to make the bed and noticed a shoe out of place in the closet.

Lula emptied the entire closet and adjusted the clothes, laced Bervick shoes evenly, and arranged everything based on how often the articles of clothes were worn. When finished, Lula stood in front of the closet looking down at Bervick's new pair of white shoes. She picked them up observing the intricate make, costing more than what they could afford. She threw the shoes back in the closet and pulled out his new white dress shirts. She sniffed that awful cheap perfume on his dress shirt, making Lula's stomach turn. She put Bervick's shirts back in the closet and lamely walked to the bed sitting down, slouching in a daze, wishing she had a pack of Doublemint gum right then and there. She needed Lillie or Samantha to confide in, or Big Ma's embrace about now. But nobody was there except for her sleeping children. Desperate for answers, Lula turned to her trusty bible and read passages to ease her mind. God was still there with her. He'd never left.

The bible gave Lula the comfort her soul was seeking. She looked over at baby Cleve, who was sleeping like a dead horse throughout the noise of her rummaging in the closet. She thought about each of her children, including Deborah, and made up her mind it was time to do something to keep her family together.

Weeks had passed since Lula's veil had been lifted to Bervick's indiscretions, and turning the other cheek in prayer was no longer an option. Every second of each day haunted Lula with thoughts of Bervick touching another woman. Her mind raced pondering ways to save their marriage and bring her lawfully wedded husband back home. She didn't want Hell, Fire and Brimstone to be neither Bervick nor her fate if they reneged on their blessed vows taken in front of God.

A passion buried long ago began to resurface. Becoming an owner of a Creole restaurant ignited a flame in Lula. This renewed zeal exploded when Lula imagined herself cooking and managing a restaurant alongside Bervick. They needed something to do together, something to bring them closer and give them financial security. Something they could sink their teeth in as husband and wife and pass down to their children when they got older.

Lula got up from the bed rejoicing at the idea that would save their marriage and stop Bervick from seeing Geneva Jo once and for all.

The sun rose and Lula opened the front door letting the light shine down upon her face. Closing her eyes, she recharged herself, already feeling her life turning in a new direction for the betterment of her family. As she took a deep breath of the fresh morning air, she closed the front door smiling, anxious to wake the children for school and do hair at Fran's house.

***

Cleve stopped on his way home from work to see Lula. He hadn't seen her or the children in a couple of weeks. He played with the kids outside for a while, and then went into the house to sit with Lula, waiting for her to put baby Cleve down for a nap in the bedroom.

She came back in the kitchen, "I wanna thank yah fo' gettin' Bervick that job at GM. There wasn't enough money in that construction work he was doin'."

Cleve smiled glancing away so that Lula wouldn't see the truth in his eyes. He never wanted Lula to find out it was he who was paying the bills all along. "Where's Bervick?"

"He should be home from work by nah. You didn't see him there at work?"

"No, he didn't start yet. They still reviewing applications."

Lula changed the subject. "Yah want coffee or somethin'?"

"Yes, ma'am. Coffee's fine."

"Comin' right up." Lula got up from the table hiding her despair and embarrassment. Even though the idea of owning a restaurant lit a spark in her life, hearing another lie knocked her confidence down a notch.

She couldn't hold it in any longer. She needed answers. "Can I ask you a question?" Lula asked, filling the coffee pot. "I kno' I shouldn't involve another man in my marriage, but I need answers from a man's perspective."

"Of course, what's the problem, Sha?"

"Remember when Hattie Ann told me people in church were talkin' bout Bervick and Geneva Jo?"

"Yeah. I'm sorry bout her tellin' you that. I told her bout herself and that big mouth of hers."

"No need fo' that, Cleve," Lula said, remembering how Cleve consoled her when she cried out of embarrassment from Hattie Ann disclosing the church folk's knowledge of Bervick's infidelities. Cleve held Lula until she stopped crying and Lula was grateful for that.

"She means well," Lula said, sitting the coffee pot on the stove.

"I love my wife, she just like startin' trouble and I don't like that one bit. Just kno' that yah in our prayer's, Lula Mae. You and yah chillun."

"Thank you, Sha."

"Nah, what is it you need a man's perspective on?"

"Do you think startin' a restaurant will help our marriage?"

"A restaurant?"

"Yeah, well, I was up prayin' and the thought of startin' a restaurant came to me so crystal clear. It's somethin' I've been wanting to do fo' years and I think dis is God's answer to my prayers."

"Where yah gonna get the money to start it, Sha?"

"I can make my sweet dough pies and save the money. It don't take much. I kno' a little bit bout startin' a business. Papa Top, Bervick's daddy, Joe, and one of my aunt's own businesses."

"And you think startin' a business with Bervick will stop him from foolin' 'round with Geneva Jo?"

"I think so." Lula looked down. "I don't kno'. That's why I'm askin' you?"

Cleve knew the answer all too well, yet he didn't dare disclose his theory with Lula. "Yah gonna have to ask him bout it and see what he say."

Lula watched the tiny bubbles floating to the top of the coffee pot as steam omitted from it. She quietly said, "But why?"

"Why what?"

"Why he lie to me? How can he be a God fearin' man and do dis to me and our chillun? I tried supportin' him, lovin' him, and being the best God fearing wife I can be. Why isn't that enough?" Lula started crying. She tried hard to maintain the internal joy of starting a restaurant, but the thought of her beloved husband with Geneva Jo pierced Lula's heart.

Cleve got up, turned the stove off and embraced Lula. He wanted to say, leave Bervick and come with him. He'll take care of her. Cleve wanted to tell Lula everything was going to be all right, it was he who kept a roof over her family's head while Bervick paraded around town with Geneva Jo. Cleve wanted to tell Lula that he was the better man and that they were meant to live in holy matrimony. Not her and Bervick.

But instead, Cleve held Lula, wishing he could turn her pain into joy. "Just be patient with him, Sha. He'll come around."

"I don't kno' what angers me most, his cheatin' or the open lies to my face! I tried to be the best wife I can be and look what happened to me! My husband's out there sinnin' with another woman. Maybe I'm not the virtuous woman I thought I was. I just don't kno' anymore. Lord, help me! Dis restaurant idea gotta work! It's all I got."

Cleve held Lula closer, hurting for her.

Joseph ran into the kitchen, pouting. He raised his elbow showing a cut to Lula. She quickly broke away from Cleve, wiping her tears away and picked Joseph up. She smiled back at Cleve on her way to the bathroom, thinking how much of a good friend he was in her moments of despair—this being the reason she visited Cleve's house often, and to catch a glimpse of her baby Deborah. It hurt Lula to see Hattie Mae's growing resentment towards her, making it difficult for Lula to spend time with her baby, Deborah.

***

Bervick sneaked in the house thinking Lula was asleep. When he thought the coast was clear, he got ready for bed and lay down quietly beside Lula. Right when his eyes closed, Bervick felt a tap on his shoulder and heard, "We need to talk."

He sat up rubbing his eyes open.

Lula said, "I kno' you didn't start yah job yet and I kno' what's goin' on between you and Geneva Jo."

"I kno' you kno' already."

"How?"

Bervick was quiet.

"If you don't wanna tell me, then fine, but how could yah do dis to me? Dis goes against everythin' we believe in, and you runnin' 'round here sinnin' with a married woman?"

"Those rules only apply to the average man. I'm God's Prophet."

"I wish you can stop sayin' that. It ain't cute anymore."

"It's the truth. It's God's truth."

Lula bit at her bottom lip looking at Bervick. It was time for him to hear her truth. "We're growin' apart, Bervick. I love you and I want dis here marriage to work! Please, I'm askin' yah, stop seein' her. Why don't we start a business together?"

"A business?"

"Yes, 'a business'. Open up a restaurant serving Creole food. You can make yah famous barbeque sauce and I can make the Creole dishes and my sweet dough pies. I've been thinkin' bout dis fo' a while nah. It's somethin' I've wantin' to do fo' years."

"And yah just tellin' me dis?"

"I kno' and I apologize fo' keepin' dis from yah, but nah I kno' I have to be honest with yah if I want you to be honest with me. I think dis here restaurant will help bring us closer together. We made vows in front of God and our kids deserve a mother and a father. We gotta trust in God and make dis marriage work to keep our family together."

"I'll think bout it."

Lula kissed Bervick on the cheek. "What we gonna do in the mean time? I've been knowing bout you and her fo' some time nah, but me being a child of God, I forgive you. Let's just move forward. No more lies. That's how much I love you. I'm willin' to give us a second chance and leave the past in the past."

Lula grabbed the bible and placed it on top of Bervick's chest. "I'm still your virtuous wife, Bervick, and I do believe God will see us through dis if we both live our lives saved and full of the Holy Ghost."

"I'm already full of the Holy Ghost. I follow my God."

Lula sat up. "No you haven't! You just said *his* rules don't apply to yah and it's not fair. We gotta trust in God and our faith in dis here marriage, not just me."

Bervick lay there quiet for a moment.

Lula waited. She wasn't about to let her head hit that pillow until he said something.

He reached an arm out for Lula. She lay down on Bervick's chest while he stroked her hair whispering, "I'll stop. I love you, and thanks be to God, we're gonna make dis here marriage work fo' the sake of our chillun."

That was music to Lula's ears as she held onto Bervick tighter, wishing she had spoken up sooner.

It exhausted Bervick pondering how to become the man of two households. Unfortunately, he couldn't turn his back on Geneva Jo. He had to obey his Lord Jesus Christ's decision. Nobody, not even Lula, could impede on the Lord choosing Geneva Jo for him.

***

Sunday morning, Lula woke up feeling a familiar stomach pain and dizziness. She woke Bervick up to take her to the hospital. He refused. She pleaded with Bervick, explaining the acute sharpness in her belly.

Bervick said, "God heals all,", and got up to wake the children for church.

Lula stayed in bed while he left out with their children to church, leaving a glass of water and the bible by Lula's bedside. She lay back and read the bible trying to pray her pain away.

***

Three Sundays passed and Lula was still in bed not feeling any better. Church members started questioning Bervick and consoled him when they find out Lula was bedbound again.

The following Sunday in the middle of a sermon, Sis saw Bervick and the children in the front pew of the church, and timed it just right to slip out the church's back door to go get Fran and see about Lula.

In front of Lula and Bervick's house, Fran lifted the mat for the extra key and opened the front door.

Fran and Sis called out Lula's name, walking into the bedroom where Lula lay with dull skin, unruly hair, and pinkish eyes.

Fran grabbed her chest. "Oh dear God," she said, running over to Lula's side feeling on Lula's head asking if she was okay.

Lula moaned.

Fran said, "We got to get her to the hospital fast!"

They helped Lula on her feet, got her dressed, and walked her across the street to Fran's car. They took Lula to the hospital where the doctors immediately admitted her.

While in the waiting room, Sis called the church where Mother Adams was on phone duty. She informed Mother Adams on Lula's condition and gave the hospital address to pass on to Bervick.

A half an hour later, it was safe for Sis and Fran to enter Lula's hospital room. The doctor came in to give Lula her test results. He greeted Fran and Sis and asked, "Are you two kin?"

Fran said, "Yes, sir."

The doctor put on his glasses and opened the chart in his hand. "It says here that you're married, Mrs. Frank. Is your husband around?"

"No, sir. I believe he still in church."

Fran said, "He'll be here shortly."

He said, "Good because he'll have to sign you out. Did your pain subside yet?"

"Yes, sir, it surely did. Thank you, doctor."

"Okay good. You have a urinary tract infection that was spreading, so I wrote up a prescription for antibiotics and it has to be taken daily until the bottle's empty. Follow up with your primary care doctor, and don't worry, the medication won't affect your baby."

Lula said, "Baby?"

"Yes, congratulations, Mrs. Frank, you're three months pregnant and very lucky to have checked in when you did. We had to intravenously administer the antibiotics to stop the infection before it put your baby at risk. Once your husband arrives, he can sign you out."

"Baby?"

The doctor nodded, "Yes, ma'am. Good day ladies."

Sis ran over to Lula's side when the doctor left. "Oh my Lord, how long yah been in pain, Sha?"

"Don't kno', lost track of time."

"Did yah tell Bervick yah were hurtin'? He should've known yah condition just by lookin at yah."

Lula was quiet. She was too fatigued to defend his reasoning.

Sis didn't persist. She already knew their religious belief on conventional medicine, but still felt Bervick shouldn't have left Lula in pain for so long. "You kno' what, I've had it with him. Wait 'til he get here, I'm gonna knock some sense into that bastard cousin of mine! Forgive me Lord."

"Sis," Lula said, "Com'on nah, Sha."

Sis was already too upset, pulling her sleeves up pacing the room. "Just wait, I'm gonna get him, Sha!"

Fran sat laughing at Sis ready to battle a man almost twice her size.

Bervick arrived at the hospital an hour later with Brother and Mother Adams. Sis backed down when she saw the Adams'. They were highly respected elders in the church.

The doctor came back in the hospital room and saw Bervick. "Mr. Frank?"

"Yes, sir!"

The two shook hands.

The doctor said, "I need you to sign your wife out. I've already given her the instructions on how to take her medication, and like I told her, it won't affect the baby."

"Baby?" Bervick looked over at Lula.

The doctor chuckled, "Yes, congratulations. She's three months pregnant."

The doctor exited the room, but turned back around almost forgetting to get Bervick's signature. Bervick motioned the doctor to follow him to the hallway. They both came back and the doctor went over to get Lula's signature.

***

For the next couple of months, Bervick allowed Lula to stay with Sis to rest and be cared for—he figured he could spend more time with his future wife, Geneva Jo, too. Sis administered Lula's medications as directed, fed Lula and kept her company. Sis lived with her husband in a one floor ranch style house with two bedrooms, a kitchen, living room, and a nice size basement where her husband held card games on Saturdays, which Ralph attended, never missing a night.

Mother Adams maintained Lula's house in her absence, happily taking care of her children, cooking and cleaning while Bervick started his new job on the assembly line at General Motors. Mother Adams took the kids over to Sis' house every other day to visit their mother up until the last two weeks of Lula's stay. After two months passed being bed bound, Lula was well enough to go back home and see about her children and why, all of a sudden, she hadn't heard from Mother Adams.

Sis walked Lula back to her house, making sure Lula got there safely before heading to church for choir rehearsal. Lula took the time to look around the house. It wasn't as clean as she kept it. The bathroom was dingy, there were no clean clothes, and the refrigerator was empty.

Opening the bedroom door, Lula sat on the bed and picked up her bible from the nightstand. A letter fell out. Lula picked it up and read the letter from Mother Adams, who apologized in the letter for her sudden absence. She explained how Bervick stated he longer needed her. The letter was dated two weeks ago, a day after Mother Adams last brought the kids to visit Lula. Lula was surprised wondering why nobody had informed her of this earlier. She put the letter up and sat on the bed, happy to be home again. She lay down on her left side with both hands underneath her head, thinking about why Bervick turned Mother Adams away. Looking over at the nightstand, Lula noticed a stack of unopened mail behind the lamp. She inched over to Bervick's side of the bed and grabbed the pile, opening the first one on top. The more Lula opened and read, the angrier she got. Every letter was a past due notice on bills and rent.

She slammed the mail on the bed and left out the house. Holding onto her stomach, Lula swiftly made her way to Cleve and Hattie Ann's house.

Before Lula could put her hand up to knock, Cleve swung the door open with a smile on his face. "Lula Mae, ain't this a pleasant surprise, how yah feelin', Sha?"

He kissed Lula's cheek and helped her in. Hattie Ann took Deborah and rushed out the kitchen to the bedroom, closing the door before Lula saw them.

Lula sat on the couch, "Where's Hattie Ann and Deborah?"

"Oh, uh, they sleep," Cleve said, even though he knew they were in the kitchen a minute ago.

"Oh, okay," Lula's heart broke. She heard the bedroom door slam shut. She hadn't seen Deborah in a while and secretly looked forward to catching a glimpse of her baby girl during visits at Cleve and Hattie Ann's house.

Cleve said grinning, "So what brings yah here t'day?"

He joined Lula on the couch.

"I kno' you a supervisor at GM, so is there any way you can get an advance on Bervick's pay? I kno' that's askin' a lot, but we really need the money bad!"

"Why? What's wrong?"

"Our bills are past due. Maybe you can help him find another position paying more money or somethin'. He's been workin' fo' a while nah and it just ain't enough."

"Bervick didn't tell yah?"

"Tell me what?"

Cleve leaned in closer. His elbows were on his knees and hands were compressed together, "He got fired in his first week."

Lula closed her eyes and waved her hand in disbelief. "Dis can't be right. When Fran and Mother Adams came by to see me, they both said he's been leavin' every mornin' fo' work!"

"I wish I was lyin', Sha, I really do. I just couldn't help him anymore. He almost put my job at risk! I haven't spoken to that selfish son of a bitch ever since, either." Cleve sat cussing about Bervick underneath his breath, forgetting Lula was sitting there, losing his composure from the resentment he had towards Bervick.

Lula grabbed hold of his hand to get his attention. She hesitated asking, "What did he do?"

"That fool started preachin' bout God on the first day! Word got back to me so I told Bervick he needed to stop and save that fo' the church. He apologized, so I thought everything was fine after that and I reported back to my manager and explained that it was all just a misunderstanding and that Bervick wasn't gonna do no such a thing again. I convinced him to give Bervick another chance, and guess what dis idiot go do again? Not only does he go back and start preachin', he gets up on a chair in front of the workers, held up a bible and start preachin' out loud angering everybody. He got the whole unit rowdy, yellin' back at him to shut up! They had to shut down the line. The floor supervisor took Bervick to the main office and he started a raucous in there! We all had to go in and try to calm him down, but that jerk didn't stop and security had to escort him out. In all my years workin' there, I got my first write-up b'cause of him! I'm lucky they ain't fire me."

Cleve scratched the side of his head, then rubbed his hands together, "I'm tellin' yah, Lula Mae, if it wasn't fo' you and dem kids, not only wouldn't I have nothin' to do with Bervick, I'd bash his face in fo' puttin' my job at risk. Yah kno' what I went through just to get him that damn position? I almost lost my job fo' referring that idiot!" Cleve's jaw clenched, breathing heavily through his nose.

Lula's head fell in shame. "I'm so sorry, Cleve. So so sorry! Is there anything I can do to make things right?" Lula knew the pride Cleve took in his job. He labored for years to earn his position as supervisor, which was rare for an African American man to attain.

Cleve leaned closer taking Lula's hand. "It ain't yah fault, Lula Mae. Don't think I'm blamin' you fo' him. If I don't come 'round as much anymore, nah yah kno' why. I need time to cool off b'fore I see him again. I'll help get yah bills caught up tho', but I'm gonna need yah to bring the bills to me. I don't want him bringing dem anymore.

You and dem kids need a roof over y'all head. Everythin' else, Bervick gonna have to figure out what he gonna do."

Lula lifted her head looking at Cleve with inquisitive eyes. "What yah mean 'not him anymore'?"

Cleve turned away.

"Cleve?"

He looked at the ground.

Lula paused, then said, "You've been payin' our bills, haven't yah?"

Cleve was quiet.

"Lord have mercy." Lula eyes closed shaking her head in disbelief again. She patted Cleve's knee and said, "It's okay, you don't have to say a word to me. I'm just gonna have to start sellin' my pies and do more hair. You done enough and I thank yah fo' that. You're a good man. The good Lord will sho' nuff bless yah."

Cleve smiled at Lula, loving her gumption. She was a person who handled business when need be, the type of woman he wanted. Cleve kissed Lula's cheek longer than usual, scooting closer to her. He no longer wanted to wait. The time was now for Lula to leave Bervick. Cleve wanted to marry Lula and adopt her children as his own, as long as he could have Lula as his wife. He knew Lula had a good head on her shoulders and Cleve contemplated many times taking her away from Bervick. Pregnant and all, Cleve still wanted his Lula.

Cleve took Lula's hand, leaned closer to her ear, and twisted his lips to whisper his heart's desires, but was interrupted when he heard his name yelled from across the room. Cleve jerked back when he saw Hattie Ann with her arms crossed, tapping her foot hard against the floor. Cleve quickly put his hands up to say it wasn't what she was thinking.

Lula saw Hattie Ann was upset and got up. "I'm gonna go."

Hattie Ann wryly said, "Good-bye."

Lula made her way to the door.

Cleve followed.

Hattie Ann grabbed his arm. "What yah doin'?"

"Seeing her home. I ain't gonna let her walk home alone pregnant."

Lula said, closing the door, "No need, Cleve. I can see myself home. Y'all have a blessed day."

When the door closed, Hattie Ann shot an evil look at Cleve. He ignored her. He opened the screen door to watch Lula leave. Deborah sneaked out the bedroom and went over to the window without Hattie Ann noticing, and pointed at Lula, "Mama".

Lula heard Deborah from outside and saw her little hands and face pressed against the window. She blew a kiss at Deborah and continued walking.

Hattie Ann screamed, "Get back in the room little girl!"

Cleve said, "Don't be screamin' at my daughter like that!"

Hattie Ann yanked Deborah away from the window. Cleve pulled Hattie Ann's grip off Deborah and picked her up, "Let dis girl be!"

Hattie Ann stomped in the bedroom and came back out with a blanket and pillow, throwing it at Cleve. "You sleepin' on the couch t'night," and went back in the bedroom slamming the door in Cleve's face.

Chapter 21

Big Ma rocked in her rocking chair on the porch, waving at the passers-by and chatted with a few who stopped to make small talk. After discussing the sermon from church last Sunday with a fellow church member, Big Ma went out back to her garden. She got on her knees, pulling small weeds trying to sprout between the carrots and tomato plants. She stopped when she saw a tall figure in her peripheral vision taking a seat on the back steps. Big Ma smiled without turning around and continued pulling as Papa Top sat admiring how great Big Ma's vegetables looked.

She plucked a few ripened vegetables to give to Papa Top and waved for him to follow her to the front porch. She went in the house to bag the vegetables and brought it out, handing it to him as she took a seat.

They sat listening to the sounds of birds chirping, laughter from neighbors, and waved at people passing by on foot or by car. They sat for a couple hours until the sun waned, leaving a reddish orange print in the sky. Before it turned completely dark, Papa Top lifted himself from the seat with help from his cane and raised his hat to say good-bye, holding up the bag of fresh vegetables to say thanks.

Big Ma said, "It's good to see yah, Oscar. I'm doin' just fine, Sha."

Papa Top said, "I'm glad to hear that. I'm just worried bout my baby gal out there with them chillun and that man."

"After hearin' bout her messin' around with Hattie Ann's husband, I washed my hands of the situation and gave it up to God. All I can do is pray fo' her and dem chillun to come home. Otherwise, I refuse to burden myself over what Lula Mae doin' out there."

"Yah never give up on kinfolk, Sha."

"Right nah, she no kinfolk of mine. Lord knows I raised her betta than that."

"That's why yah never stop prayin' fo' her. Don't mind what these people 'round here say. Wait 'til yah hear it from the horse's mouth."

Big Ma rocked in silence.

Papa Top smiled, "Take care, Louverta."

Big Ma watched him take one step at a time with his cane down the porch stairs, holding his bad knee, limping towards the road.

Big Ma stood up and yelled, "I'll never stop!"

Papa Top turned around, nodded, and continued walking.

Big Ma rocked in her chair, enthralled at how beautiful the sky looked.

Chapter 22

Lula didn't speak to Bervick about her visit at Cleve's house. She waited, hoping Bervick confessed losing his job, and furthermore, Lula wanted to know where Bervick was going during his supposed work hours.

In the morning, she shuffled her pregnant body, helping the kids get ready for school, listening to Bervick talk about how great his new job was, kissing her goodbye and leaving for work with his work uniform on. Bervick felt Lula's distant behavior toward him, except, he didn't care or bother to ask any questions.

Finishing a long day of doing hair, working more hours than usual for more money, Lula held baby Cleve while walking across the street where her children were already home from school and outside playing under Mother Adams' watchful eye. Lula said her good-byes to Mother Adams, and brought her children inside the house to prepare cornmeal couscous with milk and sugar for them to eat—the only affordable meal now that Lula was paying the bills on her own.

After they finished eating, Lula sat outside holding baby Cleve in her arms, watching her children play games together. Popping her Doublemint gum, she waited for Bervick to arrive to see which direction he came from.

By six o'clock, Bervick was a no show.

Lula took the children inside the house, washed them up, and gave them buttered sweet potatoes for dinner. After they ate, Lula told them a bedtime story and put them to bed. She cleaned the kitchen, washing dishes repeatedly and wiping the table over and over again. Her swollen ankles forced her to take a seat at the kitchen table, facing the front door.

At ten o'clock, Bervick tiptoed in the house and peeked inside the bedroom.

"Over here, Bervick."

Bervick jumped. He turned to find Lula sitting at the kitchen table. He grinned opening his arms, playing as if he was happy to see her.

Lula didn't crack a smile, "I kno' yah not at GM anymore. Where've yah been?"

He dropped his arms and smiled, "Out lookin' fo' a job."

"In yah old work uniform?"

"Yeah."

"If I catch you with that woman one more time, I'm leavin' with my chillun back to Eunice."

With that said, Lula got up from the table and went to bed, leaving Bervick to warm up leftover couscous and eat alone at the table.

He ate, fuming at how Lula had spoken to him—God's prophet, ruler of all men. *Touch not my anointed, do my prophets no harm*—the creed Bervick felt God had wrote for him. He smiled in between bites feeling comfort in the fact that God will grant him permission to deal with Lula later.

With that revelation, Bervick got up to add more milk in his couscous.

***

Brother Adams invited Bervick to their house for dinner. When Bervick arrived, Sister Adams exited the kitchen, leaving the two men alone. They sat making small talk about the pastor's sermon, eating baked chicken, green beans, mashed potatoes and gravy, and cornbread. Bervick turned down a glass of wine and drank lemonade instead. Brother Adams' fork trembled as he struggled to feed himself with his arthritis stricken hands. He rubbed between his knuckles in between bites.

Brothers Adams said, "I hope you don't have to go through this when you get to be my age."

"God heals all, sir. You of all people should kno' dis already, halleluiah." Bervick finished his plate, picking up his napkin to wipe his mouth. "Your wife sho' can cook, sir."

"So can yours. I've been eating my wife's food for over sixty years and never met a cook that measured up to my wife until I ate Lula Mae's food." Brother Adams laughed, "Don't tell the Misses." He got up to prepare coffee.

Bervick rushed to Brother Adams' side and took the bag of coffee grinds away from him, "Allow me, sir."

Brother Adams smiled and patted Bervick on the back. He took a seat crossing his leg up and said, "Have you found a job yet, son?"

"No, not yet, sir. Yah kno' of anything available?"

Bervick looked around for a coffee scooper. Brother Adams pointed to the drawer.

Brother Adams said, "I know the grocery store's hiring for baggers."

"I'm no bagger, Brother Adams. Where yah crème and suga' at?"

Brother Adams pointed to the covert in the corner and said, "Brother Bervick, you can't be choosy with seven kids and one on the way."

"Oh yes I can! God's got big plans fo' me. You'll see."

"What plan does God have for you, son?"

"You'll see, sir. God will reveal it in due time."

"God help those who help themselves first. You know that right?"

Bervick leaned against the counter next to the coffee pot on the stove, pulling at his hairless chin. The smell of brewing coffee began filling the air. He took a seat at the table and felt Brother Adams eyes watching his every move.

Bervick finally said, "You will see, sir! All in God's time. I am his humble servant."

"I'd believe you if I didn't hear this a year ago, and quite frankly, Brother Bervick, that excuse is running dry. Your wife and kids need you now!"

Brother Adams sat back in his chair with an elbow on the table, leaning his face on his hand getting annoyed with Bervick. "Son, you got to get your priorities in order. Your family comes first! Not Geneva Jo, not what you think God have in store for you, and not you wanting to preach everywhere you go. It's your family! A man's strength lies in his family, believe it or not. Nothing in this world can replace the power of love that you get from your family. All you young men do is chase women or money, leaving your families out here to suffer. Family gives you that unconditional Godly love, and when a man has this, he can go out and conquer the world in truth, integrity, honor, and respect. A man's character and how he treats his family makes a man *a man*. Anything else is a boy playing a man. I wish I had children to carry down my legacy, and here, you got a wife and children, and look how you're behaving. You're taking God's greatest blessing for granted. You got to be there for your family first and foremost, Brother Bervick!"

Bervick got up from the table, poured Brother Adams a cup of coffee and sat the sugar and crème in front of him.

"Aren't you going to have a cup?" Brother Adams said, grabbing a spoon to scoop up sugar with trembling hands.

Bervick watched, smiling wryly at Brother Adams struggle. A clear example of God's punishment for Bervick's enemy.

Bervick said, "No, I got somethin' to do. Thank yah fo' dinner." He got closer to Brother Adams, "And by the way, sir, God blessed me with a nice house that I'm bout to move my chillun in, so God already provided fo' his Prophet." He smiled, "Good luck with that crème and suga'."

Bervick walked out without looking back.

Sister Adams found her husband sitting at the kitchen table alone and pouring crème everywhere but in his coffee.

"Let me get that for you, honey," Sister Adams said, taking the bottle of crème and pouring it for Brother Adams. Stirring it in his coffee, she asked, "What did he say?"

"Nothing."

"I was hoping he'd at least listen to you. I feel for Lula Mae and her babies. I'm sorry, honey."

"No need, baby, your heart was in the right place. He needed to hear it. But that's one crazy stubborn man. It'll be best we keep our distance from him and just wish the best for Lula Mae and them children."

"We can't just leave them alone like that. What happens if they need food?"

"We'll just have to bring food over there when that fool isn't home."

Brother Adams sipped on his coffee. Bervick's words about moving into a new home with his children, and no mention of Lula, worried Brother Adams.

***

Late that night after Bervick's visit with Brother Adams, Bervick sat in the kitchen drinking a hot cup of coffee while everyone was asleep. He felt humiliated and belittled by Brother Adams insinuating that Bervick wasn't a good provider for his family. No one makes such accusations to God's Prophet without consequences. Even after his visit with Geneva Jo, Bervick couldn't shake Brother Adams' words.

Taking sips of coffee, Bervick sat in the dark kitchen, imagining a coffin in front of the church with black roses on top. In it lay Brother Adams in a three-piece suit and red tie. Bervick reversed his train of thought and envisioned a car hitting Brother Adams. He quickly dissolved that image to another vision of Brother Adams being stabbed to death, and then rested on the third and final visual of Brother Adams falling over holding his heart, a more sensible death.

Bervick glared down transporting his vision to the middle of the kitchen floor. Brother Adams' dead body floated in the air, lying in a three-piece suit and red tie as if he was in a casket. Bervick smiled taking another sip of coffee, daring Brother Adams to say another word right then and there. When there was no response, Bervick smacked his leg yelling "Halleluiah" to the victory God bestowed upon him.

In the dark, Bervick rejoiced over putting Brother Adams' words to a rest by witnessing his death through the visual. Gratification engulfed every inch of Bervick's soul as he sat in the kitchen marveling at the apparition until sunrise. The beam of light shining through the glass window dissipated the silhouette of Brother Adams deceased body. Bervick smiled, content that he was God's Prophet beholding the power to punish those who cross him. Reprimanding these individuals could be done in many ways. However, for the first time, Bervick sought out death unto Brother Adams.

Chapter 23

Lula gave birth to a baby boy she named Benjamin. She named him after their current pastor, Pastor Benjamin Cook. He was a healthy baby with big round eyes, golden brown skin, and vibrant face. As the doctor predicted, Lula had a difficult labor and she knew this had to be her last child, no matter what Bervick said.

Lula cared for baby Benjamin in the bedroom for a month, allowing her body to heal from the difficult labor. She put herself on a strict diet consisting of plenty of water, fruits, vegetables, and fresh fish. In contrast to Bervick, Lula didn't fast during the two required days of the week anymore, resting on the notion that God knew she needed to get her strength back and breast feed.

Fran, Sis, and Mother Adams supported Lula with her diet by supplying fresh fruits, vegetables, and fish for the family in order to help Lula get stronger. They took turns caring for her children while Lula got her strength. They kept her company when Bervick was gone looking for a job. He came home at a more reasonable time to prevent any suspicion on his whereabouts since church members started distancing themselves from him. He went through enough scrutiny in Eunice and didn't want his current congregation to turn on him as well. He had to ignore Geneva Jo's advances during church and delay his plans for what he had in store until God gave him the signal to make his move.

Bervick attended church with Lula, who was still in recovery, trying to portray himself as the perfect husband tending to Lula and their children's needs. Lula fought through her sickness to be present during church and found herself getting better as the weeks progressed. Observing Bervick's efforts, Lula's threat to leave ceased; she wanted to keep her family together for the sake of their children.

Lula got up Sunday morning and got the kids ready for church. She put spiral curls in the girls' hair, edged the older boys' hairline with Fran's clippers, plaited baby Cleve hair, and put a blue cap on baby Benjamin's head.

The night before, Lula ironed her children's clothes, Bervick's white suit, and her cream skirt with the flower print on the side. She was excited to wear a new blouse Sis had bought her as a gift, which matched perfectly with Lula's skirt.

Since Bervick left earlier for church, Lula wanted to surprise him with her new white blouse on, figuring if Bervick saw how good it looked, he'd pay more attention to her rather than Geneva Jo.

Lula and the children arrived at church and waited for Bervick, who said he had a few stops to make on the way. Lula left a seat open for him, and when church service began, she started to worry. Bervick was never late for church. She turned her head and relaxed when she saw Ralph and Geneva Jo seated. At least he wasn't with Geneva Jo.

Bervick raced into church an hour late, sweating bullets. He sat down next to Lula. His white suit had skid marks around the knees—a rarity from Bervick's usual neat appearance. Lula asked him where he had been, but he didn't answer.

During service, Bervick sat in a daze without listening to the sermon. Lula repeatedly glared at Bervick's unruly appearance and when she didn't hear his regular "Halleluiah" shouts. Sensing something was wrong, she offered Bervick a piece of Doublemint gum. He declined and got up from the pew, stepping around Lula and their children towards the open aisle.

He busted out the front doors, running towards the back of the church gasping for air. For the first time since childhood, Bervick was frightened. Pacing back and forth moving his hands frantically, he grabbed hold of his chest, falling against the church wall, unable to focus his attention on anything. He crunched down to his knees and looked up at the sky praying out loud until he was startled by Lula standing there holding baby Benjamin in her arms with a flabbergasted look on her face. Bervick quickly scooted himself up, brushing his white suit off, and then put his hands up to ask "What".

Lula said, "Service over. You alright? Why yah pants so dirty?"

"I followed through with one of God's plans."

"And what's that?"

"Com'on, let's go back in," Bervick put his arm around Lula and escorted her back into the church.

"You sho' yah alright?" she said, looking Bervick up and down.

"I think so," and he left it at that. He didn't explain the sudden fretful rush he felt or why he was feeling this way.

"You like my new blouse?" she said, entering in the church, pulling at her blouse.

"Where'd yah get it?"

"Sis gave it to me," Lula smiled.

"It's okay."

Lula's face dropped. She wondered why she even bothered to get Bervick to notice in the first place.

The congregation sat downstairs in the church eating Sunday dinner, talking amongst their tables as they did every other Sunday of the month. People came to Lula and Bervick's table, chatting with Lula and clowning with the children while Bervick sat in silence not touching his food. Lula spoke for the both of them to offset his rude behavior.

Their pastor, Benjamin Cook, walked into the room in a somber mood. He stood in front of the room and waited for everyone to find a seat and silence themselves. His head tilted down, dreading having to be the bearer of bad news. He composed himself enough to speak clearly as the noise faded and all eyes were on him.

He said, "I really hate to interrupt you alls dinner, but unfortunately, I have to inform y'all that...God called Brother Adams back home this morning."

Silence.

Looks of disbelief searched other's faces to confirm what they had just heard. Sounds of mourning trickled through the silence, becoming a mass influx of loud sobs. Lula realized she didn't see Brother or Mother Adams in church, and the last time she spoke to them was when she brought Brother Adams homemade soup. He kindly told Lula that he was fine and suffered bouts of pneumonia from time-to-time. He wanted Lula to go home and get well herself.

Lula's eyes watered remembering Brother Adams last words to her. She wrapped her arms around her children huddling around her. Their young minds unable to comprehend the situation. Lula noticed Bervick slipped out the room during the announcement and was nowhere in sight. Ralph and Geneva Jo were at their table, but still no Bervick. Rocking baby Benjamin and bringing her children closer in, Lula touched and smiled at each of them to ease their confusion.

She got up, no longer wanting her children to be subjected to such sorrow and excused herself out of the church with the assistance of church members helping the little ones get by.

Lula walked home with her children and no Bervick.

***

Bervick sat at the kitchen table in the middle of the night, drinking a scorching hot cup of coffee in the dark while thinking about

Brother Adams' death and the figment of his imagination that came into fruition. In each sip, his tongue adapted to the scorching hot liquid. Sneaking through the Adams' window before church and standing before Brother Adams in bed, declaring that it was time for him to go with God, was confirmation for Bervick that he was God's Prophet rising in power. The Lord granting him permission to send Brother Adams' soul away was the ultimate power bestowed unto man. Brother Adams was becoming a nuisance. No man should dare speak ill to Bervick without reaping the repercussions of their actions for going against God's Prophet. Brother Adams had to face God, and no longer be granted the air in which he breathed.

Bervick laughed hysterically at the thought of Brother Adams burning in Hell while praying for one more chance to take back the words he had spoken to Bervick.

Sitting proud for a job well done, Bervick appointed himself dispenser of the wicked and the trumpet for the sanctified. From that day forth, people who dared go against his word would be dealt with accordingly, and reap the wrath of God, facing the same fate as Brother Adams.

In the dark, Bervick concentrated on the words God spoke, readying himself to move out on his plan. Bervick watched as an apparition from God appeared in the middle of the kitchen with him and Geneva Jo living in a luxurious house with their children playing together. Smiling at the translucent image, Bervick took a huge gulp of his blazing hot coffee, burning the inner walls of his mouth until they peeled. He mashed his tongue against the roof of his mouth to increase the burning sensation, not realizing his mouth was blistering.

This moment of bliss ended when Bervick heard the cries of baby Benjamin coming from the bedroom. Lula walked into the kitchen holding baby Benjamin and turned the light, startled by Bervick sitting there. "What yah doin' up dis late sittin' in the dark, Sha?" she asked, walking over and wetting a towel underneath the faucet, holding Benjamin in her other arm.

Bervick took another sip of coffee looking straight ahead without responding.

Lula said, "Ah, I kno'. Yah takin' Brother Adams' death pretty hard, huh?" She rung the towel out and walked over to Bervick and kissed him on the cheek, "Everything gonna be alright, Sha. At least try and get some sleep, and if yah need to talk, I'm here fo' yah. I gotta clean Ben up. He's wet," she said, rubbing Bervick's back before going back in the bedroom.

Bervick got up, turned the light back off, and sat down at the table to finish his hot coffee.

***

Lula finished doing hair at Fran's house and left for the day, holding baby Benjamin in her arm and little Cleve by the hand. She returned home to find Brother Davis, a member of their church, at her door step with a TV on the ground next to him. He waved at Fran across the street who gave him a nod.

Brother Davis said, "How y'all doing today?"

Lula said, "Just fine, Brother Davis. What yah got there?"

"You know me and my wife moving and trying to get rid of a few things. Thought you might be able to take this off our hands, Sister Lula."

Lula couldn't believe her eyes, "Thank yah so much and tell yah wife thanks, too."

Mr. Davis held the door open for Lula. He picked up the TV and carried it in behind her saying, "You got something to sit this on?"

"Let me see."

Lula laid baby Benjamin's sleepy body down for a nap and sat little Cleve on the floor near the kitchen table. She popped her gum looking around and went over to the hallway closet, pulling out an old stand a neighbor gave them. Mr. Davis helped pull the stand out and carried it to the kitchen.

Bervick forbade any media outlets such as TVs or radios in the house. He believed they were devilish objects used to corrupt the minds of God's people by making them idle.

Lula was too overjoyed to turn it down. She wanted another source of entertainment for the children instead of them playing outside all the time. A TV was a luxury item that they could not afford, so Lula hoped Bervick would bend the rules for what she considered a big blessing.

After Brother Davis adjusted the antennae and programmed the channels, Lula stepped back looking in awe of the new TV. She smiled telling little Cleve to look at it. She couldn't wait to see the faces on the rest of her children when they came home from school.

Brother Davis said, "Alright then, God bless, Sister Lula."

"Let yah wife kno' she can come get her hair done fo' free. I'll do my specialty on her. That's the least I can do fo' y'all being so kind."

"I don't think that's possible, Sister Lula!" Brother Davis laughed, "My ole lady been wearing wigs ever since she burned her hair out using that lye stuff to straighten it."

"Oh, I'm sorry to hear that. Well at least let me cut your hair fo' free."

"Don't worry about a thing, Sister Lula. You've given us plenty free pies when I didn't have the money, so this the least we can do for you," he said, nodding in agreement with himself. "Fran told me y'all needed a TV and I couldn't get it here fast enough."

Brother Davis saluted, a remnant of old army days, and left out the front door. Lula stood in the doorway holding little Cleve and waving his little hand at Brother Davis driving off. She looked across the street and blew a kiss at Fran sitting on the porch drinking a cold beer. Fran held her beer up accepting Lula's thanks.

Lula closed the door and checked on baby Benjamin. She sat little Cleve down as he watched his mother bopping her head, smiling while preparing dinner for the night. Her heart melted for the rest of the afternoon, giving thanks to God for the blessing, and laughed when little Cleve yelled out imitating her.

***

After Brother Adams' death, Bervick sought out to make his next vision a reality, so when Ralph left that morning to visit his brother in Los Angeles, Bervick took the opportunity to spend time with Geneva Jo and share God's vision with her.

Returning home from Geneva Jo's house late, Bervick sneaked in the front door, reaching his hands out to feel his way in the dark. Taking steady steps into the kitchen, the moonlight shone through the window for Bervick to find his coffee pot. After he brewed the coffee grinds, he poured a fresh cup of coffee and turned the burner off while taking a sip. He turned around and jumped back, dropping his coffee on the floor, splattering it everywhere. The unfamiliar figure in the corner of the kitchen startled him. He stared at it, taking steps closer to it and turned on the light, shocked to find a TV sitting there. He observed the TV as if it was an object from outer space. He walked back over to the stove, picked up his cup from the floor and washed it out to pour more black coffee in it. He sat down at the table and took a huge gulp of coffee, burning away the rage he felt toward Lula for bringing the devil's machine into his house, purposely disobeying him. Bervick took another hot swig of coffee, now burning the inner lining of his lips, inviting in the blisters. At last, getting his fill of pain, he went into the bedroom and lay down next to Lula, falling asleep with wet coffee stained clothes still on.

***

The following morning, Lula calmly walked over to Bervick's side of the bed and stood over him watching him sleep. She waited up all night for Bervick, reading her bible, feeding baby Benjamin, and was in the middle of a prayer when she finally heard Bervick creep inside the bedroom in the early morning.

Lula stood over him. She wished there were enough bible verses to calm her fury. She bent down and yelled, "Wake up!"

Bervick jumped up startled by the abrupt wake up call, stunned that it was Lula's voice yelling.

He sat up wiping at his eyes.

Lula leaned down close to Bervick's face. "I kno' yah weren't out there lookin' fo' a job that late, Bervick!"

"I was lookin' fo' graveyard shift jobs. That's what God wanted me to do, and yah need to stop yellin' b'fore yah wake Ben."

"He's in the other room," Lula said angrily and walked out to check on her children.

Bervick jumped up following behind her. "Oh yeah, well what's that in the kitchen?"

Lula stopped from opening the children's bedroom door and went into the kitchen so that they wouldn't hear anything.

Bervick pointed. "Dis here God's house and I don't kno' where or how yah got it, but dis devil box betta be gone by t'day!" He said, hitting the top of it.

"Why? It ain't hurtin' nobody. We the only people in dis here town without a TV and the kids love it. They don't have to watch it every day, just let dem have some type of entertainment fo' goodness sake. I'm getting tired of livin' like dis! The old clothes, no car, hardly any food, and thank God fo' my client's generous tips that's keepin' a roof over our head. The whole church kno' how we livin'. We gotta do betta fo' ourselves and our chillun. We left Eunice fo' a betta life and it seems we in a bigger rut than b'fore. We don't got no money to do anything 'round here, so why not have dis here TV fo' a little enjoyment in our life fo' once? It's a blessin'."

"I'm the man of dis house, therefore, I have the final say. Take that TV back where yah got it from. God say fo' you to honor and obey, Lula Mae Frank."

"Honor and Obey? It's just a TV, Sha."

"I don't question what God tells me to do and neither will you. I answer to no man but God and I'm not gonna sit here and argue with yah," Bervick's said in a dismissive tone, taking a seat at the table.

Lula calmed down sitting across from him. She played with a hole in the sleeve of her gown and mildly said, "Can we please keep dis here TV, Sha? It's not doin' nothin' but sittin' there. If yah saw their little faces when they came home and saw it, I kno' you'd wanna keep it, too." She smiled, playfully hitting his arm. "I kno' you'll like it if yah give it try. It's not that bad when yah,—" Lula paused. Her smile dropped. She stopped playing with her sleeve. "Wait a minute. How dis discussion go from you to me? Where were you last night?"

Bervick stared off in space ignoring the question.

Lula crossed her arms. "Where was yah, Bervick? You were with Geneva Jo, weren't yah?"

Bervick stood up and went to the bedroom.

Lula followed.

He quietly got dressed.

"What yah doin'?" She asked, running behind him.

Bervick didn't answer. He slipped his shoes on and went back into the kitchen while Lula followed still asking questions. He unplugged the TV, picked it up, and headed towards the door.

Lula protested, "What yah doin'?" She grabbed at Bervick's arm, but he yanked away struggling to get the screen door open. Lula yelled for him to stop as he carried the TV out the house. She stood in the doorway watching him carry it down the street, promising herself she wasn't going to cry over a TV. Lula closed the door and turned to find Joseph, Bervick Jr., Sandra, and Gloria Jean holding baby Benjamin, standing in the hallway, watching. Lula smiled and waved for them to follow her in the kitchen. "Y'all hungry? Want oatmeal?"

They nodded in somber moods and sat at the table. Each of their faces telling Lula they heard the commotion.

Bervick Jr. asked, "Where's daddy taking the TV?"

Lula put water on the stove and bent down to wipe the left over coffee stains off the floor. "The TV stopped workin', baby."

"He gettin' it fixed?"

"No, but don't worry, my baby, after yah done eatin', I'm gonna take y'all across the street to watch Fran's TV."

They perked up.

Lula got up from wiping the floor clean of coffee spills and washed her hands, saying over her shoulder, "Baby, do me a favor, go wake up yah brother and sister and tell dem to come get ready to eat."

Joseph jumped from the table and ran to wake them. Lula grabbed the milk out the refrigerator, slamming it shut out of irritation for Bervick finagling his way out of her initial question by redirecting the issue on the TV.

Her attitude changed, smiling lightheartedly at her children, doing things to make them laugh to mask the anger resurfacing in full force for Bervick.

***

Bervick almost tripped three times carrying the heavy TV into the house. His bowlegs buckled by the time he made it into Geneva Jo's living room, sitting it on the couch and stretching out his worn out back. Geneva Jo jumped into Bervick's arms, kissing him all over his face. "You're a God send, Bervick Frank! Thank you so much! How am I gonna explain this to Ralph?"

"Tell him God blessed yah with it through a church member." Bervick looked around. "He gettin' off late t'night?"

"Yeah, but he goin' straight to card night," Geneva Jo smiled.

Geneva Jo's kids came into the living room and jumped around at the sight of the new TV.

"Is this ours?" one of them asked.

Geneva Jo said, "It sho' is thanks to yah Uncle Bervick."

Bervick said, "You gotta find a stand fo' it."

"Wow, this is such a blessing. You're such a blessing to us." Geneva Jo kissed Bervick on the cheek.

Her kids, except for her oldest son, surrounded the new TV that looked better than their own. The oldest boy stood in the hallway with his arms crossed looking angrily at Bervick and Geneva Jo.

In the middle of her glee, Geneva Jo paused. Her wide smile went flat at the sight of her unenthused oldest boy. She walked up close to him and yanked him by the chin to look up at her. "You better change that smug look on your face right now! And don't you dare breathe a word about this to your father or else I'll beat the life out of you…That goes for all of you! You here?" she said, looking at each one of her kids dead in the eye.

They said in unison, "Yes, ma'am," except her oldest son.

She gripped his mouth, pulling his face up near hers. "I said, do you hear me?"

The boy didn't say a word. He angrily shoved Geneva Jo's hands off his face and ran to the back room, slamming the door.

"Boy, I outta—" she said, starting to chase after him.

Bervick grabbed her. "Let the boy be, Sha."

She softened up and looked around at the rest of her children. "Y'all scat! Go to y'all rooms."

Her younger son said, "I wanna watch TV."

"Boy, don't make me slap the black off you. Me and your Uncle Bervick gotta talk so don't give me no lip, just go!"

Once the last kid retreated into their bedroom, Geneva Jo closed and locked the front door and ran over to Bervick on the couch, hugging up next to him.

Bervick said, "Yah ready to make our move?"

"Yes!" Geneva Jo bopped up and down like a kid in a candy store.

Bervick laughed, "Calm down, baby, yah gonna make the TV fall. I think it's time our kids meet since they'll soon be siblings. They mama turnin' into the devil. They don't need to be 'round her no more."

Bervick lifted Geneva Jo's face by the chin and looked into her eyes. "They need you, baby. My God fearin' virtuous woman."

Geneva Jo blushed turning away. "You sure you want me to be your children's mother?"

"That's right. It's what God wants, Sha."

"Why can't it be just me, you, and my kids?"

"God wants my kids with me. They my seed."

"But what about Lula Mae?"

"You questioning God, Jo?"

"No, no, no. I wasn't! Whatever you wanna do, or *he* wants me to do, is fine by me. I just feel bad for her, that's all."

"Those are her chillun no more. Dis is what the Lord showed me. They my chillun and mine only, and soon, they'll be yours, too. They don't need a mother that drink beer, talk back, and mess 'round with that devil, Cleve. She's tainted. These devil women out here done changed my virtuous wife into the devil. She ain't gonna taint my seeds. I'm gonna take my seeds and raise dem to be great Christians and give dem a real God fearin' mother. You!"

Geneva Jo passionately kissed Bervick and was honored to serve her devoted, holy Prophet of God.

***

Lula tossed and turned alone in bed. She sat up pulling out her bible for peace, but not even the Holy Book could tame her racing mind. Lula wept looking at the pillow imprint where Bervick's head should've been lying. Staring down, twisting her wedding ring that symbolized a false union of what Lula wanted her marriage to be, she realized there was no husband joining her in it. The bible reinforced religious laws, and Bervick's words solidified Lula's adherence to these rules, except, it was getting harder for Lula to tame her suffocating spirit. She mulled over each sermon she could remember, seeking the benefit of both man and woman in a marriage, only to come up short on the woman's behalf.

She got up from the bed and walked over to the crib where baby Benjamin slept and rubbed the back of his head gently, smiling at him yawn as he stretched his little body before falling back to sleep. She put the blanket over him and walked out of the bedroom.

She turned the hallway light on and went inside the boys' bedroom first, tucking Bervick Jr., little Leroy, and Joseph in tight, kissing each of them on their forehead. She picked little Cleve from the foot of the bed and placed him in between his brothers so he wouldn't fall. She kissed his forehead and left to the girls' bedroom.

Lula smiled down at Gloria Jean, Sandra, and Luvicy, giving them each a kiss on the cheek and gently rubbed their hair. Rubbing Sandra's hair last, Lula felt thick patches of flakes returning after Fran scratched and treated it numerous times. Lula made up her mind; it was time to take Sandra to the doctor, regardless of Bervick's opposition.

She quietly left out the room into the hallway, shutting the bedroom door behind her. Lula sobbed thinking of how proud she was of her children's resiliency during the ordeal between her and Bervick, and wanted their lives to change soon for the better.

She walked outside humming quietly onto the porch in her night gown, inhaling the fresh night air. She looked up at the stars, watching the clouds sail across the full moon peaking in between them. Inhaling the twilight air, Lula closed her eyes, exhaling the exhaustion of her life. She smiled down at her bare feet, almost forgetting how she went barefoot every day in Eunice. She stepped into the moist mud-filled yard, digging each foot in the soil, remembering how Beatrice took her, Mary, and Lillie out for walks to taste virgin soil, explaining to them why it was the most nutritious food on the planet. "Where you think the fruits and vegetables get their nutrients," Lula heard Beatrice's voice say. Digging her feet deeper into the soft soil, Lula realized how much she missed her mother. She yearned for her mother's sweet smile, warm embrace, and wisdom beyond years.

Lula made prints with her foot, falling more nostalgic looking down, beginning to crave the most comfortable place on earth—Big Ma's lap as she gently caressed Lula's hair while humming the sweetest tone.

Lula missed her sister's laughter and the fun they had walking to old crazy Mr. Pete's store. She missed staying up late talking to the one person in the world who understood her most, Lillie Mae—a sister who suffered so much, but still acted as a Guardian Angel who had fallen into the hands of a mad man due to the circumstances life presented her.

Lula missed Aunt Samantha's zest for life and her bravery to be herself no matter what anybody thought.

She missed Papa Top, a man of few words, yet kept a close eye out for his loved ones with Miss Colt .45 handy. She missed Grandma

Emma, who took long trips from Texas just to visit and care for her grandchildren.

Lula thought about Leroy and Beatrice, realizing that all along, throughout her marriage to Bervick, she'd been trying to replicate what her parents had. Their love for one another permeated throughout the room, making everyone take notice when they entered. Lula smiled thinking about how Leroy would come home with flowers or gifts for Beatrice, and how Beatrice showered him with love through soft kisses, sweet words, and encouragement. On Leroy's worst day, Lula remembered her father softening to Beatrice's loving touch. Even when Beatrice got feisty, Leroy couldn't help but smile afterwards, hugging Beatrice for just being Beatrice. It was Leroy and Beatrice against the world. Their unconditional love for one another was something Lula yearned for in her own marriage.

Reflecting through the lying, cheating, financial struggles, and Bervick's asinine philosophies, an epiphany struck Lula. Her marriage would never be what Beatrice and Leroy had. Being married to Bervick would not give their children the opportunity to experience what she had in her parents.

Lula walked over to the porch and sat down looking up at the sky, praying for forgiveness for her failing marriage. She rubbed at goose bumps forming on her arms by the night air, feeling like a failure to God for not upholding her vows.

Lula accepted within herself that she would never have what Beatrice and Leroy had in their marriage. She no longer saw Bervick as her savior from Grandpa Doc. Through guidance and help from God, she had to be her own savior now.

Hell, Fire and Brimstone flashed through Lula's mind. She tried bolstering her new found revelations as warranted to where Hell, Fire and Brimstone couldn't possibly be her fate under disconcerting circumstances. Be that as it may, Pastor Evans' sermon about Hell,

Fire and Brimstone still pounded Lula's psyche. She tensed in terror like the six year-old child in the pew listening for the first time.

Rigid in fear, Lula backtracked.

There had to be some way to save her marriage and stop Bervick from seeing Geneva Jo, get him a steady job, and buy new clothes for their children. They needed a mother and a father in their life. Lula couldn't back out now. Never! This was what God wanted!

Lula got up from the porch and went inside the house to clean her feet off. She checked baby Benjamin's diaper, and then laid down crying. To relieve her anguish, Lula picked up her bible and opened to a random passage, stopping at Jeremiah 29:11, *For I know the plans I have for you, declares the LORD. Plans for welfare and not for evil, to give you a future and a hope.*

Lula paused.

She sat in a daze for a moment.

It was as if God was speaking through the bible to her.

Lula laid the bible down, falling deep in thought, and suddenly heard Big Ma's voice, *"Leave him and come with me, I'll take care of you and them children. It's not you, it's Bervick."*

Fran's voice echoed, *"I don't care for that Bervick Frank."*

Sis' voice said, *"I know Bervick's my cousin but that's one crazy man."*

Cleve's voice followed, *"Bervick made me almost lose my job!"*

Samantha's voice spoke, *"It's something about Bervick that I don't like."*

Pastor Evans' voice added, *"The the new assistant pastor is, Curley Frank."*

Courage triumphed over the depiction of Hell, trampling over the affects of this forbidding apparition, now tenuous and impassive.

Lula got down on her knees to pray a prayer of thanks. She reached in the nightstand drawer, grabbed a pen and notepad, and began writing.

Dear Big Ma:

How have you been? Fine I hope! I gave birth to two baby boys name Cleve and Benjamin. (I'm sure you heard already.) Gloria Jean, Bervick Junior., Sandra, Luvicy, Leroy and Joseph are doing great and getting so big. They work together helping one another out and they are doing well in school. As for me, I'm still doing hair and making my sweet dough pies and the people out here love them and can't get enough of the pies. I have you to thank for this Big Ma. I miss you and everybody else and I want to come home soon! I was thinking about opening a Creole restaurant when I get back and I would love for the family to be a part of it. I believe this family needs something like a restaurant to call our own. We can do this together.

Everyone down there said they would help me financially if I leave Bervick. I do hope their offer still stands because I'm ready to come home, without Bervick, and need the money to help me and the kids move back to Eunice.

P.S. I love you very much and miss you. Hope to talk to you sooner than later. Tell everyone I said hello. God bless you.

With all my Love,

Lula Mae Frank

Chapter 24

Big Ma rocked back and forth in her rocking chair, sipping on a cup of water, reflecting on how she had fought for her children and grandchildren to live their lives as God fearing Christians, and how none of them seemed to adhere to the word of God.

Regrets soon followed.

Leroy was her favorite son and could do no wrong in Big Ma's eye, which made Big Ma wonder if she contributed to Leroy's arrogance and infidelities, or how she could've stopped Doc from persuading Leroy that Beatrice needed to stay in her place. Just maybe Leroy would still be with Beatrice.

Big Ma gripped her heart when Lillie, Lula, and Mary entered her mind. She stopped to pluck a mosquito off her arm, rubbed the red bump forming, waved at a few passers-by, and began rocking deep in thought again.

Her heart raced regretfully, having had to turn the other way from new bruises on Lillie's once flawless skin.

Big Ma only did what she knew best. Pray. Unfortunately, the Lord had yet to receive her prayers for her beloved Lillie. Lillie moving to Texas, having children with a wife beater and enduring the inevitable. Big Ma cringed at the thought of how Lillie and her children were living.

Big Ma turned her thoughts to a brighter situation with her youngest granddaughter, Mary, who moved out and married a good Creole man named, Alex Guillory. Watching Alex's upbringing put Big Ma's mind at ease to know that Mary was in good hands.

Big Ma got up from her rocking chair and headed towards the back, shaking her head at the trail Doc left again.

Knees cracking, back hurting, Big Ma knelt down to check her carrot plants to avoid the thought of her second oldest granddaughter. Pulling sprouts of weeds from in between the carrots and tomatoes, she stopped at a large ripe tomato and pulled it off the vine, holding it up to admire how firm and nice it was for sausage stew. She gawked at the deep red color, fine texture, and smooth exterior. She squeezed to feel the firmness of it. She squeezed more and more, squeezing uncontrollably. The tomato dripped from her shaky tight fist. Finally releasing her grip, the tomato was no more.

Big Ma put her hands over her face and fell over in tears. Her heart frenziedly palpitated. The thought of Lula's helpless face when Tauntadi closed the backroom door flashed across Big Ma's mind. Memories she prayed away flooded back with a vengeance. They never left. They lay dormant, now killing her from inside out. She had to face them. She had to make things right again.

After a silent prayer for guidance, Big Ma stood up dusting her garden dress off. Stepping into Lula's shoes for that split second gave Big Ma a new found perspective on why Lula bothered to marry Bervick in the first place. She felt a strong need to make amends with Lula and give her the support she needed, despite Bervick. It was time to put their differences aside and show Lula the unconditional love and support that should've been shown in the first place.

***

Lillie was visiting from Texas for a couple of days when she walked out Big Ma's house to go to Mr. Pete's store. The mailman passed by handing Big Ma's mail over to Lillie.

She almost fainted.

Lillie ran back into the house waving Lula's letter in the air, looking for Big Ma. Busting out the back door where Big Ma was pulling sweet potatoes out her garden, Lillie ran up unable to contain herself. She hadn't spoken to Lula in years. She ripped the letter open and began reading it out loud. Big Ma praised God listening to the letter, thanking God for answering her prayers. With no time to lose, Big Ma dropped her sweet potatoes and rushed in the house to grab her purse, and left out in her soil covered garden dress with Lillie treading behind.

Back hurting, chest pains, and hands still covered in soil, Big Ma left with Lillie, traveling to family and church member's houses to spread the word—a collection was needed to get Lula and her babies back home.

Chapter 25

Lula woke up before sunrise to get her kids ready and off to school earlier than usual so that she could do more hair for money to start saving. Easter Sunday was approaching and the church women needed fresh perms, or press and curls.

She was on her feet for eight hours straight, only stopping to care for baby Benjamin and little Cleve. Lula did superb work on her client's hair, receiving more tips to add to her stash.

In the kitchen taking a lunch break before their two o'clock appointments, Lula fed little Cleve and baby Benjamin while eating cornbread and milk for lunch, talking with Fran who drank a beer for her lunch.

Lula said, "Don't yah want food fo' lunch, Sha?"

"Nope. I do better hair feeling good."

Lula laughed, "Whatever works fo' yah, Sha." She lifted baby Benjamin to burp him after his bottle and said, "I gotta tell yah somethin'."

Fran put her beer down and was all ears.

Lula said, "I've decided to move back to Eunice."

"Why? I thought you liked it out here."

"I do. But I gotta go."

"Aww, Lula Mae, why?"

Lula got a burp out of baby Benjamin and wiped his mouth, saying in a monotone, "I'm leavin' Bervick."

Fran's mouth fell open. She took a huge swig of beer that filled her cheeks, then swallowed hard, slamming the can back on the table, "Shut your mouth, come again?"

"I've decided to leave Bervick. I can't live like dis anymore. Him sleepin' 'round on me and not takin' care of our chillun."

"By all means, Lula Mae, GO! And never look back."

Lula rocked baby Benjamin and reached over to clean little Cleve's face from cornbread. "I'm scared."

"I know you are. Divorce isn't easy, but you'll get over it. It just takes time. Trust me, I know."

"The divorce ain't what I'm afraid of. It's what's gonna happen to me b'cause of it, Sha. The walk of shame back home to a family that probably still hate me ain't gonna be no fun."

"They don't hate you, Lula Mae. They hate Bervick."

Lula chuckled at Fran's candid words.

Fran asked, "What you scared of?"

"We don't believe in leavin' our husbands. Once a vow's made b'fore God, it can't be broken. I fear God first and foremost. I've been goin' back and forth in my mind bout dis and still can't shake the feelin' that I might be doin' somethin' wrong. I want my kids to have what was stolen from me. A mother and a father, happy together."

"I'm sure *thee* will understands, Lula Mae. And your kids will be just fine with you as their mother."

"I don't have any other choice at dis point. I'm just gonna have to face Hell, Fire and Brimstone if I'm sinnin'."

"I know I'm not a religious person, and y'all Church of God and Jesus people don't hear nothing but the teachings in the church—"

"Church of God and Christ, Fran."

"My apologies. But listen to me, don't let your fears consume you to the point where it stops you from doing what needs to be done. You put up with that crazy man for many years and you finally had enough! I applaud the step you're taking. Do what needs to be done for you and them children. I'm not God, but I'm sure *thee* doesn't want you to live your life in misery just to impress others."

"I know everyone gonna be talkin' bout me back home when they find out. I'll be a marked woman. A sinner."

"Let them talk! It's your life, not theirs."

"It's not just that…I feel like a failure, too. All I wanted was a happy marriage like my parents used to have. I was so determined to get away from my grandfather, and to be loved by Bervick, that I couldn't see that I was makin' the biggest mistake of my life. I went from livin' with a mad man to marrying one. My family tried to warn me, but I saw only what I wanted to see. They were right. Oh my Lord, how could I be so blind."

Lula started to cry.

Little Cleve reached his hand up offering a spoon full of cornbread and milk to Lula, spilling half of it on his legs. Lula and Fran laughed as Lula bent down taking a bite, "Thank yah, baby."

Fran got up to get a cloth for little Cleve while saying, "Love clouds people's judgment, Lula Mae. Your only twenty-six years-old! You didn't know any better and it seems you married him for all the right reasons, so don't think ill about it. The only mistake you can make is not learning from the first mistake." Fran wiped little Cleve's legs off and put his half empty bowl in the sink. "You're older and know better now, so don't blame yourself. You're doing what's best for you and your children so you'll be fine. You're stronger than what you give yourself credit for."

Lula wiped her tears away and patted baby Benjamin's back. She smiled at little Cleve falling asleep in the chair.

Fran walked over to the refrigerator for another beer. "He sleep?"

"Yeah, Sha," Lula leaned over to look at baby Benjamin's face, "He just bout there, too".

"Can't wait to visit you down there and eat from that restaurant of yours."

"Yah think I can cook? Wait 'til yah taste my Big Ma and sister Lillie Mae's cookin'," Lula said, getting up to put baby Benjamin and little Cleve down for their afternoon nap.

It was night when Lula finished her last client's hair. As usual, her and Fran equally split their earning, gave each other a hug, and Lula started walking across the street holding baby Benjamin and little Cleve. She hoped Bervick cooked dinner since the children were home for Easter break and he agreed to watch them.

Stopping in her tracks, Lula turned around and walked back over to Fran on the porch.

Fran asked, "Forget something?"

"No, I think yah miscounted. I have more than my share, Sha."

"No you didn't. I want you to get home as soon as possible."

"Aww, Fran, I can't take dis. You got just as many bills as me. Here, take it."

"Okay then, Happy Easter. Ha! Now it's a gift so you can't give it back!"

Lula laughed shaking her head, "Thanks, Fran, you're indeed a true friend! God bless yah."

"I know."

They laughed.

Lula made her way across the street and entered her house.

She paused.

She didn't smell anything cooking. Something didn't feel right. There was silence. Lula yelled out for everyone.

No response.

She sat baby Benjamin in his basinet, put little Cleve on her bed, and ran to each bedroom, the garage, and out back, panicking when she saw no one in sight. Lula went back to her bedroom pacing the floor. The walls were closing in on her. It wasn't like Bervick to take the children somewhere without her.

Biting at her lip, scratching her head, Lula froze. Her lips tightened. Blood rushed to her head. She calmed herself down enough to pick baby Benjamin up and take little Cleve by the hand to go back across the street to Fran's house.

Fran saw Lula marching across the street yelling, "He took my chillun?"

"What?"

Fran got up from her chair and they went inside the house.

Lula handed baby Benjamin and little Cleve over to Fran. "Watch dem fo' me please, Sha. I'll be back."

"Slow down, Lula Mae, what's going on?"

"Bervick took my chillun and I kno' just where he at!"

Lula busted the screen door open, almost breaking it off, took off her shoes, and marched up the street.

Fran yelled, "Lula, wait! Wait, Lula Mae! You can't go by yourself!"

Fran went back into the house in a panic. She ran over to the phone and called her friend that was a cop and told him to hurry up and get Lula before she made it to Geneva Jo's house.

Officer Jones and his partner spotted Lula walking barefoot in a haste. When they pulled their patrol car alongside her, Lula ran up to the car. "Hi, Mr. Jones, I need yah help!"

Officer Jones said, "I already know. Get in."

Lula got in the back seat feeling a sense of relief to have the cops with her. She never felt such rage, afraid of what she might do to Bervick.

Officer Jones attended the same church as Lula and Bervick, and was already aware of the situation between them. He was just leaving the house for duty before Fran called, and when his partner picked him up, they immediately went searching for Lula.

Officer Jones was secretly pleased to help Lula out. Coincidently, he too didn't care much for Bervick. After hearing his uncle complain about a disruptive man that was preaching nonstop at General Motors where he worked, Officer Jones picked his uncle up from work and saw that it was Bervick Frank who was the disorderly man.

Lula and the two officers rode over to Geneva Jo's house. During the ride, Officer Jones told Lula to remain calm and let them handle everything. When they arrived, he opened the back door to let Lula out and they all walked up to the front door. He pounded on the door hard enough for the whole block to hear.

Geneva Jo peeked through the peephole, then looked over at Bervick, who was sitting in the living room surrounded by his and Geneva Jo's children. Geneva Jo ran to Bervick's side, bending down, facing him so none of the children heard her, "Lula Mae's at the door with two cops!"

"What?"

"She there with two cops. What we gonna do?"

Bervick moved Geneva Jo out the way and went to the front door peeking through the peephole.

"Open up! This is the police!" Officer Jones commanded, banging again.

"No crime was committed. These here my chillun, Officer Jones."

"Bervick, open the door."

"No! I'm in my house with my chillun and that ain't no crime."

Car lights came shining through the window from the driveway. Without hesitating, Bervick ran to the back room, closing and locking the door.

The headlights turned off and Ralph got out of the car, looking at Lula and the two cops. He walked up towards them with a toolbox, wearing a greased stained uniform and untied boots, asking, "What's going on here?"

Lula said, "I'm tryin' to get my kids, Brother Ralph!"

"Where they at?"

Officer Jones pointed, "We believe they're in your house."

"What makes y'all think they in there?"

Lula said, "Bervick brought dem here!"

Ralph yelled, "Bervick in there?"

Officer Jones said, "I'm afraid so."

Ralph screamed, "I knew it!"

Ralph dropped his toolbox as Office Jones backed Lula and the other officer out the way. Digging in his pocket for his key, Ralph cussed underneath his breath. When he found it, he unlocked the door and heard the latch lock back up. He unlocked it again and the latch locked again.

"Damn it! Open this door, Jo!"

He pounded on the door yelling for Geneva Jo to open it.

Geneva Jo was on the other side of the door, biting at her fingernails.

"Jo, I hear you breathing, open this goddamn door now!"

Geneva Jo backed away from the door, looking back and forth, panicking. She yelled for Bervick to come out and help, but got no response from the back room.

Ralph yelled, "I know you ain't yelling for him in my house! Damn it, open this door!"

Ralph banged on the door and tried unlocking it again. Geneva Jo ran up to lock it again, but was too late. Ralph bust through the front door causing the hallway mirror to fall and shatter. Fist balled and nostrils flared, Ralph yanked Geneva Jo by the arm and shook her uncontrollably, yelling, "You sleeping with him?"

Officer Jones and his partner pulled Ralph off Geneva Jo, restraining him against the wall. Lula ran past them into the living room, rounding her kids together, checking them to see if they were okay. She paused when she saw the TV sitting there on a stand. She held back tears and got her children out of the house fast and into the police car.

The officers tried calming Ralph down, holding him against the wall, talking to him. Ralph's nostrils flared with every breath while looking over at Geneva Jo with rage filled eyes. Officer Jones held Ralph there telling him to compose himself in front of his children. Ralph looked over at his kids who were watching in fear, causing him to calm down. He ran his hand over his face, taking deep breaths to control himself. Officer Jones loosened his grip on Ralph, and then released him. He patted Ralph's back for no hard feelings while Ralph looked over at Geneva Jo, now with sorrow-filled eyes. The back door squeaked open and Bervick came out walking towards everyone in the hallway. He stood in front of them, looking at everyone, and then rested his eyes on Ralph.

Officer Jones said, "Com'on, Bervick, you caused enough trouble tonight. Let's go."

Bervick stood there, never taking his eyes off Ralph.

Ralph pointed his finger at Bervick, saying, "Get the hell out of my house."

Bervick held his head high. "No! *You* get out of *my* house! I fear no man!"

"I'm gonna give you to the count of ten to get out before I kill you!" Ralph said, pointing at the door.

"Dis here is my house nah. God gave me dis here house, so I'm gonna have to ask *you* to leave b'fore *I* count to ten!"

Officer Jones said, "Bervick, if you don't come with us now, I'm arresting you."

Bervick didn't take his eyes off Ralph. He acted as if he didn't hear Officer Jones. This was God's plan for him. He was not going to have Ralph or law enforcement stand in the way. "Geneva Jo is my wife."

"That's it," Ralph said going after Bervick, who ran to the back room shutting the door and locking it.

"Open the door!" Ralph banged.

Geneva Jo ran behind Ralph trying to calm him down, pleading for him to leave Bervick alone.

Ralph turned to her yelling, "You're trying to protect him?"

"Please! Just don't hurt him."

"Have you lost your mind?"

"No. I'm gonna marry him. God told me so."

"You crazy bitch!" Ralph slammed Geneva Jo against the wall choking her. Officer Jones and his partner tussled with Ralph to release his hands from around Geneva Jo's neck. "Let her go, Ralph! Let go!"

Geneva Jo's face turned red, coughing, fighting for air. The officers broke her free of Ralph's grip. She fell holding her neck, gasping for air. While the other officer restrained Ralph, Officer Jones tried helping Geneva Jo up, but she backed away and ran to the living room with her kids, huddling them close to her on the couch, except for her oldest son who was leaning against the wall with his arms crossed.

Ralph yanked his arms away from the officer and started banging on the back room door, calling Bervick every name in the book and screaming what he was going to do if Bervick didn't get out.

Bervick began preaching the word of God from inside the bedroom, infuriating Ralph more.

Their oldest son uncrossed his arms and peeked down the hallway at Ralph banging on the door. He gave Geneva Jo an evil look before running out the front door to the side of the house. The oldest son picked up a crate, placed it against the wall, and stepped on top of it, getting a clear view of Bervick sitting at the edge of the bed facing the door. He quietly lifted the screen up and raised his body into the room. Bervick turned and saw the oldest boy plant his feet on the floor. They both paused looking at each other. The oldest boy darted to the door, unlocking it before Bervick could grab him. Ralph dashed in the room running over to Bervick, punching him so hard in the face, he had to shake his knuckles out. He picked Bervick up to hit him again, but heard guns cock from behind. Ralph turned around and saw two guns pointed at him. He released Bervick's collar and put his hands up.

"Go in the room with yah mama," Ralph told his oldest son. The boy shook his head no. Ralph calmly said, "Go on, son."

The boy reluctantly left out the room.

Officer Jones said, "Ralph, I want you to calm down and let us do our job. Step away and let us take him."

Ralph backed away with his hands up. The cops lowered their guns, putting them back in their holsters.

Officer Jones said, "Let's go, Bervick!"

Bervick staggered onto his feet, covering his eye. He didn't move any farther.

Officer Jones took out his handcuffs, "Now, Bervick!"

Bervick stood still. "Are y'all hard of hearin', I told y'all dis here is my house. I am a Prophet from God and what I say go. Dis here my house and Geneva Jo is my wife. You should be locking him up."

The other officer grabbed his handcuffs and started walking over to Bervick saying, "Let's book him."

Officer Jones put his arm up to stop his partner. He looked over at Ralph, and back at Bervick. "No, I think our job here is done."

"We're not gonna book him?"

"No. Matter-of-fact, we were never here."

The other officer chuckled putting his handcuffs away.

They backed away exiting the room, giving Ralph a nod.

Bervick looked up at the man twice his size.

Ralph said, "Get the hell out of my house."

"Dis here my house and Geneva Jo is my wife. Dis here is God's work and nobody can stand in the way of it."

Ralph leaped on Bervick, punching him hard in the face again. He took Bervick by the collar and dragged him out the room, down the hallway and out the front door. He threw Bervick on the lawn and watched Bervick struggle to get up on his feet.

Bent over, Bervick muttered, "Dis is what God wants. He wants me to have the house and Geneva Jo."

Ralph yanked Bervick by the collar, "If I catch you near my family again, I'm gonna kill you!" He punched Bervick in the face again, knocking him back on the ground. Blood gushed from his nose. Ralph walked over, lifted Bervick by the collar and hit him one last time in the face. He shook out his knuckles from hitting Bervick's teeth, and then kicked Bervick in the stomach one last time before retreating back into the house.

Neighbors watched. No one bothered to help Bervick. He lay there moaning and groaning, coughing up blood. He pulled his shirt off to hold against his bleeding nose as he struggled to stand steadily on his feet, spitting out blood. He began walking bent over in pain, staggering home, shirtless with a bloody face and swollen shut eye.

Bervick sat alone in the dark kitchen while everyone was asleep. Eye swollen, busted lip, bruised back and stomach didn't faze him. His hand wrapped around a piping hot cup of black coffee, welcoming the heat stinging the palms of his hand. Elbows rested on the table as he stared out into the darkness with the moonlight piercing through the dark. In pain and defeated, the vision God wanted had diminished.

His house and future wife slipped away. The congregation would soon be aware of the altercation, eliminating Bervick's chances of becoming pastor one day. It seemed the same fate he encountered in Eunice had now revisited him in Pacoima. Losing the chance of becoming a pastor made Bervick hold his cup tighter. His eyes swelled up. Streams of tears burned the wounds on his face. He quickly smacked them away, ignoring the pain from touching his wounds, and grunted himself back in order. *No room for emotions,* echoed in his head. The voice of his father spoke during times Bervick's manhood wavered.

Falling into a trance from Joe's echoing words, a bright, translucent image appeared in the kitchen of a little boy on the ground crying, and the most beautiful woman in the world walking over to the little boy, picking him up and kissing his pain away. She put the little boy on the counter and wiped away his tears with soft hands, smiling down at the little boy like Jesus to a child. Bervick reached his hand out yelling "Mama" causing the image to vanish.

Bervick sat for a second, waiting for Christina to come back, but she was gone. He downed his steaming hot coffee, feeling his insides sizzle, putting him at ease. The pain in his back was relentless, making it hard to sit comfortably in the chair, so Bervick staggered up and lay down on the floor, focusing on the evil in his life.

Bervick began praying for God to provide him with the steps needed to get rid of this devil. The same devil that destroyed God's plans, causing him to get hit in the eye and thrown out his new home; and most of all, kept him away from his beloved wife to be, Geneva Jo. The same devil who was sleeping across the hall. The same devil who bore his children and tricked him into marriage.

Bervick remained on his back, summing up the reason for his dissatisfying life. Lula, the devil, was the cause of all of his mishaps. She prevented the union between him and Geneva Jo, brought the cops to remove him from his new house, prevented him from obtaining the assistant pastor position, and committed adultery with Cleve, forcing Bervick to wed another woman.

Bervick laughed at it all, figuring everything out for himself. Lula was the devil in disguise, a test from God.

He licked his busted lip and touched at his swollen shut eye. Waving his index finger in the air, Bervick laughed hysterically saying, "Good one."

Bervick got up from the floor, wincing in pain, and fell back into a chair, enthused at the new prophecy he embarked on.

Another lucid image materialized in the middle of the kitchen, except this time, it was one Bervick was delighted to see. A young woman in a coffin, pin curls in her hair, and she wore a skirt with a flower print on the side, lying there looking sound asleep.

Bervick puffed out his chest, ready to pass God's test as a true Prophet and Chosen One, "I rebuke you devil," he sneered, pointing at the woman in the coffin, and in a split second, the image vanished.

Bervick got up from his seat, elated and pain-free. Pouring another cup of hot coffee, he sat back down taking a sip and muttered, "Til death do us part."

***

Lula didn't speak to Bervick for two weeks after the incident at Geneva Jo and Ralph's house, and vice versa. Her focus was on moving back to Eunice. She never breathed a word about it to Bervick. She confided in a few people, getting their opinions on her decision, and each one agreed it was time for Lula to leave him.

Lula sat at the kitchen table writing a letter to Lillie about her business plans, and decided to work on a business outline for her restaurant, as Cleve suggested. She wrote down an estimate on how much money was needed and what had to be done to raise the money. Lula sighed at all of the pies and dinners needed to be sold in order to finance the cost. Nonetheless, she was ready for the challenge. She considered Samantha and Papa Top as potential financial investors since they were established business owners, and even put her father-in-law down as a prospect, for he also owned a lucrative store.

Lula opted to be optimistic about her family accepting her and her children back with open arms, and they would do their part in building this family business.

Once Lula completed the outline, she reviewed and approved of her work. She took out another sheet of paper and wrote down her goals for the restaurant and the prerequisites to achieve them. After putting her ideas on paper, she sat back in her chair reading over it, then folded the papers up and went into the bedroom, hiding the business plan and Lillie's letter underneath the bible in the nightstand. She heard the front door close and steps walking into the kitchen. She checked on baby Benjamin and little Cleve taking their afternoon nap, and then went into the kitchen.

Bervick had been staying away from the house for long periods of time while Lula was home with the kids. She welcomed his absence, now indifferent to Bervick's whereabouts.

She passed by Bervick without saying a word. She put on a pot of water to make oatmeal for the kids when they returned home from school. Feeling the hairs on her neck rise, Lula jumped turning around to see Bervick sitting at the table wearing all white, staring at her with an indecipherable glare. She stared back at Bervick, waiting for him to say something, but all he did was look fiercely at her. Lula flagged her hand at him and returned back to making the oatmeal, feeling an overwhelming urge to get back to Eunice soon.

Bervick got up, fixed his clothes, and left out. He walked a few blocks to Cleve and Hattie Ann's house to begin damage control. Luckily, Cleve was home from work that day and answered the door, surprised to see Bervick standing there.

Bervick said, "May I talk to yah fo' a minute?"

Cleve stood there looking at Bervick, hesitant on letting him in. He looked Bervick up and down in his all white clothing, growing more irritated at the sight of Bervick.

Hattie Ann came to the door. "Mind your manners!"

She nudged Cleve out the way letting Bervick in.

"Thank yah," Bervick said, taking a seat on the couch. Cleve sat down on the other side of the couch. He looked everywhere but at Bervick.

Hattie Ann said, "Would yah like somethin' to drink?"

"No, ma'am, I'm not stayin' long."

"Thank God," Cleve muttered underneath his breath, sitting back folding his arms.

Hattie Ann rolled her eyes at Cleve and smiled back at Bervick, "What brings yah here t'day? Haven't seen yah in a while."

"I came here to apologize to yah both," Bervick turned to Cleve. "I do appreciate everythin' you've done fo' me and my family and I'm sorry fo' what happened at the job. I kno' we're not gonna be the friends we used to be and I take full responsibility fo' that, but I hope we can at least be civil with each other."

Cleve looked straight ahead, annoyance increasing by the minute. "What yah want nah?"

"I don't want nothin' at all. Just wanted to apologize, that's it."

Hattie Ann gave Cleve an angry look and interjected, "He accepts."

Bervick said, "I just wanna make things right again."

Hattie Ann said, "Good, and I hope things work out with you and Lula Mae. Is she still leavin'?"

Bervick's face changed from pitiful to puzzled.

Cleve gave Hattie Ann a facial expression to be quiet. She ignored Cleve and continued, "Ain't she movin' back to Eunice?"

Cleve shook his head looking away in disgust.

Bervick said, "Where yah hear that from?"

"Out the horse's mouth," Hattie Ann said, studying Bervick's body language, and then wryly grinned. "Oooh! You didn't kno'? She said she takin' y'all chillun, too."

Bervick tried his best to remain calm. He looked over at Cleve staring away with his hands folded, and looked back up at Hattie Ann. "Thank yah fo' tellin' me, but I doubt she'll be goin' anywhere anytime soon."

Cleve turned to face Bervick. "And why not?"

"She's pregnant."

Cleve looked up at Hattie Ann.

Bervick continued. "She's gettin' that sickness she always get during pregnancy again, so I'm gonna be there fo' her 'round the clock. I've been tryin' hard to be there fo' her. The thanks I get is her tryin' to leave with my babies?"

Hattie Ann said, "I'm sorry, Bervick. Is there anything we can do fo' yah?"

"No thank yah, Sha, I'm gonna take care of her myself. It's my duty as her husband to do so. Her being down is the perfect time fo' us to make our marriage work, and show her what I'm made of, so all I ask is that everyone respect our privacy so we can work on our problems alone. Our issue is between me and her, nobody else."

Hattie Ann said, "We will respect that. Cleve?"

Cleve reluctantly consented, "I reckon so."

Bervick put his hand out for a shake. Cleve shook it giving his word.

Bervick said, "I appreciate yah both."

Hattie Ann walked Bervick to the door. After closing it, Cleve got up from the couch, giving Hattie Ann an angry look.

"What?" she nonchalantly asked.

"You don't kno' when to shut yah trap, do yah?"

"Oh hush. That man apologized and he's tryin' to do right by Lula Mae, so who cares."

"I don't buy it."

"Yeah, well don't even think bout goin' over there. They tryin' to work on their marriage. You kno' betta than that."

Cleve turned the TV up, tuning Hattie Ann out.

Hattie Ann said, "Did yah hear me?"

"I heard yah loud and clear," Cleve said, angrily looking for his car keys to get away for a while.

Chapter 26

Lillie got permission from her husband to catch the first bus to Eunice when she received another letter from Lula with an outline of her plans to start a restaurant and asking the family to be a part of it.

Lillie nearly ran the whole way to Big Ma's house from the bus station with the letter in her hand that she read repeatedly during the ride. When she arrived at Big Ma's house, Lillie joined Big Ma on the porch and read the letter. Big Ma clapped her hand in merriment at the thought of the family having a restaurant to call their own, "I'm gonna start collecting donations from the church and get some money from Willie Ray and Daniel Lee to help."

"Yah sho' they gonna help? They tightfisted!"

"Mind yah mouth, Sha."

"Yes, ma'am."

"Dem my sons and they'll do as I say! I kno' they sittin' on money with that barbeque stand. Did yah see that house Oscar gonna move Lula Mae into? Got a nice cookin' stove in there and just enough yard to start another garden fo' me to teach dem chillun how to grow fresh vegetables. We gotta hurry and get dem back here soon. We got a lot of work to do."

Lillie said in her soft voice, "Can you imagine all the money we'll make?"

"More than we can count. Does she have a name for it yet?"

"How bout the family's last name?"

"No, don't sound right to call it that."

"Then we can name it after, Lula Mae. It was her idea. We can call it 'Lula' or 'Lula Mae' or 'Lula Mae's Kitchen' or maybe 'Lula, Lillie, and Big Ma's kitchen'!"

Big Ma laughed playfully smacking Lillie's shoulder.

Lillie winced grabbing at it.

Big Ma leaned forward. Lillie looked away in shame.

She said in a low tone, "Please, let it be, Big Ma! I'm okay. We'll be okay. I'm in prayer every night."

"You gonna move back here with yah chillun to help make pies fo' the restaurant?"

"That's my plan, if the good Lord say the same."

Big Ma sat back, "Or if that boy say the same." She shook her head. "Lord have mercy."

Lillie saw Doc walking towards them from the road. She got up, kissed Big Ma's cheek and said, "I'm going visitin' fo' a spell."

"Alright, my baby."

Chapter 27

Lula was over Fran's house doing hair and noticed Fran was unusually quiet. When they were done for the day, Fran walked outside with a cold beer in her hand sitting in silence. Lula joined her. They sat watching the cars go by, waving at the people they knew. Lula took in the fresh air from being inside on her feet all day as she held baby Benjamin while little Cleve was in the house watching cartoons. She smiled over at Fran, grabbing hold of her hand and gently squeezing it.

Fran started crying, squeezing Lula's hand back. "I'm gonna miss you."

Lula got up and sat at the edge of Fran's chair, wrapping her free arm around her friend. "I'll have a bed ready when yah come and visit me in Eunice. I'm gonna feed yah 'til yah pop. That's the least I can do fo' helpin' me. Our friendship won't end just b'cause I'm leavin'. You gonna come visit me?"

"Oh yeah, I'm coming! I'll be there with bells on! I just feel bad. I know it ain't gonna be the same without you. Who gonna watch the stories with me and have their children around to brighten up my day?"

Fran wiped tears away.

Lula consoled her whispering, "If there's anything yah need, don't hesitate to call me, yah hear? The first thing I'm gonna do when I get back to Eunice is get a phone and I'm gonna call yah every day, Sha. We gotta keep up with our soap operas nah!" Lula laughed, "I love you like a sister. We sisters, right, Sha?"

"Right, 'Sha'. I don't understand ya'll southern folk with that 'Sha'. Got me using it now, Sha."

"There yah go, Sha."

They laughed.

Lula saw her children walking up to the house.

"Gotta go. My babies are home." She got up holding baby Benjamin and went into the house to get little Cleve.

***

After putting the kids to bed, Bervick was gone, allotting Lula the time to go through the closet to separate everything she was taking with her back to Eunice. Looking in a shoebox on the top shelf, Lula was enraged at what she saw. Love letters Geneva Jo wrote Bervick filled the box. Lula figured Geneva Jo wasn't aware of Bervick's illiteracy, and because the envelopes weren't open, he never bothered to look at them. Lula read vivid details about their sex life, his marriage proposal to her, and what Geneva Jo was going to do to him the next time she saw him. Lula was upset, but more at herself for the anger brewing inside. She thought she was over it, but seeing it come from Geneva Jo's perspective and reading explicit details of what took place was enough to send Lula over the edge.

Securing the letters back in the box, Lula put it back up on the shelf and bent down digging for her small box underneath old newspapers. She opened it to count the money she had saved and sucked her teeth; it still wasn't enough for her and the children to leave the next day. She jumped when she turned to find Bervick in the doorway.

He looked around at the clothes on the bed and glanced back at Lula. "Goin' somewhere?"

"Gettin' my stuff situated," she said, resuming to her task.

"You not leavin' me!"

"And I'm 'pose to stay here and watch yah marry another woman? Go 'head, you can be with her, but I'm takin' my chillun and we moving back home to Eunice!"

"There's nothin' fo' you or my seeds back there."

"Yeah there is, I got my family and a business plan."

"Oh yeah, what's that?"

Lula ignored his question, neatly putting clothes away.

Bervick stated, "Honor and obey, Sha."

"Honor and obey? I'm the one takin' care of our chillun, workin' to keep the bills paid while you're off doin' God knows what with Geneva Jo. I've earned some say in dis here house!"

Bervick calmly said, "Hell, Fire and Brimstone. Remember that! Remember the word of God."

"You can do whatever yah want to me, but not even Hell, Fire and Brimstone will stop me when it comes to my chillun. I'll answer to whatever I got to if it means me keepin' my chillun safe. Yah done barked up the wrong tree bringin' our chillun into yah madness with that woman! I'm leavin' back to Eunice. Back home where we belong and I'm gonna start up a family restaurant and make money sellin' pies, dinners, and cleaning homes if I got to. And I'm goin' back to school to get my diploma, too. I'll make dis happen fo' me and my chillun, without you."

"Yah not goin' back to Eunice disgracing our marriage. I rather be dead than you go back there and make people think the worse of us. And yah ain't takin' my chillun either, they my seeds. Me and Geneva Jo is what God wants, not me, so yah just gonna have to except that and not turn yah back on God."

Lula stopped what she was doing and walked over to Bervick, standing directly in his face. "Stop blaming God fo' your selfish actions, Bervick! It was you who committed adultery, plain and simple! I'm tired of yah usin' God fo' your mess."

"You 'pose to obey me, woman!"

"Obey!" Lula stepped back putting her hands on her hips. "You kno', you must really wear yourself out being you, Bervick Frank. I tried being your virtuous wife, sticking by yah through thick and thin, through people talkin' bout us, and my family disowning me. But yah kno' what, there's no such a thing as a 'virtuous wife' dealin' with a man like you. Never satisfied. I loved you and did everythin' I can to make us work while you off trying to be with Geneva Jo. You and her can go live happily ever after and enjoy y'all TV. Oh yeah, I saw the TV in her house you hypocrite! I'm livin' fo' me and my chillun nah. I prayed on dis long and hard and kno' God is with me."

Bervick's tone turned menacing. "How dare you talk to God's Prophet like dis."

Lula stood unfazed, "All yah do is run around here playin' God, but I got news fo' yah, you ain't God! All you do is hide behind God so you don't have to face yah own reality and truth about yourself and the people around you. So while you're livin' in that fantasy world of yours, I'll be movin' back to Eunice with our chillun."

"What was that you were hidin' in that box?" Bervick asked, walking over to the closet. Lula ran over before he could get to it. She took out the money holding it up. "Dis here is to help us move and I thank God fo' it." She stuck the money in her bra, patting it, making sure it was secure. Bervick walked over to his side of the bed. He put his hand around the back of his neck, looking up at the ceiling. Lula stood still waiting for him to say something.

Baby Benjamin started crying in his bassinet. Lula quickly fell out of her rage, feeling bad for waking her baby boy. She picked him up and went into the kitchen to heat his bottle. When she came back, Lula sat on the edge of the bed to feed him. Bervick laid on the other side of the bed with his hands crossed behind his head and said, "You goin' straight to hell, devil."

Lula looked back and said, "I'm sho' you'll be sittin' on a hot coal right next to me with a pitch fork up yah behind!"

***

Bervick got up early the next day. He had to put God's work in motion fast. He made his rounds to the people in the church including Sis, Mother Adams, and their pastor, spreading the word that Lula was pregnant again and had fallen ill due to her pregnancy. He told them he was going to care for Lula and that her illness was a blessing in disguise, giving them a chance to work on their marriage. He asked everyone to respect their space. They were more than happy to oblige, giving Bervick a pat on the back for his efforts.

His last visit was at Geneva Jo's house while Ralph was at work. Bervick told her that he had business to attend to and she wasn't going to see him for a while. He left Geneva Jo crying on her doorstep, ignoring her calls. Bervick was on a time restraint and had to prepare for the future his Lord and savior Jesus Christ intended.

His next move was to reconcile with Lula, give her what she needed, adhere to her every need and be the great husband she wanted him to be. He had to build her trust again for his plan to work. It had to work. Divorce wasn't an option. Breaching a contract with God was against Bervick's beliefs.

Master of disguise and skilled persuader, Bervick was up for the challenge. He walked to the grocery store and bought very little food and more cleaning products to take over the chores.

By night, Bervick had cleaned and washed everything in the kitchen spotless, learning about each cleaning products—how well it cleaned, strength of odor, and tasted each one. Once Bervick got an idea of what cleaning products were best, he bought more the next day to compare them to the ones he had chosen.

After long nights up in the kitchen drinking coffee to kill the chemical taste in his mouth, Bervick found the perfect one. He ogled at the cleaner on the table for a moment, reading the back of it as if he could comprehend the words, shaking his head in agreement with his thoughts on what the words may have informed.

He finished the rest of his hot coffee, which tore the already scorched flesh in his mouth, got up from the table and went to the bathroom wiping down the floor, toilette, tub, and walls using the liquid cleaner.

He went into the boy's room, woke Bervick Jr. up, and told him to come to the bathroom. He closed the bathroom door and waited before asking, "Smell a difference?"

Bervick Jr. shook his head no.

"You smell anything?"

Bervick Jr. muttered, "No, sir."

"Yah sho'? Put yah nose to the sink and see if yah smell somethin'?"

Bervick Jr. sucked his teeth and went ahead and sniffed.

"Anything?"

Bervick Jr. yawned, "No, sir."

Bervick opened the bathroom door for his son to go back to bed. He smiled, returning back to the kitchen and poured another cup of coffee, ready to leave out in the morning to pick up a few more bottles of that cleaner.

Chapter 28

Leroy shaved in the bathroom and accidently nicked himself underneath his chin. He took a tiny piece of toilette paper and stuck it on the wound, then started shaving around it. The tiny piece of tissue quickly soaked in blood and fell off. He wiped the blood off his chin, noticing the cut was deeper than what he had thought. He went into the bedroom and picked up an old mirror in the corner that was turned around—the only mirror in the house—and overlooked why he had stayed away from mirrors for so many years.

Turning the large mirror around, placing it on the dresser, Leroy wiped the dust off it to get a clear view of his wound. He froze glancing at himself. His eyes fluttered, and then stopped. He backed away taking a seat at the edge of the bed still staring at himself, awakening from a long slumber. The man staring back at him had a balding head, a pot belly, wrinkled attire, and armpit stains on his undershirt. Leroy waved his hand. He watched the reflection wave back at him. His hand dropped. He stood up walking closer to the mirror, looking at a man he did not know. The reflection of this man's eyes was full of sorrow and shame. Leroy shook his head in disbelief, backing away from the mirror, taking a seat back on the bed. Beatrice flooded his mind. Her smile. Her scent. The yearning to touch her soft beautiful chocolate skin again made Leroy remember the harmonious sound of Beatrice's soothing voice, and kiss of her tender lips.

Curtains opened, allowing the bright light of shielded memories flood back in.

Leroy hung his head covering his face in shame. "What've I done." The only woman in the world who knew him best and gave him unconditional love, despite his flaws, was gone because of him. Facing the disgraceful man in the mirror, tears rolled down his cheek. The handsome, muscular built, clean-cut chef with a beautiful wife and three lovely daughters was long gone. All what was left was a balding, unkempt, miserable man.

Leroy sobbed uncontrollably, shaking his head in disbelief of what had become of his life. The face of his beloved wife made Leroy's heart ache in pain for what he had done to her. He missed Beatrice dreadfully, and the thought of his three beautiful girls made Leroy fall to his knees. His precious baby girls were now young women with lives of their own. *Are they okay? Are they married? Did their husbands treat them like the little princesses they were? Did Big Ma raise them right? Was Doc as mean to them as he was to his own children?* So many unanswered questions.

Leroy's sobs lessened at the thought of being with Beatrice again and meeting Lula, Lillie, and Mary for the first time as women. He wanted to be a part of their lives again and be the best grandfather to his grandbabies, if there were any.

Leroy sat up against the bed, hanging his arm over his bent knee, brushing dust off his pants. He got up off the dusty floor, dusted the back of his pants off and looked around, sickened by how dirty the room was, reminiscing on Beatrice's cleanliness. His beautiful Beatrice, Beatrice Harrison.

The last name, 'Harrison,' echoed in Leroy's mind.

"Harrison!" He said to himself, eyes lightening up. "Beatrice Harrison! Harrison!" He yelled and clapped his hands together. "She's still my wife, SHE'S STILL MY WIFE!" He yelled, scratching the top of his thinning hair. "My beautiful, beautiful wife," Leroy said, lowering his tone.

Without giving it a second thought, Leroy rushed into action. With no time to lose, he gathered his belongings from the closets and drawers, throwing everything out of order into two large suitcases. Leroy pulled out his three piece suit from the back of the closet, one he hadn't worn in years, hoping it still fit.

In his mist of transparency, Leroy stopped in motion. Everything hit him like a ton of bricks. Cordelia made jokes about Tauntadi, knowing more than the average person about her line of work. Thinking back, Leroy remembered Beatrice screaming about snakes and unseen bugs. Signs of foul play were right before his eyes.

Then it struck him. He too was under a hex. In his right mind, he would have been able to clearly see the obvious.

Leroy struggled getting the suitcases outside. He opened the trunk of his car and threw them in, slamming the trunk shut. He ran back in the house, took a shower, finished shaving, brushed his teeth and hair, patted on cologne, and put on his suit, carefully looping his tie in the mirror the way Beatrice taught him. He fixed his collar, adjusted his cufflinks, and stood in front of the mirror seeing himself coming back; the only thing missing was Beatrice on his arm again. He put a nice hat on, checked himself in the mirror one last time and was ready for his trip to Stolden House Penitentiary to get his wife back, praying to God for Beatrice to forgive him and accept him back.

Outside, Leroy turned the key to the ignition and began pulling off just as Cordelia pulled up blocking Leroy in. She got out her car and walked up to Leroy's driver seat window, knocking. "Where yah goin'?"

Cordelia backed away when Leroy stepped out the car looking like a new man.

She asked, "Where yah think yah goin' dressed like that?"

Leroy didn't answer.

Cordelia told her children in the car to go play at a neighbor's house while she and their daddy talked. Roseanne, their middle child, stayed back looking at her parents in confusion. Leroy motioned her to come to him, and leaned over saying, "Baby girl, go with yah siblings fo' a while, okay? Can yah do that fo' yah daddy?"

Cordelia tapped her foot waiting.

Roseanne said, "Yes, daddy."

"Daddy gotta go, but I'll be back to visit soon, okay?"

He hugged Roseanne and watched her run to catch up with her brothers and sisters. He was already pondering how he could see his children with the least bit of contact with Cordelia as possible. His thoughts were interrupted by the sound of Cordelia's voice saying, "Oh, so you ain't gonna answer me?"

"Com'on, let's go inside," he said, pulling Cordelia's arm to follow him to avoid causing a scene in front of the neighbors.

Cordelia followed Leroy into the kitchen. She yanked out a chair and plopped down with her hands crossed. Leroy sat across from her.

He asked, "What yah do to me?"

She crossed her legs, wagging her foot, looking away.

He repeated, "What yah do to me?"

Cordelia wagged her foot harder, still looking away.

Leroy calmly got up from the chair. "Thanks fo' my answer. Silence from that big mouth of yours always give yah away." He took the house key off of his key chain and threw it on the table. "I'm leavin'."

Cordelia said, "Excuse me?"

She stood up, not believing what she just heard. She put her hands behind her ears, pushed them out, and asked for Leroy to repeat himself.

He pulled Cordelia's ear close and yelled, "I'M LEAVING YOU," pausing between each word.

Cordelia slapped Leroy's hand off her ear and backed away, huffing and puffing, and said through her teeth, "I kno' you ain't just say that to me, Leroy Harrison!"

Leroy turned away and headed for the door.

Cordelia followed, yelling, "What bout me? What bout our chillun?"

"What bout you? Yah made a zombie of me to be with you. I kno' b'cause yah ain't even try to deny it. We're finished, and as far as our kids go, I'm gonna make sho' they still takin' care of."

Cordelia trailed behind Leroy to the front door, pulling him back screaming, "You're not leavin' me!"

Leroy rubbed his chin wishing he'd left sooner. "I don't got time fo' dis."

"Please, don't go, baby, please. We can work dis out. I promise! Please don't leave me! I kno' things haven't been great 'round here, but I love you and I kno' yah still love me, too. I can see it in your eyes," she started crying.

Leroy sighed, exhaling out his frustration. Cordelia wrapped her arms around his waist, trying to get him to look her in the eyes. She leaned in to kiss Leroy's lips whispering, "I love you, baby, and I kno' yah love me, too."

She lowered her eyes, winning Leroy over once again with the technique Tauntadi gave to keep Leroy in love.

Leroy leaned in closer to Cordelia's face, looking deep into her eyes and said, "Are you hard of hearin', I told yah we're done!" He moved away from her, "I gotta go."

"You can't leave me, I'm yah wife," Cordelia said, pointing at the ring on her finger. Leroy gripped her wrist and started twisting the ring off. Cordelia pounded at his back, screaming to let go. He pulled the ring off, yanked Cordelia closer to him, held the ring up to her face and said with clenched jaws, "You're NOT my wife! The woman with my last name is my wife, NOT you! I never married yah and never will! My eyes opened to the train wreck of a life we had together and I'm done! What yah did to me and my family, yah gonna pay fo' it!"

Leroy threw the ring across the hall, picked up his hat and headed for the door.

Cordelia hurried to the front door, smacked her back against it, and held her arms out wide to block Leroy's way. "Please, I'll do whatever you want, give yah whatever you need, just please don't leave me!"

"Move out of my way."

"No! Not until we talk bout dis!"

"I'm not gonna tell yah again, Cordelia, move the hell out my way!"

"Not until you give me one good reason why."

"Beatrice Harrison."

Cordelia's eyes widened. She stopped breathing. Those were the last words she thought would come out of Leroy's mouth.

"That's right. I'm gonna get my wife back. All I can do is pray the good the Lord forgive me fo' what I've done."

Before Leroy could react, Cordelia leaped on him, hitting him all over his head, scratching his face, calling him every name in the book. Leroy struggled to get Cordelia off him and lost his balance, both falling against the wall. He finally wrestled Cordelia to the ground, pinning her hands against the floor, putting all of his weight on her, yelling for her to calm down. Cordelia spit in Leroy's face and continued yelling at the top of her lungs, trying to kick him off until she started heaving out of breath tiring herself out.

Leroy lifted off her slowly and dusted himself off. He fixed his suit and adjusted his tie. He licked his lip tasting blood and went to the bedroom to examine his busted lip in the mirror. Dabbing the blood off with toilette tissue, Leroy sucked in his bottom lip so that Beatrice wouldn't notice. He adjusted his tie and checked himself in the mirror one last time and smiled back at the reflection, hoping Beatrice was going to be satisfied with his appearance. He pulled out his wallet to count out enough money for fresh roses and a gift, and started rehearsing lines to say when he saw Beatrice. Regardless of how horrible Beatrice may view him, and rightfully so, Leroy wasn't going to give up. Even if he had to be on bended knee, he was going to win the love of his life back.

Leroy left out the bedroom walking back into the hallway. He looked around. Cordelia was nowhere in sight. He pushed his hat on his head and anxiously headed to the door, full of confidence and excitement to see Beatrice after so many years.

Turning the front door knob, a blunt object hit Leroy in back of the head, knocking him straight to the floor. He tried getting up, reaching for the doorknob, but another blow hit Leroy's head again causing his body to collapse.

Blood poured from his nose and mouth. It seeped out onto the floor forming a huge puddle. Cordelia dropped the iron skillet. She nudged Leroy and turned him over checking his pulse. She gasped falling back against the wall…Leroy was dead.

***

Big Ma sat in a daze. There was no congregation, church, or sermon being spoken. As assistant pastor, Curley Frank, preached in front of the church, all Big Ma saw was her baby boy lying in a casket before the church.

She had raised her children and grandchildren, having to ask herself where she went wrong with them, especially Leroy. He went from being a family man to living in sin with a woman that wasn't his wife. No matter what Big Ma did or said, she could never get through to Leroy. Years passed without the two speaking to one another. Big Ma prayed every day for Leroy to come to his senses and be the family man he once was. When the two did cross paths, their conversation never went further than Big Ma greeting Leroy out of courtesy, then going about her business as if Leroy wasn't once Big Ma's pride and joy. Big Ma hoped to see Leroy again after years of his absence. She never thought they'd meet again like this.

Big Ma wept, blaming herself for Leroy's death. Even though she had been told his death was accidental, Big Ma should've been there to warn him about walking over wet floors; but still, something in Big Ma knew Leroy well enough to know that he was a cautious person—he knew better than to walk over a wet floor and hit his head hard enough to cause a brain hemorrhage.

Big Ma bit at the edges of her nails, a childhood habit that broke in her early teen years; except on this day, the habit revisited her more than ever. She bit down asking herself if she was too hard on her children, or maybe Doc was too hard on them, or did they witness Doc's beating one too many times? Did her preferential treatment over Leroy cause him to act out, instead of being a God fearing Christian man? Maybe too much church caused him to run away from God. Perhaps she should've taught Leroy more about adultery and how that is the ultimate sin. Was Leroy's actions God's punishment for her own sins? Is it possible that Leroy was not really dead and the funeral was just a cruel joke? Maybe he was going to wake up from that casket, laughing along with church folks who were in on it, too. Maybe Beatrice and the girls were back at home, waiting for them to return from church… perhaps.

Big Ma's thoughts ran rampant. What could she have done for Leroy to be the father and husband he once had been, instead of leaving Lula, Lillie, and Mary? What could she have said to get the old Leroy back and see him return home in his chef uniform, giving Beatrice a kiss and greeting his children with open arms? But staring at her son's lifeless body lying in the casket brought Big Ma back to the reality that, that day would never come. 'What if's' didn't matter at this point.

Big Ma rubbed at a cool breeze running up her arm. The breeze intensified, spreading down the left side of her body. A breeze she used to get as a child, prayed away by church members years ago, never to return. Church kept away the encounters that followed the breeze, only to return on this very day, which Big Ma refused to believe was happening again. She nudged Doc and told him to stop breathing so hard. Doc gave Big Ma a weird look and resumed listening to the sermon. Noticing Doc's chest slowly breathing, Big Ma glanced around at everyone seated near her. No one seemed to feel the wintery cool air. A strange feeling came over Big Ma. Goose bumps formed on her arm. A far translucent voice echoed, "Mama...Mama..." Big Ma sat up looking around at everyone listening to the sermon. Doc put his hand on Big Ma's back, rubbing it to comfort her.

She whispered to Doc, "Yah hear that?"

"Hear what?"

Big Ma looked around again, seeing people giving her a sympathetic glance. She turned back around in her seat, swallowing hard. When she finally relaxed, the cool air returned, raising the hairs on her neck. She slapped at her neck to make it go away, but it didn't work.

A faint voice said, "I'm sorry, mama."

Big Ma squeezed Doc's hand.

Her lips quivered. Tears rolled down her face. "My baby."

She spoke louder, "Mama loves you."

Doc consoled Big Ma more, hoping nobody else heard her.

Big Ma heard the voice echo, "No accident… no accident…"

Then the cool air ceased.

Her chills faded.

"No accident," Big Ma said to herself. She looked over at her son lying there like he was sleep in the casket. "No accident," she repeated.

Big Ma's eyes shifted back and forth. She bit at her thumb. Leroy would never slip on a floor, especially if it was wet. Her son wasn't a clumsy fool, and the unexplainable injury on Leroy's lip put the pieces together for Big Ma. Rage engulfed her. Doc had to wiggle his hand out of Big Ma's tight grip.

Big Ma got up in the middle of Curley's sermon, stepping over family members who assisted her out the aisle while asking if she was alright. Without a response, Big Ma marched down the aisle and stopped at the last pew in the back. Cordelia sat at the end, blotting her red eyes with tissue. She looked up startled to find Big Ma standing there with her hands on her hips.

Big Ma bent down in Cordelia's face. In a low demanding tone, she said, "What you do to my boy?"

Cordelia's face went blank.

Big Ma raised her voice, "What yah do to my boy?"

Assistant Pastor Curley stopped his sermon. He and the entire congregation focused their attention on Big Ma. A few members got up and gently pulled Big Ma by the arm. She yanked her arm away, giving them a look to leave her alone. They backed away.

Big Ma looked back down at Cordelia and bent down whispering, "I kno' what yah did to my boy. God knows, too. Everyone has their day with *him*, Sha!" She patted Cordelia's back, "Sleep well."

Big Ma walked to the exit, smacking the doors out of her way.

Inquisitive eyes were on Cordelia sitting there dumbfounded.

Lillie got up to see about Big Ma. She peaked outside and saw Big Ma sitting on a ledge against the church, holding her heart.

She ran over to Big Ma, "What happen in there?"

Big Ma looked up at Lillie, and then exhaled turning away, unable to muster up a logical response.

Back in the church, Tauntadi stood against the wall in back of the church. She wore a massive black hat covering her face. Banned from churches for decades, Tauntadi felt obligated to pay her respects to Leroy and his family. The look on Big Ma's face when speaking to Cordelia devastated Tauntadi. Heavy bags formed under Tauntadi's eyes from loss of sleep after hearing of Leroy's death, bringing back memories of the state Lula was in after leaving with Big Ma years back. Whether old age or growing a conscious, it haunted Tauntadi. The least she could do was pay her respects to Leroy in an attempt for peace, except, it made matters worse. Big Ma's face just added to Tauntadi's memory stains.

Tauntadi caught Cordelia looking at her. She squinted her eyes at Cordelia and said with her lips, "I warned you," before lowering her big black hat and exiting the church. Breezing by Big Ma and Lillie unseen, Tauntadi took a solemn walk home.

As she walked, Tauntadi took off her hat to allow the sun to shine upon her pale skin. She had practically forgot how good the sun felt since she spent most of her time in a dark house with candle's being her only light.

Once she entered her house, Tauntadi kicked off her shoes, threw her hat aside, and began scouring the house, picking up alters, tinctures, statues, candles, dolls, and bottles full of recent cliental concoctions. She piled it all into sacks and carried them out, one at a time, to the curb. No more faces were going to taint her memory bank.

When church ended, Big Ma sat outside turning everyone away. She needed time alone. Lillie was the only person Big Ma allowed close to her. Samantha walked out the church, stopping in front of Big Ma to console her, but thought the better of it and continued walking.

Lillie asked again, "What happened in there?"

Big Ma rocked humming to herself, "You send that letter to Lula Mae yet?"

"No, ma'am. Just finished writing it last night."

"Send it as soon as possible, my baby. Let her kno' we gonna get her and dem chillun home. And tell her don't worry bout a thing. We just want dem home."

"Yes, ma'am."

"You put in there Mary Lee a Guillory nah?" Big Ma asked smiling, knowing Lula would be happy to hear her little sister married Alex Guillory. Lula was fond of him, too.

"I reckon she knows that already, Big Ma? I'm sho' Sis or Hattie Ann ran they mouths over there." Lillie chuckled, "Anything else yah want me to add in there?"

"Tell Lula Mae that…I forgive her fo' elopin'. I don't care bout all that anymore. Tell her I'm sorry and I love her. Tell her I love her and will support her from here on in. I just want her home!" Big Ma wiped away a tear, "Don't mention nothin' bout Leroy! I don't want her to worry. She gotta get home first."

"Yes, ma'am."

Chapter 29

Lula woke up in the early morning running to the bathroom, unable to hold her food down. She sat for hours on her knees in front of the toilette, holding her stomach. When nothing else came up, Lula flushed the toilet and went back to bed before her children saw her. She lay in pain alone in bed reading the bible, praying for relief.

Sickness was nothing new to Lula. Bervick tried to convince Lula that she may be pregnant, but she didn't believe it. What she was experiencing was a different type of sickness in her stomach. Her previous pregnancies never felt this bad.

Bervick kept the children away from Lula and was adamant about her not breast feeding baby Benjamin anymore. Lula conceded. She didn't want them to see her sick as well, so Bervick took over getting them ready for school and walked baby Benjamin and little Cleve to Mother Adams' house, and then would return home to prepare Lula's morning tea.

Lula didn't speak much to Bervick. She took the tea from him and sipped it, leery of the way he had been acting lately.

Bervick sat next to her on the bed, moving hair out her face. "I'll understand if yah don't wanna talk to me. I kno' I deserve it."

"I'm still leavin'."

"I think yah should go. I don't deserve you as my wife anymore. But, I do want yah to kno' that I'm not seeing Geneva Jo anymore. Had to let her go. I'm ready to do whatever I can to make our marriage work fo' us and our chillun. To start, I'd like to apologize fo' all I done to you and our babies. Y'all deserve betta! All I ask is that b'fore y'all leave me, please forgive me. I betrayed you, our marriage, dis family, and most of all, God. I can't change what I did, but I'll try from dis day forward to make things right. Just allow me to take care of you and show yah the love I should've been showin' all along. Yah sickness is my punishment fo' my sins. God wants me to take care of yah. I kno' yah don't think yah pregnant, but I do, and the good Lord knows I don't want nothin' to happen to our baby. Please, Sha, give me a chance to be yah husband and correct the wrong I did. And if yah get betta and still wanna leave, then by all means, go. I ain't gonna stop yah. I'd at least be at peace knowin' I tried. Could yah at least give me that?"

Lula squinted in pain. She quickly moved her hand away from Bervick trying to help. "What yah want from me? I kno' you! I kno' yah want somethin'. You want a part in the restaurant, don't yah?"

"No. I want yah to stop lookin' at me funny, always thinkin' I'm up to somethin'! That's what I want. I want yah to trust me again. I've been gettin' the kids up fo' school, I take Ben and Cleve to Mother Adams' house so I can be here takin' care of you! I've cooked, I've cleaned, and I'm here 'round the clock makin' sho' you alright. Give me one last chance? Jesus forgave us for our sins, so maybe you can find it in yah heart to forgive me."

"I need time, Bervick. I can't just turn my feelings on and off at a drop of a hat."

"I just want my wife back," Bervick started crying.

Lula was at a loss for words. Bervick had never shed a tear throughout their marriage. Guilt began to consume her. Here he was trying to do right, and she couldn't get past the lies and deceit. In marriage, there had to be room for forgiveness. She did want her children to be raised by both parents and give them what she once had. She still loved Bervick and if he was willing to try, why couldn't she do the same.

Lula's eyes watered watching tears pour out Bervick's eyes. She put her hand out for his. If Jesus forgave us for our sins, then she could forgive Bervick.

He took hold of Lula's hand, allowing her to wipe away his tears.

She smiled, "I almost forgot why I married you."

"I love you."

"I love you, too. Only time can say what's gonna happen after I get betta."

"That's right. Time is on our side."

Knots formed in Lula's stomach. She bent up in a ball holding it her stomach. Bervick rubbed her back. He got up to help Lula to the bathroom.

***

Sis and Fran went to see about Lula after Fran noticed the children playing outside more often. Bervick was gone, dropping baby Benjamin and little Cleve off at Mother Adams' house when they knocked. Lula woke out of a deep sleep. She tried to yell out, but was too weak. Sis opened the front door and walked in yelling out for Lula. Going into the bedroom, they saw Lula squinting over in pain.

Fran ran over to Lula's side. "Come on, get up! We taking you to the doctor!"

"I can't move. I'm hurting too bad."

"Come on, we'll help you up. Come on, Sis, help me."

They tried lifting Lula from the bed.

Lula protested, "I'm fine, just let me rest."

Sis said, "We can't let you lay here like dis. Maybe the doctor can see what's wrong with yah. Even if yah are pregnant, at least they'll kno' how to help yah."

They started helping Lula out the bed.

"What y'all doin' in my house?" Bervick said, standing at the door of the bedroom.

They didn't hear Bervick come in.

Sis said, "We takin' her to get some help, that's what we doin'! Somethin' you should've done yah ole nut!"

"Let her be. I'll take her to the hospital myself."

Fran said, "When? She needs help now!"

"Cleve gonna take us."

Sis and Fran looked at each other. They hesitantly laid Lula back down.

Sis walked over to Bervick. "Don't make me beat yah the way Ralph did! Yah sho' yah gonna take her?"

"I promise with everythin' in me, I promise, Sha."

Fran said, "I don't believe him."

Sis added, "Me neither," tapping her foot with her arms crossed. She walked over to the edge of the bed and sat down crossing her arms and legs.

"I'm not movin' 'til Cleve get here."

Fran joined Sis sitting down in the same stance. Bervick took a deep breath, rubbing the back of his neck. He picked the bible up and went in front of Fran and Sis. He held out the bible, putting his left hand on it and raising up his right hand. "If God is my witness, I'm gonna ask Cleve to take us to the hospital." He hugged the bible close to his heart, closing his eyes in dismay. "I cannot believe y'all think I'd sit here and leave my wife in the condition she's in," Bervick lowered his voice so that Lula couldn't hear. "I told y'all I was gonna care fo' her during her pregnancy and to please stay away while I try to make things right between us durin' dis time! The only person I need forgiveness from is her and my God and I got that from both. We workin' out our differences and I stopped seein' Geneva Jo. So, I don't owe y'all nothin'! I owe Lula Mae everythin' and I'm takin' it one day at a time to care fo' her and my kids, so can y'all please stop tryin' to come between us? Lord have mercy!"

Fran asked, "Well why your kids outside all day, Bervick?"

"You want dem to see they mama like dis? She don't want dem to see her like this and I don't either!" Bervick shook his head and turned to Sis. "And you, yah kno' betta than dis. We weren't raised like that, to come between a man and his wife. I wonder what yah husband gonna say bout dis?"

Sis avoided eye contact with Bervick and twisted her mouth. He was right. She got up and walked over to Lula, kissed her forehead, and then walked towards the door. "Com'on, Fran. Let's go."

Fran sat with her arms crossed still looking at Bervick. "If you don't get her to a doctor soon, I'll be back. I don't care. I'll come between a man and his wife to help a friend. Lula Mae's my friend first!" Fran got up rolling her eyes at Bervick.

Fran's heart told her to stop, but if Lula obliged, Fran had no choice but to leave and allow them to give their marriage another chance.

They said their goodbyes to Lula, then left.

Bervick locked the front door behind them and went into the kitchen to fire up the stove and boil water for tea. A few minutes later, Bervick brought Lula peppermint tea with a piece of lemon on the side. Lula sat up and stirred the tea before sipping it.

She asked, "So when we goin'?"

"I'm on Cleve's schedule so I'm don't kno' yet. I'm gonna go by his house to see if he can take us tomorrow."

"Wow, Bervick."

"What?"

"That's a big change from not believin' in doctors. I was waitin' to hear yah tell dem God was gonna heal me."

"When I told yah I wanted to make things right, I meant it, Sha. Even if that means me goin' against our faith and beliefs." He laughed, "I still don't like doctors tho'."

Lula smiled taking a sip of her tea.

***

A couple days later, Lula was too sick to move. Her feet and hands were numb and she couldn't keep warm. She tried reading her bible, but the words were too blurry. Everything in the room doubled in vision. She stayed thirsty and drank very little fluids, fearing it'll cause another trip to the bathroom.

When the kids left and Bervick took baby Benjamin and little Cleve to Mother Adams house, Lula crawled out of bed to the bathroom where she stayed the remainder of the morning. She missed seeing her children, but was too embarrassed about her deteriorating condition and didn't want them to worry.

The peppermint tea Bervick made helped to cool Lula's insides for a moment, yet didn't take away the abdominal pain. She refused soup Bervick made since she couldn't keep anything down. Lula figured she would heal with or without a doctor, as she did after her previous illnesses. At twenty-six years-old, Lula felt her body was young and strong enough to bounce back any day now.

Lula appreciated Bervick's attentiveness with their children, and rediscovered the deep passionate love she had once felt for him, realizing it never left. There still was an inkling of some clandestine motive lurking underneath Bervick's palpable behavioral change, which caused Lula to deter herself from falling back into the same predicament with Bervick as before. Change needed to happen in order for Lula to pursue her dreams owning a restaurant to pass down to her children. She yearned to be back in Eunice with her family, even if it meant minus a husband.

Lula wasn't going to play a fool twice by thinking Bervick wasn't going to go back to Geneva Jo after the dust settled. She knew Bervick would resume to his old ways, using God as an excuse to be selfish. At the end of the day, Bervick was going to be Bervick. There was no changing him and Lula couldn't allow herself to be put in a position to get hurt again. Lula still loved Bervick and decided to love him from afar, back in Eunice.

Crawling back into bed, Lula settled back under the sheets and smiled picking her bible up, understanding that Bervick's unruly sin was a blessing in disguise. It was the catalyst in releasing the fear of Hell, Fire and Brimstone as an inevitable fate if she dared to challenge or leave the man she had wedded in Holy Matrimony. The burdening weight from the decision to leave lifted off Lula's shoulder as she came to a truce within herself between conflicting beliefs of what happiness was and what God expected of her. Now at peace with understanding God in a new perspective, Lula concluded that all along, God was waiting for her to help herself and do what needed to be done to embrace her own happiness in life.

When Bervick returned home, he went straight to the kitchen. Moments later, he entered the bedroom with more tea. Lula asked for another tea, sick of peppermint tea. She didn't like the strong taste and it wasn't helping to ease her stomach. Bervick insisted, but she turned her face, refusing to drink. He quickly went back into the kitchen, scouring the cabinets, looking for a tea just as strong as the peppermint. He grabbed the chamomile tea, put more water in the tea kettle and sat it on the stove while brewing him some coffee. He took a seat at the kitchen table and folded his hands, waiting. His patience was waning. The final result to his master plan should have already taken place. Going into the third week forced Bervick to take drastic measures for God's plan to come into fruition.

The tea kettle whistled. Bervick got up from the table to pour hot water in a mug, squeezing two lemons in the water before putting the tea bag in. He poured a cup of coffee and drank it down, craving the smoldering heat inside his mouth. The pain soothed his tension.

He added sugar in Lula's tea to offset the lemons, and then dug underneath the sink for the best solution to his problem. He poured mild All Purpose cleaner into the tea, mixing it in until it spilled over.

The torment and suffering Bervick was going through living under the same roof with the devil had to come to an end soon. It was his duty to suffer through hell on earth as a Prophet from God, and Bervick wanted to prove why he was 'The Chosen One'. He must do away with the devil and be with Geneva Jo—the wife God had chosen for Bervick and; in turn, Bervick must set forth to conquer all enemies holding him back. No room for error. No room for time. The job had to be done quickly and according to plan before people tried to intervene and demolish this God given objective.

Lula's weak arms trembled as she sat up for her tea. Bervick handed it to her and watched Lula take a sip. His breath stopped when she sat it down on the nightstand.

He pointed saying, "Aren't yah gonna finish that? It's not peppermint."

"Maybe later. I can hardly hold the cup to my mouth."

"Yeah, but it won't work when it cool. You gotta drink it while it's hot. It's betta goin' down hot."

"I'm sorry, Bervick, but it taste pretty nasty."

Bervick swallowed hard. "What it taste like?"

"Too much lemon."

"Oh," Bervick breathed again. He hung his head. "I'm sorry, Sha, I was just tryin' to help. I wanna see you get betta fo' our baby."

"I'm not pregnant. Why you keep sayin' that?"

"I was just tryin' to help."

Bervick stood up, hanging his head with a pitiful expression, picking up the cup from the night stand.

Lula said, "Wait, you went through all that trouble, the least I can do is drink it."

Bervick smiled kissing Lula's forehead and handed over the cup. Lula held her nose and took sip after sip until it was gone.

Bervick said, "See, it wasn't that bad nah was it?"

"No, it wasn't," she smiled.

Bervick kissed her cheek. "Get some rest my wife."

Chapter 30

Big Ma kept busy working alongside Grandma Emma, Papa Top, Daniel Lee and Willie Ray, fixing up the house for Lula's return. Big Ma and Grandma Emma painted the living room while the men fixed the pipes in the kitchen.

Big Ma painted the wall near the window and peeked out when she saw Samantha get out a car with a man kissing all over her. It incensed Big Ma seeing the man grab on Samantha, touching her in places reserved for a husband only. Samantha giggled and laughed as the two walked up to the house carrying buckets of paint. She nudged him away before entering and smiled walking in wearing overalls and an old t-shirt.

The man straightened up to greet Big Ma and Grandma Emma, sat the paint down, kissed Samantha good-bye, and then left. Samantha waved good-bye, then turned smiling at Grandma Emma and Big Ma. She pulled out paintbrushes from her overall pockets and sat them on top of the paint, pointing proudly at everything she brought. Big Ma and Grandma Emma paused for a moment. Samantha grinned, waiting for a response, still pointing at what she had brought.

Grandma Emma walked over and picked up a paint brush, "Thank yah, Sha. That's mighty kind of yah." She grabbed old newspaper and laid them out in the corner and pointed for Samantha to start there.

Samantha was still looking at Big Ma, waiting for her to say something. Big Ma pointed at the same corner for Samantha to start, then turned around and continued painting. That was enough of a response for Samantha to happily get started.

Big Ma said, "Who's that boy?"

Samantha looked over her shoulder, "A friend."

Grandma Emma asked, "A boyfriend?"

"No, just a friend, Sha."

"One of many friends," Big Ma added still painting.

Samantha painted looking over her shoulder in Big Ma's direction. "I reckon so."

"I didn't kno' friends touch like that."

Samantha's arms fell in annoyance. She put a hand on her hip and turned around to look at Big Ma. "I'm leavin' if I gotta hear dis the whole time I'm here, mama."

Big Ma said without looking up, "Nobody stoppin' yah, Sha."

"Fine!" Samantha said, dropping the paint brush on the floor, rushing out the house. Grandma Emma called out for her to come back.

Big Ma said, "Let her go, Sha. She shouldn't bring men over here disgracing herself like that."

Grandma Emma stood in the doorway watching Samantha stomp away.

A pick-up truck pulled up. Mary and Alex got out bringing more supplies.

"Hey my babies," Big Ma said, dropping everything to give them a hug.

Papa Top came out of the kitchen with his toolbox, greeting them.

"What y'all need done 'round here, sir? I'm a man of many trades. I can do it all," Alex said, smacking his hands together ready to help. He was of average height and built with reddish honey skin, and straight jet black hair cut low and combed back. A joy to be around, Alex lived for lending a helping hand. There wasn't a person alive who didn't love Alex Guillory, who told many stories and jokes, laughing harder than anybody else.

Throughout the day, Alex brightened the mood in the house after Samantha left, telling stories for Big Ma and everyone else to laugh.

Alex said laughing, "I'm tellin' y'all, that hog winks at me!" He stopped painting to imitate how the hog winked. "I gave her the name, Winkie, b'cause she wink at me all day long."

Everyone laughed.

Willie Ray chuckled, "He ain't lyin'! That hog winked at me, too."

Alex pointed, "See, told y'all. Winkie be winkin' at us men."

Grandma Emma asked, "Then what Winkie do to women?"

"Roll her eyes and keep bout her business."

Everyone laughed.

Big Ma laughed rubbing tears out her eye. "Lord have mercy, I gotta see dis fo' myself. Where that hog at?"

Alex said, "Gone, ma'am."

"Where to?"

"My fridge!"

Another burst of laughter filled the room.

Big Ma laughed, "Lord, y'all done pork chopped Winkie."

They had a good laugh, taking away the sorrow each of them felt after losing Leroy.

Working into the night, they started singing church songs, bearing their souls during solo parts, releasing built up tension and grief while others waved their hands in the air, shaking their head side-to-side, tuning into the sentimental waves. Unable to share their emotions otherwise, they released their sentiments through song, ending the session with Big Ma's solo in honor of Lula's return home.

Chapter 31

Gloria Jean held baby Benjamin outside along with Bervick Jr., little Leroy, Sandra, Joseph, little Cleve, and Luvicy. Bervick stopped taking baby Benjamin and little Cleve over to Mother Adams' house when she started asking too many questions about Lula's "pregnancy".

Gloria Jean fed baby Benjamin sugar water while little Cleve leaned against her, too weak to play. They were hungry, only eating during school lunch while Bervick cared for baby Benjamin and little Cleve at home, feeding them very little.

Bervick kept the children outside, away from Lula, while he fasted and prayed for the new transition about to take place in his life. He had the children fasting too and didn't look at them as being hungry—it was him doing God's work, cleansing his seeds of negativity from the devil, and before they went to bed, he'd give them bread and milk, which was a stretch.

Bervick kept his word, waking them up and getting them off to school, but did nothing further. He forbade his children to go into the closed off bedroom door where their mother lay sick. Incomprehensible young minds couldn't understand why they saw Lula up one day, then gone the next, retreating to her bedroom never to be seen again.

Little Leroy, seven years-old, caught a glimpse of Lula crawling to the bathroom one day, and asked Bervick in a slow tone, "Dad, why don't yah take mom to the hospital?"

Bervick replied that God was healing her and sent his son back outside with the rest of his siblings.

Bervick sent his children outside to play every day when they returned home from school, leaving the oldest to watch their younger siblings, and then he'd go inside the house to pray. After prayer, Bervick sat at the kitchen table drinking scorching hot coffee, on-call twenty-four hours, making sure nobody visited and that Lula got her tea on schedule. He broke the regiment to periodically check on the children.

Instead of their usual play, the kids stood outside at a loss, waiting for their neighbors, Jose and Maria, to return home with leftover doughnuts from their bakery. Days when Jose sold out of doughnuts made it hard for them to return home empty handed, but they figured if Bervick could bring home groceries in an expensive white three-piece suit, and Lula was in the house, it wasn't a big deal.

Bervick would walk home holding a bag full of cleaners without any food, and wave at his neighbors, especially Fran, holding up the bags, shaking his head at the heavy bags he had to carry home. Neighbors nodded, chuckling at Bervick and how he walked everywhere, never accepting any rides from neighbors. They wrote him off as just a "southern man" who loved to walk. Fran, on the other hand, sat drinking a beer, biding her time before seeing about Lula. She figured Bervick was buying enough food to feed Lula and the children, but something still nagged at her conscious to go see about Lula sooner than later.

Cleve stopped by their house one day without Hattie Ann's knowledge, breaking the agreement he made to stay away. Bervick spoke to Cleve outside, informing him that Lula's health was improving and how she would be back on her feet in no time. Cleve didn't want to be intrusive and left back home taking Bervick's word for it, even though everything inside Cleve begged him to go back.

***

Fran's instincts got the best of her a couple days after Cleve's visit to Lula's house. Watching the kids turn lethargic outside made Fran pay a visit to Bervick as well.

Bervick stepped onto the porch, closing the front door behind him to assure Fran that Lula was getting better and she would be back doing hair by the following week. Fran called the oldest children over and asked if they were okay. They glanced up at Bervick, who was giving them a stern look behind Fran, and quickly shook their heads yes. Fran left, assuring herself that if Lula wasn't up and well by the following week, she was going to return, knocking the door down to see about Lula.

Later on that day, the children got lucky when Jose and Maria's van pulled up. They came out the car holding a bag of homemade donuts baked fresh, given that they too noticed a change in the children's temperament outside.

Maria was horrified at how the children ate, chewing their food before swallowing. She looked over at Jose with a face asking if he was witnessing this as well. He nodded. In a few seconds, the donuts were gone.

Bervick came outside with another bottle of sugar water, handing it over to Gloria Jean to feed baby Benjamin. He greeted Maria and Jose.

Maria asked in a heavy accent, "Did your children eat today?"

"They're on a fast."

"What's a fast?"

"It's part of our religion."

Jose said, "Oh, Amigo, we're sorry for giving these donuts to them. I did not know."

"That's okay, they can go 'head and eat it."

Maria asked, "Where's Mrs. Lula Mae?"

Jose pulled Maria back, walking her over to their house, embarrassed for interfering with another man's religion. Maria protested aloud in Spanish all the way inside their house where they still could be heard after the front door shut.

They were the new neighbors in town, moving next door to Lula and Bervick four months ago. They had three kids who often got in altercations with Lula's oldest boys. Lula had to defend her children against Jose and Maria for yelling at them for fighting with their boys. Lula decided to reconcile, bringing homemade soup to Maria after she had caught the flu. After tasting the soup, Jose later visited Bervick, asking if Lula could make more of that soup to sell in his store, splitting the profits fifty/fifty. He was expanding on his business and loved the soup so much, there was no doubt it would be a guaranteed seller. Bervick gave his word that he would relay the message to her. When Jose ran into Lula a couple weeks after, he greeted Lula, waiting for a response. Lula waved back continuing into the house, unaware of Jose's request. Jose took Lula's reaction as a no, and had to freeze what was left of the soup to find someone who could duplicate it through taste.

***

Bervick cracked the bedroom door open, squeezing his way through, and went over to Lula's bedside to wake her up. When he shook her, she didn't move. Bervick shook Lula again, hoping God's work was complete.

Still no movement.

Bervick stood tall poking out his chest inhaling pride, exhaling further burdens. Lula moaned in pain stirring in her sleep. Bervick sucked his teeth and retreated to the kitchen, filling the tea kettle up with water, slamming it on the stove. Waiting impatiently pacing back and forth, he ran over to the stove when he heard a whistle. No more careful methodical measures taken. Time waned. Too many church folks, neighbors, and family were asking questions.

Bervick grabbed a bigger cup and poured hot water in it, spilling water all over the counter top. He threw two chamomile tea bags in the cup, squeezed a couple lemons in it without removing the seeds, tossed a hand full of sugar on top, and poured extra All Purpose cleaner in last.

Bervick shook Lula out of sleep and handed over her evening tea.

Lula said sleepily, "Sit it down, it's too hot."

"I'll get some ice."

A few seconds later, Bervick came back with a cup full of ice, placing cubes in the hot tea, listening to it crack and pop as it dissolved causing the cup to overflow.

Bervick said, "Okay, nah try it."

"I thought you said it's betta when it go down hot?"

"That was my only way to get you to drink it," he laughed. "I just wanna see yah get betta soon. I need help with these chillun. Forgive me fo' tryin'."

Lula was dizzy, falling in and out of consciousness, too weak to argue. In a daze, her hair was all over her head, lips parched, and mouth dry. She was thirsty, but didn't have the energy to swallow. Her mouth hung open. "I can't drink dis anymore."

"Yes you can. Com'on, drink up!" Bervick put the cup to Lula's mouth, spilling some on her face as she coughed and choked, pushing Bervick's hand away.

Lula held her hand out. "Please stop. I don't want no more. That chamomile taste bad."

The tea spill helped Lula regain some prudence. "Where's my babies?"

"They outside playin'."

"What they eat fo' dinner?"

"Beans and rice."

"I ain't smell nothin' cookin." Lula said slurring her words.

"Fran brought it over. She cooked it at her house."

"Good, tell her thanks fo' me."

"Will do."

"You gotta call the doctor fo' me. Somethin' ain't right. I can hardly feel my feet and fingers. Yah gotta get somebody here fast." Lula coughed.

"I already called a doctor. He won't be out here 'til next week."

"That's too long."

"There's nothin' else I can do. We just have to wait. It's in God's hands nah."

Bervick left the room closing the door behind him. He stuck his head out the front door and yelled, "Y'all stay out here fo' while, don't come in 'til I tell yah to."

The children flatly nodded their heads and Bervick quickly went back in the house, slamming the front door.

In the middle of the night, Lula staggered to the bathroom, falling on top of the toilet, and held on for dear life. Nails were hammering at the walls of her stomach. Torches burned the wounds it left. Lula sat on her knees constantly rubbing away chills throughout her body to keep warm, and then covered her mouth trying not to regurgitate. The acidic fluid burned her esophagus causing an unbearable pain, and rose out her shivering mouth into the toilet. Her blurred vision didn't notice the blood in the water as she flushed the toilet and wiped her mouth with unsteady hands. She pulled herself up on her feet, holding onto the counter, and turned the faucet on to rinse out her burning mouth. Her head was swimming in pain and the bathroom light seemed dimmer than usual. She splashed cold water on her face to cool her feverish body. The sclera of Lula's eyes, which normally was white, was now a pinkish hue, and dark circles outlined her eyes. She turned the water off and leaned closer to the mirror for a better view, but then her knees buckled and she lost her balance, falling to the bathroom floor, too weak to get up. She lay there hoping her children didn't hear, for she didn't want them to find her in such a horrible state.

Lula managed to open the bathroom door with her foot. She crawled on her knees to the girl's bedroom. In excruciating pain, Lula inched her way over to Gloria Jean, Sandra, and Luvicy's bed, kissing each of them on the cheek. Then she crawled into Bervick Jr., little Leroy, Joseph, and little Cleve's bedroom doing the same. She sat against their bed for a moment taking a few breaths, and then crawled to baby Benjamin's bassinet, rubbing and caressing the side of his face through the bassinet. She paused when baby Benjamin stirred, waiting for him to go back to sleep. Lula closed her eyes in relief and slid herself across the bedroom to the door, grabbing hold of the doorknob to pull her body up. She struggled back on her feet, closed their bedroom door, and used the wall to help her walk down the hall. Almost to her bedroom, Lula's knees gave out again. Her body collapsed on the ground, hitting her head hard against the floor. She covered her mouth moaning and crying, panting heavily in agony.

Bervick came out the bedroom and gasped, "Lula!"

He immediately lifted Lula's limp body and took her back into the bedroom. "You alright, Sha?"

"No! Take me to the hospital now," she said, having a difficult time breathing. "Please," she said in between a breath, "Take me nah!"

"Next week. I'll make sho' yah get there next week. Just hold tight."

Bervick fixed the pillows behind Lula's head.

She grabbed his arm tight while he was tucking her in and slurred, "You don't understand. Somethin' ain't right! I gotta go nah!"

"God's gonna help you. All yah need is a little rest. Wait right here, I'm gonna get yah some tea."

"No! I don't want no tea, Bervick. I need a doctor!" she said, losing her breath.

"If yah don't drink yah tea, then prepare fo' the worst b'cause the tea is the only thing helpin' you right nah."

Lula was too weak to protest.

The last thing she remembered before blacking out was that she wasn't drinking anymore of Bervick's nasty tea.

***

The following Saturday morning, Bervick left early to pick up a little food for the weekend since the school teacher had contacted him questioning why the kids all of a sudden came to school hungry.

Returning home, he put the food in the refrigerator and sent the kids outside, giving strict orders to stay put before leaving to do an odd job to make much needed money.

Lula woke up later that morning, and to her surprise, she was pain-free. Thanking God for answering her prayers, Lula felt lighter than usual after slipping in and out of consciousness throughout the night; and for the first time in weeks, Lula was able to stand on her own without any struggle. She got up feeling light as a feather, yet her feet were like anchors on the floor. She sat back down on the bed to get a tissue for her excessive hard coughs. Flabbergasted at the blood in the tissue, Lula got worried. Something wasn't right. She smelled food cooking making her stomach turn. She waited for Bervick so that he could open the windows to air out the nauseating smell, but when the bedroom door opened, Lula was shocked to see Gloria Jean come in with a plate of half burned toast, runny eggs, and bacon swimming in grease. Gloria Jean walked in proud of the breakfast she prepared for her mother, disregarding Bervick's command not to enter the room. She missed her mother and was scared of her father's strange behavior.

Lula looked down at the plate of food, unable to eat, "That's okay, baby, you go 'head and eat that," she said. It took everything in Lula not to gag in front of Gloria Jean. Lula watched her nine year-old daughter's wry smile through a worried look before she skipped out the room into the kitchen to eat her first delicious meal in weeks.

Lula sat on the bed with a sense of urgency to leave the house. No time to lose. She got up from the bed and went into the bathroom to wash off and brush her hair in a quick style. She went back into the bedroom to put on a blouse and her flower printed skirt. Her body was getting lighter by the minute as her feet felt heavier like magnets tugging at her. She rushed to the kitchen and opened the refrigerator, astound by the lack of food in it with only eggs, half a loaf of bread, butter, bacon, and baking soda. She rushed over to the cabinets and saw that they were empty except for a can of milk, tea, coffee, and sugar. Lula looked over at Gloria Jean sitting at the table with an empty plate in front of her. Her hair wasn't combed and clothes were shabby. Lula's heart sank realizing her children had been starving and weren't being kept while she was ill. Lula quickly put a pot of water on the stove, eagerly waiting for the water to boil, and then poured the last of the oatmeal from on top of the refrigerator into the boiling water.

Time was of the essence.

Gloria Jean ran up hugging Lula around her waist. Lula hugged back, realizing she couldn't feel Gloria Jean's arms. She bent down facing Gloria Jean, "Take care of yah brothers and sisters fo' me, baby, and make sho' they eat dis here breakfast, okay?" Lula didn't quite understand why or how she spoke those words. It seemed more as if they involuntarily fell out her mouth.

Gloria Jean nodded.

Lula hugged Gloria Jean tight enough to get a slight feel of her daughter's body.

Moving faster, feeling her feet drag and body lighten, Lula cooked up the oatmeal mixing milk, sugar, and butter in it, then turned the burner off. She shook up can milk, sugar, and water and put it in baby Benjamin's bottle. "Here, feed yah baby brother too fo' me," Lula said, handing it over to Gloria Jean. "I'll be back later, okay. I gotta go do hair." Lula's body got lighter. She no longer felt her legs, except for the heaviness pulling at the bottom of her feet. Time was running out. She quickly left the house, dashing pass her children in the yard without them noticing her. Lula had to get away quick!

The faster Lula moved, the slower her body followed. It took every ounce of strength to get across the street, striding in slow motion as if she was fighting against gravity. For some unknown reason, Lula felt she had to hurry away from her children, and fast.

The mailman came by whistling, handing the mail over to Gloria Jean holding baby Benjamin. She looked at the letter addressed to Lula from Big Ma and Lillie, then sat it down and tried feeding her five month old baby brother who was frantically crying.

Lula got to Fran's front door, leaning against it, pounding.

Fran's customer got excited pointing out the window. "Look, there go Lula Mae, maybe she can finish my hair," she said, nudging Fran jokingly. Fran playfully hit her client's arm and went to open the door. Before the door was completely open, Lula collapsed in Fran's arms, unable to stand any longer.

Fran held Lula up, screaming, "Lula Mae! Oh my God, what's wrong?"

Fran's customer threw her magazine aside and rushed over to help carry Lula to the couch and lay her down.

Fran screamed, "Call the ambulance?"

Lula breaths deepened. She whispered, "Call the pastor, too. Something ain't right." She looked in Fran's eyes, "I think I'm dyin'."

Fran's customer stepped back, dropping the phone out her hand when she heard Lula's words. Fran covered her mouth with trembling fingers, holding in the heaviness building in her chest, falling to her knees. Her eyes shut. The condition Lula was in, Fran felt there maybe some truth to Lula's statement.

Fran opened her eyes, solemnly looking over at her client, and nodded to go ahead and make the calls, ambulance first.

Pastor William's wife dropped the phone, jolting over to him, whispering in his ear in front of their children. He quickly got up from the kitchen table, leaving his hat, glasses, and wallet, and ran out the house with a napkin still hanging from his shirt collar. He jumped into his car heading straight to Fran's house, running stop signs and traffic lights. He pulled up to Fran's house running out the car with the ignition still running and busted through the screen door.

A few minutes later, word spread. Cars lined the block. Sis held on to Lula's hand while everyone surrounded her.

Lula felt extremely tired, finally feeling the weight lift off her feet while looking at double the amount of people standing in the room. People she never seen before dressed from different time eras, breaking the iconoclastic era of the church folks, friends, and neighbors in the room.

Lula asked Sis, "Where's Bervick?" .

Sis yelled out, "Where's Bervick?"

"Where's Bervick," voices said, rippling across the room.

Pastor Williams commanded, "Get Bervick here now please! And where's the ambulance?"

"Ambulance on their way, pastor!" A voice said from the crowd.

Cleve busted through the screen door. He pushed pass everyone to get to Lula, but Hattie Ann held him back.

"Lula!" He screamed, "It's me, Cleve!"

Lula cracked a slight smile, unable to feel her face.

Mother Adams shook her head in disbelief and could no longer witness Lula in such a state. She told Pastor Williams, "I'm gonna go tend to them babies across the street," and covered her mouth running out the house. After burying her husband, this was more than what Mother Adams could bear.

Pastor Williams screamed, "Where's Bervick! Can someone go get him please!"

A church member said, "Somebody went to go get him already, pastor."

The muscles in Lula's eyelids weakened as she looked up at Sis and the church folks flickering into misty shadows. The unknown people, dressed in clothing from another time period, became more pronounced, scaring Lula until she noticed a familiar face she had not seen in years. She smiled at the tall muscular built man dressed in his chef uniform, looking the same way he did when Lula was six years-old. Leroy warmly smiled at Lula, putting her at ease.

Bervick arrived moments later. The room quieted. All eyes were on him. Pastor Williams stood up from the chair next to Lula, and moved himself and Sis out Bervick's way, angrily. Bervick ran to Lula's side and knelt down on one knee. She looked over at the shadow hovering over her with enough form to know it was Bervick, but didn't feel him holding her hand.

Unable to fully close her mouth, Lula said, "If there's anything I've done to you, please forgive me as I forgive you. Take care of our chillun. Get dem back to Eunice, back to our family."

Lula squeezed Bervick's hand with the last bit of energy she had left. Bervick nodded.

Silence in the room.

A siren neared.

A burst of bright light shined through the room as the shadows of familiar faces dissipated while Leroy and the unidentifiable people became more prevalent. Lula's eyelids lost all strength. Her eyes closed, allowing the luminous light to absorb her.

Lula's body went limp.

Big Ma dropped a fresh baked sweet dough pie. Samantha spilled tea in her lap. Lillie sprung up out of sleep. Tobacco blew out Papa Top's pipe. Beatrice got up from scrubbing the floor and walked over to the barred window, gazing beyond sight.

The people of Eunice stopped in their tracks. An ominous cloud cast over them. The wind peaked as the soft rain began to fall.

Lula Mae Frank was gone.

***

The coroner was long gone. Night sneaked up outside Fran's house. Church members, neighbors, clients, and friends joined together comforting each other's sorrow. Bellows of grief rippled in waves throughout the day as mourners came to term with Lula's sudden death.

Fran comforted Cleve on the porch, constantly reminding him to breathe. Her own tears flowed looking across the street with false hope of Lula coming out the house popping her Doublemint gum. Fran saw Lula's neighbors come out of their house. They walked over with a frost coated pot in Jose's hand.

Maria hugged Fran while Jose shook hands, giving his condolences.

Maria said, "I'm so sorry for your loss. She was a great neighbor and a good person."

Jose added, "I've been trying to duplicate this soup Lula Mae made for us, but I thought it'd be best if I share it with you all. That's the least we can do."

Maria said, "I will heat this up."

Fran pointed for Maria to go ahead inside.

Pastor Williams said, "I'll help you," and followed Maria into the house.

Jose sorrowfully stood there looking around at everyone. "She was a good woman and a great cook!"

Cleve slightly lifted his head and muttered, "That's right, she was," the first words he had spoken in hours.

Hattie Ann came from across the street over to Fran's house. She squeezed between Cleve and Fran on the porch, leaning her chin on Cleve's shoulder, softly saying, "Yah ready to go?"

Cleve frowned at Hattie Ann.

Hattie Ann defensively said, "It's gettin' late! We gotta get Deborah in bed!"

"She's fine over there with Mother Adams and her siblings."

Hattie Ann said through her teeth, "I don't want Deborah 'round dem."

Cleve leaned his head away from Hattie Ann. "You worried bout that at a time like dis?"

"I don't want my Deborah to kno' they kin. I'm her mother!"

Cleve flicked Hattie Ann's hand off him and ignored her.

Jose put his hands in his pocket and said, "A great cook though," bringing the subject back to Lula to defuse the disagreement between Cleve and Hattie Ann.

Fran added, "Yes she was."

Jose said, "I wish she would've taken me up on my offer. It would've been good for her."

"What offer?"

"I asked Bervick to tell Mrs. Lula Mae about selling her soup at my shop, but when I saw her, she didn't bother to bring it up, so I took it as a no."

Fran sucked her teeth, "That's because that bastard ain't tell her," she said, shaking her head in disdain.

Sis came outside the house and went down the porch steps standing near Jose. She stretched looking across the street, then hung her head. Her eyes swelled. She looked over at Fran's frowning face. "What's wrong, Sha?"

"You know that fool didn't tell Lula Mae about Jose wanting her soup in his store?"

Sis looked around, "He ain't back yet?"

"No, he left with them coroner people to sign papers."

"That was a long time ago. He should be back by nah."

Pastor Williams and Maria came out the house.

"There's soup in there," Pastor Williams said, patting his stomach, "Had me a taste," he chuckled then stopped, looking around at the angry faces. "What's going on out here?"

Sis said, "We don't kno' where Bervick at, pastor."

He said, "Bervick should be back by now."

"That's what I said, sir."

Maria looked down the sidewalk and pointed, "That him?"

Everyone simultaneously turned and saw Bervick walking toward the house. Sis ran up to his face, screaming, "Where the hell have you been?"

Pastor Williams walked over calming Sis down, pulling her away from Bervick, letting other church members take Sis near the porch.

He walked Bervick closer to the sidewalk, away from everyone and asked, "How you doing, Brother Bervick?"

"Not good, pastor. Needed to walk fo' a while. Clear my head."

Cleve lost all composure. He got up from the porch, treaded over to Bervick and got in his face, "You knew she was sick! Why'd yah let her lay sick like that, Bervick? Huh? Why?"

Pastor Williams got between them, putting his hands up to calm Cleve down.

People from inside came out gathering around watching.

Cleve calmed himself down. "Pastor, please let me talk to him. I'm not gonna do nothin'. I just wanna talk, that's all."

"Just talk?"

"Yes, sir."

Pastor Williams moved out Cleve's way, staying close in case something happened. Cleve kept enough space between him and Bervick and calmly said, "Why didn't you get her to the hospital?"

"The Lord told me *he* was gonna heal her."

Fran got up from the porch and walked over to them, yelling, "Wait a minute! Wait just one minute!" She looked over at Cleve and pointed, "I thought you were taking them to the doctor? Weren't you supposed to give them a ride?"

Cleve said, "No! I couldn't get pass the front door to see bout her."

Fran put a hand on her hip turning to Bervick. "You told me Cleve was going to take you and Lula Mae to the doctor."

Bervick shrugged standing quiet.

Fran yelled, "I can't believe I fell for your shit!"

Bervick yelled back, "Lula Mae didn't wanna go! She knew God was gonna heal her."

The crowd mumbled.

Never taking her eyes off Bervick, Fran pointed at Jose, "Did you tell Lula Mae about Jose's plan for her soup?"

"She wasn't interested."

"Like hell she wasn't. Lula Mae wouldn't pass on an opportunity like that and she never breathed a word about it to me and she told me everything!"

Bervick fixed the collar of his shirt, uninterested in what Fran had to say.

Sis walked over looking Bervick up and down with suspicious eyes. "I haven't seen you once shed a tear fo' your wife."

Cleve said, "I can't believe yah told dem I was takin' y'all to the doctor? You ain't knock at my door once to ask me such a thing. How could yah just let her lay there sick all these weeks?"

Angry faces closed in on Bervick. He held his head up clearing his throat. Now that he had everyone's attention, it was the perfect time to reveal who he really was.

Backing away for all to see, Bervick raised his hands and began preaching, "Dis here was a test from God. I passed my test and nah, it's time fo' y'all to pass, too. I am the 'Chosen one'. God's Prophet who live among you people. Let's take dis time to acknowledge his work. Lula Mae is in all of our hearts, but as you can see, the Lord giveth and the Lord taketh—" before Bervick could finish his sentence, everyone started yelling at Bervick, moving in on him. Pastor Williams went in front of the crowd, holding his hands up to calm everyone down, but they resisted. Yells and screams surrounded Pastor Williams shielding Bervick. He had no other choice but to hurry Bervick into the car to prevent any physical altercation. They screeched off leaving everyone behind in disarray.

People mumbled their disdain for Bervick, grieving more for Lula putting up with him.

One of the church women repeated, "Lord know I's prayed for her. Lord know I's prayed."

Another church woman added, "I can't believe my Jesus let Lula Mae suffer like that. She was only twenty-six!"

Fran had about enough of the church folks playing the blame game with God and stood up shouting, "Why don't y'all just shut y'all mouths for a minute. Just shut it!"

Everyone angrily got quiet. Smug looks had Fran's full attention.

Fran yelled, "All I hear is 'why God' this and 'I prayed to God' that! Just stop it! God ain't cause Lula Mae's death. WE DID! Everyone out here, including myself, know Bervick Frank is one crazy bastard. And you, you, and you, all of us didn't do nothing!" Fran shook her head pulling her hair loose, "You know, just maybe God was answering our prayers all along…maybe through here," she pointed at her heart, "maybe the God within us was warning us to go see about Lula Mae. I know I'm not the only one out here that felt something wasn't right. But no! We just continued praying for some gray haired holy man to drop out the sky and make everything right, instead of us taking action based on our God given instincts. We had the power in our own hands to move that bastard out the way and get her to the hospital. But we didn't! And that's why we're sitting here in mourning now." Fran choked up. "I'm by far a religious woman, but I know God blessed me with good judgment that I failed to use in this case. Now look...my best friend gone." Tears ran down Fran's face.

Everyone stood quiet. Some angry. Others looked away in shame, wondering what they could've done differently.

One by one, everyone started making their way home. Jose and Maria walked back across the street. Fran, Cleve, Sis, and Hattie Ann sat on the porch saying good-bye to everyone leaving.

Cleve hung his head allowing Hattie Ann comfort him.

He said through tears, "I'm the reason why Lula Mae gone. I should've known betta. I should've busted that door down and got her out of there."

Fran said, looking down, "No need in dwelling on it, Cleve. You, out of everyone, did the most for her and them children. I'm sure she appreciated that."

Hattie Ann got up to leave, waving for Cleve to follow.

Oblivious to Hattie Ann, Cleve shook his head mumbling, "My sweet Lula Mae's gone."

Hattie Ann waved her hand calling out for Cleve, but all he could do was cry out. She backed away from the porch, astound at how he was acting. Hattie Ann called for Cleve one last time and saw that he never bothered to look in her direction.

Fran patted Cleve's back while he went on about what he could have done differently. Hattie Ann walked away backwards, taking slow steps, offended by Cleve's reaction. She turned around and stomped across the street to pick Deborah up and go home.

The clock waned and midnight struck. Mother Adams crossed the street over to Fran's house where a few people were left on the porch. Fran, Cleve, Sis and a couple other church members were sitting down talking when Mother Adams walked up.

Fran asked, "How the children doing?"

"They sleep for now. I don't think they got a clue what's going on."

Cleve got up and allow Mother Adams to seat.

Mother Adams said, "Thank you, baby. I'm exhausted. I cleaned up in there and I got my nephew to go to the store and I cooked them a big dinner. I can't believe how Lula Mae and her children were living. No food, barely any clothes. I had to comb all they hair. Bervick's a low down dirty man for having his family live like that. I try my best not to question God, but I just don't see the sense in taking a young woman away from all them babies, leaving them with a crazy father. I just don't know why," Mother Adams said and started sobbing over the lost of the woman she considered a daughter.

Sis shot a look over at Fran to keep quiet. Fran shook her head no. She wouldn't dare talk ill to Mother Adams.

Silence again.

Everyone sat, lost in their own thoughts about the situation.

Mother Adams broke the silence. "So, who's gonna make the call to Eunice?"

Chapter 32

Big Ma sat on the porch with a bleak face, waiting. Paper bag curlers hung out of a white scarf wrapped around her head. Still in her night gown in the middle of the afternoon, she sat staring out into the deserted road. Happiness a distant memory. A memory more like a myth, a fable, a fairy tale—an implausible story Big Ma seldom experienced throughout her life. Joy and laughter is all Big Ma sought-after; heartache and pain is what she got in return.

Partial to the tranquility of the town's stillness, a storm took place within Big Ma's heart. There was no use for tears, memories, pain or sorrow. Her aging body couldn't take any more emotional damage. Grin and bear was the lone antidote.

Doc trailed around the house, his hands behind his back and pipe hanging from his lip with the smoke long gone, never bothering to relight it.

Big Ma rocked until she perked up seeing the person she'd been waiting for. Papa Top walked up to the porch with his cane. He leaned against the post, sitting his cane down and nodding at Doc passing by. Papa Top's eyes were glassy. He yawned repeatedly from lack of sleep.

Big Ma leaned over, "When they gettin' my baby back here?"

"Couple days. What's goin' on with the funeral arrangements?"

"Mary Lee taken care of that. She's collecting Lula Mae's burial money."

Papa Top watched Doc pass by in silence.

He turned back to Big Ma, "And how are you doin', Sha?"

"If I knew how I was doin', I'd be in my own grave."

Papa Top slightly nodded, waving away the mosquitoes. He took his cane and planted it in front of him. "I guess I'll be on my way. You take care of yourself, Louverta," Papa Top watched Doc pass by again, "and him, too!"

Papa Top began taking steps down the porch and walked towards the road. Big Ma got up from her rocking chair and called out for him. She stepped down the stairs, ignoring the paper bag curlers dropping from her hair, and walked over to Papa Top, "Sis say anything bout Lula Mae reading the letter we sent her? Did she read that I love her?" She asked, clasping her hands near her mouth in high hopes.

Papa Top said, "She say Lula Mae got it and was happy after she readin' it, Sha."

Big Ma grinned, raising her hands to the sky, "Thank you Jesus!"

Papa Top smiled and continued walking, oblivious of any letter. Nevertheless, there was no harm in telling a little lie to put a smile on Big Ma's face.

Chapter 33

In the middle of the night, Bervick cleaned out drawers, closets, nightstand, bathroom, and kitchen of all belongings or reminders of Lula, and stuffed them in a trash bag along with her graduation picture and pictures of her and the children.

He emptied everything into a huge tin can in back of the house and poured alcohol on top. He threw a lit match on top, standing back to watch Lula's belongings go up in flames. He grinned glaring at the fire. God's work was finally done, halleluiah. The flames lit up Bervick's face as he delightfully watched the fire sway outside of the tin can. A neighbor's dog started barking. Bervick used a stick to mash the items down, and then put a lid over the can to put the fire out.

In the morning, Bervick disregarded the constant knocks on the door, keeping the children inside to avoid any outside contact. He told his children their mother no longer existed and left it at that. They were unable to fully comprehend Bervick's words, or begin to understand the concept of death. All the children knew was, Lula was nowhere in sight and when will she be coming back home.

Bervick refrained from preparing, scheduling, or speaking to anyone in regards to shipping Lula back to Eunice. He left the planning to Cleve, Sis, Fran, and Pastor Williams. A church collection and donations funded the cost to ship Lula back to Eunice after a viewing was held at the funeral home in Pacoima, California, where a tremendous amount of people came to say their final goodbyes.

Bervick made arrangements to return back to Eunice for the funeral without the children. He dropped them off at Mother Adams' house, dressed in all white, and took the same train as Lula's casket without anyone noticing him.

He rode long hours feeling like God's son, a higher power after defeating the evil in his life. He plucked a speck of dirt off his milk white suit, the only color capable of touching his anointed skin. White exemplified the purity of his soul, and given that colors attract energy, Bervick wasn't going to risk absorbing anything tainted.

With Lula's bible in hand, Bervick went through the scriptures he memorized best and read, believing he was reading the pages the same way Lula did at night before she went to sleep. This was one of many features of Lula's that Bervick captured and broadcasted for himself after her demise. Her social skills, cooking, and vibrancy would soon be his in due time. His God declared all of Lula's gifts to Bervick for being an obedient servant.

The conductor yelled "Eunice" as the next destination. Bervick panicked getting up, walking through the aisles in search for an accessible escape. The last train car had a side door with a high three steel step on the side, opposite the station. He stood there until the train came to a halt, and hesitated in fear of getting his white pants dirty. As an alternative, Bervick threw his suitcase out first, and then jumped, landing on his hands and white shoes. He stood up brushing himself off, hearing southern accents on the other side of the train. He picked up his suitcase, walking swiftly away in the opposite direction in which the train had come, unnoticed and unheard.

A crowd surrounded Eunice's train station for Lula's arrival. Family and friends cried out watching the funeral director and his carriers carry out a white casket from the train into a hearse. Some refused to believe Lula was in it.

When the hearse drove off, everyone waited for Lula's children and Bervick to get off the train. Voices asked, "Where's the babies" and "Where's Bervick?" The train pulled off on scheduled time as voices rose throughout the crowd, realizing neither Bervick nor the children were present.

***

In Big Ma's house, the oven was cold, chores abandoned, laundry piled high, Doc's trail deepened, and weeds saturated Big Ma's garden. Big Ma lay in bed motionless for days. Doc left Big Ma alone, closing the bedroom door behind him before leaving for work. Knocks at the door came and went. The one thing welcomed in her house was silence.

Mary collected money from church members, friends, and family for the remaining cost of Lula's burial, and Lillie assisted in funeral arrangements. Everyone came out of pocket, giving their week's pay, their savings, or selling food of some sort to partake in the contribution. Daniel Lee and Willie Ray took advantage of the chance to give as much money needed for the funeral, making up for what they didn't give to help Lula.

The money Mary collected tallied up to more than enough for Lula's burial. The community of Eunice came together to ensure Lula was able to rest in peace.

***

A summer day in 1964, almost everyone in Eunice's black community gathered in the church for Lula Mae Frank's funeral. Flowers sent from various people filled the church. The church was crowded with little room to move or sit. The only person not dressed in black was Lula, who had on a white satin dress, white shoes, and hair beautifully done in pin curls, looking like a sleeping angel.

A heaviness of guilt swarmed the air as family, church members, and friends remembered their last memory of Lula asking for financial assistance to move. The community always came together financially to help a person's desired goal, but all of them failed to assist Lula because of Bervick.

Now, there she lay.

She was their friend, granddaughter, neighbor, niece, cousin, and fellow church member. Her beautiful face, kind smile, joyous laughter, sweet demeanor, and great food never entered the people's current state of mind. Their last memory of Lula's troubled face when they turned her away created an atmosphere full of regrets as they mulled over the possibilities of what they could have done differently, despite Bervick. Family and friend's hearts were touched by Lula, whom they failed to acknowledge until this very day in 1964, when it was too late.

Big Ma found the strength to get out of bed to face her granddaughter one last time. She sat in between Doc and Lillie, wondering how she ended up in this same predicament again. The words Lula screamed, saying she wasn't returning back to Eunice unless she was in a pine box haunted Big Ma, who never in a million years took the words literally. Her heart forced her to look away from Lula in order to keep a steady heart beat.

Being as though Big Ma had not shed a tear or addressed the fact that Lula was gone worried the family. Big Ma was worried for herself, and prayed to God for her not to bury any more children or grandchildren. She would rather them bury her first.

Big Ma closed her eyes, holding Lillie's hand tight, listening to the sermon in hopes of hearing or feeling something out of the ordinary—now welcoming this clairvoyance ability that she once saw as the devil. If this was going to grant her the opportunity to see Lula one last time, then so be it.

Big Ma sat for a while holding her breath, welcoming any cool sensation to engulf her. Nothing happened. She did it a couple more times.

Still nothing.

Big Ma gave up with a sigh, leaning her head on Lillie's shoulder.

During the sermon, Big Ma looked over her shoulder in the other aisle, shocked to see a young innocent woman with her hair pulled back in a ponytail. Samantha dabbed at the tears flowing like a river on her face as she lifted her head catching Big Ma's eye. With no make-up, exaggerated hairdo, or tight clothing on, Samantha turned away and closed her eyes, continuing in silent prayer.

***

Mr. Pete opened his home to Bervick, allowing him to stay and respected Bervick's wishes not to disclose his whereabouts with anyone in town. Bervick visited a few of his family members to brief them on Lula's pregnancy that caused her untimely death, then, on the day of the funeral, Bervick fled to Lake Charles to visit his father.

In front of his father's front door, Bervick stood straight poking his chest out and knocked. He dusted his white suit off, slicking his eyebrows back with his pinky finger, waiting. Joe swung the door open and motioning Bervick to come in, patting his son's back.

Bervick took a seat on the couch.

Joe sat with his pipe in his hand across from Bervick and said in Creole, "I'm sorry, son. Is there anything I can do for you, Sha?"

Bervick slumped over. Confidence flew out the window. He couldn't bring himself to look Joe in the eye. Something in Joe's face startled Bervick, throwing him off track. The sympathy in Joe's voice and the wavering of his words was all too foreign for Bervick.

Joe asked in Creole, "Where are your children?"

Bervick answered in English, "Back in California. I'm gonna take care of dem myself, sir."

"Nine babies, Bervick?"

"Eight, sir. And they got a new mama nah."

"Is that so?"

"Yes, sir. Geneva Jo they new mama. God said so."

Joe lit his pipe and puffed on it without blinking, still staring at Bervick. He took the pipe out of his mouth and leaned in closer to get a better view of Bervick, who looked everywhere but at Joe.

Joe's deep voice said, "Look at me, boy!"

Bervick looked at him for a few seconds, and then turned away. Joe squinted his eyes, getting a good overview of his son.

Joe twisted his mouth to the side putting the pipe back in his mouth. "A new mother, huh? What happened to Lula Mae?"

"She got sick from her pregnancy. Couldn't get her to the hospital in time."

"Sick, huh?"

"Yes, sir."

"Humph," Joe said, sitting back in his chair, staring intensely at Bervick, who was rubbing his sweaty palms together. Joe knew his son all too well and didn't believe a word Bervick said.

Bervick rubbed the back of his neck looking away and finally got up, walking over to the window, putting his hands in his pocket to conceal the shaking, "Can I stay here fo' the night, sir?"

Joe nodded using his cane to stand up and retreat to his bedroom. He stopped in mid-step without looking back and said loud in Creole, "Don't bother looking for my tin can, it ain't there no more," and continued on into his bedroom.

Bervick inaudibly went out to the front porch to sit down hoping to get a whiff of smell the sweet perfume one last time. However, it never came.

***

The day after Lula's funeral, close family and friends hung around Big Ma's house discussing the possibility of Bervick being in town. Some were told Bervick was seen leaving Mr. Pete's store while others heard Bervick was seen sitting at the bus station dressed in all white.

Big Ma, Papa Top, Doc, Grandma Emma, Paul Robert, Willie Ray, Lillie, Mary and Alex, a few distant relatives, and church friends surrounded Big Ma's porch.

Junior Harrison, now in medical school, was among the younger family members standing near the road, reminiscing on how he helped Lula in school. Stopping in mid-sentence, Junior did a double-take at a figure walking up the road dressed in all white.

Putting his hand up to block the sun from his eyes, Junior definitely saw a white suit and quickly pointed, "There he go right there!"

Everyone got up from their seats and made their way to the road with balled fists and hands on hips. Seeing the crowd, Bervick stopped in mid-step, now regretting not taking the other route from the bus station.

Lillie yelled, "Aye, Bervick, where dem chillun at?"

Bervick paused, measuring his distance between him and Lula's family. Too far to get caught, Bervick took off running in the opposite direction. Junior dropped his soda water and darted after Bervick, chasing him two blocks until losing Bervick when a car rode pass. Junior smacked his hat on the ground and stood there catching his breath and waiting to see if he saw some semblance of a white suit anywhere. He gave up, picking up his hat and walking back hanging his head. Big Ma met Junior in the road with open arms. "Chin up, my baby. It's okay. Let Bervick go. God sits high, but *he* looks low."

Everyone settled back down in front of Big Ma's house discussing Bervick and his actions. So engulfed in conversation, nobody noticed Papa Top missing from his chair.

When Junior took off running after Bervick, Papa Top shuffled between houses holding his cane, making his way to the road adjacent to where Junior chased Bervick, and waited near an abandoned house. Papa Top rubbed his sore knees waiting, assuming Bervick was headed towards the train station and had to cross that path.

Bervick thought the coast was clear. He began heading to the train station until he heard a noise. He looked and saw a car turning the corner, then relaxed wiping the sweat off his forehead. He took his suit jacket off, shook it out, and then froze when he felt cold steel press against the temple of his head. He heard a gun cock. A hand pushed him behind the abandoned house into a remote area where he was shoved on the ground.

Bervick raised his hands shaking in fear from the steel warming up on the side of his face. He saw a cane drop on the ground.

Papa Top said, "Where's my grandbabies?"

Bervick panicked. Hands shook uncontrollably.

Papa Top struck Bervick with Miss Colt .45, who hankered to speak for herself. Bervick fell over in agony, holding the knot forming on his forehead.

Papa Top said, "Where's my grandbabies?"

Bervick was quiet.

The sun pierced through trees shining directly in Bervick's eye. He brushed at his now brown suit, then started laughing hysterically clapping his hands, stomping his knee and pointing up at the sky.

Papa Top didn't budge. He watched Bervick pointing at the sky repeatedly saying, "Good one."

Wiping tears of amusement from his face, Bervick picked himself off the ground, elated at God's humor. But then, in a spit second,

Bervick's face fell limp into a trance-like state. He pushed his body into the gun and said with a blank look, "I've ascended, greater than a Prophet, now at the level of my God. I await my next elevation to become...God. Killing me will resurrect me, for my spirit lives on."

A wicked grin followed Bervick's statement as he started to walk off, pointing at the sky and laughing again.

Papa Top took his cane and cracked Bervick across the head from behind, watching Bervick fall to his feet still laughing, saying, "Halleluiah!" He got up and began walking, oblivious of the blood pouring down his face, holding his hands up high praising God.

Papa Top held his index finger on the trigger, pushing down bit by bit, aiming at Bervick's head.

"Damn!" Papa Top said, shaking his head. His arm fell releasing his grip, cocking Miss Colt .45 back. He watched Bervick turn the corner, heading to the train station. Papa Top shook his head.

He'd be wrong to kill a crazy man.

Papa Top picked his cane up and shuffled his aching knees back to Big Ma's house thinking, *I'm getting too old for this!*

Chapter 34

In 1965, Papa Top and Grandma Emma got out of their vehicle and stood in front of The Stolden House Penitentiary waiting for the bus to arrive. When the bus pulled up, two guards got off and let a woman wearing a soft pink blouse and cream skirt get off the bus. She held her suitcase and purse in front of her, looking around fearful and timid of leaving Pineville, the place she called home. Dust blew as she stood gazing at an image she had dreamed about for twenty years. The two faces she prayed to see every day finally arrived.

Grandma Emma held her hands out, chuckling and crying at the same time, nodding her head that it was them. Beatrice dropped her suitcase and purse, and ran over to her parents, hugging them tight.

Grandma Emma smiled and took Beatrice by the face, pushing back her hair while Papa Top limped over with his cane to pick the purse and suitcase up, carefully dusting them off. He went back over to Beatrice, kissed her forehead and smiled the biggest smile anyone had ever seen on him. He happily put Beatrice's belongings in the trunk and signaled for them to get in the car.

On the ride home, Beatrice hung her head out the passenger seat window, catching the breeze. Grandma Emma and Papa Top never stopped smiling, patting their daughters shoulder, head, and lap in excitement.

Beatrice put her head back in smiling at them as Grandma Emma sat in the back seat fixing Beatrice's hair.

Papa Top said through his smile, "We got food ready and everybody's home waitin' fo' yah!"

Grandma Emma asked, "How yah feelin', baby?"

Beatrice smiled, "I'm doing well, mama. How did you all find me anyway?"

Papa Top said, "I woke up one mornin' and an anonymous letter was on my porch tellin' me where you was at. We searched everywhere fo' yah, Bea. Lord is my witness, that place was the last place I thought you'd be. I'm so sorry, baby gal. I'm so sorry it took us so long. I'm so, so sorry."

Beatrice smiled wiping tears from Papa Top's face, "It's alright, papa, I'm fine now. I'm just happy to be going home!"

***

Back in Stolden House Penitentiary, a man screamed at the top of his lungs in the jail cell. Two guards in black uniforms walked over and opened the cell. The man tried to escape, but was slammed to the ground like a rag doll.

The man screamed, "Please stop, please, sir! Get me out of here! I don't belong here!"

"Shut your mouth!" One guard yelled, wrestling with the man.

"Please, sir!" The man begged, "I'm not doin' too good, sir!"

Another man in a blue uniform came in with a strait jacket. They forced the man's arm inside the sleeves and tied the back of strait jacket tight as the man slobbered at the mouth screaming for help.

The man in the blue uniform motioned, "Get him out of here."

The two guards picked the man up by the strait jacket and pushed him to walk. The man tried to run but was tackled to the ground again, punched and kicked repeatedly. One of the guards yanked the man by the collar of the strait jacket and wiggled a black baton in the man's face. "You run again, nigger, I'm knocking your teeth out!"

The man pleaded as they lifted him on his feet, pushing him outside to a white van with a doctor standing next to it along with a young medical intern. The man tried wrestling out of the guard's grip while yelling out for the doctor to help. When they got to the vehicle, the guards released the man, letting him fall face down on the ground near the doctor's shoes.

The doctor said, "Get him up."

The guards lifted the man onto his feet. The doctor walked up pushing his glasses closer on his face.

The man pleaded, "Please, doctor, I'm not feelin' too good. They kept me locked in that cold wet cell fo' a week. No food. No water. I need yah help. I'm sick!" He started coughing up blood and phlegm. His head swam in pain as knots formed in his stomach from the beating. He looked up at the doctor with pinkish eyes from lack of sleep, falling in and out of consciousness all night. He begged for medical assistance from the doctor.

The doctor looked down at his clip board and read, "Is your name, Bervick Frank?"

"Yes, sir!"

"Bervick Frank, my name is Doctor Foster and you are being transferred to Pineville where there will be rules and—"

"Please, Sir," Bervick coughed, "I need help! I'm not feelin' good, I—"

"There will be rules and regulations you will follow—"

"Please, Doctor Foster, please help me!" Bervick turned away, regurgitating uric acid that burned his esophagus from lack of food. It felt like nails hammered at the walls of his stomach. Torches burned the wounds it left.

"Damn it, nigger" the guard yelled, whacking Bervick across the head for the mess he made on the guard's shoe.

Doctor Foster nonchalantly said, "Get him on his feet please."

Bervick saw double, barely holding his head up. They lifted him back on his feet. Chills ran throughout his aching body. Unbearable pain caused extreme dizziness.

Doctor Foster continued, "As I was saying, there are rules and regulations you will have to abide by—"

"Please, I'm beggin' yah, help me. I'm sick!" Bervick said through parched lips, feeling overly dehydrated.

"This conduct will not be tolerated at Pineville, Mr. Frank."

"Please wait, please—"

Doctor Foster nodded at the guards and whispered into his intern's ear. The eager medical student nodded and ran into the van, bringing back a white medical kit. Doctor Foster walked the intern through measuring the amount of liquid sedative needed in the needle.

The guards wrestled the strait jacket off Bervick and held his head against the ground with their feet, pulling up his sleeves while Bervick screamed.

Doctor Foster knelt down watching his intern miss Bervick's vein three times before finding it and injecting him.

Bervick passed out immediately.

The guards picked Bervick up and threw him in back of the van, shutting the doors and hitting the back of the van for the driver to drive off.

A week later in Pineville, Doctor Foster walked down a hall with his intern taking notes, going from window-to-window discussing each patient. Walking up to the next sealed white room with nothing in it except for a sick man screaming bible scriptures, Doctor Foster looked at the medical student and said, "Now it's your turn. I allowed you to monitor him for a week, so give me your prognosis on Bervick Frank."

The intern flipped through his notebook fast. Doctor Foster calmly took the notebook from the intern's hand and pointed at his head.

The intern cleared his throat, "Okay, um, okay. He demanded to be dressed in all white and I saw some catatonic behavior. Um, there were signs of hallucinations. Him staring at nothing in particular and waving his finger in the air saying, 'good one' and, um, his records show he hasn't worked a day in his life, so that's a sign of avolition, especially having so many children to feed. Um, Mr. Frank believes he's God or a prophet of some sort, demonstrating a delusional state of mind. Um, I saw a blunted affect when we spoke of his deceased wife and orphaned children, showing complete disregard and lack of empathy for his family. And, uh, there's no substance abuse to explain these behaviors, so I believe it's safe to say that Bervick Frank suffers from schizophrenia."

Doctor Foster nodded his head in question, "Very good observation. However, more tests have to be done to make certain. I myself observed more psychopathic characteristic patterns as well. Next question: how do these mental disorders come about?"

The intern pulled at his chin, "Childhood perhaps. Maybe a catastrophic event distorted his view on how he see himself and the people close to him. Or it could possibly be genetics."

"Looking through his records, there's no mental disorders in his family history," Doctor Foster said with his hands behind his back looking at Bervick through the small circular window. "But you're correct. People create their own fictions to escape their reality and it usually starts at a young age. Individuals such as Bervick Frank have no place living amongst people. It would be detrimental to himself as well as putting others at risk. Patients suffering from mental disorders to this degree are capable of anything, up to the severity of murder."

The intern asked, "Who admitted him?"

"We received many calls about Bervick Frank, but we didn't take them seriously until social services out in Pacoima, California, called after taking his children away, placing them in foster care. They informed us that he fled back to Eunice by train, so we met him at the train station and brought him to Stolden House. We had no choice but to admit him after social services provided us reports on how he had his children living."

The Intern peeked through the glass watching Bervick. "Don't you think he needs medical attention, sir? He's been sick for over a week now."

Doctor Foster chuckled, "One thing you'll learn in this field, turn a blind eye to minuscule issues." He put his hand on the intern's shoulder, "Come, let's see if you can properly diagnosis our next patient."

Doctor Foster and the intern walked off.

Chapter 35

Big Ma worked endlessly to get her garden back in order, pulling weeds, harvesting ripe fruits and vegetables, and discarding those that went bad. With her hair wrapped in a white scarf and wearing her garden dress, Big Ma worked barefoot since the break of dawn, oblivious of the clear blue sky, birds singing and multicolored butterflies swarming around.

In between pulling, Big Ma grabbed at sporadic pains in her chest. She looked up thinking she saw Doc in the doorway, but remembered he was in Lafayette visiting family. She got up leaving vegetable piles outside the garden and went inside the house, having a sudden urge to make teacakes for breakfast.

Big Ma's pace was slow prepping the table area. Her movements were flaccid as she dragged her feet, plopping things on the table and throwing the tin bowl over on the counter. No humming, singing, or zeal for her craft in the kitchen. Chest pains consumed Big Ma as she constantly rubbed her chest to calm the palpitations.

Mixing the dough in an aloof state, Big Ma tore a piece off to taste. A couple ingredients were missing. She went over to the wooden cabinet to grab the sugar, and searched high and low for the other ingredient. Moving everything out of the cabinet, dropping things on the floor, Big Ma searched. She smacked her hand on the table, and then threw her hands up giving up and retreated outside for air.

Big Ma rocked in her rocking chair with one hand on her hip and the other on her chest. She took a deep breath and released the irritation from her body. It took a couple more breaths before Big Ma finally calmed herself down, rocking back and forth at peace for the moment. She began to take notice of the birds swarming the yard chirping. Her eyes followed a beautiful rare blue butterfly swarming around her, landing on a bottle of nutmeg next to her chair.

Big Ma stopped rocking. She gawked at the unique butterfly flapping its wings on the bottle while wondering how the nutmeg got outside.

A warm sensation came over Big Ma. She looked out the front yard and saw a translucent figure of a familiar blue dress flowing towards her. The figure materialized right before Big Ma eyes. A beautiful young woman with tight pin curls coiled neatly around her head came walking up popping her Doublemint gum.

Big Ma stood up looking into the woman's almond shaped eyes and said, "Lula Mae, that you?"

Lula smiled a bright pretty smile, flashing her milk white teeth.

Big Ma said, "Please forgive me, my baby! I—"

"I love you, too, Big Ma. All is already forgiven." Big Ma heard Lula say even though Lula's mouth remained smiling. Big Ma burst into the tears, keeping her eyes on Lula. Lula smiled and looked over her shoulder down the road. She turned back to Big Ma, blew a kiss, and warmly smiled one last time before fading away into the summer breeze. Big Ma rushed down the porch and wiped away her tears smiling, relieved that her dear sweet Lula Mae made it home.

Big Ma looked up startled to see Samantha walking into the yard holding a bouquet of flowers in front of her. She held them out smiling a hopeful smile and waited for Big Ma to accept them. Big Ma grinned and was about to accept the flowers, but her jaws dropped at the sight of Samantha's tight fitted red dress, cleavage exposed, and pancake make-up behind the flowers. Big Ma's hands dropped. She hung her head. Putting a hand on her hip, all Big Ma could do was shake her head appalled at the sight in front of her.

Samantha pulled the flowers back nervously looking around, uncertain on what to do next.

Big Ma picked her head back up and smiled opening her arms, "Come here, my baby," she said, embracing Samantha for the first in thirty years. Samantha dropped the flowers and held onto her mother tight, straining her face from the overwhelming burst of emotion. She screamed out repeatedly. Bones shaking from feeling her mother's tight embrace again.

Big Ma whispered, "Don't ever think fo' once I stopped loving you. I love you with all my heart, Sam, and I want yah to always kno' that. Yah hear? Kno' that! Mama loves you so much!"

"I love you too, mama!" Samantha struggled to say through tears.

Big Ma put her arm around Samantha and walked her to the porch. She picked up the nutmeg and smiled at Samantha, asking, "Wanna help me make teacakes?"

Samantha shook her head yes like a little girl again. Big Ma smiled and put her arm around Samantha, opening the screen door to the house.

"Wait a minute," Big Ma said, pulling the towel from her shoulder and wiping Samantha's face with it.

"Mama!" Samantha protested, trying to dodge the towel in her face. Big Ma finished wiping and pulled the towel away, holding up the color stained towel while Samantha spit out lint from her mouth.

Big Ma looked at Samantha's face and smiled, "Ahhh, there you are."

Samantha chuckled and nodded understandably.

Big Ma put her arm around Samantha, kissed her cheek, and started humming. The two went inside to start making teacakes.

The rare blue butterfly flapped its wings on the screen door and then flew away.

Photographs

Lula Mae Harrison

Born September 25, 1937 - Died July 8, 1964

Leroy Harrison

Grandma Emma Guy

Doc Harrison

Louverta Scott (Big Ma)

Made in United States
Orlando, FL
19 June 2024

48014683R00254